SHAMELESS GAME

KELLY FINLEY

KELLY FINLEY BOOKS

ALSO BY KELLY FINLEY

Interconnected Books

The Belles & Bratva Beasts

Nash

Axel

Make Him

Tempt Her

The Six

Holiday For Six

Halloween For Six

After Him

With Him

NOTES

For content information, visit my website:
KellyFinley.com

Read, **SHAMELESS PLAY,**
the SHAMELESS GAME prequel novella for
free on KindleUnlimited.

For all who believe love should be proud and shameless.

The Alchemy by Taylor Swift
Sunburn by Nick Wilson
Teenage Dream by Stephen Dawes
You by Regard, Troye Sivan, Tate McRae
Daddy Issues by The Neighbourhood
Un-thinkable (I'm Ready) by Alicia Keys
Bounce by Timbaland, Missy Elliot, Justin Timberlake
What I Am by ZAYN
Alien Superstar by Beyoncé
Around My Neck by FINNEAS
We Go Down Together by Dove Cameron, Khalid
Shameless by Camila Cabello
Lose Yourself by Eminem
Glorious by Macklemore, Skylar Grey

SHAMELESS GAME

Blair

You'd think working in an adult store would be fun.

I get to sell the best vibrators to women, delighted by the impatience in their eyes. Like they can't race home fast enough with their new lover. I encourage husbands to play kinky dice with their wives. Nothing says "Happy Anniversary" like a game of cunnilingus. I can tell you the best-tasting lube (pink lemonade, trust me). I know the lingerie that flatters every gorgeous shape and the best book to teach you how to tickle his pickle... *if* pickles are your thing.

Don't you worry; I'll make sure you, my happy, horny customer, get the pleasure you deserve.

But me?

I'm fine.

I'm not having fun.

I'm perfectly content in my celibate misery. I dust glass

shelves with nipple clamps, BDSM collars, and blue alien cock sheaths that make me sigh, staring longingly at the toys. My pathetic sigh fills another giant penis-shaped balloon in my pity party of one over Beau Bronson.

Until…

My evil twin schemes an intervention.

"Enough!" Vale tosses a fuchsia bustier at me. "Your sad vag is a virus that's infecting us all. Put this on. The skirt, too." She flings the matching satiny garment at my face. "We're taking you to the club."

"The Club" is a private sex club.

This lingerie turned sexy streetwear is worth hundreds. Lucky for her, I caught it.

And my twin sister is a giant pain in my lonely ass.

I'm trying to have my eat, pray, love life, minus the praying and the love part.

And yet here she is, trying to bully me into kinky fun.

"I'm not going to the club, you conniving cunt." I flit my feather duster at her. "Quit trying to make me happy and shit. I've told you a zillion times, I'm fine."

There are no customers in Delta's. We just closed the store where we work for the day, but apparently, my sister is hell-bent on big plans for the night.

Because Jace, our store's bouncer or bodyguard? Hell, I don't know what his official title is. He's just a mountain range of muscles topped by a sexy face towering behind her. He wants to ruin my life with fun, too.

"You're going with us, Blair." Yep, Jace is a pain in my abstinent ass, reminding me, "It's been four months since Valentine's, and you need to get back on the horse."

I stand my ground in a showroom full of high-end sex toys, my glare landing on the shelf featuring the biggest dildos. Pointing to the long, angry pink and brown one, I snap, "The only horse I'm ever riding again is that giant stallion cock."

Though pony play is not my kink.

No, Beau Bronson is my kink.

Beau Bronson is the cocky, sweet asshole I met in college who stole my heart.

Beau Bronson is the sexiest man who appeared eight years later, like a once-in-a-lifetime sex comet, giving me the hottest and most heart-breaking Valentine's night of my life.

And...

Beau Bronson is the number one NFL quarterback who won't stop appearing in my damn FYPs, on the flatscreen, or in my mind when I close my eyes.

And the reason I'm really miserable about it?

Beau and I were meant to be together, though we never will be.

"You don't have to fuck tonight," Vale huffs, tapping her foot clad in a black, vinyl, thigh-high boot. She tops her boots off with a gothic, Wednesday Addams black vinyl mini-dress, lace collar, and braided pig-tails. Her dirty school-girl look drives men insane. "But you're going with us to the club. Your pitiful pussy party has officially turned pathetic."

Does anyone want to buy a twin?

I'll give you fifty percent off because she can read your dirty mind and broken heart, especially when you don't want her to.

Hell, I'll give her to you for free.

Because Vale is my mirror, though I work our long raven hair in a classic starlet way, and I've proudly earned more curves than her. I swear I was born in the wrong decade. I worship Marilyn Monroe. It's destiny we share the same last name.

But still, deep down to our DNA, Vale and I are identical.

She's exasperated with my vow never to have sex again. Well, sex with others. With myself? I'd make Pornhub blush. I'm such a slut, moaning Beau's name, memories of him making me come every time.

And yes, I'm guilty of trying almost every single dildo in this store. And no, I don't use the ones on the shelves.

I use my store discount and buy my own. You should see my collection. I use them as bookends on my shelves.

Big fake boners and real smutty books: that's my fetish.

"It's enough, Blair." Vale softens her tone. Usually, she's a raging bitch, and I love her for it because it lets me be a royal bitch right back.

That's called *sisterly love,* as she scolds, "You can't keep living in your books and writing about alien romance and big blue cocks and—"

"My books are finally selling, thank you very much." Sister or not, no one comes between me and my smut. "So I'm not going to the club tonight. I have another book to finish and a deadline."

"Your books are selling because Beau Bronson went viral yesterday reading one in a Charleston coffee shop," Vale snaps. "And you've been moping around all day about it because that was *it*. Beau made you a bestseller, but he didn't show up today. He hasn't called or texted or dropped in your DMs, and I swear to god, if you sigh like a pining romance heroine about it one more time, I'm cramming an alien cock sheath down your throat."

Jace chuckles. Our daily duels amuse the hell out of him.

"Go suck a box of Daddy dicks." I half laugh, half snarl at her.

"Proudly, I suck dick almost every night." She half laughs, too. "And so did you. Where is my shameless sister? The one no man could break? Since when do you crumble for cock?"

"You got as much room to talk as a cheap Vegas honeymoon hotel."

Vale narrows her eyes. "At least I don't have a dead fish city between my thighs."

"No, you got a hot Daddy treating your puss like it's his Disneyland." And I grin right back. "How many times have you ridden Mr. Allen's Space Mountain?"

I busted Vale yesterday. The entire staff did. We know she's fucking her best friend's dad, but Jace interrupts our spat.

"Come on, Blair. You know you really want to go." He sounds like an audiobook alpha male, all tempting and two seconds from making you do something dirty. He could say *vaginitis* and make you want it. "Let's celebrate," he says. "You're a bestseller now, and you've worked hard for it."

But don't worry.

Jace is like our brother.

I'm sure he's making someone, probably many people, happy with that third leg in his pants, but it ain't me.

I have zero interest in non-Beau cock, so I just roll my eyes. "Fine," I huff. "I'll celebrate. You can buy me a Happy Meal before you take my sad ass home."

But that doesn't happen because my sister is a pit bull like me. Once she sinks her teeth into an idea, she won't let go.

And Jace is quite persuasive because he's too damn big. Arguing with him is like telling Mt. Everest to step aside.

Same with his older brother, Grant, our other mountain range, who guards the front door to Delta's.

Grant doesn't miss a chance to go to the club with us. He always uses me as bait, making jealous women swarm like bees to his hulking honey stick.

An hour later, the four of us are quite the sight at this club I used to frequent several times a week. I was known for my knowledge of kink and my erotic skills, too.

What can I say? A romance author needs to do her research.

Many couples sought me as their unicorn—a bi woman shared with another man and woman already together. But often, I was wary. Their expectations were unrealistic, and I didn't want to be the reason for friction or a break-up.

I just wanted to have fun so my romantic heart didn't get broken. I usually kept it to one night only. Sometimes, I'd let couples play with me for the weekend.

But that was months ago.

Months since Valentine's. Months since my night with Beau Bronson at The Mercier Hotel. Months since I finally fucked my college enemy, who I lusted over for years, because really... Beau and I were secretly in love.

Only twice have we admitted it.

The first time was the night he showed up at my dorm room our senior year with a busted lip, fighting back tears, and I held him all night. I told him it would be okay. I gave him ice for his face. I listened while he confessed his deepest secret and kept it for him. But we never did anything about our love. Through tears shed, we confessed that, too.

Because Beau was dating my roommate, Reese. He was faithful to her, and I was loyal. I don't fuck other women over. Even though she wasn't there that night, and we could have. We never did anything about our love, our attraction.

Until eight years later.

This past Valentine's night.

The feelings Beau and I revealed, the secret fantasies we fulfilled, the kink we shared, it found Beau deep inside me, over and over again, finally confessing our love over moaning lips.

And yeah, since then, my pussy has been in a coma. Self-induced. Numb to others. The feline has flat-lined. It doesn't wet or purr or even tingle with desire for anyone else because my mind wants to live in the past.

It wants to live forever in that night in the hotel suite with Beau, remembering how I melted with our first kiss. How he kept growling my name and biting my neck. How he held me tight afterward. We weren't shy together.

Even in college, I always felt safe with Beau.

Though, yeah... we double-majored in wicked pranks on each other.

Like when he kept leaving condoms full of mayonnaise on the hood of my car, or my dorm doorknob, or my favorite... when he managed to superglue one to the bottom of my backpack without me knowing.

So, I bribed his roommates to plant rolls of fake toilet paper everywhere he went. You know, the kind that won't tear? Yep, they make it. So you have a choice: use it and clog the toilet with two pounds of paper or call for help.

Yeah, I got three of Beau's shitty situations on video until he finally started carrying his own Charmin in his backpack.

Still, I trusted him.

I secretly loved him.

Because only Beau can make me cry. Like that Valentine's in The Mercier Hotel when he gave me his Atlanta football jersey before leaving me with his tender kiss goodbye. Like when I buried my face in his hotel pillow, still warm from him, suddenly feeling cold and lost after he left.

Couples and throuples and piles of scantily clad-to-nude bodies fuck all around me. It's role-play night, and the club smells like sex and sandalwood. Music pumps. So do cocks and dildos. Whips crack the air, and moans of lust lull from every direction in the club around me, but I'm bored shitless.

No, I'm not bored.

I'm hurt. I'm confused. I'm overwhelmed that Beau did such a sweet thing for me yesterday.

He purposefully read my newest release, a paranormal romance book inspired by our Valentine's night, in public, where he knew he'd be spotted. Pics were snapped of him holding my book in his hands.

And I knew that smile on his face. His cute, cocky smile that went viral.

It's the same smile I'd bust on his sexy face when I'd catch him hiding in the library at college, reading Harry Potter or Tolkien's books. Only I knew that side of Beau.

Because, for everyone else, he's just the best quarterback in the country.

So, Beau's football fame made my book a bestseller in a matter of hours, and then...

Nothing.

Yes, I keep checking my phone. Yes, it's blowing up with notifications, new followers, and posts from excited readers. I want to cry with joy.

And I want to cry with a *What the fuck?*

"What do you think it means?" I ask Jace, sitting beside

me on a barstool while we sip virgin mint juleps. The club doesn't serve alcohol. Vodka and random sex don't mix.

Down the bar to the right, Vale's chatting with some friends, Silas and Eily Van de May. They're loyal customers of Delta's. I glance left and Grant has a swarm of women on their knees worshiping his purple throbber.

But Jace?

He's my buddy. He's here for me, chuckling. "You want me to read Beau Bronson's mind?"

"Yeah," I answer. "Beau did this really sweet thing, but why? And why, when I should be happy about it, am I feeling like shit?"

A *DUH* neon sign just lit over Jace's head.

"Because you're in love with him," he answers. "And he's in love with you. You don't do shit like that; you don't make a woman's dream come true unless you love her."

"But Vale's right. Beau's still ghosting me."

"Hang on." Jace lowers his heavy brows. "*You* said you wanted it this way. Both of you. You and Beau were frenemies in college when you really wanted to fuck the hell out of each other and when he randomly showed up at our store on Valentine's night after how many years?"

"Eight."

"Yeah, eight years later," he marvels. "You two finally had an epic night together. You said you tried to see who could out-kink the other and agreed it was a one-night-only. And that was four months ago, and obviously naive as hell because all y'all did was light a fuse. You're a bomb begging to blow."

"The only one begging to blow is Grant." I point to Jace's brother, fisting a blonde and a brunette, slobbering all over his knob like a giant grape lollipop. "Because I'm never blowing Beau Bronson again. It would be a disaster."

Even though Beau is the first and last man I ever swallowed. Even though I've been with dozens, Beau's the only man I let inside me bare. Even though Beau's the only one I ever trusted with my fantasies, with my dreams, with my heart.

"Look, I get it." Jace pats my back, and I choke on my drink. He forgets he's a grizzly bear petting a rabbit. "Dating the top quarterback who lost the Super Bowl this year could be hell. It could ruin your life, but maybe he's worth it."

"But he doesn't do girlfriends," I repeat what Beau told me. "And I don't do love," I repeat what I told Beau.

And yes, it was bullshit.

Because with the way Beau kissed me goodbye and said, "I'll be reading your books. Keep writing them about us," before he left our hotel room? I knew his heart was mine.

Because with the way I snot cried about it when he left, and for weeks, I didn't stop, even though I told him to leave? I knew it was love.

Because above all, I know what football means to Beau Bronson.

Everything.

We've always wanted to be together, but in college, when Beau wasn't playing ball, he was committed to Reese. He made fixing her problems a game he would win, too. Then, days before graduation, Reese mysteriously ghosted us, and I never spoke to her or Beau again. Reese never answered my calls, and Beau, who was drafted in the first round from The University of Alabama, disappeared into his life with the NFL.

And though I love to hate football, I've secretly watched his journey.

I'm proud of him.

Beau's well on his way to being a titan, a legend in the sport. The pundits call him "The Pope in the Pocket" because he's calm and in control, almost spiritual when everyone's rushing him, but he's holding the ball.

So, I won't get in the way of Beau's dream. He said relationships are a distraction, and he's determined to win the next Super Bowl. He came so close and lost it all in one baffling final interception that people won't stop talking about.

And I get it.

Yes, relationships are a distraction.

Because all I do is either think about Beau or write about him. Thankfully for me, I can turn distractions into fiction.

But for Beau, distractions lose football games. He's under tremendous pressure. He's the face of his team's franchise, and it all rests on his multi-million dollar shoulders.

"Well," Jace grins at me, lost in thought, "please tell your pretty face that you don't love Beau Bronson because it doesn't believe you either."

"So what? You're saying I should message him or something?"

"Do you want to?"

Hell yes.

"Do I want to get my life and heart ruined?"

"Your life?" Jace nods. "Yes. Because he's not just famous for his golden arm; he's infamous for that pretty-boy face. His dating life is a public sport, too, so anyone with him would be like a lamb led to a viral slaughter. But your heart?"

Jace rubs my back. It's in that brotherly way that almost makes you feel better. You can almost fight the tears.

"Blair, I love your books. I'm one of your biggest fans. But I suspect the love you two deny would be far better as fact than your fiction."

I think about it all night.

Should I message Beau?

Should I put my bleeding heart in the ocean full of hungry media sharks, hoping only Beau will bite?

And what if he doesn't? What if I'm the only one who feels this way? The only one who wants more than Valentine's night? What if football truly is his only love?

We purposefully didn't exchange our digits, though I know I could find him if I tried. And Beau sure as hell knows where to find me. I work at Delta's, a luxury adult store, while trying to get by as a struggling indie romance author.

Until yesterday.

Until Beau made my book go viral.

But he hasn't messaged me. Apparently, he's even in Charleston, where his older brother lives, and not in Atlanta, where Beau's team is. But he was a no-show today. So, I hear his silence loud and clear.

And it hurts.

It makes me angry.

I feel like we're back in college, and he's playing another cruel, teasing joke on me. Back then, his jokes messed with my mind.

But now, they mock my broken heart.

So, all night, I try to revive my kitty. I hope she still has a pulse. I hope she'll want to play again, but I worry.

Because watching Silas Van de May passionately fuck his beautiful wife, Eily, on the stage only makes me miss Beau. I know Silas and Eily. They shop at Delta's all the time. They overwhelm you with their love, I swear. And Silas sure does make a hot cop tonight, role-playing with Eily, who's willing to be a very bad girl to get out of a ticket.

Their marriage is heaven. Their love nirvana. Their sex is fun, too. It's obvious Silas adores Eily, and she was meant to be his.

I want that.

I want that so much.

"Does that interest you?" A baritone voice tempts over my shoulder. "Because I have handcuffs and a big baton, too."

Jace went to the restroom so I'm alone at the bar. Turning around, I confront a tall, gorgeous man. He's a hundred percent fuckable. And months ago, based on looks, I'd jump him like a polecat.

But yeah, my kitty has flatlined. No response. "No, thank you."

"Are you sure you don't deserve to be punished?" He licks his lips. "I've heard enticing, naughty things."

"About me?"

"Yes," he smirks, and I'm half-flattered, half-offended, and a hundred percent preferring a hemorrhoid to this guy right now because I can suddenly see it in his eyes. I know the difference between safe lust and dangerous lechery.

"I'm sure," I answer. "Go court a different cunt for your cop-n-cock game."

"I don't take no for an answer," he threatens, looming closer, and despite the dumbass shit you hear, that's a deadly red flag on your coffin. Check the stats.

"Then take it as a complete sentence because it is." I stab him with my glare. "No."

But he hovers at the bar, eyeing me, his sexy reeking

into sleazy, and the owner, Ms. Faye, doesn't usually let guys in like this.

Jace senses it, too, when he returns. "Hey man," he lowers his voice, threatening my icky admirer, "leave her alone and leave here now, or I'll feed your face pavement until you swallow your teeth."

The guy measures Jace up, recognizing an ass-whooping when he sees one. So he skulks away, and Jace follows, telling the security at the door to red-line him. He won't be allowed back in, but that's my cue.

This night sucks, and there's smut for me to write. At least on my pages with Beau, a.k.a. Willuf the Wilder or Valen the Vulgarian, will my kitty purr again.

In the club's front lobby, Jace waits with me. He insists on escorting me to my car, and that's fine. *All is fine*; I lie to myself as the attendant hands us our phones. They're not allowed in the club.

When I check my screen, I see all the missed notifications and messages from sweet romance readers, and a text appears, too.

It rips the breath from my lungs.

Even though it says UNKNOWN, my heart knows it's Beau. It always has. Because all it does is make me so happy and so hurt, I'm pissed as hell.

UNKNOWN

It's Willuf

And I need a wild favor

BEAU

CHAPTER TWO

YEP, WE'RE BACK IN COLLEGE, BACK TO FRENEMIES WHO WANT TO FUCK AGAIN.

The June heat in Charleston, South Carolina, makes anyone sweat. My white cotton T-shirt is already soaked.

Damn, don't let my deodorant fail me, too.

Because it's not the brutal Southern humidity or the burning sun that's drenching my pits.

No, it's the steps I'm taking up the side porch to the exclusive adult shop to see the woman I can't throw out of my mind.

And trust me, I've tried.

The truth is she's been there for years.

Then, I made it worse.

Now I know my college fantasies about Blair Monroe were a thumbnail tease to the night of the most erotic, real-life, passionate porn we created months ago.

It doesn't help that we made a video of it. And yes, I watch it. Nightly, I moan to it. Hell, I feared I ruined my phone when I got my happy juice on it.

Five times so far.

My dick keeps threatening to pop boners remembering Blair at the most inappropriate times. Like when I took my niece and nephew toy shopping, and the Hello Kitty toys threatened to turn me on.

What the hell?

After our Valentine's together, after the Bad Kitty collar and cat tail butt plug Blair wore that night; every kitty reminds me of her.

And every time I eat peanut butter, I remember her, too. How she's the hottest damn woman who likes it on her cheeseburgers. How she's the friend who's kept my secret since college.

How Blair's the beautiful woman who scored my heart.

Fuck, getting sacked by huge linemen dozens of times to the point my ribs are bruised doesn't scare me. I'd rather have that crushing pain than confront this.

DELTA'S
WHERE SATISFACTION IS GUARANTEED

That's what the brass plaque on the black door reads, and it's true.

I found satisfaction beyond my wildest dreams here. I found it deep inside Blair Monroe, but I had to leave.

And now I'm back, and my lonely dick is very happy about it.

But my worried mind? I'm dragging in a cocky-as-fuck breath so I can do this. I *have* to do this.

When I press the doorbell, a chime fills the air. When

the heavy, wooden door opens, a behemoth man greets me, "Good afternoon."

I recognize him. He's the same guy who was here Valentine's night.

I step inside, almost nervous to be caught in a high-end sex shop. My paranoia is at epic levels now, and I have every justified reason why. I'm so hunted by the press and fans; it's insane. Literally, my sanity is slipping over it.

I hide under vintage ball caps, like the TEXACO one I wear.

But I glance left, and thankfully, Blair's gorgeous twin is the only one in the front parlor. Yeah, we've met. Like an angry Uber driver, she delivered the sex toys Blair requested to our suite at The Mercier Hotel. And maybe I should've given her twin a tip then because she scowls at me now.

"Hey," I wave, "nice to see you again."

Her glare kicks my balls. "Third floor," she hisses.

Then I turn, and the bouncer at the door growls, "Hurt her more, and I don't give a fuck if I'm your biggest fan. I'll break your golden arm."

Hurt her?

What is he talking about?

Blair and I weren't a thing.

We were a one-night-only, and she wanted it that way. She insisted. She *made* me leave.

And yes, I needed to. I had shoulder surgery the next day in Boston. And no, I didn't want to leave her because I've wished for Blair since college.

Do you have an ultimate vacation you dream about? One that would make all the shit worth it? That gives you hope, but secretly, you fear you'll never go?

That's Blair.

When I close my eyes, she's my paradise. She's where I want to be.

But who in the hell gets a perfect place? Or life? No one. We just get teases of bliss while reality shits over the rest.

"Yeah, man," I huff. "I'm not here to hurt her."

I'd never hurt Blair.

Fuck her until I come seeing stars? Yes.

Play pranks on her that make me laugh-cry? You bet.

Hold her all night and never want to let her go? Twice, I've done it because she's the only woman for me.

But hurt her? I'd rather chop off my golden arm.

Trodding up the grand wooden staircase in this historic home, its traditional exterior hides its interior temptations. And though I've been no angel when it comes to sex, I met the woman who put me on my knees for it here.

Blair Monroe fucked me into a new man months ago, and I don't know what to do with him. He's hungry. He's lost. He's determined. He's desperate.

I'm a goddamn mess over her, and there's only one way to survive it again. Just like we did in college, I need to make her my frenemy again because I won't win loving her.

Winding past the second-floor showroom where I'll never forget the night I ran into Blair again, I turn and wind my way to the third floor.

I never went up here.

And holy hell.

To my left is a long hallway at the top of the landing. Its polished, wooden floors are pristine. Its white walls gleaming. But the antique black door at the end of the hall hides secrets. You can sense it. I can hear it, too. Spanking flesh and moans fill the air.

"In here."

But a voice beckons me into a third-floor parlor on my

right. It's full of black leather sex furniture and a swing and stools to watch or fuck.

And shit, I'm sweating even more because...

There she is.

Her beauty punches my heart every time.

Ivory legs crossed, sitting on a padded sex bench. Long raven hair, glamorously draped over one shoulder. Silver, enchanting eyes framed in thick, long lashes. Plump lips painted red like a siren. Curves I crave, ample breasts, and full hips bound tight in a French maid's lingerie costume.

I stifle my sudden growl, my cock instantly rousing and hungry for her.

She knows that's my kink.

Blair's my kink.

"Good afternoon, Mr. Bronson." But she sounds pissed and looks it, too. "Your text said you needed a wild favor from me, so here." She tosses something. "It's all you'll score today."

Of course, I do a basic catch. On instinct, my eyes radar-lock, my hands forming a diamond shape, soft and big, receiving the box flying into my grasp. I glance down at it.

Fleshlight Stamina Training Unit Lady in Endurance Gold

Yep, we're back in college, back to frenemies who want to fuck again.

Like when I got a voicemail saying I was "voted Bama's best quarterback and won a crimson red Toyota."

So, when I showed up on May fourth as instructed at the mall entrance for the press and gift, all I found by the glass door was a box with my name on it and a Star Wars *toy Yoda* doll painted crimson red.

"May the fourth be with you!" Blair jumped out of the bushes, snapping pics, dying of laughter.

So, the following fall semester, Blair would randomly open the door to her dorm, bathroom, or even the library office where she worked and run into cling wrap covered in Vaseline to moisturize her pretty face.

Good times. Good times.

"Thanks." I tuck the fleshlight under my arm, eyeing her role-play costume. "Will you be cleaning my lady when I'm done?"

She purses her tempting lips. "I don't do small jobs."

"Good, because I have a very big one."

"That's your infection, not mine."

"You're the one who gave it to me three, no, four times in one night."

"And yet here we are," she says. "Four months later. I'm cured and not looking for another yeasty problem."

I chuckle, actually worried if our fucking gave her a yeast infection. But with the way Blair made my dick lusciously sore for days afterward, I bet it was worth it, too.

But the afterward?

"I have another problem," I tell her.

She bats her lashes. "Can't find a kitty better than mine? Told you. And sorry, not sorry."

True, so true.

"And your kitty can't find a dick better than mine," I taunt. "I remember lots of moans and squirting and screaming my name. Even got a video to prove it."

She grins. "I remember giving you pussy so good you almost passed out."

I grin back. "I remember giving you cock so good; I'm the first you swallowed and took raw."

"And I'm the first to thrill your virgin ass."

"And I'm the one who fulfills your kinky, alien fantasy."

Damn, I love this. There are no filters, no shame between us. I hold nothing back with Blair. But everything else?

I'm struggling.

I love our games. I love our pranks and banter. I love everything with Blair, but I don't have time.

"And I really loved our new book." So, I get real with her. I lock to her gaze and share my heart with her. Deep down, she's always had it. "It was really good, Blair. Like *really* good. Thank you. I'm honored. I've read it five times already."

This hidden, tender feeling between us?

I fight it, and suddenly, it wells in her eyes, too.

She looks away, casting her gaze over the sex chaise. "Thank you, Beau," she mutters, her pretty lips trembling, fighting back tears. "That means a lot. And thank you for doing it. You made our book number one. You made my dream come true."

But something hot bites at my eyes, too.

Like we're living our dreams.

We should be happy...

But we're not.

Damnit, I've been here mere minutes, but I'm right back in that dorm room with Blair. I'm right back in the hotel suite with her, too. I'm right here again, where I've always been with her from the moment she opened her door to me.

I held her roommate, passed out in my arms, while Blair stood there, answering my knock in Hello Kitty pajamas, thick black glasses, and a tattered copy of *To Kill A Mockingbird* in her grasp.

I've loved her ever since.

And I'm right here again, wanting to hold her, wanting

to try with her, but my life is too complicated. It's not as simple as hugs and kisses and fucks and love.

I sold that for a football dream and twenty-two million a year for the next three years.

"I'm glad I could help." I shove the words up my strangled throat. "I staged it. I mean, I'd already read the book twice and knew fans were filming me, but my smile was legit because you're a good writer. You made me horny and cry and laugh and love at the same time."

She quickly swipes a tear off her cheek, still not looking at me. "That's the power of romance." Humbly, she shrugs, like she's embarrassed, barely muttering, "Of pure fiction, right?"

I swallow. I don't know what to say because it's not fiction between us.

It's a fact.

"Beau," she finally sighs, "what do you want? We were one night only. You're not supposed to come back."

She's right. If I could stay away, if I could resist the temptation of Blair Monroe, I would. I should.

But I can't.

"I need your help." And she's the only person I can say that to and not feel like a shriveled dick about it.

She looks back at me, surprised. "With what?"

For the past three days, I've practiced this. I've feared this. "I need you to go on a vacation with me. Like a work retreat. We'd leave Monday."

Her eyes widen. "This Monday? Why? Where? And why the hell are you asking me?"

I glance over my shoulder. The door's open, so I move to close it behind me. No one can hear this, and my hand, holding a male masturbator, starts sweating as I scan the room.

"Are there cameras in here?" I ask.

"No, it's totally private." Her brows furrow, her tone worried. "Beau, what's going on?"

I vomit it out. It's been sour in my gut for days.

"My coach is making me go on a retreat before we start training camp in July. It's like a vacation, but it's not. I have to go. He's making me do some counseling and shit since the Super Bowl."

She shakes her head, confused.

"The counseling is with this guy. He's a sports guru," I explain. "I have to do video sessions every morning with him and journal all day. I'm supposed to *explore my feelings* about my *performance*."

I use a mocking tone. It's how I felt when my coach gave me no choice.

"Can he do that?" Blair asks. "Can your coach make you go on some psycho-babble retreat?"

"Fuck yes," I scoff. "As he reminded me, when you're paid twenty-two million a year, you do what you're goddamn told to do to win games."

"But what does that have to do with me?"

"Because I'm not going alone." My stomach knots. I swallow hard. "I'm going with Colton Hawke." My pulse races. "You know, my wide receiver, my best friend—the one who missed my final throw, the interception that cost us the Super Bowl."

I plop down in the sex swing, not giving a damn how many people have fucked on it because, I guarantee you, I'm way more fucked than they ever were.

"Hawke and I have to spend ten secluded days together, exploring our feelings, like we're fucking married," I explain. "That's what our coach says because he knows us too well. He's had staff watching us in the off-season. We haven't spoken since the game. We haven't seen each other. We own restaurants and shit together, but I don't *want* to see him.

"Colt feels the same way, and our coach smells it like a fart in church. And there's no fucking way he'll let us start training camp until we fix the stench. We'd be toxic for the team, and he's right."

"So," Blair's voice eases, trying to understand. "You need me to go with you? Why? Am I even allowed?"

"Yeah," I answer, "because Hawke is allowed to bring his girlfriend, Amber. He insisted on it. His manager pushed back against the coach and got him to compromise, and like fuck if I'm going stag now. It'll make the fucking awkward even worse. I need a girlfriend."

Blair flinches. I search her eyes. Suddenly, they look scared.

Like she'd rather date Satan than me.

"Like a *fake* date, a *fake* girlfriend," I blurt. "Just for ten days, that's it. I need someone to be a buffer between me and Hawke."

It lands in Blair's eyes, those silver, breathtaking eyes that could always see right through me—the ones that feel like home.

"*Beau*," she aims them right at me, "why do you need a buffer from Colton Hawke?"

Why I even try hiding it from her, I don't know. I've always been safe with Blair.

Only Blair.

"Because," I confess, "he's the one. He's the guy I told you about in college."

Slowly, Blair nods, letting my past and present shit-show rain over her too. She gets it. I need to tell her so much more, but she already understands. "So, I'm your beard?"

"Yes." I shake my head. "I mean, no. You're way more than that, and you know it. I've had my beard buried in your pussy, and I fucking love it, too, Blair. I can't forget you, and trust me, I've tried. That's *not* what this is."

If you think secretly loving one person is hell, try loving two—for years. One would be a distraction, the other your destruction. And all you do is dream about her and him every lonely day because actually being with them would be a nightmare for all.

But hey, at least you can have football.

"Blair, you're not my beard." I plead, "You're the only woman I trust, and I'm so fucked if you can't help me. My career, my dream is over if you don't because there's no way I can make it ten days around Hawke without shit going sideways forever."

A tender smile ghosts her lips. "Well, I guess I owe you, don't I? You made me a bestseller, so now I'm your best beard."

Fuck, she'll be saying that for the rest of my life.

But is it true? No. I'm not closeting that I'm gay. I'm closeting I'm bisexual.

What's the name for that?

In my sport, it's called "survival."

So I roll my eyes, go with it, and smile. "Yeah, you owe me. And maybe you can write another bestseller about us while we're there."

"Where?"

A thousand pounds lift off my chest.

Is that a yes?

"Belize," I answer, almost relieved. "Our team owner has a friend who owns a private island there. No press. No cameras. No tourists. No one but a chef and maid who don't know us from Adam's house cat. We'll be trapped on it. Just the four of us, trapped in paradise."

"How many bedrooms?"

"I don't know. Why? You have to stay in mine. Fake girlfriend, remember?"

"I'm not sleeping with you, Beau." Blair shakes her head like I'm threatening her with a pit of snakes. "And I'm not fucking you again, either."

Why does that sound so sweet and sour?

"Why not?" I smirk. "We can make *fake* real fun, too."

"Because fake doesn't fuck," she says. "And you don't do *real* girlfriends, and I don't do broken hearts. Not again. I'll do this to help you, Beau, to make your dream come true, too." She draws a deep breath. "But I have to help myself as well. If we fuck, I'll feel too much again. It'll hurt too much when we have to say goodbye."

Why does her vulnerability melt my heart and surge my cock?

Oh, I know.

Because Blair Monroe was the fuck of my life, too. And though I have all kinds of feelings, a past, and a secret with Colton Hawke, when it comes to women? Blair Monroe is the one I'm supposed to be with.

I haven't been with anyone else since our Valentine's night. I know she's the one for me—the other love I can't have.

But hang on...

Tempting her?

Now, that's a game I can win. That's a distraction I crave.

"So," I stand up, "you admit my cock is king and your kitty can't handle more?"

We can't admit the truth, the real feelings that overwhelm us. But games? Like hell, we can't play those.

"We both know I won," she says. "I'll *always* win our kink game."

"Wanna play another round? Just for fake fun?"

"No," she chuckles. "I told you, Beau. No fucking, and I mean it."

"Can I tease you?'

"No."

I step closer. "Can I taunt you?"

She licks her lips. "No."

"Can I tempt you?"

"I'll win that game, too."

"Wanna bet?"

Usually, I have to be cautious, careful, and straight-laced, but not with Blair. She's my freedom. She's my survival. If Blair is by my side for this, I can win.

"I tell you what." Like she knows it, she says, "We'll make a bet."

I lord over her, sitting on a sex bench, one I'm dying to strap her to before I rip that maid's costume apart, fucking her sweet cunt again like the animals we are.

I can't forget Blair's pussy. Her thin black landing strip. Her bare ivory lips. Her soft pink petals. Her clit, a perfect blush pearl. Her opening, a dark rouge heaven. Her taste, tangy sugar until she comes, her little ocean like sweet watery milk pouring over my tongue.

Goddamn, I'm obsessed with her.

Always have been.

Hell, yes, I'm getting hard.

"What's the bet, Blair?"

I lift a raven lock of her hair, twirling it like ebony silk around my finger, and she falls silent. Her lips part, eyeing my thick erection. I can't hide it in my jeans inches from her lips.

Yes, it's June and hot as balls to wear jeans, but I wore them for her. Because I fucked Blair on these jeans like a sacred sex sheet under us.

She remembers, and so do I.

It's branded on my soul.

When the world of football falls away, I don't know why I fight this. Why can't I be with Blair when she's the one I need?

Well... one of the *two* I need?

"I bet I can resist you for ten days," she says.

I hook my finger under her chin, lifting her gaze. "I bet you won't make it five."

Fuck, I'm leaking for it. *I'm* the one who's tempted. I want everything with Blair.

She wagers, "And if I win—"

"Us fucking again is the *only* win, Kitten."

"No," she says. "If I win, you have to stop fighting with Colton Hawke. You have to finally kiss and make up."

Years ago, that night with a busted lip, I told Blair I was in love with Colton, and she held me and my secret.

So, through my tears, I finally confessed that I loved her, too.

COLTON

CHAPTER THREE

Our senior year in high school

"Dude," I adjust the focus knob on the binoculars, "forget your mom's birdwatching for a Tufted Titmouse. Look at the tufted tits by your pool. Four pairs of them."

"Yeah, Dickweed." Beau tries snatching the binoculars from my hands. "One pair is my little sister's, and I'll fucking kill you."

But I yank away. "I ain't interested in Bailey." She's hot, but yeah, she's my best friend's little sister, and I'd never do that. "But damn, look at the rack on Ashley Porter. And when did Maria and Piper grow a pair, too? Fuck, they're sophomores and so fucking ripe like peaches, I'm getting hard."

But when you're eighteen, a gentle breeze gets you hard, so I don't care.

I share everything with Beau.

Hell, I'm surrounded by swinging dicks all day in the locker room, no need to be shy about mine. It's surging hungry under my khaki cargos.

Beau growls, "Man, put that thing down."

"What thing?" I joke, scanning the glistening titties lounging in the April sun by Beau's family pool. "My boner or your mom's binoculars?"

"Both." Beau smacks my skull. "I know what you do with those hands. You touching my mom's binoculars with them is fucking gross."

"But look." I laugh, shoving them into his hands. "Piper Riggins has been begging you to pop her cherry all year, and she's right there, in a pink bikini by your pool, knowing your parents are out of town and your brother's away at college. You're in charge, and you know you wanna."

Beau rolls his eyes but can't resist. Lifting the lenses to his stare, he focuses on Piper, I can tell. I know him like the back of my horny hand.

So, I'll go after Ashley. And Maria. But I'll leave Piper to him and promise my unwavering protection of his little sister because that's what horny best friends do.

"Damn, man," Beau sighs, "Piper *is* hot. Fuck, I can see her cameltoe. I bet her carpet matches her blonde drapes."

We're such pervs and don't care.

From his second-story bedroom, where we're supposed to be playing Madden NFL on Beau's Xbox, we were lured to the window by giggles and titties bouncing around his backyard pool.

I practically live with his family, in Beau's bedroom, on his top bunk.

It's not that I don't love my mom; she's just never home. She works a lot, and I understand, but I get lonely. It's just the two of us, and we can't afford an Xbox or a pool or the steaks Beau's dad buys us, too. He says he's beefing us up for Bama.

My mom's relieved I have Beau's family, too. Hell, our moms are best friends.

"Come on, dude. It's time." I watch Beau, not the girls, while he's peeping from his window. "Since Hannah cheated on you, you haven't been laid, and I'm tired of hearing you fuck Kleenex all night."

"Whatever, man," Beau huffs. "You fuck Puffs with lotion, and I ain't judging."

"I keep telling you Kleenex is sandpaper. But Puffs with lotion is very gentle and soothing, just like a nice tight wet pussy."

Beau starts laughing. "Yeah, but not Puffs with Vicks vapor rub. You were fucking a tight ring of fire."

"Damn, dude. I didn't know that tissue box had Vicks on it," I groan. "Today, my dick finally stopped burning."

"My mom bought 'em with Vicks because she thinks you have a cold."

"She thinks *we* have a cold. We've gone through three fucking boxes of tissues this week."

Damn, the truth stirs my dick. When I glance down at Beau's, waking in his matching khaki cargos, it only makes mine worse.

He can't see me watching him. He's watching Piper, and I'll never tell him how hearing him jerk off on his bottom bunk while I lie on his top bunk drives me insane. I crave it every night. Beau's muffled grunts and stifled moans and bed springs barely squeaking make me hard as hell.

He didn't even care if I heard him the first time.

Did he want me to?

So I joined him.

I heard that subtle, seductive, *fabbing* sound. It was his fist, pumping his coming tip while he grunted with his orgasm, and I started jerking off to his sounds. I swear he could hear me jerking off, too. I didn't hide it.

I made sure the mattress squeaked to my thrusting hips. I made sure he heard my moans and grunts. I wanted him to know I was thinking about his hard dick, his creamy cum squirting over his fist. I imagined that he was coming for me.

I think he was.

It had him jerking off again minutes later and not being so quiet about it, either. So I turned over and started fucking my mattress, rubbing my aching dick on it like he was under me, my bed creaking even louder. It only made him louder, too, like he felt me on top of him. We moaned and thrust and muttered, "Fuck yeah," fucking in our imagination until we were muffling our grunts, coming together.

We've been doing it this whole week. Three, sometimes four times a night, we come for each other. We're not getting much sleep and say nothing in the morning. The only evidence?

A pile of used tissues on the floor beside his bunk bed.

Maybe it's normal.

Maybe it's not.

But it's real.

Beau Bronson has been my best friend since we were the only two sophomores playing varsity football for our high school. My mom gave up her dream job, her yoga studio, to move to the city with the best football school in the state, while Beau's family already lived here.

And from the day I puked during our first practice on

the field, and Beau passed me a berry Gatorade, he's been my friend.

My best friend.

I'm the wide receiver and Beau's the quarterback. If he throws it, I catch it. I can run, close my eyes, open my hands, and just sense him.

Every. Damn. Time.

"I thought Piper's with Mike Hernandez." Beau studies his options while I study his handsome profile.

I can't deny it.

His chestnut hair with the perfect scruffy style. His dark shadow, even for eighteen. His square jaw and full pink lips I'm not supposed to notice. But his eyes? Damn, they're so blue and rimmed by sexy lashes. When they find mine from under the shadow of his helmet, all I see is all I'm not supposed to feel.

"Mike broke up with her," I answer. "He's with Claire now."

"How do you know?"

"Because I listen to your sister while you just bitch at her about stealing your golden Oreos."

"They're my favorite, and she knows it."

"Yeah, well, let her eat your Oreos while we eat her best friends. Deal."

"I don't know, man." Though Beau's dick clearly likes what he's gawking at, he always does this. He's always cautious. "I don't need a distraction, and sophomore pussy is drama, too."

"Then pick a senior. You're taking Anna to the prom. Fuck her. Fuck someone, please, because Kleenex can't keep up their production."

"Puffs, neither, you hypocrite. Besides, we got two

months til graduation. I don't need senior distractions, either."

"Dude," I roll my eyes, "you're not marrying them. Why do you always date like it's destiny? You can just fuck girls, you know?"

"Uh-huh," he mutters. "Fuck girls like you did this season? Almost the entire varsity cheerleader team to the point where even Coach Smith told you to keep your rocket in your pocket or he'd bench you?"

"It ain't my fault my Space Shuttle makes pussies cry."

He laughs.

I always make Beau laugh.

He needs it. He's too serious. I know it's a quarterback thing. He's always in his head. He's always thinking about plays and performance and passes.

Not pussy.

And I need him. I don't have anyone else. I don't want anyone else. All a guy needs is his best friend, teammates, and mom.

But Beau is more to me. I don't have to be the fastest or the best with him. I'm just me—the best friend who always buys him golden Oreos. And he's the best friend who bought me a pair of Air Jordans for my birthday. He knew I wanted them but couldn't afford them, and now we wear matching red pairs for Bama.

Beau's always watched out for me, for everyone. It's like he has to save everyone but himself, and I've always wondered why.

Maybe it's another quarterback thing, maybe it's a big brother thing, or maybe it's more. Maybe he focuses on others so he doesn't have to be honest about himself.

I know the feeling.

I've had it since the day I warned him at practice about

the back of his neck getting sunburned. So he sat on the bench and tossed me a bottle of sunscreen. "Hook me up," he said, spinning the ball in one hand.

It hit me so fast when I rubbed his hot skin, how he barely moaned, and I definitely heard him. I definitely got hard. I had to stop. I had to leave.

"Where you goin'?" he asked.

"To squirt the dirt," I answered before I found a shitter stall in the locker room to jerk off, and I've known it ever since.

I love Beau Bronson, and he loves me.

"I say we leave the sophomores alone," he mutters. "Most pussy's not worth it."

Still, he's ogling Piper's tits by the pool, and he's hovering hard and thick and left toward me, and that feeling, the one that scares me, the one I crave, too, surges inside.

It's more than a painful urge for Beau in my hard dick. It's in my soft heart for him, too.

I can't help it. I lick my lips at Beau's desire because it matches mine.

I've caught him, flicking his glance away from me naked in the locker room. Or when I step nude out of his shower, hoping he'll do it again while he's brushing his teeth. I especially love it when we sit across each other and scarf down a dozen scrambled eggs with salsa.

The way Beau looks at me feels like home.

Because I fight it, too.

I fight how I smell Beau's pillow when he's in the shower. I fight how I'll use his soap, loving how we smell alike. I fight how we wear each other's T-shirts and grey boxer briefs because his mom is sweet and throws my laundry in with his.

The truth is I practically live with Beau because I love Beau.

"If we leave the sophomores alone." My voice gets gruff because I can't stop staring, from his hard arousal, up to his parted lips and back down again at the temptation jutting in his shorts. "Then what am I supposed to do with this?"

I'm aching. I'm scared. I'm curious. But I can't fight it because I'm in love. I'm tingling everywhere. I'm sweating. Heat coils tight in my spine. My dick aches raw and ready. It's like the first time I fucked a pussy, but it's more.

It's Beau.

He lowers the binoculars, lowering his gaze, too, and when the tip of his tongue licks his lip at the sight of my matching erection, I know exactly what comes over me.

It's lust. It's love. I won't hide it when we're alone.

It's the first time I reach for Beau, grabbing the back of his neck. It's the first time he grabs me back. It's our first kiss, which I swear lasts for hours, our tongues and lips exploring what's been building between us. It's our deep moans, our flesh burning with need. It's the first time we yank our shirts off, our hands grabbing and groping for what we need. It's our breath that can't keep up as we rip our shorts open, shucking our boxers down just enough to free ourselves.

And it's the first time I nuzzle my forehead to Beau's and fist his thick cock against mine where it belongs.

We gasp together. After all the nights of jerking off solo, we do it together. We watch our cocks together. It's beautiful, glazing my swollen tip over his, my aching shaft rubbing, pumping against his hard velvet, swelling tighter and tighter for us.

When I hear his desperate, thinning breath match mine? When I see his tempting pre-cum drip and mix with mine? When I thrust against his cock, clenched tight in my grasp with mine, I don't last.

I shake so hard I can't speak. I just groan, watching while I spill my thick pearly cum, spurting over his raw tip like it's kissing mine, and my cum makes him come.

"Fuck," he shudders. "Fuck, Colt. Fuck, baby. Yes, shoot your cum on me. Shoot it on my dick." He groans before his fat tip squirts with force, splattering my abs before coating my fist, spilling his warm cream over our raw tips, and it makes me grunt again, granting his wish, watching our slits open and spurt even more.

Witnessing our orgasms, my desire mixing with Beau's is everything I want, and I'm overwhelmed. I'm hopeful. I'm unguarded. "I love you," it falls from my parted lips.

But Beau stiffens and pulls away, his hard cock still dripping with his love for me, his blue eyes soft and filling with regret. "We can't, man. You know we can't. Not again. Not ever. They'll kill us if they know."

Who are they?

Name an out openly gay or bisexual Division 1 or top NFL player on any roster. You can't because you can have all the laws, policies, and fiction you want. It ain't reality. Not yet.

Still, that hurt like hell. My heart shatters. I shove the tears away.

I don't know what to do with my feelings or Beau's rejection, though I know he's doing it to protect me. I know he loves me, too.

So...

I stop spending the night at his house. I stop hanging out with him and the guys from the team.

I do my thing. I start fucking Ashley Porter and Maria

Thompson every chance I can. Because I still like pussy though I love Beau.

We won't survive four years at Bama together, not like this. It'll hurt too much, so I do the one thing he'll hate me for because I love him that much, too.

I make some calls and change my plans, *our plans*. I sign a scholarship deal to play for Auburn University, while Beau plays for The University of Alabama.

When you're arch rivals, you can't be in love.

Right?

CHAPTER FOUR

I'm prepared like a horny Girl Scout.

Now

"Folks, we've reached our cruising altitude of thirty thousand feet. I've turned the seat belt sign off for now, but ask that you remain seated as much as possible." The captain warns, "We might have some chop ahead."

Did he say chop?

Or death?

I tug my seat belt tighter.

"You alright there, Kitten?" Beau catches my terrified gesture.

I don't care if we're sitting in luxury in the sky. It's still the sky, and gravity still works. It's my second time on a plane, and I start regretting eating eggs over easy for breakfast.

"I'm fine," I lie, trying not to focus on our imminent plunge into the ocean.

Across from me in his recliner is Beau, smiling, looking

way too sexy, and five minutes from his forced beach vacation. He's sporting a thin, white V-neck T-shirt, giving me peeks of those carved pecs dusted with dark hair that make me feral. His khaki shorts are relaxed over his flexing quads, and his flips flop over groomed feet.

Yes, even Beau's toes are turn-ons.

Across the aisle from us in matching recliners are Colton and Amber. I gotta admit they're the best distraction when you fear death any second.

It's like studying a masterpiece painting from the What The Fuck era.

Colton Hawke looks like Thor had a baby with Ink Master. He's big for a wide receiver but still exceptionally fast—even I know that—and that's what makes him one of the greatest in the league.

But come on. Football doesn't impress me.

So, is it his dark blond hair that falls past his broad shoulders? Nope. His trim beard? No. His features that look like a Nordic god who can smash you to bits, or the tattoos from his knuckles, up his beefy arms, disappearing under his lavender t-shirt? Nah.

It's his eyes.

They're deep brown and tender. They avoided Beau but greeted me with genuine kindness as if he already knew me.

So why is this colossal, sweet hunk dating an enormous ego slut?

Don't judge my judging.

I'm using empirical evidence.

Amber Kostas has posted sixty out of the ninety minutes so far on this flight. She chats to her socials, sucking her cheeks in, sharing contouring tips and warnings like it's live news of a possible nuclear make-up meltdown.

Here I am with a ponytail and no makeup except for my red lips, though I'm so nervous I must be fifty shades of green. But Amber? She shimmers all blonde in a million shades of blended bronze.

Hell, I thought a tan was free, but apparently, as Amber informs us and her followers, her natural bronze costs one hundred and five dollars from Hermès.

Beau's killer blues threaten to permanently roll to the back of his skull. Colton tunes her out with his Bose headphones on and eyes closed. And I thought people can't use their phones on planes, but when it's a private jet to Belize, you are free to annoy the shit out of everyone.

Jimmy Williams, the head coach of Atlanta, and his wife, Maureen, are seated on a sofa toward the front of the jet while the flight attendant starts pouring champagne.

Apparently, the Williams are turning Beau and Colton's forced retreat into their vacation. They'll stay on the mainland while we are stuck on an island with Amber, the CNN of Cosmetics.

"Enjoy this round, folks." Coach Williams raises a full flute. "There's no alcohol on the retreat."

"What?" Amber whips around, snapping at him, "I didn't agree to that."

"Your ass is in that seat," Beau grumbles. "That's your cushy agreement right there."

"We need clear heads," Coach lectures, "and no distractions. That means no social media posts from the island either."

"But I have to maintain my brand," Amber whines before kicking Colton's feet. He jumps, yanking his headphones down to hear her bitch, "You didn't tell me no alcohol and social media. How am I supposed to survive?"

"On air, water, and food," Beau grumbles again, and I choke down my snort.

Clearly, Beau doesn't like Amber. In one hour, I understand why, but I suspect there's more.

"I *did* tell you," Colton glowers at her attitude. "You just didn't listen."

"Well, I don't play for Atlanta," Amber snips, "so I'll do as I please."

"When you're on Atlanta's dime," Coach corrects, "you'll follow the same rules, or you're out."

I like his version of the NFL Survivor show. Amber is definitely my first vote off the island. I won't survive ten days of her vocal fry voice and baked delusion because the world is her phone screen, and we're all just her followers.

But me?

I got my laptop, my loaded ereader, two empty journals, my favorite Micron pens, a bunch of Target sundresses and fancy La Perla bikinis Vale insisted I "sample" for Delta's.

And once Beau told me we didn't have to suffer luggage scans at a private airport, I packed a hardshell case full of sex toys, dildos, lingerie, and my hairdryer.

Don't mess with a pro.

I know how to win the Tempting Bet with Beau. I'm prepared like a horny Girl Scout. His big dick will be testing me every waking hour, so I brought vibrating survival gear.

Now, do I want to be with Beau Bronson again and always? Is this plane flying five hundred miles an hour toward my watery grave?

Yes.

Will I?

Sure.

I'll survive sex with Beau again like I'll survive wearing a little yellow inflatable vest with a plastic whistle in the middle of the fastest ocean current in the world when we go down.

But was I shocked that Beau asked me to go with him on his forced luxury vacation?

No.

I've protected his secret for so long, I understand. I may not fuck him again, but I'll always sorta love him.

A lot.

Because the tension between Beau and Colton has its own latitude and longitude.

The only one oblivious to it is Amber. But if it ever makes it to her Instagram feed, she'll dedicate the latest viral dance to it with her blonde bestie. Don't worry.

I watch Beau, who alternates his stare between me and the window. This is hard on him. I can tell.

I'll never forget the pain in his eyes that senior night in college. His lush bottom lip was busted, his eyes brimming with tears.

"Can I come in?" He trembled with torment in my dorm's doorway. "I know Reese isn't here. I came for you."

I didn't answer. I just wrapped around him while he buried his face in my neck, his hidden tears wetting my flesh.

"I just lost my best friend again," he said while we laid together on my twin bed in our shorts and T-shirts, sharing a pillow while Beau stared into my eyes. "He, uh. He kissed me, and I kissed him back. We did some stuff like we did in high school. But we can't be together. And afterward, when I reminded him, he got mad again. We got in a fight. Said some mean shit. I swear we punched each other at the same time. So I had to walk away. So did he."

I traced over his swollen lip. "Do you love him?"

The relief that flooded Beau's eyes that I wasn't judging him, that I cared, that I supported him? "Yes," he answered. "I love him. I have to secretly love him." He paused. "Like I secretly love you, Blair."

Beau's deep blue eyes vulnerably searched mine and found that place hidden in my heart for two years.

"I love you, too," I murmured, letting my tears and secret escape. "But we can't, Beau. We can't hurt Reese. She's too delicate. She's too close to graduating."

"She's been acting strange," he said. "Like she's been avoiding me for weeks, like something's wrong."

"Sadly, something's always wrong with her, and you can't fix her. Only she can."

He caressed a lock of my hair. "So what are *we* supposed to do?"

"Not get what we want." I couldn't stop touching his lips. Lips I couldn't kiss but was dying to. "It hurts, but it won't kill us."

He nuzzled his forehead to mine. "You know I give you hell because you'd be my heaven."

I nuzzled my nose against his. "You know I hate you because you kinda make me love you."

We slept like that, holding each other, but when I awoke, Beau was gone. Still, I felt so special because he left his secret safe with me. It'll always be, and that's what makes this bittersweet.

I'm here to help Beau deny his love for Colton and me.

But I won't have to do it long. We're about to die. A hard jolt shakes the plane. My stomach drops, and, "Jesus, take the wheel," I yelp.

The seatbelt light chimes, and we've flown into the eighth circle of hell. Then it becomes the ninth circle because Amber starts yapping at her phone, wrestling with the existential debate of matte versus glossy lipstick while our tiny jet is a yo-yo at thirty thousand feet.

"Hey." Beau leans forward, reaching for my clammy hand. "It's okay. It's just turbulence. We'll bounce right through it."

Another jolt smacks the plane.

Colton takes his headphones off, glancing toward the cockpit.

"We're fine," he assures. "If the crew is calm, we're calm. Besides, once you fly through a nor'easter after a loss to Boston, this little tropical breeze ain't shit."

"Now," Amber advises no one on her screen while we face certain doom, "if you're old, like over thirty, don't wear matte. It's a felony."

No, a felony is what I'll commit once I barf into the paper bag I grab from the side leather pocket of my recliner. I'll fill it with my bile and breakfast before I shove it down Amber's Botoxed neck. I swear the woman has no pores or creases like she's AI and evil.

Beau sees how I must be as green as the Wicked Witch of the West.

"Hey, babe." He unfastens his belt and kneels before me, holding my hand. "It's okay. Hang in there. We'll be fine."

He's taking this fake girlfriend thing to real levels. He's risking his safety for me.

"Get back in your seat," I tell him as the plane shakes violently, making my mouth water, but I worry. "You'll get hurt."

"I'm fine." He ignores the laws of physics.

"Dude, she's right," Colton barks at him. "Get back in your seat. The last thing we need is for you to have a head injury, too."

"Fuck you, Hawke." Beau meets his glare. "My shoulder tear wasn't my fault."

"I didn't say it was," Colton snarls back. "But a head injury due to turbulence because you weren't buckled in would be."

Coach Williams clips. "Hawke's right. Buckle up, Bronson."

"I'm fine," I lie to Beau, squeezing his hand. "I'll be oh—"

God swats the plane like a fly in the sky, and here it is. My eggy embarrassment spews into the paper bag in my other hand.

"Babe?" Beau reaches for my cheek but—

"Bronson!" Colton shouts. "In your fucking seat!"

"Fuck off!" Beau pulls away while I make sure to get some vomit on my cute white ruffled top, too. "You ain't my dad."

"No, fucker." Colton leans our way. "I'm your best friend, remember? You hurt, I hurt, so buckle up. She'll be okay."

Colton gently palms my shoulder. He's seated directly across from me, diagonal to Beau. "Right? You'll be okay, Raven." I like his nickname for me. "Just imagine we're flying on God's fingertip. We'll be there safe and real soon, I promise."

Something about Colton's warmth and Beau's concern makes me feel better—that and the eggs that can't torment my dropping stomach anymore.

"I'm okay," I mumble while Beau still leans forward, his hand on my shaking knee, though he's buckled in again.

I close my eyes and make promises I won't keep to all the gods until, finally, the hell stops.

"Folks," the captain eases like we just got a full-body

massage, "we're past the chop now. Should have smooth skies until we touch down."

But now I'm sufficiently mortified and reek of vomit.

"Blair." Beau can read me, making me open my teary eyes. "Babe, you can go to the bathroom now and freshen up. We can get a fresh shirt for you, too."

"No." I tremble. "I can't stand."

"Okay." Beau reaches over his shoulder. In a quick snap, his T-shirt is off. "Wear mine until you feel better."

I take his offer, discreetly slipping out of my soiled shirt while shimmying his on. Why? Because Beau's shirt is warm and it smells like him, and the view of his shredded naked torso across from me would cure cholera.

For the last hours of the flight, I survive with Beau as my man candy. A few times, I glance over and catch Colton doing the same.

Once we land, I freshen up in the plane's microscopic bathroom. To match my white peasant skirt, I tug on the clean white bandeau top I snagged from my carry-on before I rinse my mouth and feel human again.

After one hour on a van followed by a boat ride, we're here on the tiny private island, a five-minute water taxi ride from the mainland.

The island is tiny. It's one and a half acres of white sand, a couple of palm trees, and turquoise water everywhere. At its center is the open-concept home, with two tiny detached cottages standing behind it. That's where the chef and maid live.

Everything is luxury meets rustic island style.

The living room is really a massive covered wooden deck with sofas facing a feature wall just wide enough to fit a flatscreen. Behind it, everything is open to the pool, spa loungers, and the shimmering ocean outside.

The gourmet kitchen is at the back of the large, vaulted-ceiling living area. It's intimate and just enough for the guests, with eight stools seated around a polished white marble island.

There are four bedrooms in a Jack n' Jill arrangement. Two adjoining bedrooms are separated by a teak wood and white tiled bathroom with high, open, shuttered windows letting the light and warm breeze in.

Beau claims a guest bedroom for us while Colton tosses his duffel down on the king-size bed in the bedroom across the open breezeway.

I stand in the breezeway, laptop bag slung over my shoulder, almost amused at how they move in silent, pissed-off concert with one another.

Amber claims Colton's adjoining bedroom as her "glam room," and for once, I'm thankful for her vanity. I claim Beau's adjoining room as my "writing room" when only Beau knows I'll be sleeping here, too.

"Alright!" Coach Williams summons us like summer campers back to the living room.

The sun is starting to set. Its tranquility captivates me, but Coach doesn't share my Zen.

This is business to him. Billion-dollar football business.

"Get unpacked and rest tonight because you two start at nine a.m. sharp," he orders.

Then, he aims the flatscreen remote at Beau, then Colton, then the lavish sofa poised in front of the flatscreen with its video conference tech on top. "Every morning, you'll sit here, log on to your call, and do your sessions with Dr. Gary."

But Beau and Colton eye the sofa like a proctologist's exam table, not a plush beachy place to relax with white cushions and turquoise throw pillows.

"And you two." Coach points to me and Amber like third-string players. "Play somewhere else. By the pool. On the boat. In your rooms. I don't give two shits. Give them privacy because if I catch wind you're distractions, you're out."

Is this where Beau gets his distraction phobia? Or is it a legit football fear based on statistical evidence? Like a good dicking down that also melts your heart causes defeat?

"Yes, sir." Either way, I salute Coach with a grin, and Beau winks at my compliance.

But Amber rolls her eyes, and if she had it, she'd smack gum, too. "What's the Wi-Fi password?"

"Amber, jeez." Colton rolls his eyes. "Fuckin' chill with the socials. No one lives by what you eat for breakfast."

"I have a deal with a Total Soul Cleanse tea." She weaves her neck. "My followers need me for inspo."

Hell, I'm inspired. I'm buying. Because clearly, Amber has thoroughly cleansed, shitting her soul right down the porcelain bowl ages ago.

She doesn't get it.

She doesn't feel it.

But I do. And I respect Coach Williams because he does, too. Yes, he demands performance and perfection from his players, but he understands victory starts in the mind.

And clearly, Beau and Colton are all kinds of mind-fucked over whatever happened between them. If they start training camp with this toxic, hot tension? You can forget the Super Bowl.

It'll be a super war.

The coach is so annoyed he doesn't answer Amber. He focuses on what matters: his players.

"I'll be back in the morning to start your first session," he warns. "We're damn lucky Dr. Gary is helping us. The man is the Freud of Football. He writes books on this, and I had to bribe Jesus to make this happen. So if he tells you two to wail like banshees or fall into a fetal position while you console your inner child, you goddamn better. Am I clear?"

"Yes, coach."

Beau and Colton reply with respect. And I can tell it's not just because they're paid millions.

They want this to work. They *need* this to work.

If not, they lose their dream.

CHAPTER FIVE

After a water taxi takes Coach back to his beach hotel, I listen to him. I get busy unpacking. I can't live out of suitcases. I need a clean room to write dirty smut.

"You feeling better?"

Beau leans in the bathroom doorway connecting our rooms.

"Yeah." I unzip the last hard case resting on my bed of white linens and throw pillows. "Barfing my guts out really made my day. Time to take a shower and call it a night."

"Thanks for this." Humbly, he shoves his hands in his pockets. But he's still shirtless, teasing me with his gazillion pack of steel abs, a dark, thin, happy trail, and soft blue puppy dog eyes. "I mean it. I really appreciate this, Blair."

Sexy asshole.

He's such a pro.

Beau can be serious, sweet, and seductive at the same time. I suspect Vegas and my vagina favor him to win our tempting bet.

So I stay strong. I start unpacking my weapons hidden in black silk *DELTA'S* bags.

"Whatcha got there?" And Beau grins, spotting their obvious eggplant shape.

"My real boyfriends."

"*Really?*" He smirks. "Care to introduce me?"

I have manners. I take a few out, presenting them like a royal receiving line.

"If you please." I wave the dual-ended dildo. "Meet Mr. Glass. He dates my pussy and ass." I take out the lifelike one with a wide suction base. "And this is Sir Sticky. But I believe you've already met at The Mercier." The memory ignites Beau's eyes. "And this is Master Moan. He speaks six vibrating languages." I hold the purple and white most expensive dildo for Beau to admire before I unveil one more. "And this is Mr. Bronson. I save him for special occasions."

The dildo I named after Beau is a King Cock Girthy Ultra with a realistic curve and seven and a half inches of insertable heaven.

Beau licks his lips at it. "And on what special occasions do you date big Mr. Bronson?"

"When he spoils me, inviting me on a relaxing, tropical writing vacation."

The sudden thrill fades from his eyes. "I'm glad you'll be happy. That's all that matters because it's not a vacation for me." He mutters, asking, "Is it obvious? The shit between us?"

He knows we're good. We're safe. I'm armed with

dildos, and we're never fucking again, so he's worried about his war with Colton.

"Yes," I'm honest, putting my toys back in their bags. "It's obvious to me and your coach. There's so much tension between you two that you won't make it through training camp or the pre-season until you fix it. But don't worry. It's not obvious *why*."

He glances down, toeing the floor, so I ask, "Beau, what happened? You know this Dr. Gary guru is going to ask."

"I'll never tell him. Neither will Colt. It's career suicide."

"But you have doctor-patient confidentiality."

He scoffs, "It's the NFL. Even my stool sample isn't confidential. I signed the right to privacy away a long time ago."

I put my boyfriends in the nightstand and plop down on the bed. "So, will you at least tell me? I sorta know what happened in college. But tell me more. Tell me what happened before the Super Bowl, too."

Beau trudges over and falls on the bed beside me. He stares at the ceiling fan whirling above. "I'm afraid to tell you."

"Why?" I sit beside him, my leg touching his thigh. "You know I'll never judge. I'll put fake cockroaches in your gym bag, but I'll never hurt you."

He grins. "Remember when I filled your dorm room with ten dozen dick balloons?"

"Asshole." I chuckle. "You know I love big dicks but have a globophobia. Popping balloons freak me out."

"I know." He starts laughing. "Like you know I have a phobia for fucking bugs."

"Didn't stop you from freeing crickets in my car."

"I paid a buddy to do that."

I nudge his leg. "Then tell *this* buddy the truth. What happened between you and Colton?"

He sighs, regret and more twisting his handsome face.

"We hadn't spoken since high school," he explains. "In college, we were true rivals. We hated each other. Alabama won three Iron Bowls in a row until we lost to Auburn our senior year. And the truth is, I was mindfucked in that last game, too. I could feel Colt's eyes burning into me from across the field. I let Auburn take us into a tie game, and our kicker couldn't make the fifty-seven-yard field goal, so Auburn caught the ball in the end zone and ran it one hundred and nine yards for the win. And it was my fault, and I know it."

I nudge his thigh. "So what happened next?"

"A few months after the bowl game, I ran into Colt over spring break at a bar in Gulf Shores, and it's like our fight was over. We'd finally grown up some. We did some shots, and shit was good. So good that he showed up at my apartment later that March to talk more, but Reese was there, so we couldn't. We played beer pong instead. He got chummy with Reese, too, and we got hammered and passed out.

"Then Colt showed up again a month later." Beau sighs. "That's not true. I invited him over when I *knew* Reese went home for the weekend. I don't know what I thought would happen..."

He squirms like something's scratching inside him.

"Fuck, that's not true, either. I missed him. A lot," he confesses. "My roommates were at a party. It was just us, and we caught up about our families and the coming draft. He was hoping for Arizona. I knew I was gonna get Atlanta. It's like we were so good again; we found ourselves kissing."

I watch Beau's body, his face too. He's tense, but I swear he's getting hard remembering.

"It's like we need each other so much," he says, "we kinda go crazy whenever we're alone. So, we did our thing like we did in high school—frotting." He glances at me. "You know what that is?"

I nod, aroused by the image of him rubbing his hard cock against Colton's until they come.

"Well, Colt wanted more. He wanted us to be each other's firsts, and fuck, I wanted it, too, but I knew there'd be no going back. I love him too much. I can't be with him once and then not have him again."

My heart wrenches.

It hurts.

I understand.

It's exactly how I feel about what happened between Beau and me on Valentine's Night. It hurts too much to have love for a night and never again.

"So," Beau mutters, "I turned him down again. He knows it's us or football, so we got in a big fight. That's what brought me to your door."

"Why me?" I ask. "Why did you know you could come to me?"

Beau's deep blue eyes with those thick black lashes study me for a long, aching beat. They make my heart feel like cracking glass when he tenderly answers, "I can't explain it, Blair. I've always felt like I belong with you, too. Like you're the other one I can't have. Like I have to pick between having you or him or my dream." He's so honest and hurting. "Am I wrong?"

"No." I want to hold his hand, but there'd be no going back for us either. I can't touch him and not get lost in him. "I feel it, too. But I understand. I'm a *distraction*."

My honesty silences him, but Beau won't look away. So,

I let him see how much the truth hurts, how much that one word hurts me—*distraction.*

It reduces the tears we've shed when he was last inside me to an annoying gnat.

Yeah, it really fucking hurts.

And when Beau mumbles, "Blair, I'm sorry. It's just with you? Or with him? I'm not a perfect football machine. I'm a really fucking flawed human who feels a lot, and I don't work."

See? I understand that, too.

We share a look so heavy with passion, honesty, and pain that it's hard to breathe. The future can't be ours, so I ask about the past. "But the Iron Bowl was eight years ago. What happened before the Super Bowl this year?"

His lip curls. "Hurricane Amber."

I nod. "That woman is pure destruction."

"In a way, she cost us the game."

"How?"

He studies the ceiling again.

"I can't blame her." He sighs, "Me and Colt and our... whatever... it goes way back. But three years ago, he got traded to Atlanta, and it was weird. It was as if we never fought, we never kissed. We just started playing like we were eighteen again, and it was fucking magic. Coach was ecstatic. Our owner, too. It's like they found lightning in a bottle, putting us back together, and we were. We were perfect and best friends again til the night before the Super Bowl."

"So where's Amber in this?"

"Colt started dating her during the pre-season. The press loves it. She's some influencer from hell. But what they don't see on socials is how those two fight, and it's toxic. She's toxic. She doesn't give a shit about Colt or his game. She only cares about his clout. And I don't like her, and she knows it because she fucks with his head."

I shake mine. "She fucks with yours, too."

"No, Colt fucks with my head. Because the night before the game, it was after curfew in our hotel. I'd just taken my shower and settled into bed to start my good night jerk-off and—"

The image of Beau's fist pumping his thick, hard cock, his lips parted, his chin tossed up in ecstasy—I know what he looks like when he comes, and it electrifies my lonely clit.

Go ahead.

Paint *LOSER* on my forehead. He's going to win our bet.

Any minute, I'll be so fucked.

By him.

"And then Colt was banging on my hotel door," he says. "He and Amber were fighting like usual. She wasn't even supposed to be in his room, so he needed a place to crash. It was past curfew. We're supposed to stay on our floor, in our rooms, so I let him in, hard dick in my boxers and all, and we—"

Shouts grab our attention.

We fall silent, our ears straining to hear.

"Goddammit, Amber!" That's Colt across the breeze-way. "Coach told you no posts!"

I stare at Beau. He stares back, but we're hooked. We're eavesdropping.

"He's not the boss of me!" Amber shrieks back. "I'm Amber Kostas, and I have an image to keep. My people expect perfection!"

Her people? What is she? A filtered dictator saving the world with a ring light and make-up tutorials?

I fall back, laughing on the bed. Beau laughs, too. "See what I mean," he mutters.

"She's as smooth as lactose intolerance," I mutter, too, and he laughs harder.

"You'll get kicked off!" Colton booms. "You said you were creating content, not posting it. Keep it up, and Coach will send you packing."

"Fine!" She shrieks again. "I don't want to be stuck here with you and no Prosecco while I suffer your asshole teammate and his weird girlfriend. She's fluffy. Like Jessica Rabbit in black and white. Someone please tell her it's the twentieth century!"

"It's the twenty-*first* century, Amber!" Colton shouts back.

And I want to laugh even harder, but why did that hurt? Why do I care what a woman like that thinks about me?

I fall silent while their immature shouts continue until Beau suddenly crawls over me.

"Hey," he eases, the back of his fingers gently brushing my cheek. "Don't listen to her. You're fucking breathtaking, Blair. I love your look. I always have. It's unique. It's sexy as hell. It takes zero intelligence and no beauty to look like her, like everyone else. But you?" I gaze up at him. "Everything about you has me in awe."

He's so sweet; he takes the sting away.

I grin. "You're just trying to get laid again."

He doesn't smile. "No, I'm trying to make you realize how special you are. I'd rather have one beautiful, raven-haired, bookish beauty in glasses with killer curves than a dozen made-up fake blondes sporting trendy shades any day. And why Colt suffers a fool like her, that's his problem because you're my panacea."

A laugh bursts from my mouth. "Panacea? When did you learn Latin?"

"I didn't." He grins, lowering his lush mouth to mine. "I read it on a jar of vegan protein powder."

I smile when his whiskers brush my lips. "Beau," I lie, "this isn't remotely tempting."

"Really?" He lowers his body, too, his hard warmth blanketing mine. It's so natural how his knees spread my thighs open, and I let him. It wedges my skirt up to my hips, and he rolls his, finding the spot crying out for him. "If I don't tempt you, Blair, then tell that to the sweet, hard pink nipples I can see through your top. They want me to suck them while I fuck you again. Don't they?"

He grinds his thick erection against my thin lace panties, rubbing against my lonely clit, and I gasp, "Beau."

"See? You're tempted," he teases. "You're lying, Kitten. My cock can feel your heat. I can feel your pretty pussy getting so wet for me."

"No, I'm not," I lie. "Finish your Super Bowl story."

Beau gazes down. He and his one-eyed monster can see right through me.

"You want to know what Colt and I did in bed together?" He keeps grinding his granite cock against my soft pussy, and I moan. Beau's found my poison, *our poison,* because he confesses, lowering his lips to my ear, "Do you want to know how I get so hard for him? The same way I get so hard for you? The same way I want inside him, I want inside you? Do you want to hear how I want to fuck him," he thrusts hard, "and fuck you, Blair?"

"Beau," I gasp again.

I'm going to lose on the first night because, with me, Beau's not ashamed of his dual desires. He's safe, he's free. He wants me, and he wants Colton. It burns in his eyes, trapping me beneath him, and I can't resist his lust, his hard pressing need wanting inside me right now.

I need him, too. I reach to stroke him and...

SLAM!

Colton's bedroom door shakes the house. Seconds later, he's standing by the pool.

My bedroom lights are on. A wall of my bedroom, like all bedrooms, has sliding glass doors to the outside, and he can see in.

Colton's staring right at Beau on top of me. At how Beau's one zipper yanked down and one pair of soaked panties ripped aside from fucking me.

"Shit," Beau mutters, spotting him. "This is like the night before the Super Bowl. He needs help. He has nowhere to go where Amber won't make his life hell."

And I see it, too, how Colton looks like a caged and lonely, miserable animal.

"Let me," I ease, pushing Beau back. "Let me talk to him."

COLTON

CHAPTER SIX

I'D RATHER FUCK A FIRE ANT HILL.

The night before the Super Bowl

I bang on Beau's hotel door. I know he'll open it. I know he'll help me.

It doesn't matter how much we've hurt each other or what we hide or deny; this is best friends watching out for one another, and the wooden door swings open.

"Can I crash here?" I grumble.

Beau doesn't even ask. He knows. He steps aside and holds the door open.

Do I miss that all he's wearing are tight gray boxers over his big, raging hard-on? Nope. It only adds to my frustration.

I sit on the edge of his king-sized bed and bury my head in my hands. "I told her I needed lights out by ten. I need sleep, but she's going live, and sharing her Super Bowl looks like people give a shit. I asked her to stop, but she wouldn't, so I had to get out of there."

I glance up to see Beau rummaging through a gift basket on the table by the window. He tosses me a bottle of water from it before he cracks one open for himself.

"She doesn't give a shit about you," he mutters. "Sorry, man, it's true, and I don't know why you put up with her."

"Better than being alone like you. Besides, she understands the biz."

"Does she? Or does she understand the media but not the sport? But hey," he shrugs, "she's got a massive rack, and you're a sucker for tits and tan blondes."

"I don't have a type," I grumble. "I just need some goddamn peace."

"You won't find it with her."

I lift the bottle and guzzle it down, knowing he's right. I'm thirsty, but around Beau, it gets confusing what for. Especially when he's in the best shape of his life and in his goddamn briefs, his cock now hanging half-hard, and that's still damn big.

So I grin. "Did I interrupt your date with Kleenex?"

He grins back before downing his water, wiping drops off his chin with his forearm. "Nah, I've leveled up to a Pocket Pussy with lube."

I glance at the nightstand and suddenly clock it, shocked. "You can have any pussy you want. Why the hell did you buy a fake one to fuck?"

"I didn't. It was a gag gift from a pussy I've been dying to fuck."

"Oh?" I rest back on my elbows. I stormed down here in my grey joggers and black t-shirt, so I'm cozy and curious. "Who? Michelle, our Director of College Scouting? She's obviously so fucking hot for you. And one look at her and any senior will sign."

"Never," he scoffs. "I don't dip my pen in the company

ink. The Pocket Pussy was from a girl in college. I kinda loved her but wouldn't cheat on Reese, and I haven't seen her since."

"So now what? You only dip your lonely pen in KY and a male masturbator?"

"Yeah," he scoffs, "because you make real pussy seem very appealing right now. You're the number one receiver in the NFL, the night before playing in the Super Bowl, and yet you're the one kicked out of *his* hotel room by a hypebeast of lipliner."

Asshole.

I laugh, throwing a pillow at him. "At least I got *real* lips locked on my cock, daily."

He catches it, of course, and throws it back at my face, laughing. "Is that the price of peace? A little liplock from the most annoying mouth ever? I'd rather fuck a fire ant hill."

"At least it shuts her up," I confess. "I don't have to hear about Kylie versus Rihanna." Beau looks confused. "They have their own makeup lines."

He throws his stubbled chin up, laughing. "Never tell anyone you know that."

"My secret is safe with you."

It's sudden. The tender look in his eyes. The heavy stillness that takes the room.

Beau nods, muttering, "We need sleep. Rumor is we have the game of our lives tomorrow."

He starts shutting off the lights while I refresh in his bathroom. I finger-brush my teeth with his toothpaste, see his bottle of liquid soap on the counter, and smell it.

Memories and desire rush through my veins.

It does something to me.

Beau does something to me.

It doesn't matter the years we fought in college, the

secret tattoos on my sleeves about him, the epic Iron Bowl battles, or even the drunken senior night I regret playing beer pong with him and his frisky girlfriend. I have so many memories, and a couple were horrible.

But me and Beau?

I regret our fights, but I'll never regret our love.

We're not a mistake.

Our love just isn't allowed in our world.

I crawl in beside him, into the crisp white hotel sheets on the made side of his bed. Beau's closed the window sheers but left the heavy drapes open. He hates sleeping in pitch dark. He says it makes him oversleep, so the muted lights of Vegas filter through, and I can see his eyes are open. He's staring at the ceiling.

"Can't sleep without giving your Pocket Pussy a creamy kiss goodnight?"

I make him smile, pausing before he asks, "Why do you date a woman like Amber when you can find so much better?"

I have nothing left to lose. I can't have Beau, so why lie about this? I've always been honest with him, except for the one thing I have to hide.

"Because I can't have you," I answer, "so I punish myself with ones who'll never compare."

I don't get this anywhere else in my life. Only with Beau am I really me, am I really alive.

He turns his head, his brow furrowed. "Why do you punish yourself over us? We're not a sin. We're a secret."

"Don't you?" I ask. "Don't you punish yourself with shallow one-night stands? I see you. How no one gets close, no one's a distraction. You have a big heart, but you won't share it."

"That's not true."

"You found someone?"

Why does that hurt? And why do I care?

Why? Because I know Beau. He doesn't date. He's a forever man. He'll commit if he ever finds a woman he trusts, one who makes him laugh and love. He's just waiting. He won't be distracted now, but later?

He'll be hers. Always.

I just hope he never finds another man, one he can be open with. I won't survive it. I won't know how to breathe.

"No, I haven't found anyone," he answers. "I find my fun. I got my kinks. When we win, I reward myself with a night with a French maid, a dirty schoolgirl, or both. That's it."

"That's *it*?" Fuck, he stirs my cock. "A maid *and* a dirty schoolgirl? Damn, I never knew. Do you get the schoolgirl all dirty for the maid to clean, or are they just into you? Gimme all the nasty details. Do you spank them for being bad?"

He laughs in the dark. "Yes, and fuck no. This is what I mean. *You're* my distraction, Hawke. We need to sleep."

And this is what knowing someone half of your life and loving them, too, gets you. When we're alone, we're a hundred percent real.

"I can't." I grind into the mattress like it's his bunk bed. "Your kink made me hard."

"There's Kleenex in the bathroom."

"I don't want Kleenex."

"I'm out of Puffs."

"I don't want Puffs or pussy either."

I let the silence hang, heavy and wanting like my leaking cock.

"What do you want?" he finally asks, his deepening, gruff voice arousing me more.

"Something a dirty maid or a naughty schoolgirl can never give me." I growl low, "Something *real* fucking hard and manly and thick like me."

Again, we let the silence torment us. I can hear his breath changing. Then, I hear him rustle before tossing the sheets aside.

There's plenty of light through the window. I can see his hungry eyes aimed at me. He's taken his boxers off. His naked and proud erection angles hard, hovering long and thick over his carved abs for my touch.

"Then be a man and come and get it," Beau orders as he does on the field, and I move just as fast.

I'm on him. I'm taking my chance. I don't even tease.

I'm too hungry, too crazed to finally taste his cock in my mouth, and when I do, our loud groans could crack the walls, erupting from years of holding this lust back.

"Oh fuck yes, Colt!" Beau cries out, bowing his back, then thrusting his hips. "Fuck yes." He palms my skull like a ball, controlling my mouth. "Yes, fucking suck me. Yes, baby. That's it. Be my man. My dirty man. In your throat. All the way. Fuck yes, suck my hard cock."

And fuck yes, I do.

I don't know what I'm doing. I'm just hunched over him, plunging my lips down his wide shaft and sucking him like I love to be sucked. Hard. Gagging. Drooling and shameless.

I can't fit all of Beau in my throat; no one can, so I grab his thick base, squeezing and twisting while I lose my mind, bobbing my head, too. Gliding his swollen slick salty tip over my tongue, I want him so fucking much.

I want his pleasure because it's mine, too.

"Fuck, Colt," Beau growls. "Fuck, baby, yes. Let me suck your cock, too. I want to taste you."

We're too aroused, too familiar and foreign. We've never done this, but it feels right. I shove my joggers down, kicking them off before I yank my T-shirt off, too, and turn my naked body.

We're lying on our sides. Our cocks are hard and so desperate for each other, but it's intimate, too. The way Beau sinks his hand into my hair, watching and guiding my mouth to take him again while he thrusts his hips, not hard, just hungry enough to make me drip for him, to make me know how much he needs me.

And then he does it.

While his cock is deep in my mouth and stretching my lips, I feel his, his whiskers sinking down my shaft as he swallows my length, and my feral groan is like no other. I don't know the sounds coming from us. I've never known overwhelming pleasure like this.

I can tell he's never done this before. Neither have I, and that's what makes it too much and perfect.

My hips thrust, my cock fucking his mouth, too, and tears leak from my eyes. It's not just from his size. His cock chokes me, and I love it. I'm moaning and choking him back. I know I'm long. I know most can't take all of me, either.

But I shed tears because Beau can. He can take my body and heart because he's always had them.

My soul, too.

I don't know how long we do this. It's like we don't want it to end, but once his finger finds my virgin ass and starts teasing me, I'm gone.

"Oh shit." I drool over his tip. "Beau, please. I want you fucking my ass. Please."

"Just gimme your cum tonight," he orders. "Shoot it

down my throat, Colt. Fuck, I love you. Make me fucking choke on you. Let me finally taste you."

I give him what he wants. I palm his head between my thighs and pump my hips, watching while I fuck his sexy face. His bearded lips drool over my shaft until his gag fills the air, his fingertip sinking deep into my ass, and I'm gone.

"*Fuccck*!!" I roar. "Fuck yes. Fuck, Beau. Beau, fucking take me. Swallow." I keep pumping. I keep grunting and gasping, spilling my cum down his throat until it's drooling over his lips, too. "Fuck yes, you're my man. Take my cum. Take it."

Now it's my turn because Beau won't relent. He has to win. My cum drips from his lips while he yanks my mouth down his shaft, and I give him everything. I take him. I receive him. I open to him until I'm tasting him, too.

"Yes, Colt. Yes, baby. Take this cock in your sweet, dirty virgin mouth." He thrusts hard. "Take it. Fucking take it. I love tasting your cum on my tongue while you taste mine, too."

With five more groaning thrusts that make me gag, that make me see blissful stars, Beau's thick cock jumps in my mouth, and he can't even shout. His body just locks, his deep grunts so erotic while he holds my head still so we can't move. We're latched together while he shakes, his warm, salty love filling my mouth, and I moan, finally tasting him, swallowing him, licking every drip off my lips for him to watch.

For silent minutes, we lie together. He kisses my cock as I go soft. I do the same to him. Then I turn my body and kiss my way up his trail, one I've mapped for years, before I find his lips, and our deep kiss is new.

It tastes like us reborn, and it's terrifying.

We've crossed over again. With each rare time we're

together, it grows more intense. The deep friendship we need. The ache to be together. The love we can't deny.

But the stakes are too high now.

We can't even talk about it or fight about it anymore. We're grown men, and we know the truth.

For the first night ever, maybe the only night, I fall asleep, wrapped in Beau's arms, and I swear I feel his tears on my back. Silently, I shed them, too.

The next day, we awake, and I have to leave without another kiss. We can't speak because it'll destroy us. We don't know our world anymore. We'll always love football, but now, we hate the sport.

In our world, as teammates, we have to win today.

But the real question is, as men in love, why must we keep losing, too?

CHAPTER SEVEN

Now

Gingerly, I approach Colton, reclining on a cushioned lounger. Stars glitter above, and the moon is full, making silver light dance over the calm black water.

"Don't tell Coach Williams." I hide a silk bag behind my back. "But I brought some contraband."

He smiles, his brow raised and curious.

Don't worry; it's not a dildo from Delta's. It's a bottle of Hennessy, and when I present it to Colton, he nods, "My kinda woman," before accepting the first swig with a toast. "Thanks."

I settle on the lounger beside him, taking the bottle he passes back to me. I take a swig, too, while I catch Beau's silhouette in the dark windows of his bedroom.

His lights are off. He's watching us, but I don't mind. I'm honored he trusts me to do this.

"So," I sigh to the stars above, "got any good make-up tips?"

Colton's chuckle rumbles low while he reclines, considering the sky and his shitty relationship. "Don't do your eye makeup before your formation."

"Formation?" I laugh. "You mean *foundation*?"

"Yeah, that." He laughs back.

I pass him the bottle. We exchange a couple more burning sips before he asks, "You think I'm a dumbass, don't you?"

"Nope. I think we all got reasons for our relationships or lack thereof. Question is, do you know what yours is?"

"Uh, bad habits are hard to break?"

"Harder to break than hearts?"

"It won't break my heart to end this one," he admits. "Hell, she's got me so numb, I don't feel a thing."

Colton doesn't know I know about him and Beau. But I do, and that's not true.

He feels something powerful for Beau, and I can't sit by for ten days and watch them destroy each other and their dream over it.

"You know, when I was in college," I share, "this guy I loved to hate kept playing pranks on me. Then, one night, he showed up at my dorm with a busted lip and tears in his eyes, and it wasn't a joke. He told me about his best friend, the guy he loved, and he said he loved him, too. He just hated their world because they couldn't be together in it."

Like a comet across the sky, Colton looks at me, his huge smile beaming. "I *knew* it was you."

"What?"

"*You*. You were Reese's roommate, right? I heard about you."

"Yeah," I answer.

"Yeah, you're the one Bronson bragged about on Snapchat. The girl he played all those pranks on?"

"The one and only. And just you wait. I packed Clingwrap to put over his toilet."

"That's your toilet, too."

"That's what they make oceans for."

He softly chuckles, considering me for a moment. A long one before he gently smiles. "So, he told you about us?" I nod yes. "But you never told anyone, did you?" I shake my head no. "That's what I thought. It's *you*. He trusts you." His smile lights up his eyes. "That's why he loves you. You know that, right?"

"He doesn't love me. He loves *you*."

"Uh, you're the one he was willing to get a skull fracture for."

"I'd never hurt him," is all I can answer. "Torture him? Yes. Embarrass the shit out of him. It's my daily mission. But hurt Beau? Never. I'd never hurt you, either. Your secret's always safe with me." I shrug. "Hell, I celebrate it. I'm bi, too."

"Thanks." Colton gently pats my knee. "Thanks because God knows we fucking need it."

He lets his big, warm hand linger a little longer on my leg, and it doesn't feel wrong. It feels like *he* needs this.

"You deserve someone you can trust, too."

"I trusted my mom," he says. "She knew."

"As you should," I answer, immediately hearing the past tense. "I'm so sorry for your loss."

He winces. "I lost her last year. Brain cancer is a bitch."

I swallow hard. For such a big man who looks like he could break you in half, Colton seems broken.

"I think you found your reason," I offer, and he raises a brow, taking another swig from the bottle. "Maybe you're hanging on to Amber because you had to let go of your mom."

"Damn, Bronson," he chuffs. "The sexy lucky fucker. He gets one who's sweet, beautiful, *and* smart as hell."

"Nah," I grin, "just took a few psych classes and got a degree. But it's obvious, so let me ask you a question."

"Hang on." He aims his playful glare. "We already got mandated counseling with a sports shrink this week. So what are you shrinking?"

"Dr. Gary will shrink your balls." I make Colton grin. "But I can open your shrunken heart. Do you trust me?"

"Shoot."

"Would your mom like Amber?"

Colton's naked chest shakes so hard when he laughs. I try not to ogle, but when his body's adorned with that much exquisite ink over all those hulking muscles, what the hell am I supposed to look at? A thousand shooting stars?

"Hell, no, she wouldn't like her," he answers. "When I'd do dumb shit, my mom would smack my head and say, 'I didn't raise my son to carry his brains in his back pocket,' before she'd pinch my chin and peck my cheek. That's what she'd do right about now."

"Ummm." I take the bottle from him, then a big swig. "I like your mom."

"Yeah." He takes another long pause, his gaze my way deepening and intense. "She'd like you a lot, too."

I can see why Beau loves Colton. What's not to love? He's hot as hell, and his big heart is in the right place. He's just grieving the mom he lost and the man he can't have.

So, I share something I rarely discuss. "I lost my mom, too. Five years ago."

"Shit." He softens his face. "I'm fucking sorry. I really am."

"People who text and drive are assholes, too."

He grabs my hand and squeezes it—not in a sexy way. Grief does that. It humbles us to reach for what we have, even a stranger or a really sweet NFL player.

Or two.

We shoot the shit until an hour later when Colton sees me shiver, so he finds beach towels in a basket by the sliding glass doors. He offers a couple to me, taking one for himself.

As we wrap up, my world shifts. Beautifully. Powerfully. Inexplicably. My gravity centering, balanced by Beau and Colton's love. It pulls my heart to them. I feel warm and cozy and where I'm supposed to be.

"You know what my mom used to say?" With Colton, I like talking about her.

"Was she wicked smart like you?" With me, he's more connected to Beau.

"Yeah," I answer. "She was, and she used to say, 'Apathy is the opposite of love, not hate.'"

"So," he grins, "you're saying I'm in deep hate with Bronson because I have lots of feelings about the Super Bowl?"

"Yep. That's why y'all have your jock straps in a twist over an interception."

He laughs. "You may be right about an interception, but not jockstraps. None of us wear cups, and few wear straps."

My eyes get wide. "You free ball? Won't your meat and potatoes get mashed?"

He looks me in the eye, not too shy to explain, "A cup can pinch my potatoes, and it gets in the way. It slows me down. That's why most of us have big thighs, like pillows protecting our meat."

Don't do it. Don't look at Colton's crotch. Just accept the meaty facts.

It takes all my might not to…

Whoops, I did it. I can't fight my slutty DNA. I glance and…

Oh my god, Colton's free balling in navy cotton shorts and laying pipe like Beau. With these two, I'll have Dick Brain for days, so I force my wide pupils to lock back to his.

"You go commando?"

"Nah." He grins because he caught me drooling. "I wear the same game-day underwear. So does Bronson. White Hanes boxer briefs. We've worn them since we won state our senior year in high school."

I do the stinky math, my nostrils twitching, adding it up. "You've worn the same pair of underwear for twelve years? Eww! Talk about winning streaks."

Colton falls back, laughing. "We fucking wash them! But don't come between a player and his superstitions."

"Superstitions. Distractions." I roll my eyes. "Y'all act like voodoo wins games, not skills."

"Raven, all that matters is we win."

We curl up under our towels, talking some more until we fall asleep under the stars.

I have peaceful dreams by Colton's side. I've found a friend while our mutual love sleeps alone in his bed, and I know Beau. He wants me out here with Colton since he can't be.

But when we wake up to, "What the fuck is this?"

Amber Kostas is about to find out why you don't fuck with me until I've had my coffee.

BEAU

CHAPTER EIGHT

"Who wouldn't want to Peter, Paul, and Mary with you two?"

"What the fuck is this?"

I hear Armageddon start before it begins.

Outside my glass bedroom doors, Amber stands with fists on her waist. She's staring down at Blair and Colt, who fell asleep on their loungers.

I loved watching Blair get to know him and making him laugh. I wasn't jealous. I was relieved.

It hurts Colt and me that we can't be together, and mostly, it's my fault. I have to constantly remind him to think with his head, not his heart.

Our careers are over if we're outed.

And we didn't work this hard and sacrifice this much; our families, too, with his mom sacrificing the most, to give it all up.

But at least I can share every reason I adore Blair with Colt, too. She can make him laugh when I can't.

But now?

Amber's not laughing.

And Blair's not her bitch.

"Good morning," Blair answers Amber. "Is there a tragic problem? Did your mascara flake?"

Amber weaves her neck. "You're sleeping with my boyfriend, you fluffy bitch!"

Blair jumps to her feet, and *oh fuck!*

I yank my door open, rushing outside, but it's too late.

Blair's locked and unloading.

"Hey, Amber, since they don't sell 'em at Sephora, let me give you some BOGO enlightened thoughts for free." She points west. "That's the fucking ocean that sustains human life, not your soul-shitting tea. And that's the fucking sun rising." She points east. "And it ain't to illuminate your bleached asshole." She circles her middle finger. "And this entire planet turns whether you post about your laminated brows or not. And he," she points to Colt, "can sleep wherever he goddamn pleases, and last night, it was by his new friend, a black and white fluffy Jessica Rabbit who will fuck your rejuvenated cunt up if you step to me again."

"You little bitch—" Amber moves to leap on Blair, who's drawing her fist back to greet her face, but Colt jumps up, his expert hands knowing how to block a tackle.

"Whoa, whoa, whoa." He's half-laughing, keeping them apart while I join him.

"Settle down, ladies." I'm half-laughing, too, wrapping around Blair and scooting her back. "You turn me on when you're feisty."

"Shut up," she growls. "I'm gonna choke her on a make-up brush."

"Fuck you, you gothic creep!" Amber shouts at Blair. "Like my man would ever be interested in Casper the Cunty Ghost."

"Well," Blair starts laughing, "at least you know about alliteration. Did you learn that from a box of beige, brown, and buff bronzers from Hermès?"

Colt snorts, holding Amber back, but it's like he doesn't want to touch her. "I'm not your man anymore, Amber." His voice is calm. "We'll both be happier that way, and it's time for you to leave."

"But, but," she stammers, "I'm your date to the ESPYs. I've already bought my dress and told my followers."

"I'm sure they'll find a way to survive the devastation and so will you." He pulls away, his arms still guarding Blair, though she's safe and squirming like a snow leopard in my grasp. "I'm sure you'll find your perfect match, Amber," Colt reasons with her. "It just ain't me."

"So what? It's her now?" Amber points at Blair. "She's your match?"

"No, she's mine!" I shout before I can stop myself, so I don't. "Blair's mine and this is between you two, not us. Come on." I wrap my arm around Blair, tugging her toward my room.

She follows, muttering, "Will he be okay with her?"

"He's a very big boy," I assure her. "He's fine."

I guide her through my glass doors, then slide them closed behind us.

"So, Bronson?" Blair turns, her gaze combing my body, and that's when I remember, glancing down, that I slept nude. I still am. "I'm suddenly *yours* now?"

There's a war in my chest over Blair, but my dick has

already declared victory, raising its flag. "For nine more days, you are."

"And then what? I'd be a *distraction* again?"

"You'd be something to me, that's for sure."

"So all this." She gestures down my rousing physique, my muscles about to unleash. "I'm yours now because you're jealous over seeing me sleep beside your hot best friend?"

What did she just ignite in me?

Images of our three bodies wrapped together in bed— her sucking Colt. Then I help her, our kiss meeting over the swollen tip of his cock. Me fucking her, while he's fucking me and her....

Holy fuck, I swell so fast I get dizzy.

"Oh, Kitten, jealousy is *not* what I feel when I see you with Colt. He's the only man I won't kill if he touches you. Tell me if I'm lying." Her eyes get wide because I let her see mine narrow with lust, my hardening cock very convincing. "I want the three of us together," I confess. "A lot."

Blair licks her bottom lip before snagging it between her teeth.

I know that look, her hidden desire. The last time I saw it, I had her tied down and blindfolded, about to fulfill her secret fantasy with a huge, blue alien cock sheath on my dick.

"You'd love our threesome, too?" I lick my lips. "Wouldn't you, Kitten?"

"I'm celibate, not insane," she answers. "Who wouldn't want to Peter, Paul, and Mary with you two?"

"Marry? Let's not get ahead of ourselves."

But why does that suddenly sound like my wildest dream come true? To marry Blair? To marry Colt? To figure out some impossible way we could work?

She rolls her eyes. "Check your massive ego and erection, Bronson. Yes, I want to fuck you again. We can get all kinds of kinky together. Tell me if I'm lying. Tell me I don't make your eyes roll, your toes curl, and your thighs shake, your mind all dizzy when I make you come so hard, grunting my name."

Fuck, she's doing it to me now.

"But I'm no one's *distraction*, Beau," she insists. "I deserve devotion. Or, I'll date a dozen dildos instead."

BLAIR'S WORDS bounce through my brain all morning while I try to focus on my job.

Amber was successfully escorted off the island by Coach and Colt.

I wanted to video her bitching, stumbling departure in heels down the dock. It'd make great inspo content for her followers on how to make an ass of yourself. But Colt gave me a look that promised murder, so I was content to raise a cup of coffee to her water taxi.

Blair did it, too, before she put on a distracting red bikini, scooped up her laptop, and settled under a sunshade sail by the pool.

Our first morning session with Dr. Gary opens with formalities. Coach kisses his ass, thanking him for his time.

I don't dislike this guru guy. He's got a PhD. I respect him but don't believe he'll do any good until he says, "Coach, I invite you to enjoy your vacation while I do my sessions with Bronson and Hawke alone."

Coach clears his throat. "Of course, whatever it takes."

But he doesn't miss a chance to aim his water bottle at us, sitting side-by-side on the sofa, warning, "Be honest, or be benched."

Then he leaves, waving goodbye to Blair before the next water taxi whisks him away.

"Now," Dr. Gary studies us like we're sitting in his office, "you two have mastered the game on the gridiron. Your stats prove it. That's not why we're here. We're here to master the game in your mind."

He pauses, and I swear he's a microscope lens burning into me. I wonder if Colt feels it as well because Dr. Gary waits way too long to speak again, and I start squirming, making sure my bare leg isn't brushing Colt's. We're big men. We spread our legs when we sit, but hell no, I can't touch him.

When I touch Colt's body, I can't control mine.

No one but Blair can know about us.

I glance past the screen on the narrow wall to the sunny outside, and smile, seeing Blair content, typing away on her laptop, and that's when Dr. Gary asks the multi-billion dollar question.

"Where was your mind, your focus in the last five minutes of the Super Bowl?"

"I can't remember," Colt answers too quickly.

"I don't think," I automatically reply, "I just play."

But the tense topic makes Colt adjust his swim trunks, and on instinct, I mimic him. And, like fuck if this doctor dude doesn't clock our tension, too.

"Alright then," he eases. "Let's start there. Today, you'll remember. Write in your journal everything you recall from the morning before the Super Bowl until the final second."

"The day before or the day of?" Colt lets it slip, and I try not to roll my eyes.

"Interesting," Dr. Gary replies. "Did something happen the day before?"

"Nothing that hasn't happened before." Colt doesn't lie.

Sorta.

"Well, let's start there," Dr. Gary answers. "Write it down, from the morning of the day before the game to the final second—all of it, even what you ate. Then, take screenshots of your journal and text them to me by 2 p.m. I'll compare the two and report back."

"What are you looking for?" I'm afraid he can read between the lines of our lie.

"I'm not looking," he answers. "You are. Try to see where your mind was at the time. Then we'll talk about where it should be and how to get it there."

After a few pleasantries, I click the remote, turning off our video conference.

The sound of gentle waves and our pained silence fills the warm, salty air, and I toss my head back, feeling so fucked.

"How do we do this?" I ask aloud, not expecting Colt to answer.

But he does. "We'll be honest."

"Honest outs us."

"I trust him."

"I don't trust anyone."

"That's your problem."

"I got more problems than that."

"Well," Colt surges to his feet, "don't let me keep being one."

I jump up, too. "What the fuck is *your* problem?"

"The same one for years!" We stand almost nose-to-nose while Colt shouts, "I love you, and you love me! We always have, but it's always been a *problem* for you, while for me, it's the solution."

"Solution?" I shout back. "We're NFL players! We don't get to be anything but all-American and all-straight!"

"So what? So if we're bi, we die? You make it sound like a death sentence."

"Death sentence, no." I clench my fists. "But a distraction, yes."

He rolls his eyes. "You and your *fucking* distractions."

"You wanna see a fucking distraction?" I snarl. "Let every player on our team know, including the coaching staff, our owner, the management, the staff. Oh, they'll say they support us. Legally, they have to. But every subtle fucking way they'll ice us out, or judge, or joke? It'll fuck with our heads until all we see are phobic distractions. And you know I'm right. I'm sorry, but I am!"

And I fucking hate it, so I gotta bail.

I grab my dumbass journal and pen, then I grab a spot on a lounger on the far side of the pool and get so damn real with my memory. With everything. Even Colt sleeping in the bed with me, but not that.

Not that I love him, too.

CHAPTER NINE

Never did I think I'd be on a frickin' writers' retreat with two hunky NFL players.

Beau's on a lounger to my right with his back to the ocean, his nose down, his pen feverishly writing in his black journal.

Colton's on a lounger to my left, facing Beau and the horizon. He'll write, look up, and study Beau with a scowl, then put his face down, his pen scribbling, too.

And I swear this retreat is a pilot episode of *Mad Ballers With Angry Ball Point Pens.*

So, here I am, sitting on my shaded lounger between them, inspired to write another alien romance book, and yep, you guessed it.

It's about two alien rival warlords who are secretly lovers, too. And the one thing that will bring them peace? The human sacrifice they kidnap, the woman they have to breed together to unite their seed, their tribes in lasting harmony.

But here on planet Earth?

I do what I can to bring some peace, too.

When the chef comes by with fresh tamales for lunch, along with ceviche and slices of dragon fruit and mangos, I thank him and tell him he's free to enjoy his afternoon. I'll serve the men.

Then, I notice the basket of ingredients he's brought for dinner and tell him I'll cook dinner, too. He's hesitant initially, but I'm the guest, so he graciously accepts his day and night off with a smile.

Once he leaves, I grab the frilly apron to the French maid lingerie outfit I brought to torture Beau with and wrap it over my red string bikini.

I feel like a naughty young Martha Stewart—the goddess of cooking and entertaining who was just in the Sports Illustrated Swimsuit issue at age eighty-one: life goals—when I bend over, serving Beau from a rattan tray.

"Would you like to eat my sweet mangoes, Sir?"

Beau glances up from his journal, his ire turning into a smirk as he thanks my cleavage for lunch. When I serve Colton, he does the same.

They settle on their opposing loungers, devouring their lunch while, yes, my kitty purrs, feeling their eyes devouring me, too. Then, I bend over and serve them big glasses of ice water while chewing my bottom lip for them. Who knew serving men with your tits and a smile could make them drop their swords, pens, or whatever?

Me and every human alive.

So, while Beau's busy enjoying candied craboo, the tiny Belizean cherries I served with a "Please eat my cherries for dessert, Sir," I wander inside.

When I come back, he's downed his water. So, he gets up to grab a refill in the kitchen while I save my work, set my laptop aside, and wait. And wait. And wait. And...

"Goddammit, Blair!"

I start laughing when he appears on the threshold of his bedroom, his glass doors open, his sexy face fuming about my Clingwrap over the toilet revenge.

"I got it in my flip-flops!" He shouts, charging my way.

"My, my, someone's pissy!" I jump up. "Payback is warm, yellow, hell!"

But Beau's coming, and not in a sexy way, so I dash the other way as if I can outrun a professional athlete when I'm allergic to treadmills. I don't even make a lap around the pool before I squeal as Beau snatches me from behind, laughing with him while he plunges us into the pool.

It's a refreshing jolt, and I emerge, trapped in his beefy embrace, my black mop blinding my face.

He laughs. "You look like Cousin It with great tits." So I twist in his slick arms and dip my head back again, making my long hair flow down my back, away from my face.

I'm still laughing at my pissy payback when I find my focus. When I meet Beau's intense, dripping gaze, the heat in his eyes startling, and suddenly, I feel the heat of his wet body holding me, too.

"Damn, Blair." He mutters, "You're so fucking beautiful, baby, I'd swim in my piss for you."

"Isn't that what we're doing now?"

"Oh. Are golden showers your kink, too?"

"Hell no."

But I made Beau laugh. He's happy again, and that makes me all soft and squishy inside while he's getting rock hard against my bare belly.

"Dirty pool sex with my hot maid is about to be my

kink," he growls, lowering his lips, kissing a warm, hungry trail up my neck. He blooms goosebumps over my flesh, steaming over my ear, "Come on, Blair. You know you're tempted," he urges. "Right here in the pool; let me thank you for lunch. Let me pull your itty-bitty bikini aside and suck your sweet nipples while I slide my hard cock inside you."

Zing!

My clit screams OPEN THE FLOOD GATES, but I murmur, "Colton's right there."

I'm well aware of his presence. All I've felt today are Beau and Colton—their real fight this morning and their fictional love on my page.

I heard their shouts after their session.

Colton's not wrong; they love each other and can find a solution.

And Beau's not wrong. I looked it up after their session with Dr. Gary.

There are approximately seventeen hundred NFL players a year. And, if like national surveys say, five to ten percent identify as non-heterosexual, that means about a hundred men are closeted in the sport every year. They don't feel safe coming out.

But they're safe with me.

And I'm safe with them.

I felt it the moment I met Beau, the kind of young man who'd rescue a young woman passed out at a frat party. And I felt it last night talking to Colton, the kind of man who misses his mom so much, he's hurting, he needs love.

We all do, and it's overwhelming when I'm wrapped in Beau's strong arms because it's where I belong, and we feel it.

It thins our breath when we're this close.

Beau brushes his soft whiskers over my parted mouth. "He doesn't mind." Gently, he tickles his fingertips up my spine before tugging at the string of my apron top, freeing it to fall from my waist. "Do you, Colt?" Beau calls out, "Do you mind if I fuck my beautiful woman right here in front of you?"

"Be my guest," Colton answers, and my pussy clenches, aching with lust.

I look to my right, where Colton's lounging feet away, wearing sunglasses. I can't see his eyes, but I sure feel his satisfied smile, his arms resting behind his head, making his biceps pop while...

Oh my god, he's popping a huge boner, too?

"Whatever." I squirm, resisting the overwhelming desire to do this. To let Beau fuck me while Colton watches. Yes, it turns me on so much. Yes, it's so wrong; it's my favorite right thing to do.

Like right now.

But...

"I'm just a *distraction*, Bronson, right?"

I'm starting to hate that word. You can understand something but still resent the hell out of it.

Beau uses that word for me. For Colton, too. For almost everything in his life that's not football, and I'm beginning to suspect it's about much more.

"No, baby." But Beau's feeling playful, horny as he snaps my bikini top free. "You're the hot destination my hard dick needs to fuck right now."

I let him do it. I let Beau tug my red top off before he tosses it at Colton. It lands, sopping wet over Colton's feet, who smiles even more.

I'm not ashamed to be topless in front of them. Hell, it

thrills me. I don't know why I even bothered with bikinis for this trip. I suspect we'll be nude for days to come.

Speaking of coming...

"You want this, Beau?" Gently, I shove his concrete chest, pushing away from his grasp. I step back into shallower water until it warmly laps at my waist while cooler air excites my bare nipples, pearling hard and dripping for Beau's ravenous gaze.

Colton's hungry smirk, too.

"Come on, Blair." Beau rips the velcro to his swim trunks, reaching in to free himself. "Fuck, baby, you know I want you. It's been months. You know it's so fucking good between us. It's the best."

"No, no." I tug my nipples for him. For Colton, too.

Hell, yes, my pussy is trapped in paradise with two massive cocks, but my pride is here, too.

"Remember what I said?" I tease, craning my neck down while I lift my breast. Looking at Beau, I circle, licking my nipple for him. His lips part as I vow, "I'm no man's distraction, Beau Bronson. You want this pussy? Then devote yourself to it."

Beau lowers his gaze, glaring like he's starving. Like he has to decide what he's willing to kill, to sacrifice to feed on me.

Do I understand about distractions? Yes.

Will I be reduced to one again? Never.

I glance at Colton, who's watching us, intrigued—more than intrigued. He wants in. I can tell. I already share their secret. I protect it. And he wants to share more—with Beau. With me. And suddenly, I want it, too. It feels destined, so I make it harder for them—literally.

I turn, topless, ascending the wide steps of the pool still

in my bikini bottoms and naughty maid's apron, dripping from my waist.

"Where are you going?" Beau sounds tortured, almost angry, as if he'll attack.

I call over my shoulder, "I'm going on a date with my big, *devoted* boyfriends. I'm going to let them fuck me and take turns with me until I come. Watch, Bronson, if you can handle the distraction."

COLTON

CHAPTER TEN

"Y'ALL ARE SO FUCKING HOT TOGETHER."

"You're a goddamn idiot if you don't go in there," I snarl at Bronson because Blair wasn't kidding.

She's so shameless, so smart and beautiful. She's the sexiest woman I've ever met, and that's the greatest compliment because I've had hundreds throw themselves at me like they're the ultimate catch.

But they aren't.

Blair is.

Because she's doing it.

She's lying on her back, on her neatly made bed, on the center of her white bedspread. Her legs fall open, her feet in the air as she starts taking turns with two dildos. And what's so damn hot is even with the bright sun outside, we can see her through her closed glass doors.

It's obvious she's fucking herself, and it's fucking with us.

Beau drags his hand down his wet face. "Goddamn, that woman," he sighs, standing in the pool, staring at her through the glass.

This villa isn't that big. The pool is steps outside her and Beau's bedrooms and shit, we can hear her lusty begs, too.

"Yes! Yes!" Blair's making sure we can. "Fuck me. Don't stop fucking me! Please!"

"Dude, why aren't you in there?" I'm hard as hell but confused.

For a woman like Blair, I'd do anything. She's brave. Bold. Beautiful. She's bi, too, and most of all, she knows about us. She protects us. She celebrates us.

So, why doesn't Beau go in there and give her what she wants?

They're clearly in love. He's loved Blair since college. He may have hidden it from everyone else but not me. I could hear it in how he talked about her and their pranks during our senior year.

It's like, other than football, Blair was the only one who made Beau sound happy.

Reese, his girlfriend? Beau sounded responsible for her, like a big brother, not a boyfriend. It wasn't fair how Reese burdened him with her problems, problems she wasn't willing to fix. After meeting her one night, I understood how bad they were.

But with Blair? Beau's always been happy. She brings out the best in him. She clearly loves him, too.

"Because," he mutters. "I'm not breaking Blair's heart."

"Then don't."

"I will."

"How?"

"Because she's right. I can't give her the devotion she deserves."

"But she's your girlfriend."

He drags his hand through his dark strands. "No, she's not. I made that shit up. I wasn't going to be here stag with you and Amber, so Blair agreed to come with me. Like a fake girlfriend."

"Beau. Ummm, Beau. Yes. Deeper. Harder. Harder."

We can hear her moans—him, me and my hungry dick.

"Well then, dumbass," I say, "make her your *real* girl-friend. Clearly, it's what she wants. Don't you?"

"I can't, man. She'd be a distraction before our season even starts. We got too much shit on the line this year. We gotta win."

I shake my head, remembering how in high school, I scrolled through porn on my phone while Beau scrolled through plays. He's obsessed with football. That's what makes him one of the best and the worst.

"So," I pop up, my bare feet straddling my lounger, "she'd be a distraction for you, and then we'd lose games?"

"Yeah."

"Then how do you explain our last game? The Super Bowl?"

He aims his piercing blues at me. "That was *another* distraction. That was you and me."

"Okay, fine. Then how do you explain Green Bay last year? Or Jacksonville? We lost those games, and it wasn't because of us *or* her."

I raise an eyebrow. I'm right, so he doesn't say anything.

His stare just slides from me to Blair on her bed, moaning, "Yes, Beau, yes." Her seductive cries are clear. Like her writhing body, they're barely muted by the glass. "Make me watch you. Make me watch you fuck my pussy. Make me watch you come inside me."

He throws his chin up to the sun. *"Fuucckk meee!"*

"Yeah!" I answer. "That's what y'all should be doing. Fucking. Right. Now."

"You don't understand, man. Blair's the one."

"Mm-hmm. I can tell. She told me last night she knows about us." He looks at me, his eyes wide. "Yeah, and she's fucking amazing. She supports us. She'd never out us. And who else can we trust nowadays like that? Like her? And she's loved to hate you since college. She doesn't want your money or your fame. She just wants *you.*"

"Yeah," he rushes, "and I want her, too. I'd give everything for her, and that's what it would cost her—everything. You know what'll happen. Press will stalk her when we win. Fans will hate her if we lose. My bullshit life will be a distraction for her, too, when her dreams are finally coming true, and I won't ruin it for her."

I bark, "You're ruining it NOW! You're a fucking idiot. You're not even trying with her when you *know* she's the one. And I know you. That means she's your forever. So, this ain't about distractions. You're scared."

"Scared? Am I wrong about our lives?"

"No, but y'all would be so right, and you know it. You've loved her since college, right? All these years?"

"Yeah, so what? That's the price of winning. I don't get to have who I love, Colt, remember?"

He stares at me, defeated, and I drop my head.

Blair's got our cocks hard, but our hearts are breaking, too.

I get it now, thanks to her, why I clung to Amber though we were toxic. Some people would rather be lonely, faking it in a bad relationship than learn to be real, to be alone and happy by themselves.

But Beau's lonely *and* alone. Honestly, so am I. And to be real? We're not happy faking it like this. We'll never win like this.

Something needs to change.

"You know what really pisses me off?"

He scoffs, "Lately, everything I do."

"No, Dickweed," I answer, lowering my voice. "I *wish* I had a woman like her. One who understands me, who really loves me. One who supports me. Who supports this." I point between us. "But you're the lucky dick who does, and she's right there." Then I point to her. "She wants you. She loves you. Any man would fucking kill for her. So, like she said, go love her. Go devote yourself to her, you lucky, beautiful asshole."

He stares at me, and I stare back, shocked by my sudden realization. The one awakening my numb heart, telling him, "You say *we* can't be together, but you two can. At least *you* can be happy. *You* can have love." I urge, "Do it for us."

"Colt." His face falls. "What about you? What about us?"

"I want us, too. I always will."

"But what about her?"

"I'm not a fucking idiot like you. I'm not jealous *or* scared. Blair Monroe is goddamn amazing. I swear, if you don't claim her, I will."

His nostrils flare, his glare narrowing and deadly. "She's fucking *mine*, Hawke."

And I laugh because, yes, he'd kill for her. *Good.* "Then fucking act like it, Bronson!"

"Oh God!" Blair cries out. "Oh God, Beau, yes! Yes! Yes! Make me your slut."

I groan, rolling my eyes, my cock surging hard again. "I swear, Bronson, if you don't go in there and fuck that sweet pussy crying your name…"

I open my eyes and turn my focus on Blair's glass doors. And holy-made-in-our-cock-heaven, she's on the edge of her bed, facing us now. There's no silhouette. We can see everything.

The sunlight illuminates her milky thighs spread open. Her luscious, naked, writhing body leans back with one hand propping her up, her other hand gripping a glistening beige dildo, pumping it hard into her pretty pink pussy.

She's giving us a shameless show, and I growl, "We've died and gone to porno heaven."

"Fuck yes, we have," Beau agrees.

"Yes." Blair can hear us. "Look at me, boys. Watch." Her dark pink nipples are so damn hard, her long black mane so damn sexy. "Watch me be such a dirty little girl for you. I'm so hungry for your cock."

"Bronson," I snarl, "if you don't go in there and give that hot-ass woman the fuck she needs, I swear, I'll—"

"Fuck, yes, baby." But Beau growls, and I know that husky tone. I've heard it used with me, so I turn my stare on him and moan.

He's stroking his cock for her. "Yes, Kitten. That's it." He's taunting her, "Show us. Come on, show us what your naughty little pussy needs. Show us how fucking dirty you are for me."

Blair can hear him through the glass. She can see him, too. She cries out because Beau's summoned to her. He wades into shallower water. It laps at his thighs, and oh fuck, we can admire his raging cock choked in his pumping fist, too.

"Damn," I mutter and don't care. This is too fucking

hot, too taboo, and erotic. I rip my swim trunks open and lie back, watching him, watching her. "Y'all are so fucking hot together." I make sure they hear me. "Come on. Do it. Give me a dirty show."

"Yes!" Blair cries out again. She can see Beau jerking off, water sparkling around his tan, shredded thighs, his white bathing suit around his hips while his exposed cock screams hard and hungry for her.

And she can see me with my black trunks open, how I'm proudly jerking off for them, too. My hooded gaze slides from her beautiful pussy fucking a big dildo to Beau, twisting and pumping his hand over his big shaft.

It's like they're connected. They're drawn to each other. They can't escape their passion.

"Fuck," I bellow, feeling their lust, too, and Beau looks at me.

"Oh fuck," he grunts, realizing what we're doing together. "Yes," he growls, getting louder, making sure Blair can hear. "Fuck yes. The three of us. Come on. Watch. Watch how we come for each other."

"Oh god! Oh god!" I look, and Blair's crying out, her thighs shaking, her hand pumping that dildo faster.

"Yes." Beau locks his gaze to hers, his voice, too. "Yes, Kitten. Do it for us while we watch you. That's it. Make that pretty pussy come. Show Colt what a sweet little slut you are for me."

Blair bucks, crying out, her lungs huffing with her leg-shaking orgasm. And I've never seen a woman so natural, so beautiful, and proud of her sex. And then I stare at the hungry man so in love with her and me, too; I throw my chin up. "Oh fuck, yes." I come so hard, blinded by the sun and all we could have together.

"*Fuuckkk!*" Beau comes too. I know his sound. I live for it and it only makes me spurt more. And more. And more.

Then I just lie here, finding my breath, letting the euphoria wash over me. The hot sun, too. Cum coats my abs, and it feels right.

More than right.

It's perfect.

We're shameless together.

And when I hear a sliding glass door open. When I look at Blair standing sexy and nude. When I see her beautiful face glowing. When she says, "Despite what you say, Bronson, your cock really loves my distractions, and so does your hot best friend. Perhaps you'll learn to love it, too, one day. But until then," she tosses her raven hair over her shoulder, "don't forget to clean our bathroom."

When Blair does that?

I love our new game.

BEAU

CHAPTER ELEVEN

It must be love because I smile while I mop my golden joke off our bathroom floor, even though it was Blair's fault.

Okay, fine.

Technically, it's mine.

I tortured her with Clingwrap on the toilet in college, so here I am, thirty, and pissing my flip-flops over her.

The rest of the afternoon, she hides from me and the sun, sitting with her laptop on her bed. So, I get to work, too.

Even though Colt and I are like sandpaper, rubbing each other raw and not in a good way, we're pros, too.

Colt packed a ball. I did, too, but we use his for drills.

He goes long, running down the wooden dock. It's only twenty or so yards, but it'll do. I throw, and he goes for the catch, practicing his half-turn, snatching the ball with his long fingers before securing the tuck, making it a true vacation by splashing into the Caribbean as our end zone.

Silently, we practice for over an hour. Silently, I worry he'll slip and crack his skull on the edge of the dock or get a splinter in his foot. Silently, I've always worried about Colt.

I had privileges and parents with money, and he didn't. I miss his mom, too. Celeste was sweet. As a single mom, she sacrificed everything for her son because Colt's dad had been long gone since he was a baby.

So, of course, Colt's family became mine and mine his.

I think that's another reason we hit our stride these past few years. I felt his grief, too. I was there for him. When it's your mom dying, teammates give hugs, back slaps, and arm locks around the neck. So I could be there for Colt. I could hold him with no judgment because it was legit. Everyone in the locker room understood, and no one judged.

But I couldn't stop the inevitable.

And I can't stop studying him now.

Colt's intricate ink gleams sweaty in the sun. I know his stunning new pec art of lotuses is for his mom. But I wonder about the older minimalist designs in his sleeves, particularly the birds, and what they mean. I have suspicions, but it'll be too hard if I know the truth.

But this is easy. My timing. His speed. My placement. His catch. There's no pressure on us, and for the first time in months, I see the real Colt—the one I fell in love with.

With Amber gone, he's relaxed. He's smiling while he runs. He's fucking laughing when he splashes into the ocean. He could go til sunset, but my shoulder can't.

"Hey, man," I call out, "I gotta stop."

He jogs my way with the ball tucked naturally into his side, like a damn baby, while he worries, "You alright?"

"Yeah," I start my crossover arm stretches, "just a bit tight."

"I'll get you some ice."

"I don't need it."

"I didn't ask," he scoffs. "Sit down and take the damn ice."

He times me, giving me twenty minutes on a pool lounger with ice on my right shoulder while the afternoon gives way to dusk.

"Fuck, I'm starving." He glances back at the open living room with the kitchen beyond.

The smell of Blair making dinner for us makes my stomach growl. "Me too," I answer.

"I can't believe it. She makes us come for her, and now she's cooking for us?" He nods toward Blair, bending over, sliding a large glass pan into the oven. It looks like she's setting the timer while Colt admires, "You lucky shit, I've never met a woman like her. The ones I meet are either too shy, too selfish, or too uptight."

"Oh," I chuckle, admiring how cute she looks in her green sundress, "Blair's not uptight. She has a religion against shame. She works at a swanky adult store. You wouldn't believe that place," I pause, remembering what I've already shared with Blair in so little time. "You wouldn't believe what she can make you feel, too."

Colt huffs. He does believe me as I realize we're talking more today than we have in months, and it's all because of Blair.

"Tell me again," he asks, looking over his shoulder, watching her put dishes away, "how she'd be a distraction and not the one who can finally make you win?"

Suddenly, I can't answer.

I never thought of it that way.

All I've ever heard from coaches, my parents, or some other players is how love is a distraction and how I should wait until I retire in a few years.

But what if Colt's right, and they're wrong?

"Damn," he fills my silence, "did she really write that alien book about y'all, too?" He reaches, dragging the towel off my dripping shoulder. The ice has melted. "I started it today and got all kinds of feels and a hard-on by chapter three."

"Yeah," I answer. "You should read her other books about us. Your dick will thank you."

"Speaking of thanking dicks." He pats his knees, rising to his feet. "It's shower time."

The image of Colt, wet and nude and jerking off in the shower, does something to me. Damn, I want to join him. I want to hold him again. I want to fist our soapy cocks together while I claim his kiss and suck his tongue.

But this feels too precarious.

We're finally talking like normal again. We're finally throwing like yin and yang. We're finally relaxed and not pissed off.

So, he leaves, and I lay the wet towel to dry over my chair before I wander into my shower alone, letting the hot water soothe my sore shoulder, too.

The one thing I confess to no one—not Colt, not Blair, not Coach—is I'm not sure about my shoulder. On paper, the surgery was a success, and I do my daily physical therapy like a devout monk. But still, after today, I'm sore, and I worry.

"I gotta pee."

Blair's sweet voice lifts my gaze from the white shower tiles. She's doing a funny dance in the threshold.

"Then pee," I tell her.

"But you're right here."

"But I won't see you. The little half wall is blocking the john."

"Yeah, but you'll hear me."

I laugh. "So we can mutually masturbate and watch each other come, but I can't hear your golden shower hit the porcelain bowl?" She dances some more. "What are you, Irish? Is that your gotta-pee-jig?"

"Shut up," she whines, and it's adorable. "Come on. Hurry up and finish."

I stand naked in the shower. There's no curtain or glass wall. Belize is too hot to hold in the steam, and the open shower is deep enough that water doesn't get on the bathroom floor, so I hold my ground.

"I'm standing right here, Blair, while you pee."

"Don't make me go in the ocean!"

"Please don't." I shampoo my hair. "I hear jellyfish come out at night."

"That's not true!" She hops up and down faster, panic twisting her face. "Is it?"

"Don't find out. Just pee."

"*Beeeaaaauuu!*" She turns my name into five syllables.

"*Blaaaaiiiirrrr!*" I rinse my hair, laughing.

"Goddammit." She huffs by me, hiking up her sundress. "You're dead if there's Clingwrap on this. I mean it. I'll choke you on a starfish."

I finish rinsing while I hear her soft moan of release. "Damn, baby," I admire. "You make it sound sexual. You sure you're not hiding a golden kink?"

"Quit listening!"

"What do you want me to do? Sing the national anthem?"

"Yes!" The toilet roll rumbles.

"No can do." I turn the shower head off, stepping naked onto the bathmat. "Now let me hear you flush."

"Over my dead, squatting pussy." She holds position, all her sexy bits covered by her pretty, flowy dress while I drip naked in front of her.

"I got all night, baby."

"No, you don't." She smirks. "Your stomach will growl, and your dick will get cold."

Damn, she knows me well. She's half right.

"Fine." I grab a white towel and use it to dry my hair. In this heat, my body will dry in minutes. "Flush and join me for dinner."

"Are you asking me on a date while I sit on the toilet?"

My god, she stops my heart.

Blair looks cute as hell. She stares up at me with her dark hair twisted high off her neck. It falls like a pom-pom from the top of her head while her black glasses perch on the tip of her button nose.

"Yes, Professor Piss, it's a date. I'm taking you out for dinner fifty feet away."

"But I cooked."

"Thank you. So I'll do the dishes." I hang my towel on a hook. "What'd you make?"

"Lasagna," she answers. "Is Colt coming, too?"

I smirk, naked and amused. "Do you *want* Colt to come again with us?"

But I'm playing the GOAT of kink. She smiles at my semi and gets the point. "Bronson, it's obvious what *you* want. You want to lick both sides of the stamp so bad, your tongue is drooling for it." I raise a brow, confused. "A switch-hitter. A gate-swinger." She explains, "You want a threesome, but too bad for you, I'm swinging with dildos only."

With that, she proudly stands from her throne and flushes. I chuckle, listening to her wash her hands while I throw on clean shorts. Fuck a shirt. It's too hot.

Minutes later, we're gathered around the marble kitchen island.

"Dig in," Blair instructs with a proud smile, so I do the honors, spearing the bubbling lasagna with a spatula.

I load up my plate. Colt loads up his. But we're gentlemen, so I spoon some onto a plate for Blair, and he carries it for her outside to the table she set.

Wine would make this dinner even more romantic, but the sunset works in my favor. Something about this night feels perfect between us as I sit beside Blair, across from Colt.

We silently dip our forks into the cheesy Italian goodness, taking ravenous bites. We chew. And chew. And chew. And chew.

"Wow," Colt mumbles with his mouth full. "It's authentico. Very al dente."

I can't speak.

I'm busy choking on raw pasta.

"What the... ?" But Blair spits her mouthful into her linen napkin. "The noodles aren't cooked!"

I don't have the heart to tell her we're eating Italian rubber bands. I just try to swallow them with a smile.

"But," Blair stares at the dish, "I made it just like I do at home."

"Did you uh... " Colt's trying not to offend her either. "Did you *boil* the noodles first?"

"No," she answers. "You don't need to boil them."

I can't help it. Her cute factor is way too high. "Babe," I answer after I swallow a doughy glob, nearly avoiding choking to death, "yeah, you do."

After all the years of helping my mom cook, even I know that.

"No, you don't." But Blair is stubborn and embarrassed while she marches inside to the kitchen, and we follow, watching her dig the empty pasta box out of the garbage. "It says... " she starts reading...

"To boil the noodles?" Fuck, this is too funny.

She's still reading the instructions like it's Russian while Colt starts laughing, too. "You're a best-selling author who didn't read the instructions."

She stomps her foot, frustrated. "At home, they're no-boil noodles."

"But Kitten, home is a thousand miles away and a pot full of boiling water from here." I piss her off, winning an empty pasta box thrown at my laughing face.

"Y'all!" But then her pretty cheeks flush. "I ruined dinner, and now you'll starve to death."

"We won't starve." Colt flicks her button nose. "There's an ocean full of dinner. We just have to boil it first."

"Oh my god." She covers her face with her hands. "I'll never live this down."

So, I whip her around, wrapping my arms around her waist. "Hell, no, you won't. This is going in the Blair Blunders Hall of Fame."

"Uh!" She knocks her forehead against my bare pecs. "Kill me now."

I kiss her silky pom-pom. "Should we boil you alive?"

"Beau!" She huffs into my chest, shaking with laughter. "Now Colton thinks I'm an idiot, too."

"He doesn't *think* that, baby." I wink at Colt, smiling over her shoulder. "Now he *knows* you're an idiot."

Her shoulders start to shake with laughter, too, and Colt can't resist her either. He cups her arm, his giant hand making her seem even more petite between us.

"Raven, when you're this damn cute being dumb"—he leans over, pecking her bare shoulder—"you're worth starving for."

Something about his tender kiss and my embrace makes Blair melt in my arms, trapped by his heat and mine.

I feel it, too.

So does he.

We're the ones boiling now. With our three bodies melding together, Colt starts barely kissing her neck and Blair moans. So my lips find the shell of her ear, coaxing, "Baby, let us eat your pussy instead."

"Oh god." Blair grabs my shoulders, sighing against my cheek. Colt must be grinding hard against her backside while she can feel my growing appetite, too, but then she squirms, pushing out of our trap.

"I'm winning this bet, Bronson," she stammers.

"What bet?" Colt staggers back from our heat.

But I glance at Blair, my eyes begging her not to share. Colt's not ready. Neither am I. We're just now barely getting along. We can't force this. We may never truly kiss and make up.

This may be as good as it gets.

Blair reads my eyes, covering my ass by answering Colt, "I bet I could resist him for ten days while he bet he could seduce me in five."

My chest falls, relieved, though my dick isn't.

"So here." Blair grabs two bags of tortilla chips from a

cabinet, tossing them on the island. "Make us nachos for dinner, and I'll be right back."

In a mad swish, she turns for her bedroom.

"Are you going to fuck your devoted plastic boyfriends again?"

"You two can make me want to fuck you all you want," she answers me over her shoulder. "But I'm winning our bet, Bronson."

Colt grabs the chips, ripping the bag open, lowly growling at me, "You're a fucking idiot."

Her bedroom door closes while I grab cheese from the refrigerator. "Finally," I answer him, "we agree."

When Blair returns fifteen minutes later, looking flushed and freshly fucked by a lucky sex toy, we enjoy a successful nacho dinner outside.

Once the dishes are drying on the rack, we turn off the kitchen lights and settle on the sofa in front of the flat screen. But instead of an awkward counseling session, we start a vacation tradition.

It's Colt's idea.

We each write three of our favorite movies, ones we can recite word-for-word, on pieces of paper, and each night, we'll draw from a bowl.

Tonight, Blair tells Colt to go first since it was his idea.

"Hell, yes," he woofs at his selection. "*Sixteen Candles*. It was my mom's favorite."

"I love that movie!" Blair sounds as excited, but I confess, "I've never seen it."

"What?" Blair whips her gaze to me. She sits between us while Colt clicks the remote, getting ready to stream it. "How did you miss this romcom classic?"

Colt answers for me, "Because he watched plays, not movies, growing up."

"Is that true?" Blair asks.

I shrug. "Sorta. Once I outgrew *Finding Nemo*, I was finding football."

"Ahhhh." She surprises me, taking her hair clip out and tossing it on the coffee table before lying down, nestling her head in my lap. "That's so sad, Bronson. Were you ever a carefree teenager?"

I can't answer because I'm entranced once Blair's black silk spills over my lap. Her soft cheek rests on my hard thigh. She's so close to where I'm dying for her; in the first hour of the movie, I will my frustrated dick down while my fingers have other plans.

They lace through her hair, letting it glide like ebony satin through my grasp and her contended sighs fucking kill me. That and how her feet somehow manage to rest in Colt's lap, too.

I'm playing with her hair, and he's rubbing her feet. They're watching the movie, and I know I'm supposed to take another chance at tempting her, at winning our kinky bet. I could start playing with her spaghetti strap, lingering my touch down, over the swell of her breasts. I know how to tease her nipples to get her wet, and maybe she wants me to, but this feels too special.

I'm overwhelmed. I'm seeing years like this. Of a future I can only dream about.

If I weren't the face of a football franchise, this would be the ultimate win—a life with her and him.

A life of us.

I can't fucking believe how natural this feels, how it melts my heart, how quickly Blair and Colt have bonded, too.

But why should it surprise me?

I've loved them for years, and now they're discovering

everything I love about them in each other, and I'm not mad about it.

Real love wants the other person to be happy. The best love is when you both are. Or... all three are.

Colt keeps mindlessly rubbing her feet, his eyes glued to the flatscreen, while I keep worshiping Blair in my lap, feeling her body relax like it belongs forever with mine.

By the time the movie ends with the iconic scene of Jake waiting for Samantha outside the church, stealing her away from her sister's wedding reception so they can celebrate her birthday alone, I'm a mess of emotions I hide.

"Make a wish," Jake gently tells Samantha over her cake, glowing with sixteen candles.

"It already came true," Samantha answers him, and I glance at Colt.

He senses me and glances back. But we don't say it. We don't need to. We've known our wish since we were sixteen, too. *We* may never come true, but he smiles and nods toward Blair.

This wish can come true.

Blair's an angel, asleep in my lap, my hand caressing her hair, and yes, I'm a fucking idiot not to at least make this happen for us.

"Come on, babe." So I scoop her up, and she mumbles, barely waking.

I remember this about her, too. Blair sleeps like the dead.

That's how I pulled off so many pranks while I watched from the twin bed across from her. Reese was usually passed out by my side while I could rarely sleep. Not when I secretly wanted Blair so bad, so I'd devise the most wicked pranks to keep her attention.

Like putting liquid soap on Blair's toes and watching,

entertained for hours while she cursed and kicked her slick feet in her sleep. A few times, I tucked water balloons around her, waiting for her to roll over and pop one finally. She'd jolt up, thinking she pissed herself, and I'd die laughing.

But my favorite was putting her in a white T-shirt that read "I have pubic lice" with a smiley face.

Yeah, I had it specially made for her.

And yes, I almost pissed myself laughing while I took pics of Blair sleeping with the shirt on.

But what I really loved was touching her soft skin, admiring her cute bralette with little mountain peaks on it while I carefully tugged the shirt on her. She was a breathtaking rag doll in my grasp. I'd never hurt her. It was a safe prank and I tried not to perv about it.

She was so beautiful then, asleep in my arms, and she's gorgeous now, barely mumbling while I carry her into her bedroom.

"Isn't she sleeping with you?" Colt follows us, asking at her doorway. He's going to bed, too.

"She said she won't sleep with me again." Why the fuck lie now? Amber's gone, and so is the pretense. So I tell Colt, "She said she won't fuck me again either. That's the real reason for our bet because it'll hurt too much when we have to say goodbye at the end of this."

Colt just chuckles. I watch as he yanks his hair free from its knot. It spills over his broad, inked shoulders.

I hold my world in my arms and stare.

"You're a fucking idiot," he mumbles his new mantra while he disappears into his bedroom. "You're the only one who thinks we have to say goodbye."

CHAPTER TWELVE

Do they make Epi-Pens for pussies?

My eyelids crack open to sunlight sparkling over the pool, the peaceful turquoise ocean beyond, and raised voices echoing from the living room.

"How the fuck was it my fault?"

That's Colton. That's the sound of a man spitting glass.

"How the fuck was it *mine*? The pass was complete."

That's Beau—I roll my eyes—and that's the sound of another fight I'll have to subdue with dildos.

Rough life, I know.

My feet land on the cool tile floor. I'm not sure who brought me to my bed, but I know the culprit when I glimpse my new sleep shirt in the bathroom mirror.

And I laugh.

It's the rainbow Skittles candy logo, but instead, it says "Squirter" and "Taste my rainflow."

How the hell did Beau get this shirt in time? We had less

than forty-eight hours from when he asked me to be here to when we left.

Unless...

He knew all along I'd say yes. Or, he hoped we'd reunite in some prankish way in the future.

I'm so flattered; I roll with it.

While they shout in the living room, I shower, then brush my teeth, swiping on my red lips but leaving my hair to air-dry. Then I wet my new white T-shirt before tugging it back on, tying it real tight, right below my braless tits that are thrilled at the fact Beau must've admired them last night before putting me in this shirt.

In the dresser, I sort through the array of panties and goodies I brought from Delta's. Smiling, it's like this vacay was meant to be. I select the white cotton thong that pairs perfectly with my new T-shirt.

Why? Because it says **DADDY'S PUSSY** in red on the front triangle.

While they're still shouting, "It was a pass rush!" and "You tipped the ball!" They might as well be speaking German because I don't know what they're saying, but they need to settle down.

I get they're upset.

But I'm the only one who knows it's about more than the Super Bowl. Either way, yelling is for dumbasses who have all volume and no IQ.

They need to talk it out.

So, I slide open my glass doors and walk around the pool to the wide-open living area. From where they're sitting, shouting at the flatscreen and each other, they spot me, standing feet away on the sunny deck.

I cock my head and hip, twirling a strand of damp hair.

Running a hand down my bare belly, I make sure they read my naughty thong like classic English Pervertature.

"Fuck," Colton mumbles.

"Dayum," Beau mutters.

"Gentlemen," Dr. Gary interjects from the speakers, "am I missing something?"

I start teasing my tits for them again, training them like horny golden retrievers, learning to sit and obey.

"Uh, no. I mean, yeah," Beau stammers while I snap the string of my thong. "It's a really pretty sunrise outside."

"Yeah," Colton sighs, "it's really *rising*."

I bite my lip, holding back my laugh.

I don't want to get them in trouble, but I want them to stop fighting. If I happen to be teaching Beau that distractions like **DADDY'S PUSSY** aren't so bad after all, well, that's just whipped cream on the cup of coffee I'm dying to get, too.

So, I sashay past them, out of range of the video camera aimed at the sofa.

The large room is wide enough for me in my naughty thong to skirt the edge behind them. I know they're dying to turn around and eye-fuck me standing in the open kitchen, but they wouldn't dare. Not under the microscope of Dr. Gary.

"Well, I'm glad you're enjoying your surroundings," he says. "Today, I hope you enjoy them while you journal from the other's perspective."

"Huh?" Beau's been struck Daddy's Pussy-dumb.

"You're going to assume Colt is right," Dr. Gary replies. "That you put too much gas on the ball and imagine the game's final play from his perspective. And Colt?"

"Yeah?" His voice cracks like my cute bare ass.

"You'll assume Beau's right. That you tipped the ball out of your grasp."

"Okay." Colton sounds way too compliant. "Will do, Doc."

"Yeah," Beau agrees. "Whatever you say."

They wrap up their session so quickly that I suspect Dr. Gary doubts their sudden Solist worship of the sun.

Because once Beau clicks the screen off, he turns my way. "Damn, baby. We almost got busted."

"What?" I pop my shoulders, sipping my coffee with a grin. "Was I a *dick*straction for Daddy?"

He smirks. "Keep wearing those naughty little pussy panties, and Daddy's big dick is *on*."

"Oh," I sip again, "so Daddy *can* handle a dickstraction, after all?"

"Oh, I'll give you a lot to handle." Beau stands up, shucking his swim trunks down so fast, showing us what's already on at ten a.m.

His mouth-watering erection.

"Oh, hell no!" Colton bellows. "How can I journal when I'll be jerking off again to y'all today?"

"Do both," Beau suggests. "Because nothing's happening. Right, Blair? Daddy's pussy isn't tempted by me."

"Oh, I'm very tempted." I smirk. "But like you said, I'm a distraction. Right? That's why I'm playing solo this vacay."

"Playing solo's not as satisfying, Kitten." But Beau knows how to win, gliding his hand down his Grand Canyon of abs like a male stripper while his other hand teases, twisting over his swollen tip. *Sexy dickhead.* "You know you'd rather play our team sport."

"*Our* team?" I challenge him, amused. "But you told Amber I'm yours."

"You are," Beau asserts. "And like I told you, the only

dick I won't kill if they touch you is Colt's. That's if Colt wants to be your Daddy, too." It's not fair. Beau just has to raise his massive dick and sexy eyebrow at Colt, and he knows the play. "Whatdayasay?"

Colton smiles, slowly dragging his muscular frame up before he turns my way, ripping the velcro of his navy trunks open, letting them fall to the floor, and...

Holy Big Dicks on Daddy Gods.

Beau is so thick, and Colton is so long.

My pussy collapses to the kitchen floor. She lies, spread eagle for them to take, waving my naughty white thong in surrender while my ego stands her horny ground.

I narrow my eyes. "You forget who you're playing against. I brought a dozen big dicks and vibrators. I'm not even tempted."

"Raven." Colton's voice rumbles low, grabbing my full attention as he slowly glides his hands down his carved abs until they frame his long, hungry cock, mimicking Beau's stripper tease. "Are you saying you don't want to be a dirty girl for this hard Daddy, too?"

Quick!

Do they make Epi-Pens for pussies? You know, like a rescue shot that cures you from sudden happy sluttiness?

And do they make pills that instantly freeze your romantic heart? Ones that make it impossible to be in love *and* fall in love, too? Because we know how Beau owns my heart and now, I can't reject Colton. I don't want to.

"Yes, Daddy," I lie to him. "I can resist you, too."

"Is that the new bet?" Beau asks, making everything on their massive frame's cock—brows, smirks, and erections—waiting for my wager.

"Yeah," I counter. "As long as I resist you two, you have

to stop fighting and start talking. You can journal for Dr. Gary and jerk off for me."

With a sexy grin, Beau chuffs, "Oh, you'd like that, wouldn't you, Kitten? Me and Colt, making out and jerking off together, coming all over Daddy's pretty pussy?"

The sudden look on Colton's handsome face, whipping from my stare to Beau's, matches the one I mask.

Lust.

Longing.

And love.

The only way something like this happened so fast—me loving Beau and me falling for Colton, too—is that it must be Fate.

Don't tempt her above all.

That cosmic bitch wins every time.

So, this threeway can go two ways.

It could be the beginning of the rest of my happiest life, *our* happiest lives. I know the three of us would work, just like you know water's wet without touching it. But any fool could tell you if this doesn't work past this retreat, some-one, more than one, will get hurt, just like you know a leap off a cliff will kill you without jumping.

"I don't know. That's hard odds," I mock my view. "You're two against one."

"No, Kitten." Beau coaxes, "That's a big win. It would be three on three, and those are the best odds."

My mug shakes in my grasp, imagining our three passionate, sweaty bodies tangled together, coming together. Yes, I've had threesomes before, but not like this. Not with my heart in it, and theirs, too.

Do they feel it, as well? How we're fumbling toward ecstasy? How our win or loss will be so great?

"Time-out," I blurt.

And Beau's shocked. "Time-out?"

"Yeah," I answer. "We're not thinking this through."

"She's right." Colton considers me before he warns Beau, "You're always the cautious one, and we better be. There's a reason we're here. Remember?"

"But we know this would work." Beau points between us. "I know you feel it, too."

"Of course, we feel it," I rush. "But you two keep fighting. And you and I," I confront Beau, "said one night only for a reason. Because I'm a distraction you can't afford, remember?"

"Fuck!" Beau curses the ceiling. "Will you quit with that word?"

"I can't," I confess. "I hate that word, and now I remember why."

"Why?"

"Because of my dad."

"I'm *not* him, Blair."

"You sure sound like him."

Colton interrupts us, confused. "Who's your dad?"

"Duncan Monroe," Beau answers for me.

He remembers.

Early in college, I was gawked at and gossiped about because my PGA champion father was as infamous for his pecker as he was his putter. He was always seeking holes, so I made jokes about it to hide the pain.

But, of course, Beau saw right through me.

I heard a rumor that he told the entire Bama football team to shut the gossip down. At least, that's what Reese said Beau did for me, and it worked. After a while, people left me alone about him.

"Duncan Monroe? The PGA champion?" Colton's

shocked. "The man who won four major golf tournaments in one year? He's your dad?"

"Yeah, that's the one," I explain. " The champion who's also had four wives, six girlfriends, nine kids... and counting. And all I've ever felt like since I was a little girl was a distraction for him: me, my sister, and my mom, his first wife. But funny, when he won his first U.S. Open, he was on wife number two, girlfriend number three, and kid number four. So, it was never about distractions. It was about devotion."

"Blair," Beau sighs, his deep blue eyes searching mine. "Baby, I'm sorry. You never told me you felt that way, and I'd never hurt you like that. You're so much more to me, and you know it." He turns to Colton. "And so are you."

Beau forgets he's naked, and so does Colton.

We forget our kinky games and bets, too.

We just get real and raw.

"Okay then," I sigh. "So, time-out. If we're more than distractions, then what are we?"

"And what will we do after this?" Colton jumps in. "Because you two belong together. Any idiot can see it. And you and I," he grabs Beau's stare, "have always been together, even when we're not. But there's life after this retreat, and if the three of us fuck or... whatever... what will that be? What will *we* be?"

The need in the room is heavy. Dripping with passion. Dripping with worry. I can see their bare chests heaving with the question, and they match mine. Because this isn't college where you can fail and get a retake.

This is our lives.

This is everything on the line.

"Alright." Beau nods. He thrives under pressure. "Time out. We'll think about it today."

But still, Beau plays dirty.

And I swear he inspires Colton to do the same.

They leave their swim trunks on the floor and tempt me, strutting around naked with their cut asses and shredded bodies and dicks that remind me of inflatable tube men outside a carwash. The second they fall limp, they see me or each other and surge back hard, waving for attention.

And I'm so royally screwed because I want to be royally screwed by them.

Well, really, I want Beau first.

We have some old feelings to resolve, while Colton and I have NRE—new relationship energy. There's no baggage. But Beau and Colton have some. They have far more to resolve because Colton's right.

There are reasons they're here. There's life after passionate threesomes, even intense twosomes, whether you want to face it or not.

So, I do what I do best. I turn my troubles into tales. I write all day.

At some point, Colton serves me lunch, and I barely remember it. I thank him before I scarf down the empanadas and keep writing until my eyes can't take it. They get blurry from the screen, so I save my work and close them.

I must've fallen asleep, resting on my belly, because I awake to a gentle, warm hand on the back of my thigh. It's Beau. I'd know his touch among an orgy of dozens.

"You're getting a sunburn."

"I'm fine," I mutter into my towel. "I'm under the sun sail."

"It's not enough to protect you," Beau warns. "Your ass is getting pink."

"Liar. You just like looking at it."

"That ain't a lie, and neither is the wicked burn you're getting. Here… "

A moment later, he's rubbing cooling lotion across my back.

"Umm, that feels good. What is it?"

"Some fancy sunscreen shit Colt gave me." He huffs, "It's the only good thing he got from Amber. It's supposed to be cooling and good for your skin."

Beau's firm hands make it soothing, too, and I don't protest. I practically fall back asleep to his lavish massage.

I never changed out of my t-shirt and naughty thong, and now all I can feel is Beau's caring touch. He moves from caressing my exposed back and arms, carefully covering them with lotion, to working his way up from my ankles. I know what he's doing. He's saving the temptation for last, and it's working.

So is his tender confession.

"I'm sorry, Blair," he repeats. "I didn't realize that shit about your dad, and I get it. I promise I'll never use that word again."

I nod into my pillow, overwhelmed by his words and touch.

"The truth is…" His hands reach my thighs, rubbing, kneading their way up. "You're the opposite of a distraction. I have everything I need right here, and that scares the hell out of me."

He parts my thighs at the crease where they meet my

bare cheeks. "I know exactly what I want." His fingertips linger over where I'm aching for him. "I want you so damn much, Blair. I always have."

He melts me. I'm a puddle of love and lust. Every part of me opens for him. For his vulnerability. For his desire.

I arch my back up high to tell him, to let him in.

"Fuck, baby." His voice growls at my permission, and when I feel his gentle bites on my ass, I moan. "You're not losing our bet," he teases, dragging his tongue over my crevice, "if you just let me taste you again. Like our first time. I can't stop thinking about it. About you."

I can't either.

I've tried, but Beau Bronson is forever in my soul, so my body takes over. She doesn't care about bets, emotional baggage, or tomorrow. She needs him. She's soaked for him.

"Not like our first time," I insist, rousing and rolling over. Beau's hungry gaze hovers over me, lying on the lounger. "Show me how you would taste me if I were yours forever."

I heard every word he and Colton shared yesterday, watching me while I was on my bed. While I was caught between reality and fantasy with them. It only made me come so hard. It only made me want so much more.

Beau lingers his fingertip over my cotton triangle. "If you were mine forever," he says, "this Daddy would devour your pussy every day. Sometimes, I'd make it sweet. Sometimes, I'd make it dirty. But either way, I'd make you mine, Blair."

I spread my thighs, lifting my hips. "Show me both. Show me sweet and dirty."

"You want it sweet? Like this?" He starts rubbing my aching clit, teasing over the thin fabric. "Do you want

Daddy to get your pussy so wet I can see it soaking your naughty panties?"

I'm a loser. I'm a lusty, lewd, libidinous loser. I'm drowning in all the *L* words. Including the one that scares me the most

Love.

Because Beau's naked, and tan, and so hard sitting there, admiring what's his, admiring me. And with his parted lips at my pleasure, his stare ravenous, rubbing the tip of his finger over my hard nub, "Beau," I shudder.

He's doing it so fast to me. Shamelessly, I writhe, seeking his touch.

"That's it, Blair. Be so sweet for me. Be a dirty girl, too." He praises. "Your clit's so hard. You're getting horny and wet for me, aren't you?"

"Yes," I confess.

"Then show Daddy. You have my full attention." He's too good. "Spread your legs more. Yes, like that." With two fingers pressing down, he circles my clit even harder, taking me there. "Such a bad girl for me now, aren't you? You're getting your panties so wet. Lift your hips. Open that pussy more." I obey. "Yes, baby, show me how much you want me."

How much?

I can't measure it with Beau. It's endless. Then I remember Colton and glance left to his lounger, but he's not there.

So when Beau leans down, growling, "I'm going to taste how wet you get for me, Blair." When he starts sucking the soaked white cotton of my thong, licking, then sucking again right over my clit, I cry out and don't care.

Colton. The whole world. I don't care who can hear me.

Let them. I just need this. I just need. "Beau." I grab his head between my thighs. "Beau, please. Please. Please."

"Baby, I'm gonna show you *fucking* please," he snarls, and in one rip, he snaps the side string of my thong, then the other. "I'm gonna show you how you're mine, Blair. You always have been. Get on my fucking face."

He's too fast and strong. In one deft flip, I'm on top, and he's on his back, ripping the remnants of my thong away, tossing it on the deck before wrapping his arms under my thighs, pulling my pussy down to straddle his mouth.

"Lift that naughty shirt and show me all that's mine," he snarls with my cunt inches from his beard. "Leave it on and play with your tits. Show Daddy what a dirty little girl you are for me while I make your pussy squirt in my mouth."

"Oh god," I cry out when he smacks my ass. I do it again when he yanks me down, when his lips start sucking my clit, his whiskers tickling my splayed sex.

I obey, lifting my shirt to rest above my breasts, but I can't do it fast enough. I can't ride his face hard enough and brutally pinch my nipples to sting enough, feeling Beau's warm tongue, his soft mouth devouring my tender pussy. Will it ever be enough? I've missed him so much.

"Beau! Beau!" I watch him. He's too hungry and too good. He's made for me and doing it too fast.

Like a luscious smack, my first orgasm wracks my spine. I buck, crying out, my thighs shaking over his face. Pleasure cracks through my body, opening, pouring for him. In a haze, I'm gazing down at his hungry eyes watching me, watching how his mouth owns me.

He's growling and sucking my clit, sucking my delicious orgasm to last so long, wave after quaking wave rips through me. It won't stop. Beau won't stop.

"You've got more for me, Blair," he rumbles. "You've got everything I want. Everything I'm gonna take from you. Do it again, baby. Come all over my fucking mouth."

A groan cracks the air. In my daze, I glance up.

It's Colton.

He's standing nude at the edge of the deck. He must've been swimming in the ocean because he's dripping wet and screaming hard, watching us.

So, I hook my finger, and he stalks our way.

Beau glances, seeing his approach. With a devilish grin, he starts licking my pussy again, and now, it's for Colton's pleasure, too.

"Ummm, Colt. Our woman tastes so fucking sweet," Beau taunts between flicks to my clit. "Show him, baby." He flicks it again. "Show him how you can squirt all that sweetness in my mouth."

This time, Beau's doing it. He'll win his reward. He wedges his hand under me, sinking his thick index and middle fingers inside me, sucking my clit at the same time, and I scream. It's agony and ecstasy because it's all I want and more.

And I can't help it.

I reach for Colton, too. He's too beautiful. Too tempting and strong. He's waiting and wanting us, so I grab his hand and guide it. I guide him to palm my exposed breast, and he groans. Taking both in his massive, eager hands, Colton kneads and pulls at my nipples, too. It frees my hands to grab Beau's head.

"Oh fuck, yes, Blair," Beau growls. "Show him, baby. Show him what a real woman is." He pounds his fingers into my clenching walls. "Show him how beautiful you are when you come. Show him why your sweet pussy is my goddamn addiction."

"Damn," Colton growls, his dick surging inches from my face. I lick my lips to it because he's obsessed, too, playing with my tits. They're full and filling his expert hands, his fingertips tugging my excited nipples until he can't take it. He presses them together, fucking my cleavage with his long dick, and I moan.

"Yes." Beau's gazing up. He's watching us. I'm straddling his face while Colton stands at the edge of the lounger. "Yes, Colt," Beau urges. "Come all over her tits while I make her squirt."

Words escape me. Reality does, too. There is no world but the perfect raging storm of Beau dominating my clit and pussy below and Colton teasing my nipples above. I don't know who to look at, but it doesn't matter.

When I close my eyes to come, to scream, to survive the watery explosion releasing from my core, all I see is Beau; all I see now is Colton, too.

"*Fucckkk!*" I hear Colton praise the sight of my burst as I cry out at the spasms, at the gush I pour over Beau's huffing mouth, trying to drink me through his moans. "Fuck, yes," Colton sighs.

Then I feel Beau reaching up, joining Colton, worshiping my breasts, and my thighs shake again at their dual touch. At four hands, four rough palms of two hot men grabbing me together, so I groan, drowning Beau's mouth in another drenching release.

Tremors take my body. Time leaves me. I'm suspended in their touch until, "Blair," Beau makes me open my eyes. "Blair, baby, fuck." I can barely focus on him between my thighs. He's gently kissing my clit, palming my breasts with Colton. "I need to fuck you so bad, baby, please."

I see the ache in his eyes. I see the ache in Colton's cock. But I feel the ache in my heart, too. Desire. Devotion.

Destiny. We feel it. It's so intense, I need to slow us down. At least, that's what I hope I'm doing.

"Both of you." My voice shakes as I move my body. My cum drips from Beau's beard down his neck while I urge him to stand. "I want to taste both of you."

"Oh fuck," Colton grumbles. "I don't know if I—"

"Let's try." Carefully, Beau moves me back so he can climb to stand beside Colton, telling him, "Let's do it together. We can trust her."

Gently, I touch Colton's thigh. "Do you not want me?"

"Fuck, yes, I want you, Raven." Colton cups my cheek. "I want him, too. So fucking much. I've just never done this."

"Me neither," Beau confesses.

"I haven't either." I sit on the edge of the lounger, gazing up at them. "I mean… I've never had feelings like this, and I don't know if—"

Beau leans down, claiming my worries with his deep, consuming kiss, one I've missed so much. I taste my arousal, my trust, my love on his tongue joining mine, and I don't need to know. I just feel.

Because when Beau lifts his lips from mine, he turns and cups Colton's neck. "I've missed you, too," he pants, "so damn much," pulling him into a matching, consuming kiss.

They're beautiful.

They're moaning.

They're mine.

The late afternoon sun is a halo behind them as Colton cups Beau's neck, too, their tongues laving over the other's, and I join them.

I fist Beau's cock, then Colton's. Feral groans rumble through their kiss that won't end while I gently guide them, pulling them closer to where their swollen tips touch, my tongue gently licking the creamy drops off of Beau's slick crown, then Colton's.

"Oh god, baby." I hear Beau sigh at my tongue, gliding over his tip, then Colton's, and back to his, over and over. I can't fit them both in my mouth, but I can rub them together. I can lavish them with my tongue, my pumping fists rubbing their slits together, and Colton's thighs start to shake.

"Fuck. Fuck. Fuck, I'm gonna come," he huffs into Beau's kiss. "Fuck, I can't last. We feel too good."

So I make sure of it. I pull them even closer together and rise on my knees. Pressing the bottom of Beau's crown, his sensitive frenulum against Colton's, I fist their cocks even tighter, bound together. I clasp my pumping hands around their swollen shafts, hovering my mouth over their joined tips.

Their grunts get savage. They're gasps sweet. They're lost in this pleasure, and so am I, licking from slit to salty slit. I can hear their thinning breath and desperate kiss. I can feel Beau's adoring hand sink in my hair, anchoring me to them and Colton's, too.

Together, they hold me, wanting me, letting me take them, allowing me to share this with them.

Then, it's Colton first.

With no words, only a sudden grunt, his body jolts. He spurts, clenching my hair while he comes in my mouth, but I let it fall out. His cream drips from my lips over Beau's sensitive tip, my milky, flicking tongue taking him, too, and quickly, he does the same.

"Baby," Beau grunts. "Baby, fuck. Fuck. That's so hot. I'm coming." He does, and I love how it's the same name and need for me that he has for Colton. His desire is so intertwined for us, so is every word sighed from his mouth.

I kiss and lick and swallow, cherishing how I hold them together and how they adore me, too. Suddenly, they feel like my men. Suddenly, they feel like my everything.

"Baby." Beau gently tugs my hair. "Blair." He's seeking me, lingering his fingers over my cheek, pulling my gaze up to meet his, to meet theirs. They're two towers of muscles looming over me while Beau praises, "Damn, y'all, we're so perfect together."

The smile on Beau's sexy face is tender. It's in awe and love, but when I look at Colton, who's staring down at me, too. "Colt?" I call him by the name Beau uses because he let me into their secret but now something's wrong.

His handsome face falls. "This is too damn perfect," Colton mumbles, pulling from my grasp and Beau's. "We're too damn perfect."

He turns around and storms away.

"Colt!" Beau calls out as he disappears inside. "Colt!"

COLTON

CHAPTER THIRTEEN

"Sᴇᴅᴜᴄᴇ ᴛʜᴇ ʜᴇʟʟ ᴏᴜᴛ ᴏꜰ ʜᴇʀ."

Which is worse?

Being trapped on this tiny island or being trapped in these big feelings? This goddamn love and lust I can't escape.

I just had my dick, my kiss, and my mind blown, and now my heart's in a million pieces.

And we're supposed to be here getting our shit together, not wrecking our lives even more.

I go to slam my bedroom door behind me, but "Colt!" Beau's right on my heels, slamming it back open.

"What?" I whip around.

"Talk to me." He stands there, naked and ripping my last breath away.

"What do you want me to say?"

"How you feel."

"You know how I feel." My voice raises with my pulse.

"Since we were eighteen, you've known how I feel. It hasn't changed, Beau. I love you. I want to be with you. And now," I gesture toward the outside, where I'm sure Blair can hear me, "I want her, too. I'm falling for her, and I want to be with her *and* you, and we can't so end of fucking story, right?"

"I don't want it to be the end," he says. "I want us together, too."

"But how?" I ask. "You won't come out. We can't be out. I fucking hate it, but I get it. But at least you two can be together. And if you'd finally get your head out of your ass about it, you can be happy with her, and I want you to be. I want you to be with her, and it's gonna hurt like hell because I want us together, too, but at least fucking do that. Be with her. Make all this pain, all this shit worth it."

Fuck, it's burning my eyes.

Losing my mom. Never having him. Meeting an incredible woman like Blair.

It's all love I can't hang on to. It slips right through my grasp.

And he sees it.

Beau sees it brimming over my lashes, and he reaches for me. He buries my face in his neck, his cheek pressed against mine.

"I'm so fucked," he says. "Because I'm so in love with you and her, too, and I don't know how to be with *one* of you, let alone *both* of you."

"Just do it. Just let her lead the way." I can feel it in my heart. "Trust her. Listen to her. Try with her, and at least y'all will be okay. It'll work. You know I'm right."

He pulls back, his blue eyes searching mine. "Nothing will ever be right, Colt, if you're not with me, too."

His kiss is tender. His mouth tastes like us and Blair and everything I need.

"That's why we lost," he sighs over my lips, "and we know it."

I can relive that moment a million times—the moment Beau's pass slipped right through my grasp.

I can't tell you what I was thinking, find the words for my journal, or explain it to Dr. Gary.

The truth is I wasn't thinking.

I was feeling.

I was feeling everything I couldn't have. Victory. Love. Happiness.

None of it was mine.

"For a split second," Beau confesses, nestling his forehead to mine, "I wasn't passing the ball. It was my fucking heart for you. When I'm in the pocket, I can always find you. No matter the pressure, I can sense you. I know you're waiting for me. You'll be there. But that day, that game, and that throw, I was scared. After our night together. After I got to hold you, I didn't trust it anymore. I didn't know what to do, so I just threw the ball, like my heart, hoping Fate or you would catch it, and when you didn't, I felt it was a sign. It was our answer. We lost. That's what made me so fucking mad. Not you. I never blamed you."

"I blame myself," I answer. "I should've caught it. But it'd been a rough year. My mom." My throat burns. It strangles. "You. Amber and her bullshit. Maybe, deep down, I wanted to lose because I don't know how we can ever win."

He wedges his body even closer to mine, touching mine, and it's like we're searching. It's like only together, will we find the answer.

And then he grins. Beau gives me that sexy-as-fuck grin

that finds my heart every time. "So, you admit you tipped the ball."

"Yeah," I answer, "because you put too much gas on it."

His next laughing kiss takes me, urging me back against the bed. We fall together, and it's not about fucking; it's about forgiveness.

Naked, we wrap around each other, my legs twisting with his, my arms holding him tight. Yes, it makes us hard, but this is healing.

"So this is our breakthrough?" I chuckle into Beau's kiss. "Coach and Dr. Gary will be so proud."

He smiles, but Beau's always wise. Well, about most shit. "We still got a long way to go," he says. "We gotta figure out how it won't happen again. How to keep our heads straight when our hearts are like this."

Our bare chests press together, and yes, I can feel his heart beating against mine, wanting what I want, too.

So, I blurt out a plan—a wish I've had for months, really—but what do I have to lose?

"I'll move in with you," I tell him. "That's how our hearts will survive." Fear lands in his eyes, so I explain, "My renovation is taking forever. The contractor says nine more months, but you know that means at least a year. And everyone knows you have a big ass house on our favorite golf course, twenty minutes from our facility, and it makes sense. Players room together all the time."

"Rookies and third-string players," he answers. "Not us."

"Dude, no one will care. They know we're best friends. They know your house is fucking huge and convenient and—"

"It was an investment."

"I'm sure it was, and they know, after my mom died, I

bought a house in Buckhead as a fresh start. As an investment, too. I've been bitching about the price and remodel ever since. It can work."

"Have you been thinking about this all along?"

"No." My heart clenches. "I mean, yeah. Sorta. When Amber was in the picture? Hell no. I wanted to be alone. But with her gone, with me free and us like this?" I rub my leg against his. "It's our chance."

"So you move in, and then what?" He's not convinced.

"Then, we'll be together. We'll have the best season. We'll win the Super Bowl and the rings, and we'll figure it out."

"But... " Beau can't accept it. The solution is that simple. "But people will say shit."

"No, they won't," I answer, and he raises a brow. "Okay, fine. Some will. Some guys will always talk smack. It doesn't matter because once Blair is living with you, too, and—"

"Living with me?"

"Yeah, *living* with you. You're going to give her what she deserves. A chance. A try. Some devotion and not be like her dickhead dad."

"Fuck." He rolls his eyes, but his smile cracks through. "She already jokes she's my beard, and now you want to make it official? You want her living with us?"

I caress his chest. It's a magnet for my eyes. "She's not your beard. You love her, too. I never understood why you were with Reese because you've clearly been in love with Blair all along."

"Reese had issues," he explains. "She needed me. She—"

"She needed help," I mumble. "I'm well aware." His brows pinch but now's not the time. That's the past, and our future is right in our grasp. "But Blair takes care of you. She wants what's best for you. Hell, she waltzes that fine ass of hers around here in a sexy thong, trying to make us quit fighting, and if that ain't love..."

"She won't fuck me though. She's afraid she'll get hurt. She's afraid we won't work." Subtly, he thrusts against me. I don't think he's aware. It's instinct; his body needs mine, and I feel the same. About him. About her. "So now I have a helluva bet to win."

"Please," I huff. "You'll win. I'll help you. She'll be your real girlfriend. None of this fake shit. She'll love you and fuck you and move in with you." I grin. "With *us*. You just gotta convince her you're legit. That you're devoted. That this is about more than a bet."

"I don't know." His brows furrow. "We gotta play this right. We gotta make her think she's won the bet. Blair's too proud and stubborn and—"

I debate, "And smart, beautiful, and worth fighting for."

"*That's it*," the pranking devil says, his eyes ablaze. "*That's* the plan. We keep acting like we're fighting, and she'll keep tempting us when, really, I'm seducing her."

"Do it. Seduce the hell out of her."

He grins. "And she doesn't make you jealous?"

"Oh, I get jealous. I'll kill any man who touches you. But her? No. Question is, will you get jealous of *me* fucking *her*, too?"

He tackles me, rolling on top and grabbing my arms. I let him pin them above my head. He starts frotting me again. It's so familiar, such a fetish of ours, driving us crazy. "You want to fuck my woman, Hawke?"

"You know I do." I lift my hips to his, seeking him, matching his cadence. "Like I want to fuck you, too."

He leans down. I can smell his trim beard, and it makes

me moan. Like a feral marker on his flesh, it holds the primal aroma of Blair's cum on his whiskers. Like now, she's in our blood. Like now, she's our mate to share.

Like she's here with us while he bites my ear, whispering, "I want you to fuck my ass, too, Colt." He thrusts. "You can fuck my ass while I fuck her sweet pussy." And I groan. "Then I'll fuck you so hard while I let you fuck her, too." He thrusts again, and I grunt. "There's no top or bottom. I want us too much. The three of us. I'm not jealous; I'm in love."

And I'm losing control.

I'm getting what I've always wished for.

It has me claiming his mouth and bowing my back, rubbing and thrusting my hungry dick against his, seeking our sudden, gasping, creamy end because we want this too much.

We want our beginning.

Blair

CHAPTER FOURTEEN

"Do you have room in your clit closet to talk?"

"What are you wearing?"

I FaceTimed my sister to talk all about me and my double-dick NFL conundrum, but all I can focus on is her.

And that outfit.

"What?" Vale shrugs. "I'm dressed up."

"For *who*?"

Normally, Vale is an homage to Wednesday Addams or any naughty schoolgirl look. It's ironic because she really *is* a schoolgirl—well, a grown woman about to earn her PhD from Emory, so she does it all tongue-in-cheek.

But now?

"You look like a New York City socialite. What is that?" I press my face closer to the phone. "Chanel?"

"How do you know Chanel?"

"Because," I scoff, "I got champagne taste on a box of

wine budget. That's a couture bouclé Chanel jacket, and it's pink! What the hell? I'm gone for three days, and you've moved to the Upper East Side. I swear, if you have an ankle-biter yipping dog in your Birkin bag, too, I'm having you committed."

"I have a meeting tonight," she explains as if I didn't notice that her hair, usually in long black, braided pigtails, is twisted up in an elegant chignon.

"Who are you meeting? Anna Wintour? The President of France?"

Thankfully, I'm sitting cross-legged on my bed because I'm about to pass out. My world keeps flipping.

"No," she chews her lip, "I'm meeting with Nash."

"Who?"

"Nash." I stare until she blurts, "Mr. Allen! Nash Allen!"

"My god, he has a first name?" I fall back, laughing on the bed, holding my phone up. "What are you? Getting audited by our accountant, Mr. Nash Allen?"

"*Noooo.*"

The way Vale slowly answers, hurry, someone stamp **GUILTY AF** on her forehead.

"*Vaaallleee,*" I drawl, suspicious AF, too. "What's going on? You're not eloping with your best friend's dad or some shit like that. Because I'm your maid-of-honor no matter how fucked up the union."

"We're not eloping, you naked nosy ho. It's a meeting. That's it. Quit asking questions I won't answer."

"Quit saying you have a meeting with Mr. Allen when I know you're fucking him and someone else tonight. Probably Tarzan with the way y'all ripped the sex swing from the ceiling at Delta's."

She smirks. Her lips, which are usually a dramatic, tempting burgundy, are now a conservative, classic nude.

Yep, that's the color of corruption.

And we share DNA. My nasty-for-the-night alarm is sounding, proud slut lights flashing.

"I may be up to something tonight," she answers, "but you're the one down for a double-header vacay in the tropics."

"Wrong sport," I reply, "but right location and yes, I'm in triple deep."

"With the NFL's number one quarterback, its leading wide receiver, and his influencer girlfriend, Amber Kostas? Those two beef sticks? Yes, they're hella hot. But her? I never saw her as your type."

"She's not," I answer. "I'd pick a sweaty wedgie over her. I swear I was gonna stab her with brow scissors before Beau stopped me. But thankfully, Colt broke up with her. Amber didn't make it twenty-four hours without Instagram, so she's gone."

"*Beau*." Vale nods. "And now *Colt*, too? Mm-hmm. Someone sounds very cozy, twice over, for a fake girlfriend."

"Exactly," I confess. "There's nothing fake about this. It's getting real intense, real fast, and... "

I pause, remembering how Beau kissed me before he ran after Colt.

I wasn't mad. I urged him to do it. It felt like we could lose something before we had it. Then I heard their shouts. I heard Colt tell Beau he loved him and was falling for me, too.

I didn't want to be nosy, so I've been hiding in my bedroom, trying to give them the privacy they need, but something keeps bothering me.

"What's wrong?" And Vale can sense it.

"I hate to rain on your naughty night, but can I ask you a question?"

"You're my twin. Let me close my eyes and sense your double-dick dilemma." She slams her lids shut. "The answer is yes for peno-anal."

"What the fuck is that?"

"It's the scientific name for a DP."

"Leave it to you to ruin hot sex with boring science."

"Boring science tells me I hope you packed a cleaning kit."

"Vale!" I snap. "I don't need advice on enemas. I know how to prep my chute. I'm serious. I'm talking about my heart."

"Uh-oh. There's no douche for that." I can tell Vale's sitting at her manager's desk at Delta's. But she must be alone because she's solely focused on me. "Shoot." She stuffs down her grin. "I mean 'shoot,' not 'chute.' You know what I mean."

I sigh. I'm serious. "Did you ever feel like a distraction for Dad? Like, his job, his sport was always more important than us?"

"Honestly," she answers. "Yes and no. When we were little, yes, I don't remember him much. I just remember him and Mom fighting about how he was gone all the time, but once I started playing in junior tournaments and winning, I couldn't escape Dad's attention. I was his junior golf champ until he took all the fun out of it, and I hated the pressure and quit."

"Yeah, you got the sports gene, but not me. Or maybe I just hated it and never wanted to play because of Dad."

"And now you're in love with one of the top athletes in the country," she adds. "And you worry it'll hurt the same, that he'll be too distracted like Dad."

There's the student-loan brain I need. It makes her mountains of grad school debt sorta worth it.

"On the one hand, yeah," I reply. "That's the life of a top athlete. They have to focus. They can't get distracted. We saw it ourselves." I pause. "But on the other hand, Beau's not like that. When he gives, he gives his all. I saw how he was with Reese. Or how he tried to be. He'd never treat me like a distraction, but what if I am, and he loses and resents me for it? Like Dad did?"

"Look," she answers. "Think for yourself, not for someone else."

"That's what Mom used to say."

"Exactly, and that's what she'd say now." Vale sighs and yes, we miss her, and yes, I'm so lucky to have my sister still. "I never thought I'd say this to my boss-bitch bookish twin," Vale continues, "but just do it. Be a WAG."

"A WAG?"

"A wife and girlfriend of a high-profile athlete." She rolls her eyes. "Jeez, you act like our dad wasn't married to four of them and dated a gazillion, too."

"That's why I don't want to be one."

"Okay then, don't," she answers, softly grinning. "Be the girlfriend in love with that cute guy from college that you write all your alien porno love books about. The guy who really loves them and loves *you* too."

"They're not porn," I scoff. "They're romance. They've got a plot."

"Uh-huh. And where is this *Colt* guy in this plot?"

"It's complicated."

"Oh," she laughs. "Complicated like romance? Or like group porn?"

"Do you have room in your clit closet to talk?"

"Nope." Her eyes sparkle. "I have a big secret board room you can't even imagine."

"What?" I sit up, bare titties swinging. I don't care. It's

my sister, and she needs to stop with the jumble fuck tease. "What do you mean by a secret *boardroom*?"

"Call me in a couple of days," she sings. "You know, when you're engaged to Beau Bronson."

She ends our call and leaves me better and worse than before.

The sneaky bitch is driving me crazy with her dirty secrets about Mr. Nash Allen.

But my sweet twin is right—Beau isn't our dad.

Because, yeah, you may be born someone's daughter.

But you should live as your own woman.

BEAU

CHAPTER FIFTEEN

DEATH BY SWOLLEN DICK IS IMMINENT.

"One of the keys to the mental game," Dr. Gary teaches, "is to treat every game like it's *just* a game."

JUST A GAME

I write it in my journal, half to look like I'm trying and half because it kind of makes sense.

Out of the corner of my eye, I see Colt doing the same.

Shit, it's like we're back in high school. He took the best notes in Chemistry while protons pissed me off. I hated science, but took the best History notes, which he hated. There were too many dates to remember when Colt had lots of those with varsity cheerleaders.

Was I ever mad about it?

Yeah. I said those girls were distractions when really... I was jealous.

I wanted a date with Colt.

Last night was pretty close.

The chef prepared lobster and red snapper for dinner. Blair joined us, emerging from her bedroom in another pretty sundress. It was white, and my heart flipped. She looked like a bride. It had us on our best behavior.

We enjoyed another sunset dinner outside, did the nightly dishes, and then settled on the sofa in the same spots for another movie. It was Blair's turn, and she drew *Dirty Dancing*.

That was one of my top flicks, thanks to my sister, and besides, whose dick doesn't dance for Patrick Swayze?

We ate popcorn. I recited the whole movie. And when that iconic scene at the end happened, Blair whipped her cute face my way. "Can you catch me like that?" she asked. "Like Johnny does Baby?"

I threw a buttery kernel at her. "In the pool, Baby. Because no one puts Bronson on the Injured Reserve list."

"Got that right," Colt agreed, and we tried to play it subtly. That we sorta made amends but not too much. We tried to make Blair believe we were still fighting a bit.

Everyone slept alone last night because I'm going for the long prank.

I'm playing for the big win with her.

"So let me ask you," Dr. Gary continues our session. "When was it just a game between you two?"

"Easy," I answer. "High school. Even when we made it to the state championship twice and won twice, I never felt the pressure. It was just Colt and me, and it was fun. I used to front flip into the end zone."

"Colt?" Dr. Gary asks, "Do you agree?"

"Yeah." He spins his pen. "It was just fun. We were kids, but it ain't the same now."

"What's changed?"

I answer Doc, "Billions of dollars and millions of fans."

"Even in college?"

"Yeah," I answer. "Even then, we were under pressure."

"We were arch rivals," Colt adds. "That made it worse."

"That was *your* fault."

"What?" Colt snaps. "I'm supposed to follow *your* game plan and not *my* dream?"

Okay. What the fuck?

We made up last night. We're way past Bama versus Auburn and Iron Bowl drama.

Aren't we?

"What do you mean *my* plan?" I raise my voice. "Bama was your dream, too. We were supposed to go together."

"Well, let's explore this," Dr. Gary rolls up his verbal sleeves, and yeah, let's *explore*.

Because clearly, Colt's still pissed about it, so we start again. Shit, we can throw insults like pigskins. And we do for minutes until...

The sunrise appears again.

More like the full moon.

The full, luscious moon of Blair's gorgeous bare ass but this morning, she slays. I mean, it's full out, fucking murder because my dick swells so fast, all blood from my vital organs rushes to my cock.

Death by swollen dick is imminent.

"*Fuck,*" Colt chokes down his shock, too.

There, Blair stands on the deck, summoned by our shouts. She's lifting her long black hair off the nape of her neck, looking over her shoulder and winking at us while she shakes her long, pink and black foxtail butt plug.

Like a hunting hound, I'm about to chase her foxy ass.

Then she turns around, wearing pink and black ears, pink high heels, and nothing else but—*holy pussy goddess*—did she cover herself in pink glitter? Are her nipples darker, too? Like red rouged?

"Uh…" My brain quit.

"Um…" So did Colt's.

My only remaining thought?

Blair can't live with us.

Not when she's going to kill us daily with pornified sex temptations no pussy-loving creature can survive.

"Gentleman?" Dr. Gary studies our stupified faces.

He's got to notice us squirming like we're sixteen again in sex-ed class when the state of Alabama tried to teach abstinence, but our hard, teenage dicks wouldn't wait. All we had to do was come once to know the preaching adults were hypocrites. That shit felt way too goddamn good to be immoral.

"Bronson? Hawke?" Dr. Gary tries to grab our attention.

But Blair sashays to the side of the flatscreen, pointing at Doc like she's a XXX-rated Vanna White.

This ain't *Wheel of Fortune*.

This is about to be Wheel of Foxy Fucks.

"Uh, yeah. Sorry." I cough. "There's a dolphin outside. It's pretty cool."

"A pretty pink dolphin."

Colt doubles down on the bullshit, and he better pray such an animal exists.

"Sure," Dr. Gary scoffs. "I'm sure it's a rare visual. On that note, that's your work today: visualization. You're going to spend an hour visualizing your state championship. Give me the stats on your senior game."

Thankfully, when it comes to football, my brain works even though my dick is busy.

"I had forty-two completions for three hundred and forty-five yards. Hawke caught two-thirds of them and three out of our four touchdowns."

"Perfect," Dr. Gary admires, but I still hear his annoyance. "Visualize that game for an hour. Time it, then journal about it. Twice. The goal is to make it a mental habit."

"Gotcha, Doc." Colt tries to smooth suspicious waters. "Will do."

"Enjoy the *pink* dolphin," Dr. Gary mocks before he ends our session this time.

"Shit!" I yowl toward the ceiling. "Blair Monroe! Woman, I'm gonna tan your foxy ass!"

She clicks by us, swaying her pink tail with no care since the session is over.

"Well," she drawls, "it worked, didn't it? Y'all stopped fighting."

It's a repeat of yesterday morning. Blair pours coffee, looking like she belongs on a stage with all my millions in her non-existent G-string while she sips and grins.

Colt nudges my bare foot, reminding me of the long prank, not the rocket about to explode in my trunks.

"No," I lie. *I think.* "We're still fighting, just not yelling. Wouldn't want to scare the foxy wildlife."

"That's progress." She pops a slice of pineapple in her mouth. "Now, kiss and make up."

Every morning, the chef leaves us a vegetable quiche, fresh fruit, and juices. Colt and I already ate but now our eyes devour her eating breakfast while we sit on the sofa.

I don't know my next move.

I'm too damn turned on.

With that furry anal plug swishing from her luscious

ass, I'm reminded of our kinky Valentine's night when Blair was a Bad Kitten, and I was her toy.

Damn, if Colt knew what he's missing right now. Maybe he does because he fights the urge. It's soaring in his trunks, too.

He rises, mumbling, "No one's kissing, and no one's making up." Grabbing his journal, he heads to his lounger outside. "Let's get to work."

"Is he okay?" Blair worries after he leaves.

"Don't know." I shrug. "I might've pissed him off again. Guess your foxy ass will have to keep us from fighting all day."

Quickly, I get up, hiding my smirk. With my journal in hand, I aim for a lounger, too. A few minutes later, Blair joins us outside.

Clicking away on her laptop, she lies, tummy and tits down on her lounger under the sun sail, her long furry tail gently fluttering in the warm breeze.

Limp is not an option for my dick today—same for Colt. I catch him grabbing his crotch like he's in pain. Like there's no relief from Blair's temptation.

What makes it harder? Literally?

I know with that plug in her ass, Blair's pussy is soaking wet. And based upon our Valentine's night reunion, I know when I tug it, I can make her come. *Real. Fucking. Hard.*

Damn! It's all I can visualize when I'm supposed to recall our state championship twelve years ago.

Over and over, it's all I see when I close my eyes.

Me, fucking Blair.

Me, fucking Colt.

Us, fucking her.

Them, fucking me.

Every infinite, carnal combination of our three bodies.

It's not just the sex we can share. It's the morning coffees. The nightly movies. The laundry we can do together. The long talks we can have in bed.

I want everything with them; I just don't know how.

Colt made our part easy. He asked me about living together, and maybe it'll work for a while. For the first time in my life, I'm willing to try with him.

But me and Blair?

I've never had a girlfriend. Not since Reese in college, and no offense, I don't really count her. That wasn't two adults in love. That was me, trying to be a hero because I didn't want to save myself.

Yeah, I've fucked around since. I've swiped for some kinky nights after the NDAs were signed, but no woman has been to my house. Hookups happen in hotels.

But my home? My bed?

It's virgin territory like my heart. I've been saving it for someone—someone to dream with, someone to marry, someone to start a family with.

I thought it would be a decade from now, not in days, because the clock is ticking down. Like it's past half-time, I gotta lock down a victory with Blair before we leave.

She's my someone. So is Colt.

I realize it now. But can someone tell me how I can convince her to try? To trust?

The chef sets our lunch outside. It's amusing when he eyes Blair's bare ass and foxtail, but the guy's chill. He and our maid. They must see all kinds of stuff, so they leave us and our kinky drama alone.

"Hey, Fox?" I sit at the table, filling fresh corn tortillas with Pibil—slow-roasted pork with local vegetables. "You gonna eat with us?"

Colt's about to scarf down his meal, too, but Blair just shakes her tail.

"In a minute." Her fingernails click on the keyboard. "I'm in flow-state."

"I'm in hard-as-fuck-state," Colt mumbles, sitting beside me. "Dude, you gotta do something because all of a sudden, I have a dirty fox fetish."

"Try having a kitten fetish, too." Colt stuffs his face, eyes wide, waiting for me to explain. "The first and last night I was with her? Valentine's? Blair rocked my world wearing a Bad Kitty collar and a long black cat tail butt plug."

I want to tell him more. I need to tell him more.

About how I discovered so many erotic things with Blair that night. About how we shared more than kink. It was a soul-branding connection, *our connection*, and I haven't been the same since.

I found myself inside Blair—myself who loves Colt, too.

But it's not for me to share. Not all of it. If Blair wants Colt to know her fantasies, too, she'll tell him. Or show him.

Hell, is that what she's doing now? Waiting us out? Trying our dick patience?

Watching her feet kick in the air, I nudge his. "Eat up, then play along. Let's see if we can tempt the fox out of her den."

When we finish our meal, we dive in the pool to refresh.

I jump out and plop down on the lounger beside Colt to dry off. There's not a cloud in the summer sky, and soon we're bone dry and boner hard, our desire for Blair scorching far hotter than the sun.

So, I disappear inside and make myself at home, rummaging through the bathroom Colt and Amber shared.

Amber left in such a huff; she left all sorts of lotions and potions behind, and *Bingo*, I grab a yellow bottle of "Glow Oil" that says it has SPF 50.

"Here." I tap Colt's arm with the bottle as I settle back beside him. "Oil up," I whisper. "Let's give her a helluva slippery fight."

Colt smirks before he straightens his face.

We start on our arms, pouring puddles in our palms, slowly rubbing glistening oil over our flexing biceps.

Blair tries hiding it, but we're stirring the pheromones in the air.

She glances our way while I prime Colt. "You know what I visualized today? The option route in that game. The state championship." I eye Colt. He's rubbing oil over his delts and ink while I rub him the wrong way by adding, "The route you missed."

"The *only* one I fucking missed." He starts on his beefy pecs. They pop with the tension in his voice. "You threw it out when I was breaking in."

Out of the corner of my eye, Blair tilts her head, her foxy ears perking up at our tone.

"Nah," I argue for the hell of it, caressing my pecs, too. "The way you juked. The way you dropped your hip. It signaled you were running out."

Tipping the bottle, I drizzle a long, oily stream of coconut seduction down my abs.

"Like hell." Colt gets riled up at the sight, grabbing the bottle from me and coating his washboard, too. "I was running in, and you threw out. That's on you, dude. It was a rare time you couldn't decide."

"So you're in my head now?"

"Yeah, I live there rent-free."

"Then freely tell me what I'm thinking now."

I'd really like to know because my brain is multi-tasking a lubricated prank, a pseudo fight, and a raging hard-on. Seducing Blair seduces me, too. Colt looks good enough to glide across.

Or down.

Or inside.

Fuck, what game are we playing?

"You're thinking nine times out of ten; we think the same way," Colt argues, polishing his abs, his big hands inching closer to his trunks like he's itching to rip them open.

Or me.

Or Blair.

Or both.

"But it's that one time out of ten"—he keeps tempting—"when you know you're wrong and you miss."

"*I'm* wrong? *I* miss? Fucker, do you know my pass completion percentage?"

"Yeah," Colt woofs. "It's seventy-one percent, thanks to me."

"And you lead receiving yards, thanks to me."

"Nah, baby," Colt mocks, stroking his glazed abs and pissing me off. "All this body control. All this stamina. All this strength and agility." *And turning me on.* "It's all me."

"Exactly," I snarl. Half of me wants on him. Half of me wants in him. "It's all you, and so was the Super Bowl interception."

Touchdown.

I didn't mean the insult, but I take the point. It was too easy.

"Fuck you, Bronson!" he barks. "That's not what you said last night when—"

"Hey!" Blair jumps up. "This ain't daycare! Stop fighting."

Our plan worked, but it went too far. She swishes our way, but now we're angry with oil and sweat glistening over our tense muscles.

"Face it, Fox." I glower. "We'll never stop fighting over this."

She arches her dark brow. "*Never* and *always* are irrational words for lazy minds. There's only once they apply—*never* does anything stay the same because things *always* change."

Damn, I love her sharp mind. I love her smart mouth. I love her sweet heart. I love her rousing curves. I love her dark landing strip.

My brooding glare aims for it.

"Don't know, Raven." Colt caresses his slick pecs, admiring her nudity, too. "Who can ever make us agree?"

I smirk because he's going for the win.

"As foxy as you are," he baits, "I still ain't inclined to see it his way. Wonder what could make us stop fighting?"

"Yeah, Blair." I pile on, going for the ultimate mind-fuck. "Who could ever make us *feel* the same inside?"

"God, y'all got jock itch of the brain." She laughs. "I know what you're doing."

"What's that?" Colt grins.

"You're fighting to make me stop you."

"Don't flatter yourself," I mock. "Colt and I were fighting long before we ever knew your foxy ass."

"Yeah," Colt tags in, "and I bet you can't ever stop us."

Oh shit. Like a bomb, his dare lands in Blair's sexy eyes. It's about to be D-Day all over Colt's dick because she won't lose a sex war.

Leaning over, she smirks at me before crawling over Colt, lying on his lounger. Her lips cunning. Breasts mouthwatering. Hips heavenly. Pussy luring. That foxtail way too dangerous.

She coos, batting her long lashes at him, "Do you want to try me, Colt?"

Lazily, she rings her tongue around his hard, innie belly button. Colt has no chest hair. Dark blond dusts his legs and arms, while he has a sexy thin line that tempts you down from his belly button to the trimmed patch framing his long cock. With Blair's tease, it's rising for release from his swim trunks.

Colt gazes down at her, then at me. So, I rip open my swim trunks and shuck them down, kicking them aside. I'm as naked as a glistening jaybird, hard as a steel rod, and fisting my cock while I raise a brow at them.

"Yeah," Colt answers, his voice gruff. "I really want to try you, Raven."

Blair goes for his nipples next. His ink stops just above them, and I swear the woman is a sex savant. She knows they're his trigger because when she slowly rings them, he moans. When she gently blows air over them, his hips thrust. When she finally licks, then sucks, then bites one, he grunts, "Fuck, woman. You're hot as hell."

Yes, she is.

I'm entranced watching her seduction. I'm light-headed, watching his pleasure. He has no idea how, in a moment, he'll be forever marked by Blair. And she has no idea how, once she tastes Colt's lips, she'll be hooked.

She's about to kiss him. He's about to let her. She's about to give him her beautiful body. And he's about to take it. To love it.

This was supposed to be a bet, a prank, a temptation but now it's more.

So much more.

Watching them together is everything I want, but not like this. I don't want to trick her. I don't want a joke. I want everything to be real and right with her. With him. With us.

"Come here, Kitten." I leap, hooking my arm around Blair's waist, snatching her body off his. "We need to talk."

"But… "

I don't know who stammers it first.

Her? Colt? They're both shocked by my reaction, and I don't care. I can't stop it. I'm a fucking caveman, and this isn't about jealousy. It's about survival.

"I need my woman for a minute," I explain, taking it back to my prehistoric roots by slinging Blair over my shoulder.

Colt starts laughing while she squeals. "What the fuck, Beau? Put me down!"

But I go full Cro-Magnon. I slap her ass. Not hard. Just enough to stake my claim. "Never, woman. I'm never putting you down."

"Y'all go settle the score now!" Colt calls out as I stomp away.

He gets it. I can hear it.

But Blair?

She dangles over my back, smacking my naked ass back. "You wanna play, Bronson?"

So I smack hers again. "You're the one with a furry plug in her ass."

CHAPTER SIXTEEN

"You tinkle like a little princess."

I barge us through the open living room, down the breezeway to my bedroom door, and I win an Oscar. I kick it open—not that it was shut—I'm just committed to the barbaric performance.

Blair shrieks, "Have you lost your jealous mind?"

"I'm not jealous." I toss her on my bed. She lands with a bounce, her bare breasts and rouged nipples adding to the primal spectacle. "If you want Colt, too, baby, you know I'm game," I tell her. "But this is about me and you first."

She jolts to her knees, her fists on her waist. "What about us? There is no us. We're fake. Remember?"

"There is an *us*." I rule. "There always was an *us*, and there always will be. The bet is over, Blair. You won, and I'm for real."

"Real about what, Beau?" There's no light in her eyes,

only sparks of fear. "Real about how you're the hottest quarterback and everyone, especially the media, wants you? Or how you want the Super Bowl so bad, you won't stop until you win? Or how it's your dream? You love football and no one can be a distraction? No one gets in the way."

"No, Blair." I grab my chest, my pounding heart. "You're right here. You get in the way, and I want you to because you're my dream. I want you to be my girlfriend. *For real.*"

Send a rescue chopper.

Blair Monroe is speechless.

Her brain blitzes. Her breath stops. Blinks are her only sign of life.

"Say something." I stand at the edge of the bed, my heart clenching at the sight. "Say yes."

"But... but..." she stammers. "But you don't do girlfriends, and I don't do love."

"There's a first time for everything. It's like you said— never say never. We always change."

Like I struck her dumb, she plops back on her pink-tailed ass. It's cute until she starts scooting toward my headboard.

Scooting away from me.

"Blair," so I lean over, crawling after her. I won't let her escape. This time, no one's leaving. We're doing this. "It's okay, baby. I mean it. I want this for us. I want us to try."

Her silver eyes get so wide. "But what if you hate me?"

"I'll never hate you. Prank you, yes. Fuck you, please. Date you; it'd be my honor. Get pissed as hell when you fill my Golden Oreos with toothpaste again. Damn, right. But baby, I'll never hate you."

Tears fill her gorgeous eyes. "You will, Beau. I know you're the best. I know you're a winner, but everyone loses a game or two, and what if you lose them because of me? Because I'm a distraction?"

I keep coming for her, and she falls back, her raven hair fanning over my white pillow. I trap her between my locked arms, my nose nuzzling hers.

She's not going anywhere.

"Blair, I'm not your dad, and you're not a distraction. Maybe everyone's been wrong, including me. Maybe the only way I'll ever win and the only way I'll never lose is if you're with me. If you're mine."

Her tear escapes and I kiss her temple, catching it.

"Where is all this coming from?" She doesn't trust me yet, and I get it. We all have wounds one kiss can't heal. "Months ago, this wasn't you. You said one night only for a reason, Beau, and I understood. I want you to have your dream."

"Exactly." Softly, I kiss her lips. "You understand me. You want me to have my dream, like I want you to have yours, and my dream involves *you*, Blair. I don't know the rest. I can't control it. But Colt smacked my head enough to make me realize I can control this." I kiss her again and again until she kisses me back. "Say yes, Blair. Give us a shot."

"But Colt?" She worries. "You love him. You need to be with him."

"Yeah, I do. I've kinda had my head smacked about that, too. I need him like I need you. I don't know where he ends and you begin in my heart. You're both just there. I'm just made that way."

She reaches up, touching my lips like she can't fathom my words. "But how? How can you be with us when you said you can't be with anyone? Not now. Not when you're at the top of your career. Beau, I understand. I know how hard you've worked and all you've sacrificed. I know what foot-ball means to you. I won't take it away."

This is the reason I can't breathe. This is why I'm scared. This is the feeling I didn't expect to hit me this hard, this fast.

This is why I love Blair Monroe. Always have. Always will.

And this is the part I fear will freak her out.

But I can't imagine a life without her.

"Come live with me," I urge. "Come live with me and Colt. In Atlanta. For the year. Let's try and make it work. That's how we'll have football and each other."

In a whirl, Blair tackles me. With my heart in my hand, I'm caught off guard while she flips me over, straddling my waist.

"Live with you? Is this a fucking joke?"

I laugh because, yeah, it'd be a good one.

"No, baby, it ain't a joke. I'm as serious as my seven thousand-square-foot home. I've got plenty of room for you and your alien romances. You can have my office and all my bookshelves. Hell, I even have a telescope on my bedroom balcony for you to find more alien lovers."

"So, I'm just supposed to give up my life to be your WAG?"

"*WAG*?" I snort. "What alien snatched you? Since when do you talk like that?"

"Since my sister told me that's what I'd be. And Jace, too. If I'm your girlfriend, I'll be stalked and dragged and trolled and—"

I cup her cheek. "If you don't want my bullshit life, I understand."

Though it will kill me. Though I don't want another

Valentine's without her. I never want to let Blair go again, but I won't trap her in hell with me.

"Beau." She sits up, breath-taking, topless, sparkling with dusty pink glitter. She's on my naked dick that soars for her while my heart threatens to drop. I can't lose her. "It's not bullshit," she says. "The press and fans are part of your life, and I get it. It's not your fault. You've earned your success."

"Then let me spoil you with it. I can protect you some and keep you out of the limelight. You don't have to come to my games and—"

"But I'll want to." Her hands fall on my pecs, her arms pressing her breasts together, and I try to stay focused, but damn... *I need her*. "I'll want to go to your games—and Colt's. And... " The other half of the proposal dawns on her. "Are you and Colt coming out?"

"Hell no. We can't, and you know every reason why."

"I do." She nods. "So, how do you expect to get away with him living with us?"

I grab her hips. "Is that a yes?"

Half of her lush lips lift. "Answer my question first."

"He's remodeling his house. He just bought it and had it gutted with all these plans drawn up that'll take a year to finish. He can rent somewhere, but everyone knows we go way back, and I live near the team's facility. It's convenient. It kinda makes sense."

"So... " Her eyes narrow, but her lips grin. "I *will* be your beard."

Aw, hell. Here we go again.

I tickle her waist, and she squeals.

"Do men want to fuck their beards?" I laugh. "Do they want them making raw lasagna and pissing like a racehorse while they try to take a shower in peace?"

"I don't piss like a racehorse."

"No, baby, you don't. You tinkle like a little princess."

She laughs, too, making stars explode in my chest. I feel lighter and hopeful. Like for the first time in my life, I've found a way to be me.

Reaching up, I lace my hands through her ebony hair, tugging her lips to mine. "Blair, say yes to us. Please. Years ago, you won my heart. Now, let me give you my devotion."

She kisses me, her tongue answering mine before she teases, "Are you giving me this, too?"

With a firm grasp, she grabs my dick, and I groan. It's as desperate for her, too. Pressing it to her opening but hovering, she keeps me waiting. For her. For her answer.

"Yes." So, I grip her hair tighter. "It's yours. It's Colt's."

She rings her wetness around my tip, torturing me. "Are you sharing me with Colt?"

She's fucking killing me. I try thrusting inside her, but she lifts just enough, keeping me right where I need to be for the rest of my life. "This is *your* sweet pussy," I coax. "It's up to you."

She circles. "Does he want me too?"

"What man doesn't want this?" I lift my hips again, trying to nudge in, but she moves. "Yes, he wants you, but I get you first." She holds me on the edge of her and her answer. "Fuck, Blair. Baby, come on. Give it to me."

"Does it make you jealous? Me with Colt, too?"

"Fuck no," I growl. "It turns me on. It feels right. I want the three of us fucking forever."

She's so wet. She's making everything harder. "Can you feel what I want, too, Beau?"

Barely, she lowers on my crown, taking me into a hint of her tight heat, and I groan. I could abuse my strength. I could yank her hips down. I could flip her over and bury my aching cock so deep inside her, but her tease is hell promising heaven.

"Goddammit, Blair." I thrust my hips again, chasing her, needing her. "Let me inside. It's mine."

"Is it the only one?" But she's in control. "Do you need a condom?"

"Fuck no." I keep a fist in her hair while I grab her hip. I'm losing it. I'm in pain. "Only you. I've only been bare with you and haven't been with anyone since. No woman but you. Because I only want you." Reason hits me. A shock of jealousy, too. It makes me growl, "Am I the only one for you?"

"Yes." She swirls on my crown. "There's never been anyone but you, Beau. From the moment we met." She wraps me so tight. My heart. My body. "You're the only man I've swallowed. The only man I've allowed to come inside me." Her lips dust mine. "The only man who really knows me. Who sees me. Who has my heart. Always." She kisses me and kisses me again, promising, "I'll try with you. You *with* Colt. Is that how you want me? Like this?"

She takes my tip all the way, hovering, leaving my bare shaft aching for her. It's perfect torture, and from somewhere deep, I need her so much. It's not just the swollen slick heat of her tight cunt that awaits me.

It's Blair.

It's the life I'll have with her. The dreams. The family. The forever.

"Blair, I'm about to fuck you." I anchor my feral eyes to hers. I grab her hip so hard I'll leave bruises on her perfect milky flesh, and I'll love them. I'll kiss them when I'm done. "I'm about to fuck you so hard and now and forever. Say yes."

"Yes, Beau." She sinks so fast, taking my cry, my cock, my sanity, too. "Yes."

I don't know the sounds we start making. I don't know this animal craze, this fierce passion for claiming every part of her, my mouth taking hers, then her nipples, then her neck. I'm dying under her ruthless, riding fuck and let her take me. Wet. Hot. Hard. Blair has me, my breath, my body, my life. I don't know who I am, but a moaning man grabbing her, plunging so deep inside her where I belong and only seeking more.

"Beau." Wetness drops on my cheek. I lick, and it's salty. It's her tears.

"Blair." I open my eyes to find hers crying above mine.

"I'm scared," she whispers, her mouth brushing mine. "I love you so much."

"I love you, too." The truth rushes over my lips. I kiss her and kiss her again. I don't hold back. I know it. "We'll be okay because I love you, too."

And I need to hold her, to take her, to prove it to her. I flip her over, and I do. I devote myself to her. To her pleasure. To making her come. To making her scream, scratching my back. To making her come again after I flip her. I tug her tail when she's back on top. I thrill her ass while her pussy takes my cock. I make her walls spasm, her cum streaming down my shaft. It makes me cry out to finally come inside her again, to fill her with the flood of emotions we've been afraid of for so long.

When we're done, all that's left is me, holding Blair in my slick arms, the afternoon sun spilling in through the glass doors, and her kissing my oiled, pounding chest, asking, "Did you really mean it about your bookshelves? That I can have them? Because I've never been so turned on in my life."

I laugh, squeezing her tight. "Yes, baby. You can have my shelves, but I control the remote, and Colt claims the thermostat. That hot motherfucker needs the Arctic Circle to sleep."

We kiss to the deal. We fuck again to seal our promise.

We got this.

It's just everyone else I fear who can take it away.

COLTON

CHAPTER SEVENTEEN

"Okay, bend your knees. Good girl. You ready for it?"

"But," Blair protests, "Baby ran from the stage, and Johnny caught her."

I keep my hands on her waist while I echo Beau, "Look, baby. We can have the time of our lives, but no one puts Hawke on the Injured Reserve Injury list, either. We do this in the pool, but he's not allowed." I nod toward Beau, standing by the edge. "I won't let him. His precious shoulder is worth too much."

Beau's grinning, recording us with his phone while mine plays that infamous song from *Dirty Dancing*.

The sun is setting. The horizon is electric pink. These two fucked so hot and loud all afternoon; even the elusive pink dolphin could hear them, and I'm happy, too.

It seems we're going for it.

The three of us.

And this iconic shot.

"Alright." I squat, holding her tight. "Let's do this—on the chorus."

We wait for it...

"And go!"

I lift Blair, bracing my arms, using all my might. She's not heavy. She's dripping wet and cute as hell in a red and white polka dot bikini, her hair a black silky sheet down her back.

It's just I don't want to drop her. I care about her, too.

We sort of just met, but it's like I've known Blair for years. I knew Beau had a crush on her. Blair made him happy, so somehow, that made her my secret college crush, too.

Yeah, I fucked around. A lot. Almost to a pathological degree. But I was young. I was trying to compensate for the love I wanted with Beau but couldn't have.

Maybe that's what Beau was doing, too. He was committed to Reese, but it wasn't love, either. It was about him focusing on her problems so he wouldn't have to confront ours.

Maybe if he knew back then how it wasn't mutual. How Reese wasn't faithful. How she cheated on him and with whom he would've been with Blair years ago.

But here we are. Like the three of us were written in the stars, we just had to wait for our worlds to turn to see it.

"Okay, hold!" I brace my core while Blair drips over me, locking her frame. "Hold, baby. Hold!"

Beau keeps filming. "Don't fall," he jinxes us.

"Don't do it," I huff, feeling Blair tilt and giggle. "Don't—"

But she squeals, and my back arches, letting her swan

dive over my head. Then I whip around because the water is shallow.

We can't break our baby on our first night together.

Laughing, she emerges. She's fine, insisting, "Again!"

So, the song loops while I let her fulfill every woman's fantasy five more times before Beau declares, "Dinner time."

Wrapping towels around us, we drip dry, scanning what the chef set out for dinner before he left. I'm a pro athlete. My priorities are my body, my food, my rest, and my dick, in that order.

I focus on the chicken stew, spooning it over rice and beans with fresh salad on the side, while I sense Blair's burning focus on me.

"Yes?" I turn, finding her studying my face like a puzzle.

"Hmm," is her suspicious reply.

"What?" I pinch my nose. "Do I have a rose in the garden?"

She grins. "A what?"

"A rose in the garden; a booger in my nose, or spinach in my teeth. That's what my mom used to call it, and you better tell me. That's part of the code."

"What code?"

"Our code." I gesture to the three of us with a dripping spoon in hand. "It's a code I'm sure we'll amend daily."

"Hourly," Beau suspects.

"No, you don't have a rose in your nose," Blair says. "You have a perfect nose. It's straight and symmetrical. It's not too big and... "

Her voice trails while her stare remains. It's shameless and adorable, marveling at my honker like God's gift.

"Uh, thanks." Guess I should return the compliment.

"Your button nose is cute. And you've got a sexy bow in your lips. Your lashes are long and dark and—"

"What is this?" Beau chuckles. "An episode of *Dr. 90210*? Is someone about to get their one flaw fixed?"

"No." Blair shrugs, turning to study Beau with equal scrutiny. "You have a perfect nose, too. It's all straight and kinda narrow with a ski slope tip."

"Baby?" Beau grins. "Did you get too much water up *your* nose? Is your brain flooded because you're making no sense?"

"You two just refute my theory, that's all."

Beau cuts a curious look at me, then her. "What theory?" he asks.

"Me and my friends at Delta's," she answers, "and some of my romance author friends, too, we have a theory: big nose equals big dick."

I set my sloshing plate down because I gotta laugh my ass off. So does Beau, who howls, "Damn. I guess Tom Cruise is hung like a crooked horse."

"Exactly!" Blair exclaims. "And Adam Driver must need a crotch wagon for his!"

And I laugh harder. "So what are you saying?" I gotta know. "We have smaller noses and smaller dicks?"

"No!" She's dead serious. "You got a python, and he has a pile driver. You destroy my theory with your bush beaters."

I glance at Beau, tipping my neck. "How many words she got for the male organ?"

"She's a romance author." He grins. "We've won the penile lottery. It's endless."

"Just as long as they're *big* words." I can't help it. I lean down, kissing her cheek. "Got any other theories? Like blonds have more stamina? Or men with beards make better mouth music?"

Blair's eyes get wide. "Is that true?"

"I haven't tested the theories," I answer. "My blondes are usually bottoms, and I skew the stamina sample with my athletic training. And I've only had one beard on my dick." I wink at Beau. "His."

"And now you got two beards," she jokes about herself and Beau...

And I'm going to like this.

I'm going to love us.

Yeah, we'll be taking a big fucking risk, the three of us living together. But if we're smart, if we're careful, we can sell it.

Later after showers, Blair makes it official when we're cuddled together, watching *Pulp Fiction*. I'm falling in love with her, too, because it's her flick pick, and she can mimic Samuel Jackson to a dick-stiffening degree.

"Say *what* again." She's entertaining, impressive until I hear a phone chiming in the distance.

"Whose is that?" Beau glances toward our bedrooms where we've left them for days.

"It sounds like mine." I jump up to check it.

When I do, I'm blind-sided. Though...

I should've seen it coming.

"Uh, Houston," I announce, returning to the living room with my phone. "We have a pissed-off ex-girlfriend problem."

"What?" Blair chuckles. "Is Amber's lipstick bleeding?"

"No." I hate doing this, but I show her the screen. "She's bleeding bullshit about you all over her socials."

Amber has no shame. She's hash-tagged me, Beau, Blair, *and* Blair's books. She's making fun of them, saying romance books are dumb, that they're not real fiction, and that Blair's paranormal fantasies are obviously inspired by her weird alien fetish for Beau Bronson.

Then Amber included the viral shot of Beau reading Blair's book and some posts from Blair's Instagram, where Blair posted pictures of her writing it.

The cruelest part?

In the comments, Amber's encouraging her followers to leave one-star reviews of Blair's books.

Blair swipes through my phone, taking it all in, and the hurt look that breaks across her face breaks my heart.

And the rage that twists Beau's? It scares me.

"I'm so sorry, y'all," is all I can say. "I should've known she'd do this. The only thing Amber influences is low self-esteem."

"Even so," Blair sighs, "it's not your fault. You can't stop her."

"The fuck we can't," Beau snarls, jumping up, aiming for his bedroom.

"Where are you going?"

"To call my lawyer," he answers me. "I'm about to influence a lawsuit against Amber Kostas."

While he's gone, I kneel in front of Blair, sitting on the sofa. She's staring into space, blinking back tears, I can tell.

"Hey," I soothe gently, brushing her hair back. "Tell me how I can make this right for you."

"You can't." She shrugs. "I can't put my heart, soul, and art out there and expect everyone to love it."

"But they don't have to be hateful."

"They do if they hate themselves."

I nod because she's right. I have my critics, and I don't mind. But I also have trolls who think I breathe wrong. I try to reason that they're so into trashing my life because, sadly, they have none.

But still.

We all have hearts that can hurt.

"Come here." I pull her into a hug. She's so petite, and I'm so tall; her face nestles perfectly against my chest while I'm kneeling. "I'm really sorry." I hold her. I kiss her hair. "I'll tell Kylie to throw Amber some shade."

She mutters in my embrace, "You know Kylie Jenner?"

"Met her at a Clippers game. She liked me more than Amber, but that's not a stretch. Amber's got the personality of hiccups. You hold your breath until she's gone."

I make her laugh and she pulls back, gazing at me. "Thank you."

Ice blue and white mix in her teary eyes, making them that captivating silver color, and "I really want to kiss you to make it better" escapes from my lips.

"You can," she softly answers. "But let's wait for him."

I rise, sitting beside her, protectively wrapping my arm over her shoulder. She nestles into me until Beau returns.

The good news is Beau has enough money to sue someone for defamation and libel to the point where you'd slander yourself to make him stop. The bad news is...

Blair can't win.

"My lawyer said since it's not a false statement," Beau explains, taking his seat on the other side of her, "we won't win, but we sure can scare her."

"It's kinda sexy," I admire. "Hell, I'd want the whole world to believe someone wrote a hot romance book inspired by me. The bigger the blue alien cock, the better."

You'd think they'd answer with laughs or laments, but they're silent.

Stone, cold silent.

"What?" I ask as a chuckle starts in Beau and carries to Blair. "What did I say?" They're acting weird. "What the fuck did I say?"

They keep laughing, and I keep getting annoyed until finally, Blair exclaims, "We did it! Okay?"

"Did what?"

"Beau fucked me wearing a big blue alien cock sheath. He even blindfolded and tied me down. He was Valen, the Vulgarian, and he abducted me, planting his milky alien seed inside me."

"*And...* " Beau adds, "We made a video of it."

"Oh fuck," I mutter. "Y'all are gonna kill me with kink, aren't you?'

Blair nudges my ribs. "We can be vanilla with you."

"Vanilla?" I scoff. "Hell no. I'm gonna banana-split your asses and give you both my thirty-one flavors with whipped cream on all tips."

"Oh!" Blair sounds excited and intrigued. "Is food your fetish?"

"No," I answer. "I got a fetish for latex and being tied down. But hell. We've been here how many days, and now I got a dildo kink, a Daddy kink, a foxtail kink, a watching kink, and—"

"Fuck," Beau growls. "Stop, man. You're making me hard."

"And I'm taking notes," Blair blurts. "Latex and dildos and being tied down? I got you covered."

I adjust myself; I prepare myself for what? I don't know. It's probably going to be everything between us and sign me up.

I've never felt this safe and free to be me. And yes, I'm now rhyming. So, it must be poetry and romance and all that shit I love.

Beau presses play on the remote. I learned long ago he wants control of the clicker. Usually, it's to watch ESPN, but as we finish the movie, no one's watching because it's not long before Beau's inching Blair's dress up.

Tonight, she's wearing a short white one with a cherry print on it. It's a lethal dose of cute and sexy.

When Beau hikes it further, I glance down at Blair's exposed lap and groan. Like from the tips of my toes to the tip of my hard dick because she's wearing another naughty pair of panties. And these were made for us, for any fan of football.

"**GO DEEP, DADDY,**" they demand in hot pink ink on her white cotton thong.

It's hot as hell, making Beau dive his hand under them. "Our. Dirty. Fucking. Girl," he growls, taunting her while his hand slowly rustles under her panties, making Blair pant.

Her thighs fall open while her body drapes back on his. "Yes, I am," she sighs. "I'm feeling so dirty for my daddies. Fuck me. Make me your dirty girl."

Goddamn.

Grab a defibrillator.

My heart can't take it while my cock rises to the occasion because Beau doubles down, demanding, "Colt, taste her flavors. Why don't you see how fucking dirty she'll be for us?"

Don't ask me to eat pussy twice.

In a flash, I'm kneeling before Blair again. This time, I tug her naughty panties down, the eager rise of her hips to let me spurring me on.

I do it fast because I'm fucking starving.

I heard her moans and his grunts and their fucks this

afternoon. It made me hard, happy, and hungry, and now I get to feast.

Spreading her thighs wide, I gaze at my glistening, pink meal. Blair's huffing, her body open for me to take. The gleam in her eyes watching me is pure lust, and I want to hear her filthy mouth seduce me, too.

I demand, "Tell Daddy what you want me to do to your pretty pink pussy, Blair."

She smirks, heavy with desire, dripping with no shame. "Lick my pussy, Colt. It's not gonna lick itself."

"You wish," I mutter, smiling before I obey.

Spearing her entrance, I want a taste of her cream first, and she cries out. I fuck her hard with my tongue, rubbing my nose against her clit, taking in her smell and taste and everything about to be my woman, too.

"Oh god," she writhes. "Oh my god, yes."

I glance up, and Beau's tugged her dress down. He's twirling her nipples to hard pink peaks while I devote my ferocious mouth to her clit.

Then I remember what I saw Beau do. It was so fucking hot. How he already knows how to unlock Blair's squirting lust, so I do it, too.

Slowly driving two of my longest fingers inside her cunt, I curl them hard against her wall while my tongue won't stop toying with her clit, and the way she moans, she cries. She does it so long and so high it's almost a wail. Her thighs shake, clenching together, getting ready to jolt with an orgasm. She tastes so good, I'd let her break my neck between her legs as she braces for it, grabbing my hair so hard.

It starts with her pulse around my fingers. So, I stroke them harder inside her, my tongue flattening, unrelenting, and taking her clit because I want this as much as she does.

"Coolllttt!" A scream finds her voice. Tremors take her thighs. She's coming, and I'm found. I lap Blair up, drinking her sweet gush in my thirsty mouth.

The sensation of her desire dripping from my chin, from my beard, makes me fucking feral to fuck her, but Beau takes over.

"Now, baby." He rips his shorts open, lifting his hips and shoving them down. "Fuck us now." So I help him kick them away. Gently, he lifts her while he orders, "You're gonna come on my cock, then you're gonna come on his. You're gonna shower us in that sweet squirt all night like our good little slut."

Blair catches her breath before she yanks her dress off, dragging it over her head. She's found her second wind while I stand and strip my trunks off, too.

Then I remember, as I watch her straddle Beau, how she sinks on his bare cock, so I head for my bedroom.

"Where are you going?" Beau growls. "We're fucking her. We're taking turns with her."

"Until I get tested, I need a condom," I explain.

After what Amber did, my trust is thin. And though it was done to me, I won't do it to another. I don't risk my lovers or me.

The rule in the locker room is you wrap until you wed.

Clearly, that's Beau's plan with Blair because he's taking her raw. By the time I'm back, taking my seat beside them on the sofa before sheathing my cock, Blair is riding him hard.

She's playing with her nipples for him, making him grunt while she moans.

Damn, she can work those hips. She makes a stripper look like a nun. She makes my lips part; my jaw slack with awe.

So is Beau's. He demands, "Hold still, baby." She obeys. "Yeah, just like that. Sit right there and don't move. Just let us watch you be a dirty girl." He sucks his thumb. He gets it dripping with spit. "You want Daddy to go deep? Like your naughty panties say?"

"Yes." She takes him all the way to his thick base.

"Then sit right here," he says, "and don't move. Feel Daddy's big dick deep in your pussy while I play with your naughty clit."

Damn, he's dirty, and damn, I love it.

I never knew.

I stroke my cock, but have to pace myself. I know Beau and I will finally have a chance this week, too, but this night's for her. We're devoted to Blair's pleasure, and it's so erotic, so trusting, too.

I don't know how Blair can take Beau, but she does. She leans back, her hands behind her, bracing on his knees, but she doesn't ride him. She doesn't move. She's sealed to him, letting him thumb her slick, exposed, hard clit until she's shaking.

It's so damn hot. It's beautiful the way her back arches, her ample breasts swelling more, I swear, while her nipples ache for attention, but Beau's in control.

He wants her like this; how she trusts him like this.

"That's it, baby," he coaxes. "Show us how you want it. How you want every dirty thing we're going to do to you." She moans, and his thumb presses faster. "*Yeah*, you do. You're creaming on my cock for it, aren't you? Your clit's so hard. You want it so bad. Don't you, Blair? You want my cock. You want Colt's, too. So, fucking come for us. Show us. Come for your daddies."

Blair convulses. With a guttural groan, her orgasm quakes through her. She can't speak. Her primal sound is like a mating call. She wants more, and damn, I need her now, and I get my wish.

"Fuck her." Gently, Beau lifts her off his cock. It falls out, still swollen and glistening, his shaft dripping with her release. "Fuck her, and keep making her come."

My heart melts, my dick surging at the way Blair reaches for me. She trusts me, too. Her hands wrap around my neck while her body leaves Beau's to straddle mine.

I lift my cock for her, holding it up, and she takes me with a moan. She's a woman on a mission, seizing what she wants. She starts riding me so hard and fast, too; it's like a defensive tackle hits my chest. I grunt at the shock, at the force of her, but this is pleasure. So much fucking pleasure, I plunge my hands in her raven hair to hang on. Her strands feel like silky reigns in my grasp while I force her hooded stare to mine.

"You like riding Daddy's dick?" *I'm gonna take her there, too.* "Feel it. Feel how it's so hard and fucking long for you, isn't it, Blair?"

"Yes," she gasps.

"Say Daddy's name."

"Yes, Colt, yes."

I kiss her. I take that mouth with my name, sighing over it, and I share Beau's addiction. Her kiss is sweet, so open and sharing like her. I feel seen. I feel safe. I feel seduced. She doesn't hold back. Blair lets me take her, and that owns me.

"You want it all?" I huff over our lips. "Can you take all of me, Blair?"

She already has my body and now my heart. She keeps riding. She keeps claiming more, way more than my cock. I gaze down at our bodies joined, and there's only an inch left of me that she doesn't fucking own. *Yet.*

"Oh god, Colt." The sight of me inside her, the heat of her receiving me, the sound of my name, strained with Blair's desire; it burns my soul. I'm branded. "Yes," she huffs. "Yes, make me yours, too."

"Oh, Raven," I swear to her hooded eyes, my fists gently tightening in her hair. "You have no fucking idea how I'll fuck you every day."

"*We* will."

It's Beau's baritone voice. I lost him in the haze. For a moment, I was so buried inside Blair's gaze and cunt, I lost track, but now he's behind her. He's easing her forward on my chest.

"You want this, Blair?" Beau asks while something cool drizzles over my balls. I know the lush sensation. It's lube. He's pouring it over Blair's crack, letting it coat her ass while he gets ready to claim it, too. "Say you want this, baby. Say you want both of your daddies to fuck you."

"Beau, do it," she tells him, groaning into my shoulder. "Do it, but be gentle. You're fucking huge."

Beau straddles my legs and hers and I hang on. I groan back my release, my breath thinning to their warm bodies urging against mine, but I hold tight.

The way he enters her, the way Beau carefully stretches Blair's ass to take him while I'm slowly pumping into her pussy, my cock feeling his pressing claim...

Holy fuck, it's like our first touch.

It's like the first time our dicks rubbed together, but now, Blair's joining us. She's connecting us. She's giving her pussy and ass to us, sharing our pleasure, and my eyes roll. I sweat. I'm going to lose it all in this heaven.

"Fuck, Beau," I groan, reaching for her hips and his. "Fuck yes, rub your dick against mine. Oh, fuck yes. Just like that. She's so fucking tight, I can feel you, too. Do it. Do it."

"Ahhh." Blair's shaking. Her face is buried in my neck; her thighs won't stop quivering against mine. "Oh god. Oh god."

"Baby?" Beau presses his lips to her ear. He holds my hands, too, securing them on her hips. Together, we go slow while he makes sure. "Does it feel good? Do you like my cock in your ass? Do you like Colt's cock in your pussy, too?"

"Yes." Her lips steam over my shoulder. She gently bites it, too. "Yes, fuck me. Both of you. Do it harder. I fucking want it. Give me your cocks."

I share the feeling. I have the same desire, and I deliver. I lift my hips, driving them harder into her strangling, wet heat while Beau goes slower. He won't hurt her. He'll only kill her with pleasure.

"You want our cocks?" I tease her. I'll give her kink. I'll be her fantasy, too. "You want your daddies to go deep? To fuck you like a dirty little girl? To make you ours?"

"Yes," she pants, staring into my eyes. "I want it. I want you both so much."

With my hand on her hip, I'm holding Beau's too, our fingers twined together, claiming her flesh while he moves his other hand, teasing her breast. So, I gently grab her neck. I make her watch me while Beau claims her, too.

"Then fucking take us," he growls. He goes faster, and my toes curl. "Take our cocks like our good little slut. Take one in your pussy and one in your ass because you love it, don't you, Blair?" *Fuck, he's taking us. We're going.* "You love that we want to fuck you. That we want to fuck each other." *Oh god, together. Here we go.* "We're gonna fuck every night. Right, Blair? The three of us?" Her lips shake. Her eyelids drop. Mine do, too. "You're gonna be a sweet little slut for your daddies while we fuck too, and you come with us. Come on." He spanks her. "Come on our cocks."

He spanks her again as I gently squeeze her neck harder, and she screams.

It's exquisite. It's awe in my grasp. It's how I've never seen a woman before in all her raw, natural power, her primal pleasure because the shameless animal sound from Blair's throat in my hand calls every brute cell in my body to her.

My neck strains with a roar. I come inside her, my cock pulsing into her and against Beau's, and it takes him.

"Goddamn, we're coming." He marvels. He groans. He grunts, and I grunt, thrusting together until there's nothing left but our bodies in a panting pile. It's exactly where we belong.

CHAPTER EIGHTEEN

Please tell me I don't look like I had a date with Elmer's Glue.

"Ahem."

It's too early.

"Ahem."

I don't care if it's Beau or Colt.

"Ahem."

I'm not cracking my eyelids for either because they cracked me open last night. My kitty sends her thanks, but my ass is hanging the **DO NOT DISTURB** sign for at least a day.

Or at least… this morning.

What time is it?

And who turned on the heat lamp? Oh god, I'm sweating like a whore in church.

I shove a body off mine. I think it's Beau's. He's sweating like a pig, too, and…

"Y'all are paid to leave it on the goddamn field, not the goddamn bed!"

What the fuck?

My spine shocks up, my eyelids exploding open. Unfortunately, I find my focus squarely on Coach Williams.

He's a volcano, his red face spewing fury at the edge of our bed.

I glance right, then left, and yep, it's *our* bed. Beau, Colt, and I are naked and tangled in the white sheets.

"Shit!" Colt jolts awake beside me. "Coach? What are you doing? What time is it?"

"It's time for me to run a goddamn ball down your goddamn throat!" Coach shouts. "Dr. Gary called and said you missed your session. It's ten in the goddamn morning. You two have milked the fucking clock and all my goddamn patience."

Goddamn. How many times can he say goddamn?

I reach for the bedsheet, covering my breasts, though clearly I left my modesty in Charleston.

Hell, who are we kidding? I never had it, but still, I'm trying to be a respectful ho.

Because Beau and Colt are in deep doo-doo.

"We're sorry, Coach." Beau sits up, tousling his hair. "We're really sorry. I thought I set my alarm and—"

"Oh, you're set, alright!" Coach barks. "You're set to ride the bench so goddamn long, your ass will go numb. And you, missy... "

He points to me, and I fight the urge to wipe the corners of my mouth. They feel crusty. Probably because we took a shower before I let Beau and Colt finger and fondle me while they knelt over my face on the pillow, giving me a good night sip of their milk before we fell asleep.

Please tell me I don't look like I had a date with Elmer's Glue.

"You missy," Coach shouts, "are outta here! Pack your bags."

"Coach, wait!" Beau goes to jump up, buck naked, but Coach gives him the hand.

"I've seen enough of your helmets!"

"Coach, look," Colt jumps in, "we're sorry. It's the first time we've ever overslept, and it won't happen again. Ever."

"Goddamn right, it won't." His finger points at me again. "Because she's outta here. You two can't get your shit together, but you'll team play with her? I pay you to give me one hundred and ten percent in every play, not every pussy!" He coughs, addressing me, "Sorry, ma'am. No disrespect. I'm just old-school and ornery."

"None taken," I reply. "I'll start packing."

"No, you won't." Beau reaches for my arm. "Coach, she can't leave. She makes us grind it out."

Colt coughs at Beau's unfortunate pun.

"I mean," Beau explains, "we're talking because of her. We made amends because of her. We're over the interception bullshit, and now we're working with Dr. Gary to make sure it won't happen again."

"You don't get a goddamn trophy for doing your goddamn job!" Coach shouts. "That's what you're paid to do without double poking a pussy!" He coughs again. "Sorry, ma'am."

And God, forgive him.

Coach is actually a nice guy. I can tell. He just really likes your damn name.

"I know. I know." Beau surrenders. "We *are* doing our jobs. We got our shit together. Me and Hawke are finally playing together like we used to."

Beau keeps stepping into puns, and Coach arches a brow. It's more dramatic because it's the only hair on his shiny, bald head.

"So, this is a habit of yours? This is how you play?" Coach jeers. "Y'all *used* to do threesomes, and we lost the Super Bowl because of what? You missed your goddamn gangbang buddy?"

I purse my lips to keep from laughing.

Poor, Coach. He's so irate and innocent. He's fucking up all his fucking references.

I want to enlighten him; a gangbang is three or more on one or more than one. We're just a wholesome little throuple. But hey, who's counting or correcting him?

Um, Beau.

"This isn't a habit." Beau reaches for my hand. "This is private and between us. And we don't *gangbang* her. Hawke and I haven't done this before. I've been in love with Blair since college, and I guess she takes me back. She takes *us* back to when we were happy, and it was just a game. When he and I were best friends and shared everything."

It's so sweet how Beau is proud of us.

It's so bitter how he has to hide him and Colt.

And it's so funny how he keeps stepping into puns like cow patties.

Coach shakes his head. "Bronson, you're not popping my cherry. I've seen all kinds of shit with players. And yes, in your home, it's private. But you're here on my time and Atlanta's dime. You two are marquee players. Everything rests on your shoulders. Literally, that's why I'm doing this guru whatever retreat shit. No one can afford to have an open mind about your threesome."

"Why not?" Colt surprises me. "Why can't you have an

open mind? Why can't you keep this between us?" He reaches for my other hand. "If we tell you that we work better like this and play better like this, then why can't you support us?"

It's so sweet, too.

And so embarrassing.

Holding their hands drops the bedsheet to my waist, adding my tits to this argument, but the girls are in it to win it, too.

Coach rubs his head, like he's rubbing a genie's lamp and wishing our throuple would just "poof!" Disappear.

But we're not. We're here—me, Beau, Colt, and my tits —asking for a chance.

"I promise I won't distract them." So, I gotta fight for my guys too.

That word makes Beau squeeze my hand, but I get it. I grew up with it. I drop their hands to grab the bedsheet again and cover myself while I plead our case.

"My dad plays in the PGA and—"

"He's Duncan Monroe," Beau interrupts, which makes Coach raise his eyebrows, very impressed.

"Yeah, him," I continue. Never have I used my dad's name before, but at least now he can be useful. "I grew up with a professional athlete. I understand the lifestyle. The schedule. The sacrifices. So I won't get in their way. I'm not some needy, pining piece of ass. I support them. I want them to win."

I'm so glad Vale isn't here. She'd run a replay, in slow motion with arrows drawn on the screen and shit, of my last four months where I was a pathetic pining piece of lonely ass missing Beau, but now?

I'm doubling down on happiness.

"And I have a life and career, too," I argue. "I'll make us

work—the three of us. Just give us a chance. If they don't prove it by the end of training camp, I'm out."

Beau protests, "No, you're not."

But I look at him because I mean it. If my living with him and Colt negatively affects their game, I won't do it.

I'll never forget the 5-iron my dad broke in the driveway, cursing his first U.S. Open loss. I stood on our deck and heard him shouting at my mom. He blamed it on me and Vale. We had a stomach bug earlier that week, and Dad swore, "They distract me! And now, they got me sick!"

Maybe it was true.

But my six-year-old heart will certainly never forget it. The guilt. The shame. The hurt. I was his daughter, not a distraction.

At least now, the experience can help me.

Funny how pain can pay off sometimes.

"You think this won't distract the media? The fans?" Coach gestures to us, sitting in a post-coital row. "You think our owner? Management? Staff? Hell, everyone and most players won't have a field day with this?"

See. Told ya.

Distractions are death in a sport.

And Beau's right.

It feels nearly impossible that we can get away with our secret triad, let alone with Beau and Colt coming out, too. It's ironic that an all-American game hasn't caught up to the rest of America.

"They won't know," Beau explains. "We'll be discreet, we promise. Blair is my legit girlfriend." His hand lands on my thigh. His touch and words make my heart flutter. "And Colt is my best friend. He's crashing with me for the season, so he won't be miserable waiting for his house to be done, and she's moving in with me, so I'll be happy. *That's* what people will see."

Coach sucks his teeth.

He's not convinced.

"I need this, Coach," Colt chimes in. "I had a shitty year losing my mom, and maybe that's why I tipped the ball. Maybe my head wasn't in the game. Maybe if I'm happy now, we'll win."

"I need it, too." Beau gets his back. "Maybe I put too much gas on the ball because I've been stressed out. I didn't allow myself to have love in my life. I always said it was a distraction, but maybe it's not. Maybe it's the answer. Maybe *she's* the answer."

Cue the violins because Beau leans over, kissing my cheek, and Colt does, too. My thumping heart and blushing face are sandwiched between their adoring beards and Coach groans.

"For goddamn sake." He rolls his eyes, too. "You three look like a goddamn Hallmark card for *Hustler*."

Beau chuckles. "Really showing your age there, Coach."

"And your porn preference," Colt adds. "Mad respect. *Hustler* was a classic."

"Hey, Pornoisseur," I joke with Colt, "they still publish *Hustler* magazine."

Yep, I have to be a kinky know-it-all, and now is probably not the time.

"Goddammit, fine." But it makes Coach half grin. "Ms. Monroe can stay, and you two better play. You'll finish your sessions with Dr. Gary, and you'll get your heads screwed on so tight, Lawrence Taylor can't knock 'em off."

I glance at Beau. He side-mutters, "Taylor was the hardest hitter in the NFL."

Coach hears him. "Yeah, well, fuck up again, and *I'm*

about to be the goddamn hardest hitter. I'll leave you three be. I'll keep your secret. And I'll take your promise." He wags his finger at us. "I want consistency, effort, and perfection in camp, or this is over before the pre-season."

"Will do, Coach," Colt assures.

"Thanks, Chris." That must be Coach's first name because Beau shares it humbly.

"Yes, thank you, Coach Williams." So, I put some skin in the game, too. "Goddamn, you have my goddamn promise."

Coach chuckles, swatting the air as he turns and leaves us to the rest of our retreat.

BEAU

CHAPTER NINETEEN

"LET'S GET HIM READY TOGETHER."

"You're squeaky clean, and it's a good deal."

I roll my eyes to the blue sky.

If my agent only knew.

Kelsie Ryan is one of the best at scoring endorsement deals for players, but if she knew how I'm about to make her job hard, she'd drop me cold.

"The Fry House?" I stand at the edge of the dock. Not because the reception is better here. It's because Colt and Blair are having an annoying one-hit-wonder playlist party by the pool, and I'm about to volunteer to swim with the fish—permanently. "They want me? Why?"

"They're launching veggie burgers and nuggets, and you score trustworthy with soccer moms and ultra fans, mainly men. You're perfect."

"I'm not a vegetarian. Not strictly."

"Yeah, but you and your shakes have paid off for Plant

Power Protein, and that caught the eye of The Fry House. They're offering two mill."

Sure, I rake in on endorsements. Lots of players do, especially those of us with clean reps. I've never been dumb enough to get caught with my hand in the kinky cookie jar.

But now?

I never had to worry about my personal life. I didn't have one.

"Hey, Kelz, I gotta fill you in before we take this deal."

"On?"

I turn around and face my new world.

Blair's riding on a giant white swan float, and Colt's on a gold one. They're singing "Baby Got Back" while Colt's trying to mount his float on Blair's. They're laughing their asses off. They're my wildest dream and greatest liability.

"On my new girlfriend," I tell Kelsie. "I've known her for years, so don't freak. I can vouch for her rep. There's just one thing." Whoops, I forgot how to count. "Make that a few things."

I tell Kelsie about Blair's infamous PGA father, her career as a struggling author, her current job as a sales associate at a luxury adult store, and, "Her latest romance book just became a best-seller, and it's about me. Well... it's about *us*."

"Please tell me we're talking Nora Roberts or Nicholas Sparks romance."

"No," it makes me smile, "we're talking about an alien warlord who falls in love with his enemy, a woman, a human he has to tie down and breed to save her people and his."

Silence. Waves. "Has your girlfriend got the butt?" and Colt's "Hell yeah!" fill the air.

"Kelz? You there?"

"I'm looking her up, but I'm not finding anything."

"She writes under a pen name, but that secret is burned. Her readers figured it out, and Amber Kostas made it worse."

Kelsie's frustrated sigh hits me before, "Bronson, please tell me you love her. This is two mill or more you may lose over her."

I watch Blair, who's now watching me. Her head tenderly cants, like she can sense my distress, asking, "Babe, are you okay?"

So I let her see how she makes me smile, answering, "Yes, I love her. I love her books. I love her job. I'll punch her philander dad in the face before I'm sure I'll hate to love him, too. So any endorsements I lose over Blair Monroe can kiss my ass. I'd be ashamed to be associated with them anyway."

"Damn," Kelsie marvels. "That shrink's really doing a good number on you, and it's about time. You deserve some love." She laughs. "Maybe we'll sign all the sex-positive companies needing endorsements."

Though I'd be proud, I have to be careful.

"Nah, just keep me to sports brands. I may not be squeaky clean enough, but I sure win enough."

Over dinner, I bring it up. Since Coach and Kelsie, I've been thinking about it all day.

We'll be back in Atlanta in no time and have to be ready.

Scratch that.

We have to be careful.

I know Colt feels the same way. He earns millions and donates his fame to raise money for cancer research. Endorsements are not his priority; football is.

But Blair has a lot to think about.

I can't lie to her about being my girlfriend. I've lived in a fishbowl since I was eighteen, and it's only gotten smaller. You can't tell someone how it is until they're stuck, swimming in it, too.

"It'll affect your career and your books," I tell her. "Some will buy them because of me, and some will hate them because of me. You'll gain just as many haters as fans, and some won't even be romance readers. They'll only associate you with me, and I'm sorry."

She reaches for my hand. We're finishing off the bottle of Hennessey she snuck in while Colt tosses back a sip.

"Fine then," she answers. "I had loyal readers before you, so as long as I keep them, I don't care. I don't write to be a best-seller. I write because it makes me happy."

"Like ball." Colt understands.

"Yeah, like big blue alien balls," she jokes, and I hope she doesn't lose her sense of humor.

She's going to need it.

"So what do we do about dates and shit?" Colt asks. "You two are about to be the *it* couple, for better or worse, but what do I do?"

It clenches my heart. It feels like we're teens again. Like Colt's dating another cheerleader while I have to watch.

"Do you want to date even though we're... "

I point between us and don't know how to describe it. I just worry. I'm just jealous.

"Nah, man." Colt reaches for my hand. "This? You and me? Her and us? This is my dream, but we're no fools. I can't be stag in public forever. Rumors will start."

"He's right." Blair sucks a creamy bite of flan off her fork before wagging it between us. "We have to make it look like you and I are America's sweethearts, and he's our best friend, America's bad boy. And on one meet-cute sports romance day, our wholesome love inspires Colt to fall in love with his sweet someone, too. There's your happily-ever-after. It's a classic tale, and folks literally buy it all the time."

"But," I stammer, "it's just the three of us. We haven't even moved in, and now we're adding a fourth? I don't want a—"

"Slow your worried roll," Blair soothes. "We'll give it a month or two. He's still brokenhearted over Amber, right?"

Colt laughs. "Yeah, I'm devastated. I'm gonna get nine cats and date Ben & Jerry's."

Blair scoffs, "That's such a cliché. That's what they make wine, vibrators, and smutty books for."

Colt toasts his tumbler. "Touché to your cliché."

"So then what?" But I can't joke. Routes, playbooks, and drills rule my mind. We gotta win. "What's the plan after he's done with his pity party?"

No one answers.

Water sloshing ashore is all we hear.

Then Blair sighs, her shoulders sagging. "Fine. We gotta do it."

"Do what?" I'm afraid when it comes to Blair and what we have to do, sex toys will be involved.

"We give it a couple of months," she answers, "and then we find Colt a legit beard. A woman who knows our secret and keeps it."

"And one not interested in my dick," Colt adds. "Damn thing attracts pussy like catnip, and I don't cheat. When I'm single, yeah, I fuck around. I got some mean booty on call. Sometimes two. But once I commit, I'm legit."

"Okay, okay." I don't want the image. "We get the idea."

"Two?" But Blair smirks, intrigued. "What did they do? Dress in latex and tie you down? Use your cock and face like amusement park rides? One got off while the other got on? I bet you licked their boots. I bet you loved being their big, bad-boy toy."

Colt smacks his palm on the table. "How did you know?"

My eyes get wide. "She's right?"

"Yeah." Colt grins with pride.

"I can read someone's kink a mile away." Blair pops in another bite of flan. "For example, Coach is into a natural muff and playing Barry White while he opens his burgundy silk robe, rubbing his cute little belly, and—"

I burp. "Blargh." It threatens barf. "That's how I'll see him on the sidelines now. Like a goddamn nineteen seventies Hugh Hefner."

Colt drops his voice low, his eyebrows dancing. "Oh, you got it together, baby." He mimics Barry White, and I throw a Creole bread roll at him.

He laughs, catching it. "Damn, Bronson. Someone's jealous, and it turns me on."

"I'll show you jealous. Who's going to be this beard? Because I'll never hurt a woman, but I won't like her."

"Sheathe your sword." Blair rubs my leg. "I know who to ask."

"Who?" I ask. "Cuz' she better look like she fell out of the ugly tree and hit every branch on the way down."

"Oh, hell no," Colt woofs, "I don't date ugly."

I half snarl, "You fucked Amber."

"Yeah," Colt lowers his brow, "because I couldn't fuck *you.*"

Yes, I'm getting mad about a woman he's not even dating. Yes, Colt with anyone but Blair and me makes me see red. Yes, we haven't even started yet, and I'm about to kill for him.

So, yes, it's love.

"You wanna fuck, Colt?" I leap across the table, grabbing the back of his neck. Plates and cups crash to the deck, but all I care about is, "You'll fake fuck whoever because Colton Adam Hawke, you're mine."

Don't grab a wide receiver. He'll always be faster.

Colt surges, grabbing my neck, too. "Then finally fucking prove it, Beau Willuf Bronson."

I crash my lips over his, our tongues tangling, my hands grabbing his hair, taking him even harder.

"I think you two need this night." A silky voice wraps around us, and I glance. Blair's watching us with nothing but heat and love in her eyes.

"No," I answer. "I want you with us."

She softly argues, "But you two need privacy. You've been waiting a long time and—"

"You're with us," Colt interjects. "At least watch us. It feels more real that way, like we're not hiding anymore."

Blair nods. "Then y'all need to be ready."

"He's so hot and jealous," Colt growls, "I'm damn hard and ready."

"Have you done anal?"

Colt answers, "Does a finger in the ass count?"

"Not when you compare it to his big man bone," Blair warns. "Or yours. If you want me there, it's not gonna be an amateur anal hour. It's your first times, so we gotta do it right."

Never in college, when I was tying anal beads to Blair's license plate, and she was sending me weekly shipments of maximum strength hemorrhoid cream, did I think we'd be here. With her, handing me a little rubber blue ball ear syringe and Colt a red one.

"Just put a little warm water in it," she advises, "not a lot."

We're standing in my bathroom, and it's obvious what we're supposed to clean with them, but it's not obvious, "How did you know to bring two of these?" I ask.

She smiles, pecking my cheek. "Because I'm Noah of the Ninety-Nine. I loaded up two of everything."

Colt cocks a brow. "Ninety-nine?"

"Anal sex." Blair sighs, "Y'all have lots to learn."

"Oh," I laugh, "forgive us, dear Oracle of the Orifices, that we don't know every term."

She asks, "Do you know if you're using condoms?"

"I am," Colt says, "until I'm tested. But he's not. I know he's clear, and I want to feel him inside me."

Damn, that stirs my cock. It races my pulse. There's an edge of fear in this, too, but with them, I feel safe.

"I want to go first," I tell him. "I want you inside me first."

Only a few times have I felt this rush of nerves. Of fear. Of lust. Of a first.

Colt was my first love. All those girls in high school? He thought I was fucking them, but no. I pleasured them. I gained great digit and tongue skills while I got enough blow jobs to last ten lifetimes.

Okay, that's a lie. You can never have enough blowjobs.

I told girls I rarely fucked (meaning *never* fucked) because it was a distraction. I guess that's where my fear started.

So, Colt felt like my first because he was. It was love.

My first woman was Reese. I was twenty. I waited that long because I was waiting on Colt. It was awkward and fast at first. Eventually, it got good, but it was never great.

No woman—even with all the kink I dabbled with— was great, mind-blowing, heart-melting, toe-curling, and soul-altering until Blair.

The way she touched me, kissed me and took me, I was like, "Oh fuck, this is what it's supposed to feel like. This is what people lose their minds for. This is what loving a woman is like," and I was found.

I'm forever found inside Blair.

With Colt now, too?

It's going to overwhelm me. I'm going to drown. Being with him. Having her there. I'm not going back, and I know it.

Blair leaves me in my bathroom, and Colt disappears to his. It's weird as hell getting ready for this, but it feels special, too.

We're adults now. We're grown men, and we want this. We love each other, and there's no shame.

In fact, we have a woman who makes us proud. Who loves us, too.

I find her waiting on my bed, and she rips my breath away. Blair's wearing a soft, lacy, black teddy. It's elegant, sexy, and perfect, like her.

On the nightstand, she's arranged several bottles of different lubes, a row of condoms, a few toys, and some wipes, too. And I'm overwhelmed.

What man is as lucky as me? Who gets a woman this damn beautiful? One who knows what I'll need before I do?

I drop my white towel on the tile floor and hook my finger. "Crawl to me, baby." She obeys, her gaze on me until I cup her chin and lift her lips to mine. "Please know what this means to me—to have you here, to have your support."

"You have my love, too," she answers. "You always have, Beau. I've always wanted this for you."

I dust my lips over hers. "I want you, too, Blair, and I want forever. I know we need to go slow, but I can't share something like this with you and ever let you go. I'm not made like that. I'm made like this—"

I kiss her and find that feeling again—the one that explains everything, the one that reveals the power of this.

And then I feel a big warm hand on my backside, cupping my ass. Colt kisses my neck while he must be caressing Blair, too, because she moans into my mouth. So, I turn and kiss him and find it here with him, too.

Every reason why.

Every wish I have.

Every need met.

Slowly, Blair retreats from our touch, and it's just him and me, and we take our time.

Quietly, Colt maps my body with his hands, like he's discovering me—like I'm the treasure he's been searching for. His fingertips brushing over my flesh feel like light dancing across my skin.

I do the same to him, but not his cock. It's hard and waiting but I want every part of him, too.

I trail down his abs, gently quivering at my touch. I stroke his thighs that flex against my palms. I caress his pecs and kiss them, too. Then I glide my hands up his corded arms, over his ink, finally asking him, "What do these mean?"

I ask about the primitive birds that soar up his arms like a flock storming the sky, and he answers what I already know.

"They're us," he says. "From the first time we kissed. They're finally free and flying home, where they know they belong together."

Hot rocks strangle my throat. Hot tears bite at my eyes. I can't believe we've waited this long. I can't believe we're finally here.

Colt's kiss takes me back, making me fall on the bed. He's over me, crawling while I crawl back. I rest at the top, where Blair is waiting for us. I reach for her, and she kisses me, too.

Then Colt reaches for her, and she rises, answering him.

The way he kisses her. The way he's on his knees, between mine. The way his hard cock is about to take me while his mouth takes Blair's, his hand palming her breast, teasing her nipples, making her moan.

We. Belong. Together.

"Get me ready to fuck him," Colt orders her, and now it's so damn erotic, too.

Blair turns and rips a condom from the row. But before she rolls it down Colt's length, she leans over and takes him in her mouth.

"Yes, Raven," Colt sighs, praising her, fisting her hair. "Yes, baby. Fucking suck me. Get my cock so damn hard to fuck his ass."

She makes his eyes roll before her touch takes me, too. Stroking Colt's cock, glistening with her drool, she takes mine next, as much as she can, then she's rubbing our tips, slick with her spit, together.

She knows us by now. She knows what drives us crazy, my back bowing while I groan. "Baby, fuck, that feels good, but you gotta stop. I come too fast like this."

With a glistening grin, she lifts away. Rolling a condom down Colt's shaft, she only turns me on more—*my woman is getting my man ready to fuck my ass.*

My cock drips for it.

"Let's get him ready together," Colt tells her.

Then he makes it more taboo, more thrilling, telling me, "Spread your legs for us. Hold your knees back and give us that ass."

Obeying his commands makes my arousal soar. He and Blair cover their fingers in lube, and when Colt slowly plunges one in my ass, and Blair follows, gliding her finger in, too, "Oh fuck," I growl. "Fuck yes. If you both could fuck me, hell yes."

"One day we will," Blair promises. "That's why they make strap-ons."

But now, they make me sweat. They make me ache. They make me feel so dirty and special while together, they finger me, stretching my ass open while they kiss, too.

"Now," I pant. It's too much. They have me too hard. "Colt, baby, fuck me now."

They leave me barely gaping and prepared, but I'm not ready. I could never be ready for the first burn of Colt. The first press of his sheathed cock into my virgin ass. The first look of pure animal lust, then tender wonder in his eyes, watching him stake his claim. Or, the first time I watch Blair fingering herself to the sight of our fuck.

For minutes, Colt can't speak.

Neither can I.

He braces over me, breaching me. He kisses me like we can't believe this... because we can't. He feels too good; he burns too much. I love him, and I can't breathe. I can't take him, and I want to.

"Fuck, I don't know. I don't know how I... " I stammer and search for Blair.

So does Colt. He turns, and she's by our side.

"Give him a little break," she eases. "Gently, take it out and slowly start again."

I could be so goddamn jealous, fucking raging actually, of where Blair got her knowledge but not now. Now and forever, I'm so thankful for her.

Slowly, Colt pulls out, and I groan at the odd sensation,

but then Blair's stroking me. I'm half hard, my body not sure how to react, but quickly, her warm touch has me firm and wanting it again.

"Go slow, Colt." She kneels where we're about to join again. "Like this. Can I guide you?"

"Please," Colt's gruff. He sounds so aroused. "Please let me watch you hold my cock while I fuck his ass with it."

It turns him on. Me, too. This time, he goes much slower, guided by Blair's small hand wrapped around his scary length. She starts stroking me harder, too, and, "Oh fuck," we growl.

It gets us there. It gets Colt easing in, past the ring of fire that burns so good because Blair's touch makes me crave it. Then it's Colt's touch. He starts stroking my dick too while he's fucking me, while he sinks so deep inside, he's in my chest, my heart, my throat. His body inside mine is all I can know while seeing stars and only wanting more.

"Fuck me," I beg, my legs shaking in my hold. "Fuck me, Colt. Deeper. You feel so good."

In my haze, Colt is over me. He presses his lip to mine. Blair lets us go, and it's just us.

"You like this, Beau?" He kisses me. "Do you like me inside you? Like you've always wanted? Like *I've* always wanted?" He thrusts, and I grunt. "Damn, I love you," he says, thrusting again and again. "Damn, you feel so good taking my dick. You're so tight. Your virgin ass is mine." His next thrust is brutal. He's almost seated inside me, and I love it. I cry out. "Isn't it? Do you like my dick? Is your ass mine now?"

"Yes!" I growl. "Fuck yes, Colt. Take it. Take my ass. Take it hard."

"Blair," Colt pants her name. He's serious because he rarely uses it. "Blair, fuck him, too, baby. Fuck him slow while I fuck him hard. We'll make sure he knows who he belongs to."

Blair glances at me. I'm sweating. I'm desperate. And hell, yes, I want this. "Do it." I nod. "Ride me while he fucks me. Give me what I've wanted for so long."

Colt leans back, and I let go of my legs. I let them fall open, and the pressure of his cock in my ass becomes immense. It's so much and so good while Blair straddles me. She reaches, tugging her teddy aside, exposing her breasts for me to suck, and damn, she's hot. So is how she reaches down, sliding her lace aside.

Running my tip through her slick slit, she leans over. Offering her nipple to my mouth, I suck it while she takes my cock and Colt takes my ass.

A thunder, a deep guttural roar from a primal place I don't know, escapes my soul. I don't know who I am, but this is right. I don't know where we are, but their bodies take me. They're all I need.

Blair slowly slides her tight wet cunt up and down my dick. I can feel her hard clit, rubbing on my shaft while Colt's luscious long cock stretches, driving into my tender ass and...

"Oh god." I gasp for air.

I drool over Blair's nipple and need it again. With each thrust of Colt's cock, with each claim of Blair's cunt, I grunt. I grab air with her nipple in my mouth.

When I tease Blair, calling her our sweet slut, I do it because it gets her off. Now, it gets me off, too. I feel like a slut for this, a slut for a cock in my ass and pussy choking my dick.

And I have no shame about it.

I want it—all the time.

"Damn, Beau." I hear Colt growl, "Damn, my cock looks

so hot fucking your tight ass while your dick looks so good, so creamy fucking her pussy." He pumps harder and harder. "Damn, we're hot."

Blair's breath is thinning. She's writhing, grinding her hard little nub on my raw length. I love how I can feel it. I can feel her. I can feel him.

"Fuck yes." I cup her cheeks. I lift her. Then I grab her neck, insisting, "Let me see you both fucking me."

Blair barely leans left while Colt presses to her back, leaning right. He's so much taller than her; we both are. He kisses her neck, eyeing me while he grinds his dick in my ass, and she grinds on my dick, and I'm going. The lightning in my body ignites every nerve, pleasure flooding my muscles, lust driving my bones.

Colt fists Blair's hair, yanking her neck open.

She's so beautiful.

She's mine.

She's his.

"Fuck him, baby," Colt growls in her ear. "Fuck him with that wet pussy. Take his big dick and grind on it. Show him you love it."

She obeys, her hips popping, my dick swelling. I reach up and pinch her nipples, loving her moan.

"I'm going to make him come in your pussy." Colt keeps pushing us. Taunting and taking us. "I'm going to fuck his ass so hard he's going to come inside you." He reaches around, his hand finding her clit rubbing against my cock. "That's it. Keep going. Be our good little slut. Open up for his cock and cum. You want it, don't you? You want it while I fuck his ass."

"Yes!" We both shout.

We're going fast and together because Colt drives us. He delivers, his thrusts coiling a new white heat, a new rousing sensation in my core. I can't control it. Not like I can my dick. I have to take it. I have to take him and her.

"Such a good girl." He's pinching Blair's clit. "Yes, fucking take him. Ride that dick and take his cum." He's making her shake. I'm shaking, too. From my jaw to my chest. The fire. The pleasure. The need. It's cracking my flesh. I can't hold back. "Fucking take it. Take it, Beau. Take my dick in your ass and come inside her, loving my fuck."

"Baby, yes! Yes!" I shout. I explode. I erupt. I come for him; I come inside her. I hear Blair coming, too, her sultry wails calling my soul, and I can't see. I can only give; I can only receive. I can only take Colt's pounding, and Blair's pumping ride as my dick won't stop pulsing. "Fuck!" I cry out, grabbing Blair's hips. She stills over me, but Colt doesn't.

"Drip it on him," Colt snarls. "Lift up and drip it on his dick. I want to see how I made him come."

Blair's trembling, but she obeys. She gets off on it. She lets me fall out of her while she reaches down, strumming her clit, clenching her pussy to make my arousal glaze over my cock that's still swollen. I'm still taking Colt.

"Oh god," Blair gasps. She watches herself do it for him, for us. It's so shameless, she's proud. She's sharing our lust, and she comes again to it. "Oh god. Oh god."

"Yes, Raven, lean forward." Colt gently guides her to rest on my body, so I hold her while he demands, "I want to watch your pussy drip with his cum while I come inside him, too."

We're so connected, so raw and real, it doesn't take Colt long. Not when I reach down and spread Blair's cheeks for him to gaze at her ass while he fucks mine, groaning, "Fuck yes." He grunts, "Oh fuck yes, you two are mine."

"Yes, we are." Blair sighs in my chest. It's our truth. It's our new life.

With two more brutal thrusts, Colt roars. The sinews on his neck strain, and I fall in love, all over again, with the sight of him coming inside me, with the weight of him while he drapes himself over Blair, resting on me, too.

"I don't care who I have to fake it with," he huffs, kissing Blair's shoulder, then her cheek before leaning, seeking my kiss, and I lift, giving it to him.

"This is real between us," he sighs. "And no one else."

COLTON

CHAPTER TWENTY

WE GOT UP BEFORE THE ASS-CRACK OF DAWN FOR HER.

"Two sugars, right?"

I hand Blair a steaming white mug. Then I hand Beau his. I know how he takes his coffee—black. But now, I want to know everything about her, too.

"Thanks." Carefully, she takes it. "We only have a few more minutes," she says. "Look. You can see it coming."

Blair insisted we get up to watch the sunrise over the ocean. That meant a five a.m. alarm, but YOLO.

Because this is worth it, too.

Carefully, I settle in beside Beau on the double lounger he carried to the dock's edge. When the alarm sounded minutes ago, we threw on swim trunks, and Blair put on a blue summer dress. We grabbed some fresh towels and made a little bed together to watch this.

We nestle together, balancing hot coffee mugs, but Blair's too excited. She sits cross-legged by our feet, her gaze eagerly awaiting the giant orange orb like she's never seen it before, so I glance at Beau.

Yeah, she's fucking cute. We share the look. *Yeah, she's fucking ours.* We half grin. *And yeah, we got up before the ass-crack of dawn for her.*

But we don't bitch. We don't say anything because we're happy.

I know we—the three of us—won't be perfect. Hell, it won't be easy either.

The friendships? Those work. The love? It's growing. The sex? I'm like a kid in a candy store. Even football, the sport? We'll win.

But it's the secrets that are gonna get us.

Yeah, the three of us are smart. We can be discreet and play some things off as just-being-friends, and Blair can find a nice woman to help us...

But who can help me?

How long can I keep my secret from Beau?

How mad will he be?

Worse?

How much will it hurt him?

We watch the sun rise and Blair takes pictures, videos, too. She's horrible at selfies, but I've had too much practice with fans. So has Beau, so we do it. Holding her phone, it captures us, nuzzled together, the sky glowing peacefully behind us while I can't fight this dark fear.

While they start breakfast and we wait for our session with Dr. Gary, I hide in my bathroom with my phone.

> I can't do this anymore

> I have to tell him

REESE

No

We made it this long. He never needs
to know

He's my best friend. I can't keep lying to
him. He deserves to know

REESE

It's not worth it. You know the stakes

It's my call

Don't do this to us

Not once have I had control over this.

At first, it made me furious and enraged, but then I had to get over it. I had to honor Reese's wishes until lying to Beau became a habit that's killing me. I used to have my mom. She knew. She gave me advice.

But now?

It's just me, about to start a life with an honest woman I'm falling for and the man I've always loved.

The man I'm lying to.

Blair rubs my arm like she can sense it when I join them for breakfast. "You're quiet this morning."

I peck her cheek. "Y'all wore me out."

"But I thought blonds have more stamina."

She makes me laugh. "But this blond never had *him* before."

I grin, pointing my fork at Beau, and he grins back.

He's changed. I've changed. Our sex rocked our world in the best way.

Yes, I want him to have me, too. It's my turn, but part of me feels I don't deserve him. Like I should punish myself.

A phone chimes in the living room. It's Beau's. It's his alarm for our session. "Come on." He pops up. "Doc will be on in fifteen."

Beau does his usual, taking over the remote to click on the flatscreen and logging on to our session.

I help Blair clear the dishes while I catch her smirk. It's devious.

We pile the dishes in the sink while Beau starts cursing, "Dammit!" He aims the remote like a gun. "What the fuck?' He's clicking, but nothing's happening. "Do we have batteries?"

"Here." Blair opens a side drawer in the kitchen.

But it's too convenient.

How did she know where the AAs were being stored?

Quickly, Beau changes the batteries to the remote and steps toward the flatscreen, clicking some more. "God-dammit!" He sounds like Coach. His face is getting red like his, too. "Goddamn fucking remote."

But he looks sexy when he's mad, so I play along. "Maybe *those* batteries are dead, too."

"Here." Blair fishes for more from the drawer. "Try these."

She sounds too sweet. She looks too helpful. Yes, our woman is a good one, but she ain't innocent, and I adore that about her. I like her experience. Actually, I'm damn impressed with the professional working her craft before my eyes.

Beau's a puppet, and Blair's pulling his strings.

He rips the remote open again, tossing the innocent batteries to the floor before cramming in another pair.

"Damn," I tease. "Is someone blowing a gasket over a gadget?"

"No, he's an *expert*," Blair coos like a desperate housewife. "What's wrong with it, honey?"

Beau clicks the remote at the blank screen, spouting off, "Could be it needs reprogramming, or the infrared sensor has an issue, or another device is causing interference, or maybe it's a firmware issue—"

Blair rolls her eyes at his mansplaining. The man prides himself on being a techie when really...

"Or maybe it's the tape on it?" Blair chirps.

And I fall on the sofa, laughing so hard I cry.

With a devilish smile, she rips off the clear piece she put on the remote's tip, the one Beau holds, speechless as he realizes he's been played.

"Now." She presses the clear tape to his nose. "See if that made your little gadget work."

He logs on, "I'll show *you* how my big gadget works later," half-smiling, half plotting her demise.

This morning, our session with Dr. Gary focuses on mindfulness and I get it. My body is in top form. I know my craft. I run routes in my sleep.

But my mind?

It's all kinds of fucked up. Mostly, I'm ecstatic. I can't wait for our new life. Our new season. But in the back of my mind, my secret looms on the sideline, sitting on the bench, waiting to rush the field.

Waiting to ruin everything.

We make it to our last day, our last session.

We've had productive mornings, fun days, and hot nights. Though Blair insisted we abstain these last two.

"Celibacy makes the cocks grow stronger," she joked, but she meant it, so we just held each other, ignoring our hard-ons.

While she clicks away on her laptop outside, Dr. Gary greets us with a genuine smile.

"Gentlemen, I'm impressed with your progress." It's like he's giving us gold stars, and we've earned them. I'm not the same man I was ten days ago. "But tell me how *you* feel about it."

"I feel great," Beau answers. "We've cleared the air and our minds. I got my new mantra: it's just a game. I'm ready to win and—"

"And I got my best friend back." It blurts from my mouth.

"Yeah, and that." Beau smiles, glancing my way. "We're best friends again."

Maybe we share a smile too long. Maybe our knees brush too much. Or maybe Dr. Gary is just too damn good at reading minds.

"Will you ever tell others how you're more than friends?" His tone is gentle—not condescending, but compassionate.

Still, it shocks the shit out of me.

"Say what?" I whip my stare to the screen.

"You're safe with me," Dr. Gary assures. "I'd never betray your trust because you deserve it."

Beau scrubs his face. Glancing at me, terror fills his eyes before he asks the Doc, "How did you know?"

"You told me," he answers, "in how you wrote about each other. How you care for and love each other. Usually, teammates focus on tactics and blame, but you went straight to the heart. You care about his, and he cares about yours. I won't pry into how you express your love, but I support it."

Beau murmurs, "No one can know."

"We're not out," I state the obvious. "We can't be."

Dr. Gary nods. I wonder how he's trained his face to stay so calm while inside; my nerves are blowing bombs.

"I'd never out you," Doc promises. "Never. Just know I'm here for you if something ever happens. You're not alone. There are hundreds of players, mostly men, just like you. I can put you in touch with a few of them if you like. They've formed a private support group of sorts."

"In the NFL?" There's hope in Beau's voice. "Who?"

"I'll give you a number," Doc answers. "It'll be anonymous at first. Trust needs to be built. But he can be trusted. You just have to earn his."

"So what do we do in this *group*?" I ask.

"You talk," he answers. "You support each other. You share how it feels so you don't feel so alone. Look. Everything changes, but it doesn't change fast enough. Most players come out after they retire, if at all. But together, you can get through. It's always your choice, your life, your career." He pauses. "Your love."

I've been thigh-tackled. Like the truth has attacked me, grabbing my legs, and I'm trapped as it rolls, slamming me to the ground, flipping my world before I can even react.

"So whatdawedo?" I ask Doc.

"Nothing," Beau answers. "We stick to our plan."

"So, we lie?"

My life is a fumble pile. One lie is piling on the other, and I'm at the bottom, trying to breathe.

"Gentlemen," Doc eases, "perhaps 'lie' is not a fair word. If your truth isn't safe, it's not a lie to protect it. To protect each other, and that's all I ask. You're some of the best players in the league, but you're even better friends. You don't have to lie about that. So, be best friends on the field and remember... it's just a game. It always ends, and life goes on. Right?"

"Right," Beau answers while gently reaching for my thigh. It's odd because it's new, but it's affirming.

So is Doc. So is knowing we're not alone. So is the woman waiting for us on a sun lounger.

On our last day, Blair writes, Beau studies our playbook on his iPad and I read Blair's book, *their* book.

I need a love story with a happy ending because I sure as hell don't know if we'll get one.

CHAPTER TWENTY-ONE

"**D**id he read these books, or did his interior designer buy them?"

"They're Beau's. He can read." I mock my twin, "His favorite book is *Dick Fucks Jane and Tom*."

Vale laughs, shifting Beau's books to the bottom shelves in his office, per his insistence, while I load the top and middle shelves with mine.

"He has all the dead white men classics." Vale lines them up neatly. "But I'm impressed with his contemporary authors: Morrison, Ishiguro, Lee, Hollinghurst, Díaz. My literary panties are wet."

"Suck a bag of big books," I tease her, but I'm impressed, too.

Beau's home—correction: his seven-bedroom mansion on an immaculate golf course—belongs on one of those reality shows about luxury real estate and nepo-baby agents.

My new closet is the size of my former bedroom. His kitchen looks like a Michelin chef's dream. I keep expecting pink dolphins to leap from his giant pool. And last night, I discovered the thrill of a bidet and why the French say, "Ooh, là, là."

Beau even insisted I take a guest bedroom for my "overflow." He did the same for Colt, who's neatly arranged his Air Jordans in a guest closet like a shrine.

My bedroom? It's a shrine to dildos, of course. Ones that will collect dust because Beau's bed feels like a cloud. Every night, I sleep in man-body heaven.

But it's his office, now mine, according to Beau, that makes me want to start writing Hallmark Valentine's cards, not paranormal romance books.

There's a white marble fireplace in here. The white shelves have two frickin' ladders like a vintage library. In addition to a desk for ruling the world, there are two cozy ivory velvet chaise lounges where I can sit for a decade.

And my favorite?

In the week it took me to get home and move my life to Atlanta, Beau made me an acrylic desk plaque.

DESK OF A SMUTTY GENIUS

"This is love, you know." Stacey, now my former boss and forever friend, stacks my books neatly on a shelf. "He's giving you his desk, house, and cars."

She just had her daughter last month but insisted on helping, saying she needed a change of scenery. So, two of her husbands, Ford and Mateo, joined her and their daughter for our caravan from Charleston to Atlanta. They turned it into their first family trip.

"I have my car," I answer, though Beau gave me the keys to his white Mercedes G-Class SUV. "My Kia has four working wheels, too."

The only time I'm comfortable with having a sugar daddy is when I'm in bed with my men. Those two are welcome to shred my ego with their dirty talk. When it comes to sex, I have no shame.

But when it comes to money, I have pride.

"I get it," Stacey answers, moving books. "I've been there, believe me. You want your freedom, your money, and your dignity. But any man who owns a book by Virginia Wolfe is worth letting him care for you, too."

"Besides," Vale adds, "what are you gonna do now that they started training camp? Or when they're at practice or away games? This is a big house to have all to yourself."

"I'll write." I cut open another box. "They have jobs, and I have mine."

"Is it something in the Charleston water?" Stacey almost laughs. "You, with your two men? Me, with my three husbands? Luca Mercier and his subs? Silas Van de May and that group of six? I guess birds of a *group* feather flock together."

"And fuck together," Vale jokes.

"Some of us do." Stacey shrugs. "Some of us don't, but we protect our network. It's about more than sex. It's about support. Do you know the looks I get with my husbands and now our daughter? Lucky for me, I have so much love and friends in my life, and I'm immune to hate."

I sigh, neatly arranging my favorite books—the ones I've read—by trope and color. Don't judge. I like a rainbow of romance.

"That's why I need help," I reveal. "I mean, other than insisting on helping me move and being a badass boss."

"Ahem." Vale clears her throat.

"And being the perfect twin," I add for her sake. "Y'all, I need a beard for Colt."

"A beard?" Vale scoffs. "That's so antiquated and phobic."

"In your world," I answer. "You're getting a PhD in Human Sexuality. You live in an ivory tower of progressive pussy and pricks and preferences. But down here, on the gridiron, that's not reality. Millions are still phobic. Some shit hasn't changed."

"You're right, you're right." Vale dusts off her overalls. "Sorry. I get it."

"So, you need someone you can trust who'll date Colt?" Stacey's already stroking her chin, scheming plans. "But someone who'll respect your triad and won't get feelings for him?"

"Yeah," I reply. "Not like tomorrow, but soon. I thought we'd have time, but Amber Kostas won't shut up about me and Beau and my books. She just outed us as a couple last week, so it's a matter of time before she drags Colt, too, especially when people find out we're living together."

"Ugh," Vale declares, "women like her drag us back a century. She's gotta put a woman down to lift herself up. I bet she doesn't vote. I bet she calls other women 'bossy' and uses 'pussy' and 'girl' as an insult."

"Probably," I huff impatiently. "But I don't have time for her ignorant politics; I need a plan. The clock is ticking."

"I think I know someone." Stacey plops down on a chaise, kicking her feet up. New moms are allowed to rest. "She's a friend's sister, and she's been coming into the shop a lot lately. I trust her."

"You trust her not to fall for Colt?"

But could I blame her?

Long ago, in college, I fell for Beau. Even though he changed all the notifications on my phone and laptop to sound like farts, I know he's also the one who anonymously left a T-shirt on my dorm bed for my birthday.

"Until I feared I would lose it, I never loved to read."

He had it made with one of my favorite quotes from my favorite book, *To Kill A Mockingbird*.

That's Beau.

And Colt?

He likes turning the air conditioner so damn low we have to cuddle when we sleep to stay warm. He and Beau alternate who's in the middle, one spooning me while he gets spooned. I tried the middle, but now I know how cheddar feels in a panini press.

Maybe this winter, they can sandwich me.

But it's also how Colt pours my coffee. How he rubs my feet. How he pinches my ass in the kitchen, but how he's been shy, too. He still hasn't given himself to Beau like Beau lets Colt take him and me. I can tell Colt's afraid of something.

And it only makes my heart soften for him. Faster than the speed of sound, I'm falling for Colt, too. That's why I worry.

Who wouldn't fall for him?

"Yes, I trust her," Stacey answers, adjusting her blonde ponytail. "She's part of a secret group. I can't say much, but she'd care about this situation. She'd help."

Stacey owns Delta's, the most exclusive sex shop in the South. She would've gone out of business on day one if she had loose lips. The woman is a vault of intriguing intel.

"A secret group?" My author ears perk up. I abandon my books for more of this story. "What group? Come on. You know I won't tell. I bet I know them anyway. Everyone who's anyone shops at Delta's, and I know their kinks."

"You know I can't answer." Stacey yawns. "Groups are secret for a reason."

BAM!

I jump.

So does Stacey.

We snap our glance at Vale, who's dropped a stack of leather-bound classics. But it's the fresh look on her face that grabs my attention.

"A secret group?" I dig. "Like the secret boardroom someone has meetings in. Right, Vale? You and our accountant, Mr. Nash Allen, add up to many secret sins."

"Quit being an ingrown pubic hair," Vale snaps. "You're annoying me *and* my crotch. It's like Stacey said, some things are secret."

"Secret like how you pluck your nipples?"

She snarls, "Secret like how you make tit butter when you sweat?"

"Yeah, twin." I laugh. "We got matching Ds."

"No, we share DNA, not dicks."

"Dicks? So you're marching in the poly parade, too?"

"Charleston's not that big of a city," Stacey interrupts. "I suspect groups and secrets intermingle."

"Not down here in Hotlanta," I worry. "I feel like a castaway. Like it's me, Beau, and Colt against the world."

"You're not alone," Stacey assures. "You remember Scarlett, right? Luca Mercier's new wife?"

"Of course," I gush. "I can't forget her. She ordered a gold chain ankles-to-anal-plug locking bondage kit for their honeymoon last month."

Vale sighs, "Scarlett's my idol."

"Yes, her." Stacey smiles. "She's Mrs. Luca Mercier now, and I met her sister, Ruby, at The Mercier Hotel and their Charleston wedding. Ruby's amazing. She's one of us."

"So, I can trust her?"

I'm sweating. Yes, the A/C is cranking for Colt when he gets home, but it's July, and I feel like I'm starting training camp, too.

Throuples training camp where the opponent is the general judgy public, and I don't like our odds of winning.

"She won't fall for Colt? Or Beau?"

Vale sings, "Someone's sounding *jelly*."

"I'm not jealous," I blurt. "I'm worried. This isn't a game for us." Vale grins like The Joker. "Okay, fine. It's an *NFL* football game, so I'm worried. We need help."

"Ruby will help," Stacey promises. "And she won't want a quad with you and your men. She's kinda got a thing of her own."

"Like?" I'm so intrigued. I had no idea all of these secret groups were hiding amongst Charleston's elite.

Then again, it's called "The Holy City," so that only means it's brimming with secrets and sinners and hypocrites.

But for our groups, love isn't a sin. So, we protect those who have to keep theirs a secret.

"Like it's not for me to say," Stacey answers, "but it's why I think she'll help. And she'll be fun. She's a huge football fan, too."

While they take a break, Stacey shares Ruby's contact

information with my phone, and I fetch lemonade from the kitchen.

Before I call Ruby, I'll run it by Beau and Colt. They told me I'm in charge of Operation Beard, but I need to consult with my troops.

They'll be home this evening. Since they're veterans, they don't have to stay overnight at training camp. Plans of greeting them at the door, holding a tray of cocktails, and wearing naughty panties make my kitty tingle.

But when I check my phone, making sure I have Ruby's contact, there's a missed call that's an immediate lady-boner killer.

"Great," I mutter while Vale and Stacey recline in my new office, enjoying their lemonades. "Dad called."

"Imagine that." Vale chuckles. "Word is out you're dating the NFL's top player, and now our dad, a former top player, too, wants to coach you. Watch."

"I'm not taking advice from him." I sit on my desk, polishing my hand over the burl wood. I went from an old IKEA desk to something that looks like Jane Austen was here. "Dad's a pro at cheating, divorce, and child support. I'll do the opposite of whatever he says."

"Was he abusive or something?" Stacey sounds concerned.

"No," I answer. "He's just an unfaithful horn-dog who tries to lie about all the kids he has. Every year, we discover a new half-sibling."

"He's actually mellowed out." Vale sounds sincere. "Since Mom died, I think it changed him. I think he's trying to be better. So, just see what he wants. The worst that can happen is you hang up on him."

The worst that can happen?

I look around the sun-filled room, taking in my new office, home, and life. I'm waiting for my new hunky boyfriends to get home, and hopefully, one of them snores tonight, and I can't sleep.

Hopefully, that's the worst that can happen to us.

BEAU

CHAPTER TWENTY-TWO

"I'M READY FOR THE BUTT BALL."

Coach took it easy on us at first.

Camp started with slant routes. Colt and I can run those diagonal drills blindfolded. The same goes with Goodwin, Martinez, and Smith. The whole offensive line was in the zone.

Then we ran post and corner routes, and my completions looked good.

But today, Coach wants to run go routes. Is he testing me and my shoulder? Definitely. But I want to know, too—do I still have a golden arm?

Colt goes deep, working on his speed while I drop back, waiting, knowing he usually takes five seconds before I go for yards, thirty yards each time.

For a while, all's good.

Our coaches are pleased. "Hawke!" They shout because that's what he is. Colt flies down the field, able to glance, attaching his eyes to the ball like a hawk, tracking his prey until it's in his grasp like talons.

We're in the zone. We're perfect. We're in love. We're happy, but I'm sore by the end of the day. My shoulder is tight.

Diggs, our athletic trainer, has me wearing ice packs like a frozen T-shirt during our afternoon offensive team meeting.

Colt sits next to me. We're freshly showered. But I catch him eyeing my shoulder while our offensive coordinator reviews our drills.

"Good job." Coach Purnell watches the screen on our playbacks. "Ball security is job security," he praises Colt and Smith, who crushed it today.

But Colt nudges my foot, jutting his chin like, "You okay?"

I grin, shaking it off. I won't admit to him or myself that I'm not, that I'll suck it up all season. As long as I can pass, I'll take the pain. I'm not going on Injury Reserve. Ever.

When we're dismissed for the day, we head to the parking lot, tossing our bags in my Ford Super Duty cab. But then Jasper and Perry, two of our defensive linemen, spot us leaving together.

"What's up, Bronson?" Perry calls out. "You Hawke's chauffeur?"

"Yeah," Colt answers, jerking his passenger door open. "And he's my butler, too."

Jasper looks confused, and so does Perry.

Colt and I have made it over a week at camp without questions, but it's time to test the waters.

Let's see if we can sell this.

I shout, "I'm letting the asshole bunk with me while he plays HGTV designer on his fancy-ass Buckhead house."

"Man?" Jasper sizes up Colt. "You ain't got enough green to rent?"

"Why should I?" But Hawke's a pro smartass, too. "When I can crash at Bronson's rent-free? He's got a chef, a maid, and a view of my favorite eighteenth hole. I ain't ever leaving. I'll just keep flipping houses for millions."

"The fuck you say." I play along. "You got five months before I toss your shit to the curb."

"Who was your Buckhead agent?" Jasper starts chewing the fat with Colt about Atlanta's highest-end real-estate investments, while I hope Colt never finishes his remodel.

These past two weeks with him and Blair in my home have me smiling all the damn time.

I don't know why I was so afraid.

Love isn't a distraction. I'm more focused than ever. I have someone to fight for, to bust my ass for.

So far, we've kept our deal with Coach. Colt and I are the best we've ever been on the field.

And when we get home?

We start Blair's Training Camp.

First, she jumps in my Siberian cold plunge therapy tub with us. It's cute how quickly her shivering, blush lips turn blue. It's adorable how Colt wraps her tight in a plush white robe when we get out.

Then, she makes us sit at the table like a family, eating the recovery meals my chef prepares. She even makes us use linen napkins on our laps.

Before bed, Blair joins me for a round of heat therapy in the hot tub. Though, that usually threatens a hot fuck, too. At least, for me.

But who knew?

My Coach of Kink is also the Diva of Dick Denial. Since

training started, Blair has a new two-nights-off-one-night-on rule. She says we need our sleep.

My mind and muscles agree, though my dick has a very firm, contrary opinion.

Honking my horn, I end Colt and Jasper's yapping. It's an "on" night with Blair, and we need to get home. I'm sporting live ammunition in my boxers.

"Whatdaya think?" Colt tugs my truck door closed. "You think they bought it?"

"Yeah, just keep being a lying asshole." I joke. "You know, like normal, and they'll never suspect."

But Colt doesn't laugh. He mutters, "Fuck you. I ain't a liar."

Ouch. Someone's hangry.

We sit in silence while my truck crawls down the interstate. Thankfully, home is only a few miles away. Still, Colt takes over the tunes, filling the awkward air with his playlist, a mash-up of rap and country.

Something's been bothering him lately.

Yeah, we've had a stellar couple of weeks. We play ball all day, chill together all night, and we're happy when we go to bed.

But I know him.

He's usually a ray of fucking sunshine, in a sexy pain-in-the-ass way, when I'm usually the serious one.

Maybe we've switched roles. Maybe I'm so damn happy now, so he's serious. Still, you don't love someone this long and not ask.

"Hey," I take the next exit ramp, "what's bothering you?"

"Nothing."

"Liar."

"I don't wanna talk about it."

I turn left and let it brew before asking, "Is it about Blair? Or us?" I pause. "Or your mom?"

Last week was a year. It was a year since she died, and I held Colt at her grave. The entire organization was at her funeral. The team office canceled camp for the day so we could support him.

I remembered, so Blair and I bought flowers. Yellow roses were Celeste's favorite. We drove with Colt two hours to Alabama to visit her grave this past Sunday. We refreshed the vase at her headstone and said some prayers, and that night, Colt held Blair while I held him. He'd never been so quiet before.

Yes, time heals, but it doesn't happen overnight or in a year.

"Whatever it is," I tell him, "I got you, man. There's nothing we can't talk about."

"Thanks," he mutters, staring out of the passenger window.

I can't tell if he's crying, but he should. He should get it out. So I reach across the wide console, trying to find his hand.

"Dude," he huffs, "two hands on the wheel."

"We're fine."

"We've got a winning season before us." He sounds okay. "So don't wreck it. Hands on the wheel and eyes on the road. Atlanta traffic is where the dumbasses come out to play."

He's right, so I retreat.

"But thanks," he says. "We can always talk, no matter what happens. Right? You won't give up on me?"

I try teasing, cheering him up. "My ass is always here for ya, man."

Holding the wheel, I steal a glance, and he looks at me.

In that way.

Pensive. Possessive. Passionate.

"I know what's on your mind." So I keep poking, trying to make him smile. "You're finally ready for me, aren't you?"

It works. He grins. "You running a high temperature for me, Bronson?"

"Hell yeah, I'm hot for you. For twelve damn years. I'm so ready to blow."

"You can blow in my mouth."

"Been there. Jizzed on the T-shirt. Loved the jaw fest. But now I'm ready for the butt ball."

A deep laugh erupts from his scruffy throat. "You sound like Blair."

"Our woman rubs off on us, alright."

"She keeps making us wait two nights."

"But she's right. If we fucked like we want, our asses would be dragging at camp."

"Speaking of asses and camp." While I pull into my garage, he insists, "No anal before camp. We're sore enough as it is. We gotta wait until Saturday."

What?

Are Colt and Blair in cahoots? Are they secretly meeting in the shower without me? Because she signs on to his no-anal-before-camp rule, too.

We shiver in the ice bath, her teeth chattering while she proclaims, "Anal, only before you have a day off. All season."

"Damn," I groan, freezing, squatting to where my shoulder is underwater because it's so painful, it's good for me. "Your asses have more rules than the NFL."

"No," she snuggles against my chest, "I'm freezing my ass off, trying to support your asses *playing* for the NFL."

I wrap my arms around her. Colt joins us, trapping her

between us. Staying warm together defeats the purpose of an ice bath, but our bodies can't resist.

"But, *Baabbyy*," I try whining, making a puppy-dog face for her, "you got us all kinky for the boom-boom, now."

She pops her smiling blue lips. "Nope."

Colt presses into her. "But *you* don't play for the NFL. Why can't we play in your backyard tonight? We promise we'll play nice and take turns."

She laughs, reaching, double-fisting our cocks. "You can't play with these wet noodles."

"This water is forty degrees," I inform her. "Every man's soft cock retreats up his ass to stay warm."

Colt laughs. "I don't know how the Vikings did it."

"They fucked by the fire," I answer.

But I try obeying Blair's rules.

She understands us. She keeps us on a regimen. She makes our care a top priority. She's even got our dicks on a strict routine.

Hell, she's got our throuple covered, too. Blair's arranged for us to meet Colt's beard this weekend.

I don't know who Ruby Jones is, but Blair says we can trust her. So much so that Ruby's flying to Atlanta. We have a double date this Saturday night. My publicist will leak it. The damn paparazzi will be there. We'll be busted, leaving some fancy restaurant, me holding Blair's hand and Colt's arm around Ruby.

We'll debut our girlfriends, and that should shut down Amber Kostas and her Insta bullshit.

She's relentless. She found out about Blair's dad, and now she's riled up my fans, posting, "Blair Monroe is a sports sl*t like her PGA dad. She'll kill Beau's game."

We ignore her, but it gets to Blair.

So, every day, Blair's new fantasy alien quarterback

boyfriend has something blue delivered to our house while we're at camp. Blue iced cupcakes. Blueberry muffins. Blue slippers. Blue soaps shaped like roses. A blue heart jeweled anal plug.

I'm driving my personal assistant, Matt, crazy, but it's what I pay him for.

I even encouraged Blair to invite her dad over for a Sunday cookout. She said he wants to meet me and give us relationship advice, which is rich coming from him, but I love her.

It should be okay with Ruby here for that, too, acting as Colt's girlfriend. Blair's dad will have no idea, and then he'll leave us in peace.

See? She's training me.

I listen to Blair.

Who, by the way, takes half an hour to get ready for bed. Is that normal for women? It's like she's warming her face up for an overnight workout.

It finds Colt and me, usually half asleep, waiting for her to turn off the lights and join us.

But tonight, he's quiet again, and I can't shake the feeling that something's wrong.

"Hey." I kiss his shoulder. "I meant it. I'm always here for you."

His back is pressed to my chest. I reach, tucking my arm under his to caress his pecs, like I need to rub his heart so he'll know I'm sincere.

He cups his hand over mine. "What if I piss you off?"

"You do it all the time." I wedge into his heat. "If you and Blair pull that shit again, leaving fake cockroaches in my gym bag and a goddamn fake spider on my ear when I wake up, I'm never speaking to you again."

I feel him laugh, barely. "What if it ain't a joke?" His voice gets gruff. "What if it's serious?"

"Then we work it out." I press into him, kissing his neck. I'm getting hard, and I don't fight it. When it's me and Colt, the feelings run too strong. "Don't ever doubt me." I squeeze him, gently biting his neck and rutting into his tempting backside. "Don't ever doubt *us*."

His breath changes. Heat rises from his flesh pressed to mine. "Promise?" he asks, squeezing his hand over mine and guiding it down over the granite ridges of his abs. "Promise I'll always have you, Beau."

We sleep nude, and as he urges my hand down to his cock, I sigh into his skin. "I promise, Colt. I promise I'm yours, and I'll prove it."

I grab his swollen length, guided by his hand. Moans erupt from our chests as I stroke him, my body needing him, too. This maddening urge has me grinding into his backside, my hard cock wedged between his cheeks. "Take me," I steam over his ear. "Take me and my promise, Colt."

"Fuck," he mutters, arching his back, opening for me. He grinds, matching my tempo, his cock, hard but like velvet, swelling in my grasp. He wants me so bad, I know it. For so long, we've wanted this. I don't know why he keeps denying us.

"Do you want me?" I nip his ear. "Do you want to take me?"

"Yes," he growls. "Yes, so fucking much, Beau."

"Then do it. Take what you need from me. I'll prove I'm yours."

Colt twists in my grasp, his lips quickly seizing mine. Our deep kiss is our promise. It always has been. His tongue finds mine while his fist grabs my cock, and I pump his.

Groans fill our mouths, our breath intertwined, our tongues laving over the other.

"Beau," he growls over our lips. "Beau, I want to take you now."

"Do it," I urge.

"But—" Colt's worried about our rule, about camp tomorrow, and so much more.

"Do it." A gentle voice urges, and we turn our cheeks, pressing together to find Blair by the edge of the bed. She's nude, her curves breathtaking, her hand offering a bottle of lube. "But use lots of this." She hands it to Colt before turning to leave.

But Colt demands, "Stay, Raven. Stay and watch us. I want you here."

She turns back, arching a brow. "You sure?"

"Yes," Colt insists. "It feels right. I want you to see me, to see us together."

Quietly, Blair eases onto a spot at the edge of my bed. She gives us room while I rest on a pillow and watch Colt. He wants control of this.

Kneeling over me, he fills his palm with lube. With long strokes, he coats my hungry shaft, and I fight the sudden urge to fuck his slick fist. "Damn, Colt," I growl. "Damn, I want you."

"Oh, you'll have me." He demands, slinging his leg over mine, straddling me. "And you'll take me raw. I got tested. I'm clear, and I want to feel this. I want to feel you come inside me."

With a deep inhale, I find my control. It takes so much for me to hold still, for me not to thrust or grab while Colt reaches behind him, slowly trying to wedge my hard cock inside him.

But I'm so sensitive. I've wanted this so much and for so

long, and he's so fucking tight, I'm panting. I hold still, sweating and staring up at him. He's beautiful, ripped with muscles and ink, *our ink*, but he's trusting, receiving. He's taking his time; he's taking me in.

"Ah," he keeps groaning at my penetration. "Ah," he keeps stretching at my width. "Ah," he winces before exhaling, barely sinking an inch, then lifting on my glistening shaft.

"Colt," I growl. I ache because he's so hard. His cock is swollen, jutting high and hard, trapping my stare while his ass strangles my crown, his fist squeezing my shaft. It steals my breath. It's more than I ever imagined. It's the ultimate surrender and seizure, his body finally taking mine. But he's trying to take all of me and sink to my base slowly.

"Ah," but his face twists, his massive quads straining. He squats, then quickly lifts, trying to take my dick, but he can't.

"Colt, baby," I huff. "Is it good? Do you like it?"

"Fuck yes," he growls. "Fuck yes. I want you in my ass, but you're so fucking huge."

"Take your time," Blair eases. "Breathe. Start over and go slow. Use more lube."

Colt listens to her. He rises, holding my swollen dick that's begging for him. He pours so much lube over it we'll need to change the sheets, and I love it.

I love how he slowly takes me this time, my crown dripping like honey, ready for his sweet ass. I love how he gazes at me, his face relaxing. The muscles ripping across his chest and down his abs release their tension as he exhales and lowers, taking more of me than before.

It makes me fist the sheets to keep from grabbing him, from taking him. For so long, I've wanted Colt; I've needed him just like this, and I groan. The urge to thrust is overwhelming, but I fight it, gnashing my molars to keep from driving into him while, inch by inch, my cock disappears inside him.

A luscious smack fills the air, and I glance, called by the sound. My heart, my body can't resist it. It's Blair's wet pussy. She's fingering herself, plunging two inside her beautiful, pink cunt. She's spread her legs so we can watch her while she watches me fuck Colt.

She only makes this harder—she only makes me harder. Instincts, urges, and hunger rage inside me. I can't hold back.

"Damn, Colt," I growl. "Damn, baby, I need to fuck you."

"Do it." Colt groans. He holds still, half of me inside him, half of me begging to enter. "Please," he begs. "Fuck my ass now. Do it."

I grab his hips. "I don't want to hurt you."

"You won't." He stares at me, hovering over my shaft, rubbing his pecs and pinching his nipples. I'm drawn, knowing how sensitive they are. I'm anchored to his breath, shallow with lust. I crave how raging hard, how swollen his dick is for me. I relish his tight virgin ass clenching my cock. "I'm about to come," he grunts. "Do it, Beau. Fuck my ass and make me come."

With my first hard thrust, his cock spurts. It shocks me. It shocks him. He cries out, splattering my abs with his cum, but he's still rigid, veins swollen, his length bobbing.

"Fuck," he growls. "Keep going. Keep making me come. I'm not done."

I pump my hips, unleashing the strength I have in my glutes, in my flexing thighs, taking his ass. I've never seen his thighs twitch so hard. His breath heave so much. His body shake so hard. His bouncing hard cock drips while he keeps pinching his nipples, staring down at me in awe.

"Fuck," he shouts again at my next brutal thrust, his dick spurting even more. "Fuck, Beau, I can't stop coming. I can't stop coming. Keep fucking my ass."

"You're hitting his prostate," Blair praises. "You're giving him the ultimate orgasm."

"Fuck, yes, I am," I growl. I deliver. "Is that right, Colt? Am I the best? You're coming so hard with my dick fucking your tight virgin ass?"

"Yes!" He cries out, more cum blasting from his cock, splattering my pecs and driving me insane.

"Fuck!" I can't stop fucking him.

"Damn," Blair stammers at our passion. I glance over, and her thighs quiver. She's coming to it. To our bodies. To our fuck. To our love. To Colt's hard bouncing cock that clearly loves this, too. He loves me fucking him.

"Baby." I grab his hips tighter. "Baby, I'm gonna come. I'm gonna come so hard in your ass, Colt."

"Do it. Do it," he begs.

I lift my hips, pumping so hard inside him, unleashing everything I've held back, everything we hid, everything that hurt, and everything that's healed. It's here, burning through me like white fire in my veins, and I let go. I let go inside Colt. With a brutal thrust, I still, my hips lifted off the bed. I bury my cock, so deep where it belongs. It pulses, making stars fill my vision while I roar, while I release, while I come inside Colt with no shame.

"Ugh," he grunts, releasing once more, spilling his cum over my abs. "Ugh, Beau, yes. Yes."

He collapses over me, braced on his arms, our lungs still huffing for breath while he seeks my kiss, and I give it. I give him everything. I give her everything. All I need is them. Nothing else.

"Dayum," he sighs over our lips. "Fuck the training camp rule, we're doing this every night."

It makes us laugh, which makes him wince with my dick still inside him. Then we kiss again while I cup his cheek, caressing his whiskers, before I hear her soft moan.

We turn and answer Blair's call. We need her, too. We disconnect our bodies to seek hers, to spread her thighs wide open while we lie on our stomachs, side by side, devouring her pussy. It's erotic. It's intimate. It's our bond. It's my tongue, slowly rolling over her hard clit, before I kiss Colt, and he does it too, tonguing her clit.

We take turns. We make Blair fist our hair. We make her lift her hips. We make her pussy come on our kiss. We hold each other later while we make her agree, "Okay," she says, "maybe a little anal training camp is okay, too."

"Hear that, Colt?" He rests on my shoulder while Blair lies on my chest. "Coach Kink said we can play all season."

"Just as long as you *win*," she says.

When I hold my world in my arms, I believe. "Oh, we will."

COLTON

CHAPTER TWENTY-THREE

"You know that saying: having skin in the game?"

"What's foie gras?" Ruby leans my way, side-whispering behind her menu, "Is it like fancy French grass clippings?"

I laugh. I like her. Immediately, I trust her.

"I think it's duck liver, but I was raised on hot dogs and Cheez Whiz, so I ain't sure."

"Me, too!" She beams.

Actually, I know this menu. Beau and I are co-investors in this French restaurant and two others. But it's fun joking with Ruby.

Our vibe is informal, though Beau and I are dressed in dark suits and Blair looks elegant, kicking her curves in a red flare dress, and Ruby stuns in a sapphire, backless number. We're relaxed, Ruby and I on our side of the four-top table and Beau snuggling Blair on their side.

We're seated in the center of the room, where everyone watches us, but Ruby doesn't care. Neither does Blair.

They hit it off immediately, like an instant trouble-making duo, so God help us.

Blair smiles, conspiring across our table. "Let's get the snails, the frog legs, the sea urchins, and the blood pudding. Let's go all French tonight."

"Let's go all hell-no tonight." Beau laughs. "I don't care how much melted butter you drown it in, I won't eat it."

Blair challenges him, swirling her white wine. "Where's your adventurous side?"

Beau lowers his voice. "In bed, where I'll put anything in my mouth, but here?" He glances around the crowded room. It glows with amber light. The tables, the furniture, the walls, everything is the color of a flickering candle. "We're here to get busted, not sick."

"Yeah." I set my menu down. "We're tossing salads tonight, not cookies."

"I knew it." Ruby laughs. "Y'all are my people. You're gonna fit right in."

"Just uh... " Beau fiddles with his bourbon tumbler. "Just when do we meet *your* people?"

"I had to meet you first." Ruby's tone gets softer but serious. "It's part of what I do. I do the munches."

"Munches?" I ask.

"I do the first meet-up," she replies. "In public. Informal. Usually, over brunch. But," she gestures to the posh room, "not always, but you get the idea. I vet the people. I ask and answer questions. Then we review the basics if we agree to proceed."

"Proceed to what?" Beau sounds worried.

"Proceed to whatever makes you comfortable," she

answers. "For all we invite, we talk first. Mostly, we're about support; we're about protection. But for others, it goes further if they want."

"Further how?" I'm worried like Beau.

And curious.

"Further, if you want to meet more professionals like yourselves," Ruby reveals, and like lightning, my brain does the logic.

I flick my stare to Beau, and he does the same.

It can't be? Is the world that small? Could Ruby be part of the same group Dr. Gary mentioned?

Beau hasn't reached out to the contact Doc gave us yet. We've been too busy with training camp.

But if Ruby is my beard, if she'll really get my back and be my friend, it starts now. So, I probe, "What do you mean 'professionals like us.'?"

She drops her voice, glancing around, making sure no one is eavesdropping.

"I mean, you have to know, by sheer numbers alone, you aren't the only ones, right? There are lots of... *pros* in your situation."

Pros? She means gay and bi pro ball players. NFL players who don't feel safe coming out. So far, there have only been a few out of thousands, but none have been marquee or Top 100.

"Like who?" Beau's cautious.

"No names, not yet," Ruby answers. "Only in person. Only over a handshake and a vow to protect each other. No matter what. You'd want the same assurance. Right?"

Beau nods.

So do I.

"But," Blair inquires, "you're a woman. You're not a...

professional. How did you get involved, and why do they trust you?"

"Mutual friends," Ruby answers. "Family, too, you could say. We met and got close. I've never judged and always understood. I love them and want to protect them, too."

Beau gently kisses Blair's cheek, pulling her gaze his way. "Sounds like you, baby," he says. "Like us and the night I came to your door."

"What night?" Ruby sounds sweet with her question.

"The night I sorta told Blair about me and him." Beau nods to me. "We go way back. Colt and I have always been best... *friends.* And Blair was the only woman I ever felt safe with. I couldn't help it. She wore cute glasses, and I fell in love with her, too."

Beau makes a show of squeezing her hand, held in his on the table. Blair squeezes it back, and I get that fuzzy feeling again.

Not once has their love made me jealous. It's the opposite. It makes me happy.

The other morning, while Blair and I drank coffee, she asked about the difference between a cornerback and a safety. So, after I bored her to death with my explanation, I asked her about my feelings—the one I got when Beau served her a blueberry muffin with a kiss, and then he kissed me, too, all while she sat on my lap.

"Y'all," I asked, "why don't we get jealous? Isn't it weird? Because all I feel is happy when you kiss."

"It's called 'compersion'." Blair brushed muffin crumbs off my beard. "It's when you feel happy seeing the pleasure your partner gets from another partner. Like in a relationship. It's not technically a word, but people like us use it."

People like us?

Of course, I knew I wasn't the only man with feelings for another man. But in the locker room or on the field? I always felt so alone until this season. Until Beau and I decided to try.

But is Ruby saying there are others like us, too? Ones who have more than one love?

She turns to me, tenderly asking, "And you? How do you fit with them?"

"Me?" My answer's simple. "I've always been Beau's, and now I'm falling for Blair, too. It took us years to get here, in our own ways, and we're not going back. But we need help going forward."

"I'll help," Ruby offers, tilting her head. Her hair is twisted up, pieces falling, framing her face. A face that reminds me of an auburn-haired Tinkerbell.

She's cute in that sexy-as-fuck way.

But then, she has a rebellious tiny diamond pierced to the left, just above her pillow lips. And she wears a rose gold diamond ear cuff from Tiffany's. I know how much it is. Amber wanted me to buy one for her. I never did, but I can sense it; *someone gave that to Ruby.*

Ruby's a score. She's got an edge. She's got lady-balls, I can tell.

"But," Blair asks her, "*why* do you help? No offense, but what's in it for you?"

Our eyes aim at Ruby, and she chews her lip. It's not coy, it's careful. "I do it for someone who stays hidden because I believe in what he does. So we have to be careful. We have to protect our group, and that's where I come in."

"So, you're protecting... *professionals* like us?" Beau asks.

"Yes," she answers. "Pros like you and others, too. Others who have to stay hidden, so they need a public face, and that's where I help. I help in different ways, so when Stacey called—she helps us, too—of course, I said I'd return the favor."

I clue her in. "I think we've already heard about your group."

"I think you did, too." She surprises me. "I bet you journaled about it."

Holy shit. Beau and I exchange another look. *We're right.* It's the same group of NFL players Dr. Gary mentioned.

And for the first time in weeks, I'm relieved. The pressure in my chest feels lighter. I've been so damn happy but hiding my dread, too. I keep waiting for my secret to explode into my life, but maybe this is a sign.

My mom believed in signs, and I do, too. You just have to be open to seeing them.

"Can we meet them soon?" I ask. "Your group? Like, how do we start?"

"We can meet sometime this season. You can take our private jet to Charleston, and I'll take it from there."

"A private jet?" Blair shares our shock.

"Yeah," Ruby chuckles, "I grew up on rusted bikes and Greyhound busses, but now, I hitch a ride on a new Gulfstream."

"What if we meet and... " Beau lowers his brow. He's always cautious. "What if it doesn't feel right to us?"

"Then you stay on the first floor," Ruby answers.

And Blair smiles. "Like at Delta's."

"Yeah, like at my favorite store." Ruby shares a knowing grin. "It's all chill on the first floor. Just folks having a beach house barbecue."

"But then?" I ask and...

Why do I already know her answer? And why does it make my cock twitch when I only want Beau and Blair?

Don't get me wrong. Ruby is captivating, but she's just that—I can tell—completely captured by another, in the best way, and she doesn't want to be free. That's why she's perfect for us. She belongs to someone else.

Someone willing to share her this way. Someone with power who's willing to help us. And why? Why do I fear we're going to need it?

Oh, I know.

Because Beau and I are bisexual NFL players, in a throuple with a woman, while we're about to begin the biggest, most winning season of our career. I can smell the Super Bowl in the air. I can feel the one hundred and twenty-three million fans of the game and their eyes already watching us.

And I can read the posts of my angry ex-girlfriend, blasting shit on socials. She's on a mission to ruin our lives.

And then... there's my secret. The one ripping me apart inside. Now that I'm living with Beau and falling in love with Blair, I don't know how long I can keep it.

It's a bomb, ticking on the sidelines.

But this group feels like a solution, a way out of the closet.

"But then, if you like the party and feel comfortable," Ruby answers me. She has a way of making this feel safe. "You can go upstairs and explore. You can meet others like you, but there's one rule."

"Which is?" Blair asks, and I cock a brow at her tone.

Is our woman twitching hot and curious like me?

With her fingertip rimming her crystal goblet of merlot, Ruby answers, "You know that saying: having skin in the game?"

"Yeah," Beau answers, his voice gruff. I know his tone,

too. He's aroused. "In this case," he says, "you mean literal skin, right?"

Proudly, Ruby lifts her chin. "If others show you who they are and how they love—consensually and safely, of course—our one rule is you show them your skin, too. Even just a little, but with no shame."

Now Blair's leaning over, kissing Beau's cheek, her lips brushing his ear. She lets us hear her say, "Imagine being safe and free enough to show everyone how beautiful our love is—the three of us. Imagine not hiding it."

I watch the idea land in Beau's blue eyes. They're a storm of desire, hope, and fear, and I'm in the hurricane with him.

All we've ever known is hiding who we are, living as half of ourselves, cutting off our truth to fit into someone else's narrow definition of love.

It used to piss me off. It made me silently rage. Sometimes, I still do.

But the older I get, with my love with Beau and my love blooming for Blair, too, I understand.

I don't accept it, but I get it.

The only people who judge the love of another are those who have no love of their own.

As we leave, it makes me proud, wrapping my arm around Ruby's bare shoulder. She may not be my girlfriend, but she's my friend.

I trust her.

I can feel my mom smiling down on us.

It's the same way I felt the first night Blair sat by the pool with me. I felt my mom guiding me to Blair, like giving her to me like a gift, and I feel her now, blessing our foursome as the maître d' holds the glass doors open for us.

Beau exits first, holding Blair's hand.

The flash of lights, the wall of hissing camera shutters, and shouts of, "Beau! Beau! Colton! Over here! Over here!" are instant.

We're greeted by the swarm of paparazzi we summoned.

I squeeze Ruby tighter. I'm six-five, and she can't be over five-five; I got her covered. She turns her face toward my chest, acting shy and surprised, but it's a performance. We don't want to look staged.

"Beau! Colton! This way! This way! Are these your dates? Are they your new girlfriends?"

The paps shout questions we don't answer.

Beau blocks, and so do I. We try smiling through the swarm, making our way to the end of the sidewalk while the valet signals for the limo we left waiting for us.

"Ms. Monroe! Ms. Monroe!" Some dude with a Nikon shouts. "Is it true? Do you write books about Beau Bronson? Is he your alien fantasy lover? Does your father approve of your kinky romance?"

What the fuck?

I whip my glare to the asshole trying to goad Blair.

So does Beau. "Back off," he growls. "And show her some respect."

We know better. Opposing fans heckle us all the time. The worst you can do is answer. The dumbest you can do is insult back. The rookie mistake is letting them provoke you into a fight, which is exactly what they want.

But the surge of cameras gets worse, blinding and blocking our path. It's like pushing through a rush of defensive linemen. I hold my palm up, expertly shucking them aside while clutching Ruby tight.

Beau does the same for Blair. He's protecting her, but that same Nikon asshat gets in her face.

"Are you just like your dad, Duncan Monroe?" This pap pushes too far, jeering, "Blair, are you a sports whore like your dad? Will you ruin Beau's game? Is he your first of many husbands and a dozen baby-daddies? Will you have little blue alien babies with him?"

Fucking dick.

This shitface sounds like Amber sent him.

CHAPTER TWENTY-FOUR

I'M ABOUT TO HAVE A VIRAL VAGINA.

Beau leads me toward the limo, his big hand sweating and tugging mine. By the veins popping on his neck, by the clench of his jaw, he's fighting every instinct to kill the shouting shithead with the Nikon.

I love Beau's maturity. His restraint. It's sexy. It's powerful. He could write a check for that guy's existence, or he could beat him into a coma. He's too good for him.

But me?

Caution, meet the this-bitch-is-pissed wind.

I whip around, aiming my glare right at the guilty lens.

This little dick on two legs smells like you'd expect. Showers? They repulse him. Toothpaste? Who needs it? Getting laid? He's never been so lucky.

I smile, beaming for his Nikon, twitching my nose for a cute effect.

"Why yes!" I answer. "Thank you for asking, Duncan.

Monroe is my father, so yes, I can bag *any* baller I like and make *all* the pretty blue Bronson babies I want." Then I rake his short stature, from his greasy head to his gnarled toenails in dirty flip-flops. "But bless your shriveled little dick. With the way you smell, no one will help you empty your saggy blue balls."

I kiss my middle finger for his lens.

Ruby laughs.

Colt chuckles.

Beau gently tugs me toward the open limo door, and victory tastes sweet in my mouth. Pride lifts my D cups high. Triumph guides my teetering high heels.

But...

They're high heels made by men like the clicking dick. They serve their purpose. They make me an idiot. They make me trip, stumbling back in slow motion with my drawling, "Ahhhhhhhh, sssshhhhiiiitttt," shout filling in the air.

In one plop, I'm on my ass. Thankfully, it's padded. My fluffy cheeks do their job. They protect my assets, but my short dress decides to show my pride to the world.

My panties, that is.

Clicking shutters catch my kitty flash before Beau can scoop me up fast enough.

"Blair," he rushes, lifting, practically cradling me. It's so damn sweet, and making it worse, exposing all my lady goods to the lenses.

"Baby, are you okay?" But Beau's just worried. He's protecting me while Colt does, too.

Colt shoves the photographer away like he's a corner-back, making him fall back on his ass, too, while Ruby stands over the guy. She twists her face, mocking him, "Ewww. You smell like you wanna be left alone."

I want to laugh, but Beau hikes me like a football, tossing me gently inside the limo before he slides in behind me. Ruby then Colt join us before the chauffeur slams the door.

Beau brushes back my hair. "Are you okay?"

"No," I answer.

"Where are you hurt?" He inspects my hands, looking for abrasions, then my wrists, as if he'll find a protruding bone.

"On my pussy."

"What?" He moves to lift my dress, but I shoo his hands away.

"I mean my panties," I huff. "My panties aren't fine."

"Oh no!" Ruby gasps. "Girl, is it Aunt Flo? Do you have a tail flower? Did that dickhead start the Red Rage, The Blood Bath, The Estrogen Exodus, The—"

"Jesus of the pink lady jizz." Colt laughs. "You two are just alike. How many names you got for your period?"

Ruby shrugs, reaching into her clutch. "I'm always packin' cotton. Whatdayaneed? Regular? Super Plus? A wad of tissues?"

"No." I want to cry, but I start laughing. "No, I'm not flying the red flag. I'm wearing these."

I might as well show them because I'm about to have a viral vagina. One no penicillin can cure.

And yes, dammit. I know that's not how that medicine works, but wait til you see my injury.

Lifting my dress, I reveal what was meant for Beau and Colt tonight, not Instagram and ESPN.

My men tilt their heads like puppy dogs. You'd think I'd have them trained by now, but they're slow to read my panties.

TOUCHDOWN

My white triangle reads in bold, black ink with a red football that also looks like women's lips. I ordered a dozen pair from Etsy to get fucked, not be fucked.

"Uh-oh," is what falls from Beau's sexy lips.

"They're Atlanta's colors," is all Colt can confirm.

"Well," dismissively Ruby shrugs, "at least they don't say 'ball control' or 'huddle up boys' or—"

I laugh, recalling all the football terms I hear Beau and Colt shout at games on the flatscreen while I snicker, dying not to make the puns.

But now I toss 'em out.

"Yeah," I add, "or 'man-to-man coverage,'" I'm crying, "or 'in the pocket' or 'face mask' or 'smash mouth offense' or—"

"Quarterback sneak," Colt jumps in, "or 'running up the score' or—"

"Two-minute warning." Beau's laughing, too.

"Damn." I swipe away tears and mascara. "I could put all those on panties and open an Etsy shop."

"You should!" Ruby scoots to the edge of her seat. She's across from me and beside Colt. He's so big he makes her look like an elfin fairy with an evil plan.

"That's how you'll spin it," Ruby says. "You'll say you bought the funny panties since people make jokes about women who date ballers." She pauses, finger in the air. "*Ballers!* There's another pair we can sell. We can put it on boxers, too. But see what I mean? You can say you wore them as a joke, but since you fell, making fans fall in love with your touchdown panties, you're opening an Etsy store and donating the money to charity. You'll be fine."

"But I'm not fine," I sigh. "I'm fucked."

"And it could backfire." Beau wraps his arm around me. "This will go viral for a hot second, but we got this. Okay?"

My phone?

You can have it. I can't watch my vagina go viral. From here on, I'm using messenger pigeons and learning Morse Code.

After we get home and say goodnight to Ruby, who bunks in one of Beau's lavish guest bedrooms, my sense of humor fails me. The magnitude of my panty problem settles in.

So, my plan is to set up camp under the covers of Beau's bed for the next three years.

Who needs sunlight and joy when you can get dragged down the pavement of public opinion online for years?

"I can't believe I did that."

I bang my head against the shower tile. Colt's combing conditioner through my hair. Usually, it relaxes us, but not tonight. Even when Beau replaces the polished marble walls of his spa shower with the wall of his pecs for my doofus forehead, I can't escape my panty predicament.

"It was cute," Beau assures, brushing the back of his fingers across my cheek.

"It was dumb," I argue. "I should know better, especially in a short dress. If it wasn't that dickhead photographer, it could've been a gust of wind."

"Now, *that* would've been sexy." Colt caresses my shoulders. "So Marilyn Monroe, but Blair Monroe and way hotter."

"Nah." Beau kisses the tip of my nose. "It *was* hot and sexy. Do you know how many wish they had a woman like you? One who makes sex what it should be? Natural? Fun? Passionate and whatever? Blair," he lifts my chin, "it'll be okay."

"You're sweet, but you're lying. You both are. This is about to get feral. Your fans will eat me alive."

"No," Beau brushes his lips over mine, "*we* eat you alive. No one else."

"Y'all, I'm serious." But I pull away, squeezing out of their muscle sandwich. "Your season hasn't even started, and I've already ruined it. It's all they'll talk about. Watch. Every touchdown you make, they'll throw panties on the field."

"That'd be fucking awesome!" Colt laughs. "That's way better than plastic bottles and cups. Or my favorite: used toilet paper."

"See!" I cry. "That's what I mean. Your fans are going to kill me, and you'll be heckled. You'll be mocked."

"We'll be *winning*." Beau stays calm. "They'll get over it."

"Fine. They'll love you but hate me."

"Do you care?"

"No," I answer Beau honestly. "After Amber's one-star review shit, I have so many haters; stand in line. But it's not fair to you." I reach for his hand and Colt's. "This is going to be your winning season. You guys are crushing it. You're gonna win the Super Bowl."

Looking back at Beau's blue eyes, I see so much and tears bite at mine.

"You've worked so hard for this. All the years you got up early for practice. Then, you went to all your classes and stayed up late, studying in the library. You—"

"And the only way you know that," Beau interrupts, cupping my cheek, "is because you always saw me. The real me. Colt and I were fighting, Reese was a mess, and I was alone. I always felt alone unless I was with you. So I'm not letting fuckers mess with my woman."

"*Our woman*," Colt corrects him. He doesn't sound mad. He sounds sincere.

I squeeze Colt's hand, then cup Beau's on my cheek. Steam billows around us. Water gently rains from the shower heads. Rivulets stream down our bodies. Colt's long blond strands fall in golden wet ropes, and Beau's brown waves drip like his trimmed beard.

"Yes, I'm yours," I answer them. "But I should go. I'm not going to be a di—"

"Don't say it," Beau growls. "Don't say that word, ever, Blair. It's not true. These have been the best weeks of my life with you two. So no one's leaving. Not again. Walking out of those hotel rooms before the Super Bowl and then after our Valentine's night felt so wrong, and nothing felt right until I got you back. Both of you." He reaches, cupping Colt's shoulder. "Yes, we started as some fake-girlfriend-temptation bet bullshit, but that didn't last because we're too real. And we feel it; we're in this together."

"Raven." Colt grips my hand tighter. He towers over me. "Don't ever go. Don't leave us. I feel like my mom finally sent you to me and—"

"That's too sweet!" A burst of tears escapes with my blurt, "Y'all are being too sweet! Stop. You'll always outnumber me, and a woman needs to win."

Colt smiles. "Oh, you've won. I fold my boxers because of you, now. I put your peach lotion on my feet before bed, and you make me eat Icelandic yogurt with chia seeds and—"

"It's good for your poop," I remind him.

"See?" He laughs. "You care about my ass more than I ever did."

"So do I," Beau teases Colt before he kisses my cheek. "See, baby? You've got us loving ass and each other in all kinds of ways, so your touchdown panties are going in my trophy room."

I grin, narrowing my eyes. "Did you just call me a trophy?"

"Mm-hmm." He smirks, all cute. "Blair Monroe, you're our prize piece of ass, our championship cunt, our title titties, our—"

"Say one more sexist word, and I'm calling the feminist police."

"Please do," Beau mocks. "Just make sure they dress in latex and bring rope because that's Colt's kink, and this is mine—"

Beau whips me around, grabbing my hands at the same time. He's too fast and trained. My wrists are pinned above my head, my palms pressed against the wet tile before I can protest.

"You're staying right here, Blair," Beau demands, his mouth steaming over my ear. I'm gasping with his chest pressed to my back. I'm suddenly turned on, and so is Beau. He's getting hard, urging into his claim. "You're staying right here with two NFL players who love you. Who'll give your sweet pussy so many touchdowns, we'll lick our creamy trophies as they drip down your thighs. Like this... "

Beau keeps my wrists bound with his hand. "Colt," he growls, "care to lick our trophy while I fuck it?"

"Make it drip in my mouth like champagne," Colt taunts while he lowers. Spreading my thighs, he makes me sway my back, giving him enough room to kneel between my legs.

Beau can't hold our position with his hand pinning my wrists to the wall, so he grabs my hips, demanding, "Stay just like this, Kitten. Keep your hands there and bend over.

Open up your pussy for us to play with. We're scoring touchdowns with you tonight, baby."

I grin, loving him. Loving how Beau is turning my mortifying moment into a hot memory, and I love how Colt agrees. How he starts kissing my clit while Beau taunts us, "Grab my cock. Suck it while you tease her pussy with it, too."

"Oh god," I moan to Colt's warm tongue, rolling over my clit before he presses, rubbing Beau's hard, slick tip over it, too, sending sweet shivers through my flesh, moans crawling out of my throat.

Then Colt teases Beau's crown into my entrance, making me ache for it before he takes it out, taking it into his mouth and sucking my arousal off his tip.

They drive me crazy. They make me feel so loved. They give me so much pleasure; who cares about pain? Who cares what others say when I have this?

"Yes, Colt," Beau hisses, squeezing my fleshy hips. "Keep sticking my hard dick inside her pussy so you can take it out and suck off her cum."

For minutes, they play with me and each other until Beau growls, grabbing my hips so hard, he'll leave bruises. He loves kissing them afterward, and I do, too. I love the marks he leaves.

"She's so wet for you," Colt teases over my clit, sensing Beau's urge. "So fucking sweet and open and ready. Take her. Fuck our little trophy."

Colt guides Beau's cock inside my cunt, and it's ferocious how Beau starts pounding. I cry out, loving it while he praises, "So good, Blair. So good. So perfect and beautiful. You're our sweet little trophy to fuck all night."

Like a hammer, Beau fucks me hard while Colt's mouth, with his tickling whiskers, tenderly sucks my clit. In seconds, I scream. Pleasure. Tension. Worry. My wanton lust. I release it all. It pours down my thighs, streaming with the shower from above.

I come so hard, with a deep grunt, I make Beau come, too. His cock is seated deep inside me. Then I feel him drag his length out. It jumps like he's still coming, and Colt moans between my thighs.

In a haze, I open my eyes. I glance down at my shaking legs, at how Colt's waiting, at how Beau gently demands, "Drip, Blair. Drip our cum into Colt's mouth."

With a wanton clench of my sex, I obey. I feel Colt's husky moans. They're primal, vibrating deep to my core while he buries his face where I'm so open for them, where Colt's licking and slurping, giving and taking.

The taboo, the thrill, the sensation of it makes me come again and so fast, all in Colt's mouth as he growls to it. Like my pussy, dripping with Beau's cum mixed with mine, is a drug, and he needs it. It fuels him.

"Now," Colt suddenly snarls. "She's fucking mine. Give her to me." In a switch that makes me dizzy, Colt rises while Beau falls.

Like he can read my body, Beau steadies my shaking thighs. I'm weak with desire and only want more, and Colt takes it. He drives in and buries himself where Beau just left me so open, raw, and ready for him.

"God! God! God!" I cry out. I belong. Where would I go but here? Where do I belong if not with them?

My clit, which Colt left lavished and tender, Beau takes it. He licks it while Colt thrusts into my cunt, making moans sing from my soul.

Where Beau stretched my cunt to take him, Colt's length finds new spots to claim. They're so different and perfectly matched. I'm aching and shouting for more.

"Yes, Raven. Keep screaming for us because you're ours to fuck." Colt reaches around, palming the weight of my breasts, swaying with his thrusts. "Aren't you? Aren't you our prize? Our dirty little trophy to use? We'll make every touchdown, so we can come home and fuck this sweet pussy and ass every night. Say it." Colt hammers his hips. "Say we won. Say you're ours."

"Yes!" I cry out. Calloused fingertips pinch my nipples. Whiskered lips suck my clit. A long cock pumps into my pussy. "Yes, fuck me," I demand. "Turn me into your trophy to use. Fuck me like your little cum slut after every game you win."

"Mmmm, yes, baby," Beau moans against my nub. "Colt, let me taste her. Let me suck her cum off your dick."

Colt grunts, pulling out to oblige, leaving me open and waiting. The smacking, slurping, and sucking sounds Beau gives us make me groan, and Colt growls, "Fuck yes, Beau. Yes, baby, suck that dick. Let me feel your beard on it. Yes, like that. Suck that sweet pussy cum off it before I fuck her more for you to clean up."

White light fills my vision, my nerves, my heart. I groan, not believing our sex. Our pleasure. Our trust. Our bond. Our everything as Colt drives back inside me, and I brace for his power.

I want Colt.

I want Beau.

The sensation of taking dick and receiving tongue is maddening. It's ecstasy with them. I come to it, falling into its depths. My knees buckle, but Beau holds my shaking thighs while Colt wraps his arm around my waist and the other around my chest.

He grabs me so hard, holding me so tight that my feet lift from the floor. In a whirl, I'm held, my back to Colt's chest while he drives inside me, and Beau delivers. He licks my clit, then Colt's cock, back and forth, right where we join.

"Oh fuck yes, take me," Colt huffs. He fucks, Beau licks, and I coil tight, getting ready to come again. It's almost too much, and I can't stop it. "Take me. Take my cum. Take every drop."

With a violent shudder, Colt's coming, too.

He grunts, and I receive him. I'm panting and pulsing when Colt pulls out. I'm dripping over Beau's waiting mouth. I'm groaning and shaking, coming on his creamy tongue, cleaning my pussy, grateful for our gift.

Our bodies become a wet tangle of huffing breath and kissing lips and limbs intertwined. We hold each other and shower in the aftermath until the hot water runs out, and Colt jokes about Beau not paying the gas bill.

Later, we're curled in bed. I make them turn on the ceiling fan to full blast so I can lie between them. Still, they won't stop melting me.

In the best way.

"I'm gonna do it," Colt murmurs into my neck. "I'm gonna put a tattoo of a stack of books and a little gold trophy in my sleeve, right next to Beau's birds. Because he's my life," Colt kisses my cheek, "and you're my gift."

"And I'm giving you something that'll make you smile, and my fans love you, too." Beau twirls my hair, curling his leg over mine. "I'm giving you your first book signing."

I should be worried.

I should learn my lesson.

I should leave my touchdown panties collecting dust in the drawer.

But when I feel love like this?

Fuck that, and fuck me. I'm wearing a pair everyday.

BEAU

CHAPTER TWENTY-FIVE

"I'll mind my manners when you mind your dick."

After weeks of training in the sweltering Atlanta summer heat, I don't even sweat standing over my BBQ Guys gourmet grill.

I set the timer for the steaks, and I sip a beer. I grin when Ruby elbows me, muttering, "Way to go, champ. I heard your touchdowns last night."

"Shit," I whisper. "Really?"

It's only been me in this house. I've never tested the acoustics before.

"Hallelujah." She chuckles. "I heard Blair praise God many times."

"Sorry if we kept you up."

"Blair left a gift bag from Delta's in my guest room, so I had a good night, too. And I suspect it won't be our last."

She winks, and I wink back, intrigued by our meeting in

Charleston in a few weeks. But now? I'm focused on this come-to-Jesus.

Glancing over my shoulder, I watch for the dozenth time as Blair tries not to roll her eyes at her dad.

I know she loves him. She told us she did in bed this morning. "He's my dad. I'll always love him," she said, "but y'all watch out. Today, you're about to discover why I don't always like him."

And we have.

Duncan Monroe entered my house like a Presidential candidate. The kind with a winning agenda, a big ego, and an even bigger mouth that won't shut.

"Now, you let me handle this." Blair's dad leans back in his chair, telling her, "I know what to say to the press. They'll listen to me."

"Dad," Blair sighs, "I got this. I never took your help and I'm not starting now. *I'll* fix my panty problem."

Behind his beer bottle, Colt smirks.

He sits beside Blair at my round, outdoor dining table, under the shade of my back porch ceiling with fans whirling above. My chair, on the other side of Blair, is empty. But once I'm seated between her and her dad for lunch, I'll experience trench-level warfare.

"You and your sister are identical in every way," he chides. "You never listen. You always have to break the rules. Don't you?"

"Hey, Kettle," Blair scoffs, "wonder where this pot gets it from."

"I'm a man," he replies. "I can break the rules. I made them."

"Uh-oh," Ruby mutters beside me. She's staying out of the line of fire, too. "We're dancing in a hog trough now."

Non-southern translation: Get ready for some shit.

"You sure did make and break 'em, Dad." Blair laughs. "Like how you made holes in more than one woman and broke so many condoms, you got more offspring than you got balls."

"Mind your manners," he scolds.

Blair smiles. "I'll mind my manners when you mind your dick."

Colt spews his beer. "Oh shit," he rushes, reaching for napkins. "I mean... sorry about that, Sir."

"Quite alright," Duncan Monroe drawls. "I'm used to my daughter's drama."

"Dad," Blair helps Colt sop up his beer with paper napkins, "quit acting like your shit don't stink."

He rips the Aviators off his face. "Quit wearing dumbass undergarments while you galavant around Atlanta on the arm of NFL's finest, acting like you have no sense. Like you're wilder than an acre of snakes and not my daughter, who was raised better. Your mother would be embarrassed."

"No, my mother would be proud. I did just as she taught me." Blair beams. "My panties were cute and clean and color coordinated to match my boyfriends' team."

Blair jokes, but that stung.

She misses her mom. She and Colt talk about their moms a lot, bonding over them. I can tell it helps. Colt's starting to smile about his mom again.

But I know Blair, too.

Just like in college, she jokes to hide her pain. That's why we pranked each other. We hurt, wanting to be together, but we wouldn't do it. I wouldn't cheat on Reese, and Blair is loyal to her core.

But this stuff about her parents hurts her. It's obvious. It's the reason for her snark because her dad left scars.

"Well," he digs deeper, "I'm glad she's not here to see your scandal. Though I'll sure never hear the end of it."

Blair looks exactly like her father. Same jet black hair. Same thick lashes. Same nose with a slope. Same lips, twisted in a snarl.

"Yeah, Dad, it's all my fault." She's wearing a pink sundress and a playful ponytail. It's a harmless look while sarcasm fires from her mouth like ego grenades. "My panties bring you such shame because the world holds you, your champion putter, and your purple-helmeted seed spreader in such high esteem."

Colt spews the rest of his beer, quickly wiping it up with a napkin. At this rate, we'll go through a twelve-pack in an hour.

"Steaks are ready!" I shout.

They're not. We're about to eat Wagyu beef that's still mooing, but someone needs to stop this blood bath.

"I'll get the potato salad." Like a true wide receiver, Colt sees an opening and runs for it.

"I'll help." Ruby bails, too.

I can't be mad. They're supposed to look like a couple while I stand by my woman, who's ill as a hornet.

"So, Mr. Monroe." I set the tray of steaks down, half expecting them to still move. I sit beside Blair, offering her dad, "Congratulations on the U.S. Senior Open. Crooked Stick is a helluva course."

Blair snorts at the pun she's dying to make.

And our woman says the athletic gene skipped her. Please. She has a gold-medal tongue. You can't make a phallic reference about sticks or balls or holes without her going for the winning point against her dad.

"Why, thank you, Son." Blair chokes on her beer. At how her dad talks like we're married and not barely dating a month. "Twenty under par with a six-stroke difference is a record for me."

I nudge Blair's foot, knowing she wants to score a point with a *stroke* pun, too, but she holsters her pistol. I guess she won't risk hurting me with friendly fire.

But she does clarify, "Dad, his name is 'Beau,' and he's not your son. You have four of your own. Remember?"

Her dad smirks. "Well, he'll be my son when he makes an honest woman of you soon."

Lucky for Blair, I'm used to pressure in the pocket. Though oddly, the idea of marriage makes me happy.

But Blair runs interference, trying to protect me.

"Too late," she sings. "I gave my flower to Bobby O'Connor in the back seat of his Honda Accord at the mall. It was real romantic. He banged me and my head against the backdoor. I was gonna save my precious gift as part of my dowry, but Bobby wooed me with a large popcorn at the movies. But hey," she smiles, "you raised me right. I didn't give my milk for free. I made him buy me a large Dr. Pepper with free refills, too."

I chuckle, nudging her foot again. I'll have to take care not to break our woman's toes when she's on a roll. And yes, I'll be asking more about that story later, but her dad rolls his eyes for now. "Just don't write another damn romance book about it."

"Oh, it'll be my next one," she chirps. "The sexy alien will kidnap the sci-fi obsessed virgin from the movie theater, luring her with popcorn, before they fall in forbidden love."

It's a Monroe thing—the dramatic silver eye roll. Her dad does it again, so I play Switzerland.

"Why don't we play here sometime?" I gesture to the course I live on.

"I'd be honored to show you a thing or ten," Duncan boasts like every true pro. "But how's the shoulder?" He also knows our greatest fear: injuries.

"Perfect," I lie. "I think we'll go all the way this year."

"Again?" Not-so-subtly, he mentions our Super Bowl loss.

"Yeah... again."

He points to Blair, not smiling. "Just don't get distracted."

That jab makes her twist by my side, my heart flinching for hers, so I reach for her hand. It's so warm in my grasp.

It's always been the little things about Blair. Her small hands. Her big glasses. Her red lips. Her tiny gold earrings shaped like books. Her evil giggle when she pranks me. Her mini vibrator collection. I've been so wrong because she feels so right.

"I'm not distracted, Sir," I answer. "I'm in love with your daughter. I've loved her since college when she super-glued pubic hair to my phone."

"Blair Madison Monroe!" He's shocked. He's appalled.

"It wasn't pubic hair." But Blair laughs, turning to me. "It was my hair from the shower drain. I just cut it to look like pubes."

"If it was in the shower drain," I laugh with her, "it could've been from your landing strip."

For a moment, I got lost in Blair's eyes. I just smile at her. I just remember my sexy frenemy, the one person who brought me joy in college. Without Colt, I only survived because of Blair.

Her dad must clock it. He gets quiet, watching our laugh, hearing our connection, his stare studying my hand holding hers.

"Y'all haven't hit the worst yet," he warns. "By the time you reach the Super Bowl, you'll be hunted like prey."

"Who's being dramatic now, Dad?"

Blair dismisses him, but her dad is right. I also warn her, but we're too in love for her to listen.

Just in time, Colt and Ruby return and we finally relax. We enjoy our meal until Blair's dad worries aloud.

"This, uh, Amber influencer, whatever the hell you kids call it." He stabs his steak. "She's raising a ruckus online. About me. About my daughter. About y'all." He points to me, and *oh shit, he loops in Colt.* "My publicist is having a fit. What's going on?"

"She's my ex-girlfriend, Sir," Colt answers him. On cue, Ruby caresses his shoulder.

"But something's fishy." Duncan asks Colt, "Why is she going after me and my daughter when Blair's dating your best friend, not you? And why isn't she going after her?"

He points to Ruby, and sweat hits my pits. My pulse triples. Blair's dad may have been a horn dog, but he's not a dumb one.

Is he on to us?

Are we that obvious?

Colt tells the truth. Some of it. "Because Blair helped me realize how toxic Amber was for me, and now Amber's pissed about it."

Blair scoffs, "Amber's pissed about that and all cosmetics not tested on innocent baby bunnies. You know, to make sure her eyeshadows don't fade."

Ruby laughs, but Blair's dad is not amused.

"Laugh all you want." Duncan points his fork at Blair. "But someone like that will steal the flowers off her grandma's grave to make herself look pretty."

"Dad, quit talking Southern and speak plain."

"I am speaking plainly," he replies. "It's universal what a woman scorned will do. Trust me, I know. Amber's put a target on your back, and your panty stunt made it worse. You need my help. I'm gonna release a statement about this mess."

This morning, my publicist called about Blair's viral panties. I put her on speakerphone with Blair, and we made some plans to spin it positively. My idea of a book signing for Blair became part of the play. And, of course, Blair had the idea to take it to the next level.

But still, Amber's on a witch hunt for Blair.

So, we spend the next hour trying to convince Blair's dad to leave Amber alone. Blair starts a long chat with him. "Dad, sometimes saying nothing says everything," she explains while my eyes signal Colt to meet me inside.

We clear a few plates, dropping them in the sink. I aim for the walk-in pantry, and Colt follows, letting the door swing closed behind us.

"We're fucked," I mutter. "Blair's dad is a loose cannon."

"He's just protecting his daughter."

"She can protect herself," I answer. "And the last thing we need is to fan Amber's flames. It's exactly what she wants."

"I know." Colt leans against the pantry shelf, guilt sagging his shoulders. "I'm sorry. It's like I regret every woman I was with until Blair."

"Bullshit." I laugh. "All that pussy? You can't regret it."

"Yeah," he crosses his arms, "sometimes I do."

"Well then, let's just focus on the one we love. Go out there and tell Blair's dad you'll call Amber. You'll kiss her ass and eat crow and try to get her to stop. And I'll play the good boyfriend. I'll try to calm down Blair's dad."

"Good luck with that." Colt chuckles. "Blair riles him up. Her offensive lines are hilarious. He needs the ego check."

I chuckle too, "Purple-helmeted seed spreader," repeating one of our girl's zingers.

That just makes us laugh.

"Shit," Colt tosses his chin up, "is that what they look like? Our dicks? Purple helmets?"

"Nah." On instinct, the image of his is instant. The urge and memory make me reach for his waist, pulling him near. "Yours is pink."

"Pink?" He grins, all sexy, moving his lips toward mine. "Wanna know what color yours is?"

"Big and beige." I tease my lips over his. "And getting bigger."

"Is that so?" Colt taunts before his kiss.

He grabs the back of my neck, his whiskers brushing mine, his tongue searching, taking me too. It's always been like this, magnetic the way we're drawn together. The pull Colt has over my heart, my body. The way we ease and soothe and take each other.

"Tonight," I demand over our kiss, "it's your turn. I'm fucking *you* in the shower."

Our moans get loud, mingling with our mouths, sealing the promise until...

"Is that so?" A deep voice snarls, and we snap our shocked stare at Blair's dad, slamming the pantry door open, his glare ripping down us. "Does my *daughter* know you're fucking him in the shower tonight?"

I stagger back from Colt. He does the same, crashing into the shelves behind him and knocking over jars and cans.

I exclaim, "Mr. Monroe, it's—"

It's what? Not how it looks? Not what he obviously over-heard? Not my dick hard in my shorts for Colt and Colt's is the same? His long Johnson points proud and my way.

Fuck it.

"Blair knows," I answer him. "She's with us."

"The hell she is!" His face, handsome for a man his age, any age, fumes angry and red. "You're not using my daughter. You're not dragging her into this! You'll ruin her life."

"It's my life, Dad." Blair's voice sounds behind him.

He whips around, pointing at us but shouting at her in the kitchen. "You knew about this? You knew they're gay?"

"They're not gay," she answers. "Though if they were, that would be beautiful, too. They're bisexual like me. We're together. The three of us. We love each other."

"And his girlfriend?" Duncan asks about Ruby. "You're lying to her?"

"She knows," Colt answers him. "She's my friend. *Our friend.* Ruby's helping us with the public part of it."

"Public?" He mocks. "Men like you can't be public. You're athletes. It's not right. It's not traditional. It violates all morals and ruins lives. Careers. Everything."

"So you get to be public and proud?" Blair goes right at him. "Men like you get a pro career and a back-slapping 'attaboy' when you go from woman to woman, making more babies than you can raise like a true father? You know, like being there at night when we cry or packing our lunches? You know the stuff real dads do? You can abandon mother after mother and kid after kid and *that's* moral? *That's* tradition? *That* makes you a man?"

"I provided for you," he snarls. "I provided for all my kids."

"We didn't want your provisions, Dad. We wanted your love. We wanted our father. And those two," she points at me and Colt, "are real men. They don't abandon the ones they love. We're not distractions to them. We're a family."

Colt coughs like something's strangling him, and I feel the strain, too.

"Mr. Monroe," I control my fury, "I'm trying to show you respect, Sir, for Blair's sake. But by God, you will give it to us, too. We're not ashamed of our love—me and Colt, us and Blair. So accept it and respect it, or get the fuck out of our home right now."

"But you can't come out," he pleads. "You're NFL players. You'll lose everything, and so will she."

"We know the world we live in," I answer. "And together, we'll figure it out."

COLTON

> "YOU BETTER GIVE ME A BIG BLUE COCK. BIGGER THAN
> BEAU'S."

Beau said to eat crow, and I'd rather.

I bet it tastes better than the words I have to swallow, listening to Amber. For her, trauma is a hangnail that requires an emergency room visit. Perspective escapes her.

"I lost a sponsorship because of you!" she exclaims. "I lost the Faux Sun account and followers because I was contracted to go to the ESPYs with you, wearing my white Balmain dress and a fresh Faux Sun tan."

Amber tosses back her Prosecco for emphasis. So, I swig my beer, fighting not to say it.

But I do.

"Maybe it was a blessing in a Balmain disguise because that Faux Sun left real brown stains on every white bedsheet and towel I owned."

She narrows her eyes. "You're a millionaire. You'll be fine."

"Is that what you want? My millions?"

"I deserve to be compensated for what I lost."

"Yeah," I scoff, "me, too."

"What's that supposed to mean?"

I glance around the trendy Atlanta bar where I agreed to meet Amber after practice. Of course, she picked a spot where everyone's snapping pics of us. Our first pre-season game is Friday, and Atlanta is buzzing about it.

Me and the whole city want that Super Bowl ring on my finger so bad, it feels naked without it.

I want to blame Amber for that loss, but I won't. I gotta own my shit.

"It means we were toxic, Amber. We fought all the time. We wasted months together when I should've been focused on the game."

"Fights are how people show their love."

"No, that's how people show they've lost their goddamn mind." I huff, "If I want to live on the edge of my seat, worried about what daily argument is going to jump out and give me a mindfuck, I'll watch a horror flick."

She sighs. "We weren't that bad."

I cock a brow. "We weren't that good."

She snaps her fingers at the bartender. This is her third glass of Prosecco, so she's either about to get nicer or nastier—it depends on her shapewear.

Yep, I'm serious.

She flat-out blamed three of our fights on her bad mood due to Spanx. Or was it Skims? Fuck, I don't remember which brand she was wearing, but her brand of bullshit was unforgettable.

"Look," I soften my voice, "I'm sorry we didn't work out

and I'm sorry I ended it so abruptly. We should've talked about it."

"Why?" She tosses her blonde hair. "It wouldn't change anything. Once that gothic freak got her nails into you, you were pale pussy whipped."

"I'm *not* with Blair."

Amber smirks while the bartender replaces her empty glass with a full one.

"Yes, you are." She's got those super long fake lashes glued on today. I stare at them, reminded of a black widow waiting in her web. "You're fucking Blair Monroe, you and your best friend. I know how close you are and that you're living together. I have my sources."

I try to hide my deep inhale while forcing my eyes to stay on hers. While I make myself lie when I hate to.

But unfortunately, I've gotten pretty damn good at it.

"Beau's in love with Blair. They've been in love since college." The trick is to pepper in some truth. "Hell, they'll get married soon. They belong together, and I'm happy for them." And pepper in some authentic emotion because I wish I could marry Beau, too. "I'm only living with him until my house is done. And... " But here's the real gamble. Pepper in a diversion. "I'm kinda seeing someone."

"That little redhead?" Her smirk drops. "The one on your arm when Blair fell on her ass? Gawd, that was priceless: her touchdown panties. My posts about it go viral, and I bet your new girlfriend hates her guilt by tacky association."

Shit, I lit her fuse. I just hope she doesn't blow. An Amber bomb is really ugly.

She likes creating collateral damage. Like smashing glass and throwing phones.

My favorite was when Amber threw my phone at my car

window, pissed by a text she thought was another woman, but it was my cousin, Alicia.

And it was karma calling.

My Range Rover has bulletproof glass. My phone only bounced back, hitting Amber's shimmery Hermès nose like a beacon light and making it bleed.

Yes, I was a gentleman and gave Amber my sweatshirt to catch the blood. And yes, I'm only human because I wanted to laugh my ass off the whole time.

"It was just a date," I tell Amber about Ruby. "We're not serious. The truth is, I never really grieved my mom last year, and now I'm taking the time to do it."

See? That was true, too. It's Blair who's helping me heal.

"So just leave Blair alone," I tell her. "Quit dragging her on your socials."

"If you're not with her, why are you here defending her?"

"Because she's my best friend's girlfriend. She did nothing wrong. And honestly, I'm defending you, Amber."

Her chin shocks back. "Defending me from who?" Her neck weaves. "That bitch can't do shit to me."

"She doesn't need to. You're doing it to yourself. Talking shit about other people says more about you than them." I pause. "It's making you look bad. It's hurting your brand."

She purses her lined lips because I'm right.

So, if I can't appeal to her better half now, I'll appease her bottom line.

"Look, I'll pay you back. I'll give you some money to cover what you lost in sponsorships over me and a bit more to start something new. You used to tell me about all kinds of makeup you wanted to create, so do it."

"That costs millions."

"Come up with a business plan, and I'll silently invest

the seed money. Then, court other investors. You're a businesswoman. You can do it."

Will I probably lose my money? Yes.

Is it worth it?

I'd give it all away to protect who I love. To have a chance with them. It's all I want.

When I politely escort Amber to her car, I peck her cheek goodbye. I hope I've inspired her to leave Blair and Beau alone. Don't tell her, but I'd give her all my millions to move on.

Because I can't.

Once I jump in my Rover, I don't leave. I'm suffocating in lies. In secrets. In shame. So, I make a call. I reach out for some good news.

"Hey," Reese answers.

"Hey." I stare at my steering wheel. "How's he doing?"

"He just made a second base hit."

"Just like his dad. Teeball leads to baseball, then football one day."

"Hmmm," she answers. "He has talent."

I smile. I can hear happy kids screaming in the background. "Send me more videos."

"I will."

She's not saying much, so I whisper, "Is he there?"

"No, it's just me at evening practice. Jake had to work."

Jake is Reese's husband. He's the man who thinks he's the father of her son.

"Can I come see him again? Before the season starts?"

Reese's sigh is long, and my heavy heart hangs by a thread. Her whim holds it. She's always had control of it.

"Colton, he's getting too old. He asks too many questions, and you're too famous now. We can't just sneak around like before."

"But... " I almost choke on my words. They strangle and burn in my throat, tears biting at my eyes, "I miss him. I want to see him. I need him to know I love him."

I do. I don't care how that little boy came into this world. He's just that—an innocent little boy I love.

"I know." Reese sighs, "And I'm sorry, Colton. You know I am. For everything. It's just not safe anymore."

"Reese, we can just tell everyone. We can just tell the truth. Please, it's fucking killing me."

"No. That'll hurt Jake, and that will hurt Forrest. He loves his dad so much."

I clench my jaw, throwing my chin up, fighting the tears that want to fall. "Jake's *not* his dad."

But he is.

It's like what Blair yelled to her father.

Jake is Forrest's dad because he's there. He was at the hospital when he was born. He held him, giving him late-night feedings. He bandaged skinned knees, packed kindergarten lunches, and taught him how to throw. He's a real man. He raised his son.

Yes, I've done everything I can for Forrest. For the rest of his life, he's set. But Reese won't allow the one thing that boy deserves, too.

He deserves to know who his father is.

And so do I.

"Colton, I'll send more videos, I promise." Reese has always felt guilty about this, and she should. It's her fault.

"Bring him to our games," I make myself answer. "I got more season tickets for y'all this year. They're closer. He'll be able to see us better."

And I'll be able to see him.

"We will," gently, she agrees. "Atlanta's his favorite

team." She gets quiet. "Forrest wears your jersey to sleep. Or Beau's. That's all he'll wear."

I nod, swiping away tears. I can't speak. I've never had much say in this. But when it comes to football, I do.

I take control. "Come to our home game against Philadelphia, and I'll set something up with our publicists. I'll get you club seats, field level, behind our bench. We'll say you won them. Then he can meet me and remember me. I want him to feel special because he is. I want to give him a game ball and take a picture with him and—"

"Colton, that's too risky. What if Beau sees—"

"Reese,"—I stifle my rage; I always have—"you *owe* me this. I've always been good to you despite what you did to me."

"Okay." That makes her softly agree. It always does, so I end our call in a storm of emotions.

Reese is a good mom. I'm sure she's a good wife, too.

But she was a troubled young woman with a drinking problem, and that still doesn't make it okay.

Because it's not.

I didn't want to have sex with her. I thought I was dreaming. I thought I was with Beau. We were finally friends again, and I'd missed him so much.

It was our senior year in college. I was in Beau's apartment. We'd played beer pong with Reese all night, and I was still half drunk. I woke up on his sofa, smelling his cologne in the fabric and thinking it was him touching me, getting me so hard, and about to come, but it wasn't.

It was Reese on top of me. She had me inside her with no condom.

If the tables were turned, and I did that to her? My ass would deserve to rot in jail. Then hell.

But she did it to me, and it was too late by the time I

realized what was happening. And I hated her for it. I worried I'd lose Beau again over it, too. That he wouldn't believe me.

Weeks later, Reese told me she was pregnant and begged me not to tell anyone. She realized what she did was wrong and hated herself. So she went to rehab, where she met Jake. They've been together ever since.

When Beau called me to visit again, I wanted to tell him. I almost did, but then he said we could never be together. We were about to be drafted by the NFL.

And I stood there, losing all hope.

I couldn't have the truth. I couldn't have him. I couldn't have a baby that may be mine. I had no control over my heart, so I snapped, and we fought.

That's the night Beau and Blair talk about. The night I busted his lip, and he busted mine. I'm glad Blair was there for him. I love her for it. I always will.

Because I drove home and found the only support I had back then, too. I went to my mom that night. I told her my two secrets—Beau and the baby—and I've been hiding them ever since.

By the time I get home from my evening with Amber, Beau's on the sofa. He fell asleep studying our playbook, so I lift it off his chest and set it on the coffee table before tucking a blanket over him. And I can't help it; I kiss his forehead.

Then, I search the house for Blair and see a light shining under her office door. Gently, I knock.

"I'm writing about you," she answers, and I smile.

"You better give me a big blue cock. Bigger than Beau's."

She laughs. "Enter and find out."

I adore the sight I find: Blair on her chair, her hair piled in a cute messy knot, glasses on the tip of her nose.

She sets her laptop on the side table. "How did it go?" she asks, patting the spot for me to sit beside her. "Did you bring me more makeup tips?"

"No. But I threw Amber a big enough bone to chew on instead of you."

I plop down on the end of her chaise, and she crawls my way, her hands landing on my T-shirt, giving me the shoulder rubs I love. I close my eyes and let her. I let Blair heal me the same way Beau does.

"Thank you," she whispers, kissing my cheek.

I grin at the floor. "You owe me the next two movie nights."

"Done. I'll watch Fast & Furious: The Geriatric version with you on repeat."

"Don't be hating on The Rock. Dwayne's my boy."

"I love The Rock. It's just men compensating for their small dicks with fast cars that's an old cliché."

Barely, I chuckle because Blair's feminine touch mends my broken pieces. It's not just her massage; it's her warmth and care. It's who I share with her, too. It's everything I don't have to hide from her except...

"Did you hear from your dad?"

"Yeah." She sighs. "He said he was sorry. That he's not a biphobic asshole. He's just worried we're doomed, so he swore he won't say anything."

"Do you trust him?"

"We have to."

"I know it's easy for me to say, but give him a chance. At least he was here. At least he's trying. His dick may not be in the right place, but somewhere deep down, maybe his heart is."

She rubs my neck, squeezing hard as hell at the topic of her father. It feels so damn good, her voice softly lulling, "Okay. For you, my sweet Colt, I'll give him a chance."

I hang my head and let the silence settle around us until I feel her arms try to circle me from behind. It's cute. She can't because I'm too big and she's too small.

"Hey," she whispers in my ear. "What's wrong?"

Everything.

But this...

I reach, turning to guide her around me, to let me pick her up until she's straddling my lap. Snapping her hair clip out, I toss it on the floor before lacing my hands through her raven silk.

I wonder if she hates my nickname for her—Raven— but I love it. I love Blair's every color, curve, and come back.

"Just promise me one thing." I anchor to her eyes.

"Anything but the laundry." She grins. "Because you guys are Pure-T filth after practice. No human alive should have to clean that nuclear waste you call your socks."

I laugh. "I'll always clean up my mess... if you promise you'll always forgive me for it."

She cocks her head, suspicious. Like she can see my secret but doesn't ask because she sees my pain, too. How I'm hanging by a thread for *her* now.

"I promise." Softly, she kisses me. "I'll always forgive you if you'll always believe in me. Just like you believe in Beau. I love how you love him and how he loves you."

"I love how he loves you, and I know why." I softly kiss her back. "Because I love you, too, Blair."

Our next kiss is slow. So is the way I tug off her dress. So is the way she reaches inside my shorts, finding me needing her. So is the way I ask to be inside her. I want this with her. I want her yes, and I want to give her mine, and she takes it. She takes me deep and slow and with kisses that don't stop until she's gasping and I'm grunting, giving what I want her to have—my body, my heart, my smile when we're done. When I insist, "Tell me what you're writing about me."

She's still wrapped around me. I'm still inside her. "You'll only want to fuck me again," she beams. She's so beautiful. She's right, and she's all ours.

"Only if you make my alien cock bigger than Beau's."

"It's not bigger." She laughs, and I raise a brow. "It's longer. Like to his knees."

"Whose knees?"

Did she just blush? Did she just get shy?

"*Raavveennn*, tell me my alien name."

"You'll laugh at me."

"No, I won't. Just don't give my character a long nose to match his long cock, and I'll be happy."

She presses her lips together, so I tickle her waist. "Stop!" She blurts, giggling. "What if I pee?"

"What if I get hard again when you tell me?"

"Fine." She smashes her hand over my mouth. "But not a word once I do."

I nod, kissing her palm.

"Beau was Valen, the Vulgarian, but in my new series, he's Willuf, the Wilder, and now you're Valr, the Vicious." I wrinkle my brows. "Valr means 'hawk' in old Norse, what the Vikings spoke. You seem to have a thing for them. Hell, you look like one."

I sputter against her hand. "How is Valr vicious?"

"He kidnaps our heroine, Falcon, the woman Willuf loves. He holds her hostage and falls in love with her, too, while trying to tempt Willuf to his lair, where they can form a truce. They're attracted to each other but hate each other. They're rival warlords. But they're tired of fighting, of the pain of war, and the only way to seal their peace is—"

I grin. "Plant their seed inside her."

"Yep." Shamelessly, she smiles, removing my muzzle.

"Now, who's cliché?" But I pinch her nose, loving her story—*our story.*

"Touché to my cliché." She shrugs. "But romance readers love a good, hot breeding."

"*You* love a good, hot breeding."

Yep, she blushes again. Yep, she makes this fun. Blair makes me feel right. She makes me want to take and give, and we do.

We fuck again, and like her book, our love summons Beau to her lair. We finish just in time to find him rustling his hair in the doorway of her office.

"When y'all are done writing her next chapter," he smiles, "it's time for bed."

CHAPTER TWENTY-SEVEN

"Oh my god, look at all these people!"

My jaw hits the floorboard of Beau's fancy truck.

My deodorant quits her job.

I suck my teeth, worried the broccoli I didn't eat is stuck in them, too, while my bare legs in white vinyl thigh-high boots feel too exposed in my Galaxy babe cosplay outfit.

"Take me home," I rush. "I gotta change."

"Babe, you look awesome." Beau drives toward the back of the bookstore, where the line of people wraps around the large brick building. "You look like the badass astro babes you write about. Better yet, you look exactly like Azora Reign, the bestselling paranormal romance author, and all these people want to meet you."

"Where did you get your pen name from anyway?" Colt asks from the back seat.

"Azora was my mom's middle name."

My hands are shaking. How can I sign books when I'm about to pass out?

"Then you got this," Colt says. "She's smiling down on you."

Gently, he cups my shoulder, clad in a white bodysuit. It's more like a long-sleeved, one-piece swimsuit with a silver turtleneck, intergalactic epaulets, and a black harness for my laser blaster. But instead of a plastic gun, I'm loaded with black Sharpies.

Colt's right. I think of my mom and clench my fists, lifting my chin.

I can do this.

Mom used to pay me a dollar for every short story I wrote on an old typewriter. I loved tapping away on that thing, and she loved supporting my dream. She raised me like a pro.

"You sure you don't want us to stay with you?"

Beau sounds worried, not about my outfit celebrating my genre. It's for his fans, who have been rabid for me since their three pre-season wins.

Why?

Because when a reporter shoved a microphone in Beau's sexy, sweaty face in the locker room after their first win, asking why Beau kept smiling on the field, he answered, "What can I say? I love the game. I love my team. And I love who's waiting at home for me."

I haven't been able to leave his house since. There's no way I'll go to their games.

Not yet.

When Beau had the idea of my first book signing to cheer me up, I decided to turn it into my debut. I want to be surrounded by *my* kind of people in *my* favorite world—a bookstore brimming with romance readers.

But some people in line are wearing his Atlanta jersey, and some are press for sure. So, that's why I came up with the plan with his publicist to give away signed Touchdown panties to every reader and fan here, too.

What can I say?

Go shameless or go home.

"Nope, I got this," I answer Beau while he stops his truck in front of the back door. "Vale's in there to help me. Ruby, too. There's a shit-ton of security. We're giving away romance books, football panties, blue alien sports bottles, and purple penis-shaped iced sugar cookies to all. What could go wrong?"

"Okay. Go for the win, baby." Beau leans over so I meet his lips halfway. "Text us if you need us."

We kiss, then kiss again. And I want to kiss Colt too, so I glance and make sure no paps are hiding. We're clear, so quickly, I lean toward the backseat, and we steal a kiss.

"Proud of you," Colt whispers over my lips.

"Where are you taking him?" I ask.

"Top Golf," Colt answers. "I'm taking him on a date so your dad won't hand us our asses the first time we play."

"Sorry, guys." I grab my Hello Kitty backpack. "That's the one thing my dad does better than you."

Beau grins as I open the door. "You saying you doubt our strokes?"

"Not if you keep practicing your strokes with Colt," I tease back. "See you in four hours."

"We'll be right here," Colt answers.

THERE ARE moments you want to slow time and this is one.

I don't want this afternoon to end. I'm overwhelmed by meeting my readers. I can't give enough hugs, signatures, and selfies because I cherish them.

All those lonely days when I felt like the geeky author in middle school, the one not invited to sit at the popular romance girls' table. The one who barely made ends meet, so I sold dildos to get by.

Little did I know it was fate all along.

Because that's where I met my friends at Delta's. That's where my twin and I grew even closer. That's where I proudly sold vibrators to pay for kinky, cute alien book cover art. And that's where this guy I loved to hate in college stumbled in on Valentine's Day, buying a French maid's outfit and stealing my heart all over again.

And now, he shares it with his best friend.

"What's your name?" I smile, asking the next reader in line.

"Brittany," she answers. "But can you make it out to 'Lore'? That's my BOB's name."

"I sure can!" I start signing the title page of her copy of *Willuf the Wilder*. "You know I have lots of BOBs, too."

"BOBs?" Vale sits beside me, prepping the next book for me to sign, while Ruby's on my right, handing out my gift bags. "I thought his name is *Beau*."

"BOBs are battery-operated boyfriends," my proud reader explains, and I high-five her with Sharpie in hand.

"But is it true? Is Beau Bronson really your boyfriend? Is he really Valen and Willuf?"

Heat flames my cheeks. She's the fortieth person or so to ask me, and finally, I'm not shy about it. I'm proud. I just hate the half-lie. I hate hiding Colt while revealing Beau.

"Yes." I close her signed book, handing it over with a wink. "The sexy bastard inspires all my alien smut."

She giggles, her inked hand hiding her pretty smile. She can't be barely twenty, wearing rainbow-framed glasses, cute blue lipstick, and two neon green star pimple stickers. I love her. I'm looking in the mirror ten years ago.

"You know," she shares, "I started watching football because of you and him. I hated it, but now I'm an Atlanta fan."

"Oh, then you'll love the Touchdown panties in your gift bag. I signed those for you, too. But don't tell anyone." I hook my finger, drawing my kindred spirit in. She leans forward with eager eyes while I whisper, "I hated football, too, but then I saw his ass in those tight white football pants, and I fell in love."

Who?

Beau and Colt have peaches I bite every night. Seriously, I do it in bed and drive them crazy.

"Are you going to his games?" Brittany asks, tightly clutching my book to her chest. "I'll look for you on the screen if you are."

"Soon," I answer. "Probably his first home game."

"Is your next book about him too?"

I chew my lip. "Yep."

It's about my men.

She bounces in her Doc Martens, so I stand and hug her. Then I walk around, and Ruby snaps a photo for us, too. "I'll be back in a few months," I promise her, "to sign my next book for you if you want."

"Want?" She exclaims. "I can't wait!"

The afternoon goes by too fast. By the time I've met everyone in line, I have four gift bags left, an exhausted twin, and an efficient new friend packing up my remaining supplies for me to pick up tomorrow.

"Y'all saved my ass today. Thank you. Let me buy you dinner," I offer. "Girls night out. We can do a strip club to celebrate. Seriously, they have the best sushi. Pun intended."

Ruby grins, her face tilting with regret. "Sorry. I can't. I have plans."

"Me, too," Vale replies. "Maybe next time."

What? Since when does my twin pass on a VIP table, rainbow rolls, and nude bodies?

Vale's staying at the Ritz. Ruby said she is, too. When they turned down my offer to stay with us, I was too nervous about today, but now?

"What are y'all hiding?"

Vale bats her lashes. "Nothing."

"Please. I can smell your cunty conspiracy."

Ruby laughs. "If you can smell me, tell me. That's serious Girl Code."

"All I smell is a secret queef between you two."

My eyes bounce from Vale, her hair in another elegant twist, and Ruby, who looks equally glamorous, and that's when I notice.

"Wait," I ask Vale, leaning closer. "When did you pierce your face?"

"A few weeks ago." Blood rushes Vale's guilty cheeks. "It's no big deal. It's a Monroe piercing. You know, for our name."

"Uh, you know, for your bullshit." I laugh, pointing to Ruby. "It matches hers. Same diamond. Same place. And you're both staying at the Ritz and bailing on me tonight. I know you're in a pussy pact, planning something. What is it?"

It's not a stretch. Vale's the manager of Delta's and Stacey, the owner, said Ruby shops there a lot lately.

Want more clues?

Vale's been fucking and falling in love with Mr. Nash Allen during his secret meetings. And Ruby fronts a secret group of closeted NFL players and other professionals who host poly parties.

Professionals? Parties? Meetings? Poly?

"Oh my god," I gasp. "Please tell me you're in a three-decker with Mr. Allen. Please tell me you're the only human alive who'll marry Vale." I grab Ruby's hand. "I've always wanted a badass sister."

"You cum sponge," Vale scoffs. "*I'm* your badass sister. And no, we're not in a three-decker with Nash."

But I glance at Ruby, searching her eyes.

My twin is too good at lying to me. For years, she denied brushing our dog with my hairbrush.

But Ruby is new to our deception. Something glimmers in her dark blue eyes. "Ah-hah!" I point. "I knew it! You're up to something."

"Not everyone eats three-layered cake." Vale sounds annoyed, which means I'm right.

"Uh, obviously." I laugh. "You two are with more than three. You're in a baker's dozen. Question is with who? Who gave you matching Monroes?"

Ruby shakes her head. "We were warned you'd do this."

"Do what?" I flex my hand over my chest. "Spot a cocks

and cunts party a mile away? Sorry, not sorry, I'm a blood-hound for kink."

"No." Vale jumps in. "We were warned you'd ruin the surprise."

"What surprise?"

"The one waiting outside the back door for you," Vale confesses. "The reason we have plans tonight and aren't staying at your house. The reason I've been a mule of sex supplies for your horny boyfriends. So shut up and go have a cocky celebration." She kisses the air. "Love you, bitch."

"Love you, cunt." Ruby does the same.

But I wag a finger, walking backward toward the storage room door, hoping to glimpse their true conspiracy.

"Okay," I say. "I'll go get surprise fucked, but I know you're up to some fucking, too."

They don't answer, and my wheels are still turning about my twin and friend while I wave goodbye to the store manager and her staff.

Then I push open the back door. It slams behind me as I step into the Atlanta night. It's warm. It's dark. It takes a second to see...

Beau's truck isn't here.

No one is.

"What the fu—"

I don't even finish my curse before I'm grabbed from behind, a hand covering my screaming mouth. My pulse explodes, my ears ringing in terror as lips press to one.

"What's your safe word, Kitten?"

I sag, "Kumquat," muttering into Beau's big hand. I'd know his safe sound, his smell, his voice at a swinger's party.

"Good girl," he jeers. Headlights flick on in the alley. A truck engine roars to life. A blindfold falls over my eyes while Beau taunts, "You're ours now. We're kidnapping you. We're taking you to our lair, where we'll tie you up and fuck you in every dirty way possible. You're our little human slut to breed tonight."

Oh, good Goddess of My Kinkiest Fantasy.

I'm naming our first daughter Ruby Vale.

I'm so damn thankful those bitches sold my ass out to alien whoremongers.

Blair

CHAPTER TWENTY-EIGHT

"Please tell me you're taking a video of this," I beg, blindfolded as a seatbelt clicks me into the backseat of Beau's truck.

"Hush, Human, or we'll muzzle you, too." That's Beau, trying to sound stern. "Now, sit on your hands and don't move."

He closes my door and must be switching with Colt, who was driving, because another door clicks open, then slams shut. The heat approaching me in the backseat wafts of Colt's cologne: citrus and bergamot.

Beau smells like apples and sage.

"She's pretty." Colt tucks my hair behind my ear. "Drive while I play with her."

Atlanta traffic is forgiving at night. Our trip home will be thirty minutes of this panty-melting, kidnapping role-play.

"Look at these naked thighs I'm spreading." Rough hands splay my knees open. "Look at her boots. They're sexy." Colt brushes his hand up my inner thigh.

"They stay on tonight," Beau taunts from the driver's seat.

Then turn signals and road noise are all I hear. Beau's not playing music, while Colt's touch makes me gasp.

He skims his fingers over the silky crotch of my bodysuit, muttering, "Mmmm, it's getting wet. I've never had human pussy before. I bet it's tight. I bet I can barely fit inside it. I bet she'll feel so good; we'll breed her at least twice tonight."

Thank you, Oscar Orgies.

Colt's acting. He's getting into his role. Maybe he'll do porn once he retires from the NFL? He's got the cock for the career, that's for sure.

"What are these?" He pinches my erect nipple, then my other pearling under my suit. I didn't want panty or bra lines to ruin my cosplay outfit, but now my lady cream will.

"Stop," I moan. "Don't touch me."

"Sorry." Colt withdraws, stammering, "I didn't mean to—"

"That's not her safe word." Beau breaks his performance, too. "She likes it. She'll say 'kumquat' if she wants you to stop."

"Oh," Colt rushes, "that's right. Sorry, I forgot. I just thought you didn't like it and—"

"I don't like it," I protest. "I hate you. You're so big and disgusting. Don't you dare touch me, you vicious creature."

I swear I can feel Colt's smile and the thrilled laughter he's choking down. We all are, but my clit is clapping for blind groping. I goad, "Go to hell, you nasty beast."

"Oh, I'm a very vicious beast." Colt gravels his voice, his

words steaming over my ear. "But you're the one who's about to be nasty for me." His fingers find my hard, covered clit. "I heard human pussies love alien cock." He spanks it, and I moan. "Is that true? You secretly love alien cock?"

"No." I start writhing against his touch, teasing over my pussy. "I hate it."

"Mmmm, you hate how long it is or how thick it is?"

"We'll have to prepare her," Beau warns, turning left. "She has to be ready to breed."

Ready?

I'm already there, bent over and spreading my cheeks with a red target tattooed on my pussy, letting them mate me for life.

"Wonder how you get a human ready?" Colt tugs at the center zipper of my suit. Slowly, he drags it down from my neck to my cleavage to an inch below my belly button. "Wonder how we get her wet enough to take our huge cocks?"

Tugging my suit aside, he exposes my breast, then my other. But the fabric is tight. I'm sure it only presses them together, creating a helluva show for him.

"Goddamn," he growls. "What are these juicy things to suck?"

Suddenly, a warm mouth is claiming my nipple so hard I cry out. Then he takes my other one, his hands squeezing them together. Rolling his tongue over my nipples, he brutally sucks them, too.

"Colt," I gasp, then he bites, and I remember. "Valr, you vicious beast, stop."

"Stop sucking these sweet titties?" Evilly, he chuckles over the drool he's laving over my nipples. "Never. You're our little human slut to play with."

Colt doesn't stop, and I can't stop moaning. I'm aching,

loving it, sitting on my hands, and wanting to grab him, but I don't. I love being trapped in this pleasure.

"Mmm," Colt plops his lips off my breast, jostling their weight together. "I heard you can fuck human titties, too. Is that right, Falcon?" He uses my new heroine's name. "Little human sluts love having their titties fucked? Then their tight pussies filled?"

"No!" I gasp. "We hate our asses being fucked, too."

Colt chuckles at my pathetic attempt at reverse psychology. "I can't wait to see my creamy alien seed spilling out of you, Falcon." He pinches my nipple. "Your ass. Your pussy. Your mouth. We're going to share your holes and fill you up and—"

"Fuck, y'all are turning me on too much," Beau growls from the driver's seat. With a jolt, his truck sways right, like he's taking a hard turn.

"What are you doing?" Colt huffs, pulling away from my breasts.

"Shut up, Valr," Beau answers in character. "We're making a pit stop." In a lurch, his truck stops.

"What if we get caught?" But Colt's not in character.

"We're fine," Beau answers. "I have tinted windows, and this gas station is so busy no one will notice us parked here."

The engine cuts off. Beau's door opens, then slams shut. "I can't believe he—" Colt starts to marvel as I hear the backdoor open.

"Move over," Beau demands as the door closes.

"Oh fuck," Colt mutters, his arm pressed against mine while I hear fabric rustling and muffled grunts.

"What are y'all doing?" I'm trying to stay in character and be a good little silent human slut for my alien abductors, but this is too damn real.

"Oh fuck," Colt mutters again. "He's gonna suck my cock in a parking lot."

That's when I feel another touch. It's Beau rubbing over my fabric, seeking my pussy. He must be kneeling on the floorboard between Colt's thighs pressed against mine.

"I'm going to taste his seed," Beau taunts, "then he'll taste mine. And you'll be a dirty little human, listening to us suck cock right beside you."

"I want to watch you. I want to help you."

"No," Beau demands, "you're going to get so wet hearing us. But if you're good, we'll let you taste us, too."

"Oh fuck," Colt keeps huffing while a zipper drags open. "Oh, fuck yes, I can't believe you're doing this, Beau." He groans. He's way off-script and turning me on even more when he growls, "Yes, that's it. Suck it. Mmm, let me feel your tongue. Damn, you look so hot with my cock in your mouth. Let me feel your beard on it. Yes, like that. Rub your cheek on it. Yes, look at me. Keep looking at me while you suck my cock."

Then there are *slurps* and *gulps* and the deep *glucking* of Beau's throat filling the air along with Colt's groans.

All I can hear is their pleasure. All I can feel are their hands together, rubbing over my pussy. All I can imagine is what Beau looks like, choking on Colt's cock in the backseat of his truck parked in a gas station with customers and cars roaming outside.

It's so forbidden; I can see it blind. It's so hot, I'm going to come. I'm so close, but Colt beats me to it.

"Fuck yes. Fuck yes, Beau," he grunts. "Open that mouth. I'm coming in it."

With a buck, Colt's body jumps beside mine, his deep grunt filling the cabin.

In a moment, I feel bodies moving before lips are pressed to mine.

They're Beau's while Colt growls, "Open your mouth, little slut, and taste my cum too." With his deep kiss, Beau shares Colt's cream with me, and I moan. It's salty and erotic, Beau's tongue laving over mine, sharing their lust, before it's Beau's turn.

Their bodies rustle and move, switching beside mine. A horn honks in the parking lot, and a man shouts about a six-pack.

"We're fine," Beau barks. "That's not for us." I hear another zipper open before he growls, "Now fucking suck me, too, Colt. Wrap your lips around it. That's it. You can take it." He groans before praising, "Yeah, baby, choke on it. As much as you can. Goddamn, y'all made me so hard."

It's Colt's sounds now. His *slurps* and *licks* and *glucking*. It's Beau's *mmmm*, his hand cupping my pussy again, rubbing my clit, matching the tempo of his hand with the sound of Colt sucking his cock.

"Our little slut is so wet for this," Beau taunts. "She gets so wet at how we love cock, too. Don't you, baby? You love us sucking cocks." But then he stops. He leaves me writhing. I'm about to come before it sounds like Beau is. "Yes, yes, you love my cock, too, Colt. Take it," he growls at him. "Fuck baby, take it. Take it. Gimme that tongue. I'm coming."

Beau's thighs shake against mine, and a deep grunt erupts from Colt's choking throat. I'm soaked. I'm aching. I'm blindfolded and sitting on my hands, needing relief, but I won't do it.

I love this too much.

I love us too much.

Their bodies move. Then, Colt's salty, creamy kiss takes mine, too.

He keeps kissing me while a door opens and shuts and opens again. He doesn't stop taking my lips, my neck, my nipples again while Beau revs the engine back to life and races us home.

THE LAST MINUTES there go by in a shameless blur. The taste of Beau and Colt on my tongue drives me mad. I'm insanely thirsty for them.

Then we park. The truck engine turns off.

I feel Colt's hands silently lifting me into Beau's arms. I'm draped in Beau's embrace as he carries me through his home.

We're climbing stairs. We're going down a hallway. I know his house. We're stepping into the guest bedroom I use.

Like the team they are, they work without a sound, which only heightens my suspense. I'm manhandled, lifted, my bottom set on a swinging padded strap while hands guide mine to hold handles at my shoulder height. My legs are lifted until my heels are secured in stirrups, too.

"A door swing," I sigh, elated, gently letting myself fall against the cool wooden door behind me. "Someone got a Delta's special delivery," I tease.

"Hush," Beau barks.

"We warned you," Colt adds. "Now we'll have to tie you in it, too."

Oh darn.

Silk wraps my wrists, binding me so I can't let go of the handles. Tugs at my boots bind my ankles, too. I'm stuck, suspended above the floor, my back to a door with a lover's swing secured to it.

I know the swing well. I've sold dozens of them.

But I've never had this happen.

"Let's admire our little human to fuck," Colt says, committed to his performance. So is Beau.

Hands grope, and fabric rips. My one-piece costume doesn't stand a chance against their brute force. They shred it into remnants that sway from my remaining long sleeves, the rest of my body exposed and open, the rush of air thrilling my naked flesh.

But of course, they left my boots on.

"Damn, she's wet." Colt tickles a fingertip over my vulnerable clit. I moan while he taunts, "We can breed her all night tied up like this."

"Umm," Beau agrees. "Then, leave her like that. Let her get really wet while we get ready."

Get ready?

Who the hell isn't ready?

But I don't protest. I just listen to them leave the room. *I think.* I just hang in a door swing with my pussy wide open, and yes, it makes me even wetter if their phones are on tripods somewhere, recording this.

I have no idea how long they're gone. It feels like forever when you're waiting, blindfolded and horny as hell for a good double alien cock breeding.

"Fuck!" I hear Beau in the hallway, the sound returning my way.

But he's laughing, not mad. So is Colt. It sounds like they're wrestling, like playing grab ass when mine needs a good fuck. *Now.*

"Whoops." Colt laughs, too. "Call the house painter. You just got it on the wall. And look. It's getting on the carpet."

Got what on the wall? On the carpet?

"Fuck it. It's worth it," Beau replies. "Come here. You need more on your abs." He pauses. "Turn around. You need more on your ass, too."

I hear silence, then a smacking spank of flesh before Colt huffs, "Don't get it *in* my ass, too. It's not made for that."

What in the hell are they doing?

I have no idea, but I sense them entering the room again. I sense them drawing near.

"Dayum," Beau sighs. "Look at her now. She's so fucking open and swollen for us."

"Fuck, she's ready. She's in heat. Look, her pretty pussy's so pink."

"No one's ever ready for Willuf, the Wilder, and Valr, the Vicious." I can hear it. Beau's choking down his laughter. "Or are you, Falcon? Are you ready for us to breed you now? We need a good little human to take our cocks and share our seed."

"No," I huff, trying to twist in my stirrups, but I'm trapped. I'm about to be fucked senseless. *Thank God.* "No. Don't touch me."

"You mean... " Hands tug my blindfold down. It's Beau, taunting while I blink, trying to focus. "Don't fuck you with our huge alien cocks?"

Holy.

Blue.

Boyfriends.

"What the alien fuck?" I'm shocked. I'm laughing. I'm touched. I'm so turned on.

Where are my pom-poms? I'm going to cheer because I'm about to be fucked by two huge hot naked men—*my men*—covered in blue body paint.

You know the kind of body paint football fans use?

Yeah, Beau and Colt are haphazardly smeared from feet to neck in it. They swiped some across their smiling faces, too. It's in their beards. It's in Colt's hair knot and Beau's waves.

They're as cute as they are hot-as-blue-fuck.

Hell, they've left a trail of blue everywhere. Footprints across the carpet. Handprints on white doorjamb.

I bet it looks like a blueberry exploded down the hallway with their wrestling and fucking around. I can't imagine what Beau's bathroom looks like.

I want to laugh and kiss them. I want to love them forever. I will never forget this.

They look like massive shredded porno Smurfs in love with me, with each other.

They're stroking off, standing shoulder-to-shoulder between my swinging legs—half smirking, half aroused.

"I love you guys," it escapes my smiling lips. "I love you so much." Hell, I'm crying happy, horny tears, too.

"Hush, Human," Beau barks, but his eyes laugh. They match his splotchy blue body. "We're about to breed you."

"Yeah," Colt reveals what he's hiding behind his back, "so whose seed you want first?"

In one hand is Colt's real cock. It's long and hard and turning blue with twists from his painted grasp. In his other?

"Oh my god," I sigh. "A bull sheath."

"Such a kinky girl," Colt chuckles. "You know your dildos."

"It's not a dildo," I gasp while he drags it down my

cleavage. "It's an eight by two-inch cosmic purple bull sheath penis sleeve with a flared head and prominent medial ring. I sold seven last year. They're mouthwatering."

"Did you sell any of these?" Beau reveals what he's hiding behind his back.

"An Ice Barbarian Sheath? In nebula blue?" I've died and gone to alien porn heaven. "Its widest girth is almost four inches. I only sold one to a courageous man. I was so jealous."

"Hope you don't mind. We snuck a peek at your current draft," Beau confesses. "We knew Willuf was big and blue. But who knew Valr was so long and purple?"

"Oh my god." Shyness hits me—stupid emotion. I can't stand it. "Did you read the last chapter? The one where they—"

"Sure did," Colt replies, grinning. "Damn, woman. Way to make us happy, hard, and honored."

Beau cocks a grin. "Is that your fantasy, Blair? That last chapter, and how they do it?"

"No," I lie. "I don't know what you're talking about."

"Good." Beau starts stroking his cock. He's getting so hard. And blue. "Because no more talking." He drops his voice. "Watch while we mate you together. While you can't fight us. You have to take us until you fall in love with us, too."

Too late. No matter the universe, I'm so in love with them.

I'm shaking with anticipation. With fear. With lust. With love, they did this for me.

This is so damn cute and corny and erotic and...

Holy porno we're about to make.

I glance over their beefy blue shoulders. They have their phones on tripods, strategically placed. They're recording my ultimate fantasy.

I can't believe my eyes as Colt kneels, teasing, "I gotta taste how sweet this little human pussy is first." He spears his tongue into my cunt, and I moan, so desperate and ready, while Beau turns for my nightstand. He knows if it's in my room, there will be a cornucopia of sex supplies in it.

"Stop," I sigh to Colt. "Stop. That feels too good. Valr, you're making my pussy so wet, and I hate it. I hate you."

This performance? This pleasure? I'm gazing down at Colt. He's getting blue paint on my thighs and the carpet, but we don't care. He starts sucking my clit, staring up at me, making me shake while Beau stalks my way.

"Dirty little girl," Beau taunts. "Look at what Daddy found in your nightstand." He holds a big bottle of lube and a little pink fingertip vibrator. "Have you been a bad girl, playing with your pussy while your daddies were gone?"

"No." I love my fib.

That's the smallest toy I play with when they're gone, when I miss them so much.

"Mmm," Colt hums over my clit. "Her little lying human pussy tastes so sweet."

"Get up!" Beau shouts at him. "And fucking share her with me. She's mine, remember?"

"No." Colt rises. "She's mine now, too."

I want to say, "Now, now, boys. Share and share alike."

But that's not in my book, and saying, "No. Don't you dare share me. Don't you dare fuck me with those huge cocks," is equally fun.

"Oh, but secretly," Beau pours lube over my mound, "you're a dirty little girl, and you want these huge cocks, don't you?"

He lets the lube coat my sex until it's dripping from my tingling, exposed flesh. He hands the bottle to Colt, who glazes his cock, too, before he secures the long-hanging sheath around it.

Lube and blue paint are everywhere. We are definitely replacing the carpet with hardwood floors, and who cares? Who cares when it's all fun and love and trust? Who cares when Colt's cock looks part alien, part human, and part stallion about to mount me?

"Fuck her first, Valr," Beau commands Colt. "That's the Wilder custom. I give you my wife, my woman, and she gives us peace."

Oh my god, they did read my draft.

They do love me so much.

A happy tear escapes because they're gonna make me so damn dirty, too.

And to hear Beau say *wife*. To watch him rub his thumb with the fingernail vibrator attached to it slowly over my clit as we gaze down at Colt, who slowly lifts his wide, flared purple tip to press inside me?

"*Yeeessss,*" I moan because smutty fact is so much better than science fiction...

Sometimes.

"Damn," Colt groans, watching his obscene length enter me. "Fuck this is hot," he marvels, and we agree. Our gaze is trapped, looking down while he penetrates my vulnerable entrance.

"You're too long," I protest, twisting in my restraints. "Your cock is too long."

It's not. It's perfect. It feels incredible. My pussy feels electric with desire. It wants more, but his sheath won't fit all the way. Still, it's the naughty thought that counts.

Because Colt leans forward, gently kissing my adoring lips while Beau rubs my clit, his body pressed to Colt's between my thighs.

Then Colt lifts from my lips, staring down, admiring while he flexes his abs, slowly gliding more in. "Fuck yes, take me," he growls. He doesn't stop. I don't want him to. I'm not using my safe word. I trust him too much. I want him too much. "Look at your little pussy taking my inches. Damn, you're creaming on it. You want it."

"She loves it," Beau coaxes, thrilling my clit, too. "Such a dirty human for us, loving that long, purple, alien bull cock fucking her pussy. Damn, she's gonna come on it."

I start shaking. It's the taboo. It's the care. It's the full sensation. It's the forbidden, sexy sight when it's just an act, but it's not.

It's our truth. It's our love.

They overwhelm me.

The orgasm exploding through my sex is sudden and severe. It's a million shattering sparks of pleasure, and I can't speak. I just watch, trapped in the swing, trapped by the sight, then trapped, screaming, shaking while I hold on to Colt's adoring stare. He's in awe, watching me. "Yes, Blair." He breaks character. "Yes, look at me making you come so hard."

"Please!" I scream. "Please, I can't take any more."

Yes, I can, and they give it.

Colt carefully pulls out, and Beau gently eases in. They feel so different; it's perfection.

New sensations storm my pussy.

Beau's blue sheath isn't long, but it's obscenely thick, as inch after widening inch stretches me to receive him.

This is like our Valentine's night. The first time Beau gave me my fantasy, the one he inspired.

Then he took my heart and left me with his.

Now, it's his forever. It's Colt's forever.

It's us. It's who we are together; we are so kinky and cute and fun. I can't believe my luck.

Colt rubs my clit with his bare thumb this time as Beau pushes in, then drags out, then pushes in again. I moan, loving it. Loving how he can't go all the way. The foreign-looking ridged blue appendage on his real cock barely fits into my slick pink dripping cunt, but it drives us crazy.

I can tell by Beau's ragged breath, trapped gaze, and Colt's, which matches his; they're feral for this.

We can't stop staring at what we're doing, at what they're doing to me. It's so damn lewd and luscious, and we love it.

"Yes, look at her," Colt urges, circling my wet, tingling nub, making my thighs tremble. "Look at her taking that big alien dick like a sweet slut." He rattles my clit, ruthlessly teasing, "Baby, you're so dirty for your big daddies, aren't you? Loving all our cock inside you? You come so hard for it, don't you, dirty girl?"

Colt's naughty words and a ridge on Beau's sheath hit a sensitive spot inside and it's euphoric. It's explosive again. Another orgasm drops like a bright bomb through my body, and I jolt. I buck.

"Fuck!" I come so hard screaming, "Don't!" I'm trapped in my fantasy, so don't take me out. "Don't fuck me anymore. I can't stop coming on your big cocks, and I hate it. You're making me such a whore. You're taking turns with me."

"Damn, Kitten!" Beau throws his chin up. He's fighting the fantasy, too. "Fuck, yes, we will. We're gonna take our real turns now."

Carefully, he withdrawals before tugging the sheath off his cock with a *slurp,* dropping it on the carpet. So does Colt.

They stand so close, their muscular blue bodies touching between my thighs, bound open for them to begin.

They start the most carnal, savage, and sweet sight of my life. The most feral and base and beautiful sensation I've ever felt.

They give me my final chapter.

Colt drives his bare cock inside me and pulls out. His length hovers long and waiting while Beau goes next.

Slowly, Beau penetrates me, open and dripping, my sex splayed and glistening for their exploit. Then he pulls out while Colt's tip slides along Beau's length, aiming for me again. He takes his next turn while Beau rubs his swollen crown against Colt's base.

Then, in and out and in and out, they slide inside me, watching as they alternate. They take. They give. They share. They shamelessly rub their cocks together while they fill my aching pussy, my sensitive walls clenching, thrilled with every penetration.

I moan at their relentless entrance and exit, at how they use me. They claim me, and I don't want this to ever end.

Please, don't let us end.

"God, yes." I start crying in pleasure, like actual tears of rapture, of ecstasy. "Take turns. Share me. Oh my god, Beau, Colt, don't stop. Please. I want you. I love you. Oh, my god, look at us."

We're connected. We're captivated. We're forever bound by the primal sight, by the natural sin that isn't one.

Nothing this intimate and intense is wrong. It's so right.

"You love this, don't you, Blair?" Beau grabs the strap holding my leg. Colt grabs the other. Their other hands hold their shafts, guiding their claim, sharing their fortune. "You love our dicks taking turns with your pretty pussy.

Fuck baby. You're so beautiful. Look at us sharing you." He grunts with his next thrust. "Damn, we fucking love you."

He pulls out, staring into my eyes as Colt takes his turn, thrusting inside me. I cry out while he growls, "Fuck yes." Colt starts shaking. "Fuck yes, we do. We love you, Blair." He doesn't pull out. "Fuck, Beau, let me feel you rub your dick on mine while I come inside her sweet pussy."

Our alien fantasy is gone. Because this is us, raw and rough and real, it's so beautiful.

"Do you want it, Blair?" Colt drives his length inside me, his thrusts deep and seeking. "Can I come inside you because goddamn I need to? I need to give you everything I have."

"Do it," I beg. "Do it."

Feverishly, Beau thrills my clit with his finger vibrator, his hard cock rubbing against Colt's exposed base, against the veins swelling in Colt's shaft. The sight. The pleasure. The sensation. It binds so tight in my core, coiling tight, waiting...

"Watch yourselves come," Beau says. "Both of you. Do it. Come so hard for us."

I am. I shake. It's building. It's so intense, I'm afraid to let it go because Colt's shaking too.

We're watching where we're joined, where Colt's pumping inside me, where Beau's cock is rubbing on Colt's. Colt is so swollen, and Beau is so hard, waiting for his turn.

I'm the turn. I'm the one. I'm the woman they love and share and give and fuck and come inside...

And my entire body erupts. My eyes roll. My edges crack. I'm about to burst through my flesh.

"Come, baby." Beau spanks my clit. "Squirt your love."

I do. So does Colt. We burst. We cry out. I gush, pouring over Colt's dripping length. It makes him growl, burying every inch inside me while he grunts, leaning forward, cupping my face before claiming my gasping lips with his kiss.

I can't find my breath or sanity and don't want it. I only want this, and I only want more. I'm not done.

I'll never be done with them.

"Hurry," Colt huffs over my mouth. "Keep her coming." He pulls away. He leaves my shaking body, and Beau takes it.

Gone are the sweet blue men who gave me my fantasy because Colt looks possessed and Beau looks savage. He's ferocious. His angry cock claims what's waiting for him, what's his, too.

"Fuck, Blair," Beau snarls with primal thrusts, driving into me, slamming me against the door. I'm shaking, an orgasm still screaming through my sex while he demands, "Yes, keep fucking squirting for me. Goddamn, baby, yes. All over my dick. Fuck, one day, we're gonna breed you for real. You're gonna have our babies."

I'm not in control. Beau is. He's taking me again. I can't stop it. I *am* in heat. I *am* an animal for him.

"Beau, please! Please!" He knows how to do it. He knows how to end us, how to satisfy this maddening hunger for each other while Colt takes us there.

He squeezes the base of Beau's cock so tight, his other hand strumming my clit, and it's an eternity of bursting lights.

I can't see.

I can only explode again.

I can only come, helpless, while I hear Beau coming inside me, too, with his pained, driving grunts. Then he stills, buried inside me, while I feel Colt lean down, tenderly kissing my clit.

Bliss won't stop shaking through my bones. Heaven lights up my veins. Euphoria drips down my cheeks, the ones suspended above the floor and those suspended above my crying smile.

My panting lips receive Beau's kiss, Colt's, Beau's, then back and forth; they kiss me until we're laughing.

Until I'm completely covered in their blue paint and love.

BEAU

CHAPTER TWENTY-NINE

"**Break out our poly playbook.**"

Four games may not be a winning streak, but... yeah, it is.

We're crushing it. We dominate on the field. Everyone is saying this is our year, and we feel it.

Atlanta is hyped. We're a well-oiled, sweaty machine on the gridiron. We beat Carolina, Green Bay, Detroit, and then Jacksonville. Away games or home game advantage, it doesn't matter.

"Goddamn!" Coach Williams slaps my back. "Bronson, I don't care how you're doing it, but keep it up. This is your best season yet."

I glance across the locker room at Colt. He just smirks, naked, slinging a towel over his inked shoulder before heading to the showers.

The press is interviewing Martinez and Goodwin. They

executed a helluva trick play to secure our win against Jacksonville.

It was late in the fourth quarter. We were down by three in the midfield. I held the ball, and everyone scrambled, thinking I'd throw to Hawke as I have for most plays, but I called a new one. I threw thirty yards to Martinez, who, instead of going down with the ball, passed it to Goodwin, who was wide open, streaking down the field for the touchdown.

Hell yeah, they deserve the praise.

That shit was incredible.

"Goddamn! Way to execute." Coach Williams slaps their shoulders, too. "Sorry," he says to the reporter. "You filming?"

She laughs, shaking her head no while I try sneaking by her. Not because I'm naked and need a shower, too. It's because the press and fans are feral for Blair.

They won't stop asking me about her.

Thankfully, some fans with a box suite in our stadium are also big fans... *of Blair's.* It seems the CEO of Atlanta's famous beverage company is also a romance reader. She saw the frenzy Blair experienced in the stands during our first home game and invited her to join her in their company's suite.

So, our woman is safe from the crowds and fans, but not the press.

Neither am I.

"Bronson. Bronson." The reporter snags me sneaking by.

I turn, nude and smiling. "Yeah?"

"It's your fourth straight win," she says. "Can you talk about your confidence in Colton Hawke? He's leading in receiving yards. Are you surprised?"

"No. He's a big part of our offense. Our players are really showing their blocking skills and their flexibility, too, this season. Martinez. Goodwin. Smith. Everyone. Our defense, as well. We got some damn good players."

"And you?" She looks me in the eye, not at my naked body. She's a pro. "Are you looking forward to Philadelphia next? They're 4-0, too."

"Yeah. Should be a good matchup."

"Speaking of matchups," she has to ask. It was all over ESPN this week. "Is what Duncan Monroe said about you and his daughter, Blair, true?"

I don't have to force my smile. "It's true I'm in love... " I pause, "...with the game." Then, I wink, ending the interrogation.

Off camera, the reporter winks back. It's not unprofessional. She understands I'm trying to respect Blair and protect her privacy.

The hype about us is out of control.

Then, her father bragged to a reporter last week that Blair and I are getting married, like any day now, and he made it worse.

It's not that I don't want to get married. I do. But not now.

Something special like that? I want to make a romantic proposal. I want to do it right. I want to give Blair her dream wedding with no expenses spared. So, it has to be done in the off-season, which is months from now.

Besides, where does that leave Colt?

I suds up beside him. Being naked with Colt and dozens of men in the shower is nothing new. It's part of the job. It never fazed me.

But reporters asking about marriage?

That's awkward.

Even our teammates feel it.

"Bronson!" Goodwin shouts across the tiled room. "Marry that hot Monroe woman, so they'll quit asking about her and focus on the *real* story." Goodwin beams, shampoo suds streaming down his brown skin. "Me and my Good Wins!"

I laugh. So does Colt.

"Come on now!" I shout back. "You know the only fucking ring I'll score this season!"

And the team hollers, "Rise up!"

It's the Atlanta slogan and true. At this rate, Super Bowl rings are in our grasp.

Colt laughs about it on the way to the players' parking lot. "Just elope over Thanksgiving," he says. "Do a vacation wedding on the beach so I can be the best man in a tight white Speedo."

I'm holding Blair's hand. Fans are waiting by the fence, wanting autographs and shouting our names.

"Oh," Blair jokes back, "I don't want a wedding, but I'm all about a topless beach vacation. Or a fake wedding role-play. Some golden cock rings. Some diamond anal plugs. A wedding dress we can trash while I'm the naughty bride, and y'all are two dirty grooms. Wait? Please tell me you own tuxes."

"Two grooms? I like that idea." I lift her hand to my lips, planting a kiss. "And yeah, we own tuxes."

"Hell, no," Colt scoffs. "I'm not ruing my Dior with cum stains. We can rent role-play tuxes."

"So," I laugh, "you'd rather start wild rumors when Atlanta's QB and running back rent tuxes from the mall and return them covered in cock snot? I can see the Touchdown panties *and* tapioca pudding fans would throw on the field after that."

Blair starts laughing, too, but then Colt stops, pointing to the fence at the edge of the lot. "Dude," he says. "Look at all those kids. We gotta say hello."

"We will," I answer, beeping my truck remote. "Let's toss our shit in the cab and get the A/C running. I don't want more swamp ass."

September is still hot as hell in Atlanta. We're showered and fresh, and I'd like to stay that way.

I open the passenger door for Blair, but she rummages through her purse. "Just a sec," she says. "I gotta make sure I didn't leave my phone in the suite."

I think nothing of it, aiming for the driver's door while Colt opens the back door. But he also hangs back, checking his phone.

"What are you doing?" I climb in, starting the engine. "Watching the postgame already?"

But Colt doesn't answer. Neither does Blair. They don't get in the truck. *Something's off.* I sense it, pressing the big A/C button, and BOOM!

The A/C vents explode with confetti. Red, black, silver, and gold glitter showers my truck.

Blair starts howling. So does Colt. He's got his phone up, recording my face that looks like a million sparkling fairies farted on it.

"Okay, Ziggy Stardust!" Colt laughs, his phone shaking. "*Now,* let's sign autographs."

These fuckers.

Think I'm afraid?

Hell no. I grab the Sharpie I keep in my center console and proudly jump out of my truck, strutting toward the fence and our fans.

"Beau! Beau!" Two boys shout. "Will you sign our T-shirts?"

"Will do, little buddy."

I reach through the hole in the fence, signing T-shirts, balls, and more, until one girl asks, "Are you wearing princess makeup?"

"Sure am," I answer. "I borrowed it from Colton Hawke. He loves glitter."

The crowd laughs, and Colt joins me. Other players gather at the fence, too.

It's funny. Blair makes sure of it. She laughs all the way home while I bitch, "I'll be cleaning up this glitter shit for months."

"Nope. Years," Blair corrects me, sitting in the passenger seat, sprinkling some in my hair. Like it needs more.

"Let's scoop it into a bag and save it for your wedding," Colt jokes.

"Alright," Blair almost scolds. "Enough wedding talk. That's just my dad having diarrhea of the mouth. Ignore him. I do. No one's getting married. You're winning the Super Bowl."

But I'm quiet, half-focused on the traffic. Sometimes, I wish I had a chopper to take us home—it's that bad. We're crawling in six lanes down the interstate, and it's awkward.

I'm making it awkward, I know.

But I don't want to marry Blair without Colt. There's no hierarchy in our relationship. It's the three of us, equally. If we marry, it won't feel right. I won't leave Colt out. I can't. Half my heart beats for him, the other half for Blair.

I'm about to say something about the big pink poly elephant in the truck when Colt's phone sings "I Touch Myself" by the Divinyls.

"There's my girl!" Colt accepts the call, putting it on speaker.

"Good game," Ruby sings. "I'm so proud of my man!"

"Uh, thank you, darlin'." Colt impersonates Elvis. "Uh, thank you very much."

"Hey, cunt!" Blair calls out so Ruby can hear her.

"Hey DP Duchess!"

I roll my eyes, grinning. They do this every time. Ruby calls, and it's an hour of verbal grab ass—oh, and vaginal jabs, too.

"Hey, next week," Ruby says. "After you beat Philadelphia and get a Victory Monday off, fly to Charleston to celebrate."

I wince.

It almost feels like a jinx.

Yeah, I'm confident in our team. But making plans to have Monday off after a Sunday win? That feels like flirting with bad luck.

"Can we play it by ear?" Colt asks. He feels the same.

"Sure," Ruby answers. "We'll send the jet. *If* and when you win, jump on Sunday evening after the game, and we'll fly you back early Tuesday morning before practice."

"So, we spend two nights in Charleston?" Blair clarifies.

"If you want," Ruby replies. "I can get you a suite at The Mercier. Or you can stay at the beach house."

"Oh, we know all about The Mercier," I say, tossing a grin to Blair. She blows a kiss back, remembering our Valentine's night there, too. "But whose beach house?"

"No names yet," Ruby teases. "Other pros are coming that Monday, too, and you'll recognize some. You beat three players in our group already."

"Shit," Colt huffs. "You sure we'll be welcome?"

"More than welcome. There are too few of you not to stick together. That's what we want to talk about."

The more Ruby talks about her secret group, the more it feels like salvation and sin at the same time.

"Will my sister be there?" Blair asks what is often the topic of our late-night chats in bed.

She'll rest on my chest or Colt's, wondering aloud if her twin is secretly in an "intimate network" with Ruby.

Blair's teaching us all kinds of terms for our lifestyle.

It's only fair. We teach her ours.

Our woman now knows what the red zone is, and I now know I'm a bi-monogamous man. I want only one man and one woman. Forever.

I assume that's not rare in Ruby's world, in her group, but she doesn't answer Blair.

"I can't... *shh*," Ruby replies, "My signal... *shh*...breaking up....will.....*shh*...have a good...*shh*...later." But then her giggle is unmistakable. "Bye."

"The sneaky little cunt candy. She hung up on us." Blair laughs before she declares, "Okay. New rule!"

"Oh shit," I mutter. "Break out our poly playbook."

"I'm serious." Blair sorta sounds it. "Add this rule right under how all toilet seats must be left down and—"

"I still object to that," Colt interrupts. "You're outnumbered."

"And you'd like to fuck a clean pussy. Not one dunked in toilet water, so you decide, your Highness of Hygiene."

I laugh. "She's got you there. But—" I insist, "I'm dead serious about your fake eyelashes. Damn things look like attack spiders on the bathroom countertop. I about shit my shorts."

"Fine," Blair agrees. "I'll put them away, but I'm serious about my new rule, about Ruby and Vale. If they're muff-munching, I support it but don't want to see it."

Colt snorts, "Won't you get kicked out of lesbian land for saying that?"

"No!" Blair turns in her seat, telling him. "I've muff-munched. I'm bi. All love is beautiful to me. I just don't want to see my *sister* do it. My ovaries will shrivel into raisins at the sight."

"I suspect Vale feels the same," I say, taking the exit ramp. We drive by the gas station I'll never forget, so I wonder aloud, "But do you ever miss it?"

"Miss what?" Blair asks. "Having a twin so identical that people treat us like the same person?"

"No," I answer. "I mean, if Vale's with Ruby, do you miss it, too? Do you ever miss being with women?"

Colt calls from the back seat, "Please answer yes, and please let me watch."

"I don't know." Blair pops her shoulders. "Not really. I'm so dick-drunk in love with you two; I'm happy. I don't miss anything."

"Well, Raven, you have my vote," Colt assures. "If you ever get hungry for another bikini burger, you have my permission. I won't mind."

"You *won't?*"

"Why should I?" Colt answers me. "I get you and her. You get me and her. It's kinda unfair in our bipoly world that she doesn't get to satisfy her needs. I get it. I like pussy, too. I want her to be happy."

"Babe?" I ask, worried. "Are you satisfied with just us? Do you want to be with a woman, too?"

Blair throws her chin up, laughing. "Oh, I'm satisfied. It takes me a day to recover from your double-dicking. My vag needs a vacay. There's no way I could squeeze more orgasms into my weekly calendar. I'd never get books written."

"I'm serious. Colt's right."

"Usually am," he adds.

"If you want to be with a woman, too, we need to talk about it."

"Oh?" Blair sounds intrigued. "But would you get jealous?"

"Yep."

"Nope."

Obviously, Colt and I differ.

"He's okay with it," I say, "but honestly, I'm… "

What the hell is this emotion? Jealousy?

No, not really. It's deeper. It's not negative. It's not ugly or insecure.

It's…

I pull to the side of the street. We're in our neighborhood. No one cares, but I do. I turn to her.

"Babe, I love you. I always have, and I always will." I look over my shoulder and tell Colt, "And I love you, too. Always. I just want us. The three of us. That's what I'm saying. But if you… "

Shit, it hurts my heart.

The idea of Colt with someone else or Blair.

"I… " I try to explain, but Blair reaches, brushing her fingers through my glittery hair.

"It's okay," she says. "I understand. I'm serious. I just want us, too. The three of us. I'm just joking about the double-dick stuff."

"No, you're not," Colt chuffs. "Double with our big dicks is no joke."

She grins, turning to smack his knee while he laughs.

"No," she says. "Our anything is no joke, and neither is our love. I only want you both. I'm not missing out because I have more than I could've dreamed for with you two."

"Same." Colt gets serious. "I like watching. I'd like being

watched. Whatever we do at this beach house, I don't care. I'm proud of our love, but I don't want to share it."

"Me neither," I sigh, relieved. "People keep asking about the future. About games. About the Super Bowl. About marriage. They ask like we can be sure when I'm sure of one thing—our future is together."

Blair climbs over the console. She gives me a tender kiss. Then she turns and offers Colt an even bigger one. I'm not jealous. She's making sure he's equal and not left out, even though he insists on riding in the backseat because he won't let Blair do it.

"Fine." She plops back in her chair, smiling, looking cute in her Atlanta jersey. She won't wear one with my number or Colt's, either. She won't choose. "Our future is together," she declares, "but only if you put the toilet seat down."

"Oh, something's going down when we get home," I tease. "We have a big win to celebrate, and it's Colt's turn."

"Yeehaw!" He howls.

And once he sees our surprise—the black leather chaps Blair bought for me and the bare breast and crotchless latex lingerie set Blair bought for herself? Once we tie Colt's wrists to the bed. Once he begs to suck me, then lick her until his beard is glistening with our cum? Once I'm between his legs, fucking his ass while Blair rides him?

"Goddamn, don't ever stop fucking me," Colt roars as we give him the ride of his life.

Goddamn, I won't ever stop loving them either.

COLTON

CHAPTER THIRTY

I'M SO FULL OF LOVE, BUT THE LIES DRAIN ME.

> After the game, stay there
>
> I'm giving him the game ball

I texted Reese before the game, but she never answered.

I keep glancing back from the bench, looking over my shoulder, searching the small crowd in the club area on the edge of the field.

Men don suits. Women wear dresses. It's an exclusive crowd that pays for this level of close access to us.

Like a bar, they lean on the silver metal half-wall with their snacks and beverages, cheering as we take on Philadelphia.

We're down 23-20 in the fourth quarter, and the tension is high.

But all I care about is seeing one small tawny head. Forrest would barely be tall enough by now to see over the railing. So maybe Reese would hold him on her hip. Then, I'd easily spot them. But I don't see her either.

Maybe she said no.

Maybe Reese was too afraid when our publicist, Scott, approached her and Forrest in their season ticket seats, congratulating them on winning club seats for the game.

Maybe she broke her promise.

Maybe she'll leave me sitting here, waiting for our offense to take the field, to fight it out with Philadelphia's crushing defensive line while I fight the crushing break of my heart.

This feels like my last chance. This feels like I'm losing him. The older Forrest gets, the more questions he'll ask. So will his dad.

Does Forrest look like me? Or like Beau?

Tough to say.

He was born with a tuft of brown hair. I took in every detail while I held him when he was three months old. Reese let me come by when Jake was at work, and I cried. Forrest was so tiny in my arms, and I fucking cried at how beautiful our little boy was. Holding him healed what Reese did to me.

Then, she let me see him again when he was thirteen months old. I had to miss his first birthday. Reese said it was too risky. So I met them at a park. Forrest had just learned to walk. All his brown hair had fallen out, replaced by wisps of blond like mine. And I cried again when he held his arms out, laughing, toddling my way with a big smile.

But Reese is blonde, too. The truth is, Forrest looks a lot like her.

Three, maybe four times a year, Reese lets me see him.

And I wanted to hate her for all the time I've missed with him.

But when she found out about my mom's illness, Reese came through. She brought Forrest to see her when I wasn't there. They explained their relationship as family friends, and they were. Reese was so good to my mom in her last year. She let her see her grandson every chance she got.

That's what my mom died believing—that Forrest is her grandson.

"Hey," Beau plops beside me on the bench, "let's do a Lucy."

I snap my glance his way. He's chewing on the tip of his mouthguard. He does that when he's up to something.

"A Lucy?" I ask. "You sure?"

It's a trick play. It's our code word for a left-handed throw.

"Yeah. I've been throwing to Goodwin and Martinez this whole quarter," he says. "So act gassed out. Act like you're tanked, and I'll throw to them again for the first down. Then I'm throwing left to you for the second. They won't see it coming."

Beau can do it. In a clutch, he can throw left-handed, but it's risky. With his right, his aim is razor-sharp. But with his left? It's a gamble when we need a sure win.

But I nod, checking the clock. It looks like we'll have two minutes left in the game to score.

I feel the pressure. The worry. The disappointment. The possible loss. It's clawing inside my skin.

"Hey." He juts his chin. "You alright? You've been fucking quiet all day."

"I'm fine," I lie, glancing up at the club box on the visitors' side—the one on the fifty-yard line. I can't see her from here, but Blair's in there. I can feel her watching us.

So, it's instinct. I glance back over my shoulder, worried Blair's spotted Reese behind us.

Are Reese and Forrest here? Could Blair see them from there?

"Who are you looking for?" Beau glances over his shoulder, craning his neck, too.

Oh shit. "No one!" I answer quickly.

"You sure?" Beau laughs. "Careful, if you get too close to our fans when we win, you'll get pelted with Touchdown panties."

I lighten my tone. "No, *you* get pelted with panties." I try distracting him.

If Beau spots Reese in the crowd, it's over. If he sees her with Forrest, we're done.

Usually, Beau doesn't go to the midfield, where the richest seats are, after a game. He goes to the end zone, where he gives a game ball to a kid waiting there.

That's what I'm counting on.

"Alright!" Coach approaches us with his laminated play sheet in hand. "It's magic time."

Beau nods, hopping up and slapping his hand. "We got this," he promises.

"You goddamn better," Coach says, watching while I slowly rise like lead is in my veins. "Hawke!" He barks, "Light a goddamn fuse. It's time to hustle."

"He's acting," Beau says.

No, I'm not. I can sprint, but I can't run. I can't escape this ache in my heart.

We take the field, still three points down. Our defense did the job. Philadelphia didn't score, but now we have to.

It's all on the line. The roar in the stadium sounds like a jet plane.

I glance again after we huddle, after Beau calls the play to the offensive line.

The crowd in the club area shifts. They gather near us at the forty-one-yard line.

I don't see him.

I squat into position. I put my nose down, my eyes up. Beau takes the snap, and we're off, but I'm not. I make it look like I have nothing left in me because sometimes... it's how I feel.

I'm so full of love, but the lies drain me.

Beau throws the first down to Goodwin, and we rush to huddle again, the clock running down. I search the club sidelines while Beau calls the second play, "Phili. Bagel. Lucy. Sixteen. Discount."

That call is all gibberish code except for the third word —the play—and the fourth word—the player. "Lucy" is a left throw. "Sixteen" is me for my favorite movie, *Sixteen Candles*. It's also Martinez's number and decoy if the other team overhears.

I knew what Beau would call for our second down, so I glance up, searching again.

And my chest, heavy with pads and worry, falls, relieved.

There he is.

I spot Forrest's little tawny head peeking over the railing. I see Reese behind him, her long, blonde hair tucked into a ponytail under a black Atlanta baseball cap.

I see Forrest watching me, and light explodes in my heart. It lifts my chin and shoulders, too, and I smile...

Because it's fucking on.

Let's win this.

We jog into position and hold, my muscles pulled like a rubber band to snap. Beau takes the hike, and I bolt, my peripherals clocking the blur of players while I block. They pivot away, assuming Beau will throw right again, but he falls back.

He's the *Pope In The Pocket.*

It gets tighter and tighter around him, but he's calm. He won't crack under pressure.

He shifts his shoulders right, and the defense runs that way, covering Goodwin and Martinez.

I'm wide open as Beau, lightning fast, switches the ball to his left hand, throwing fifteen yards into my waiting hands.

There's no stopping me. All my stress from before explodes through my muscles. I use it to drive down the field, shucking the cornerback before I juke the safety with a quick right, claiming the end zone with a subtle swagger, but not enough to get fined.

The crowd erupts, their roar deafening. A mob of players pile on me, slapping my helmet and pads. Cameras and boom mics rush the field, surrounding our cheering huddle, while Beau huddles in, smacking my helmet, too.

"Fuck yeah, man!" he shouts. "That's how we win, baby! That's how we win!" He's on fire. So am I.

More press and players storm the field. Proud slaps hit my pads and ass as Beau turns to run to the visitor's sidelines. He always shakes the hand of the opposing team's quarterback first, then other players.

Usually, I do, too, but not today.

I throw my helmet on the field and tuck the winning ball under my arm. Slapping players' hands, I give props, but I'm searching. When my eyes land on Reese, she nods, seeing me, too.

She knows to wait.

She lets me give a quick interview and three quick

comments in praise of Beau and our team before I jog her way.

"Hawke! Hawke!" Other press flank me. They want comments, too, but not now.

All I can see are those big hazel eyes gazing up at me, surprised as I jog his way. They're so full of innocence, joy, and pride. It suddenly makes my eyes burn with tears. The rocks in my throat make it hard for my heaving chest to breathe. I'm still amped from the game, but this has my nerves alive.

My heart pounds harder than ever before.

Everything falls away but my little boy.

"Hey there!" I run to the edge, to the metal half-wall. Reese lifts Forrest in her arms. He's getting big, but he's still small enough for her to hold.

"Are you a big fan?" I ask, hoping he can hear me above the cheering crowd.

He beams, his eyes locked on mine. "I'm your *biggest* fan!" he shouts from two feet away.

"You are!"

"Yeah! You and Bronson! I'm gonna be you one day! I'm fast, *and* I can throw!"

I play along. "What's your name?"

"Forrest!" He shouts. "For Forrest Gump. Bama's fastest player ever."

I swallow hard. *That's Beau's favorite movie.* Beau is number four because of it, and that's where this little boy gets his name.

Did Reese name him after Beau? Did she do it out of guilt? I ask myself all the time.

"Well, I played for Auburn," I tell him. "Do you like them too?"

Reese beams at our exchange. Her smile lights up with her son in her arms.

"No," Forrest answers like a kid, brutally honest. "But you play for Atlanta now, and they're my most favorite, so it's okay. You're my favorite, too."

"I am?" I laugh. "You sure? Do you even know my name?"

Please say it. Please know me. Please have one piece of me in your heart.

"You're Colton Hawke!" he crows. "You're the best! You're the fastest like me!"

"Well, now I'm *your* biggest fan." *I want my son.* I want to reach across and hold him in my arms, but I can't. There's too much press gathered around. "Do you want my game ball, Forrest?"

His eyes get big, lighting up like I'm Santa. "Really?"

"Yeah!" I hand it to him. "Keep it safe for me now. Okay? I'll come throw it with you one day."

"Will you really?" He smiles so cute.

He's lost his front tooth. He's getting so big. I'm losing so much time.

"Yes," I promise. "Let's take a picture. Then I'll remember you and come visit. Okay?"

I turn, and there's Scott, our publicist, waiting with one of our team photographers, just as I begged him to. I told Scott this kid is special, but he has no idea how much.

"Look at the camera," Reese coaches Forrest.

They turn right, and I turn left, trying to stand shoulder-to-shoulder with him, but the barrier is in the way.

I need my son. I need to hold him.

The grip on my heart is suffocating while I force a smile as the big lens aims our way before the photographer gives a thumbs-up. He got the shot for me.

"When will you come see me?" Forrest asks. "I'll tell my dad, and he can play with us, too."

His dad?

I search the crowd, looking over Reese's shoulder. I don't see her husband. Jake travels a lot for work. I know because that's when I usually get to see Forrest.

"How about after the season?" I answer.

"After you win the Super Bowl?" he asks.

"Yeah!" I smile. "After I win the Super Bowl for *you!*"

Hands start tugging my arm. I look, and it's our staff. They're huddling us back into the locker room.

"Okay, Forrest." I turn back to promise him, "I'll see you again. Okay? You take care of our ball, and I'll come play with you."

"Can he mom? Can Colton Hawke come play with me?" he asks.

I stare Reese down.

You owe me this. You better say yes.

She reads my eyes and nods, smiling.

Another hand tugs me, so I wave. "Okay, Forrest. I'll see you soon."

He smiles, waving back, and I hate this. Tears burn my eyes again.

I hate leaving him. I hate saying goodbye to him.

Every time I do, I ache. I feel like my heart gets ripped out of my chest.

But when I turn and see Beau standing there, frozen with a swarm of people around him. He's staring at me, then Reese, then Forrest...

I know that look in his aching eyes.

I've ripped *his* heart out.

CHAPTER THIRTY-ONE

RUBY

Limo is waiting outside

Jet is fueled and waiting

And I'm up for anything except...

RUBY

???

Catching you mumbling in the moss with my twin

RUBY

Girl, you got a one-track beaver

No, I got a proud beaver with boundaries and hearing you make mouth music with my twin is one

RUBY

I'm NOT dining at the Y with your sister, bish

> But you're having a moresome with her
>
> Don't lie

RUBY

> See you at The Mercier lobby bar. 8 ish

I feel buzzed. I feel like I rolled the perfect life in a piece of paper and smoked it.

I'm high on happiness and horniness, bouncing in my heels, waiting in the wide corridor outside the locker room for my winning men to emerge. For them to hurry the hell up so we can celebrate.

Our bags are packed. They're waiting in a stretch limo parked outside. I met our driver. I asked him to order pizza. It's waiting in the limo, too.

Pizza is Colt's celebration meal, while Beau likes to celebrate with Glenlivet whisky.

Me? My lips are shining with oral pleasure lip gloss in Strawberry Wine flavor.

Don't use the cherry stuff. He'll think his dick is on fire.

But my men love the little tingle and lots of drool I create when I wrap my pleasing glossy strawberry lips around their winning cocks, pressed together, congratulating them with a dual, creamy knob job.

That should take up our time in the limo.

Now, for our one-hour flight to Charleston? Is that long enough to join the mile-high club?

There's only one way to find out.

Players wave at me as they leave. Their wives and girlfriends do, too. Reporters try getting my comment, but all I'll say is, "I'm so proud of the team."

But a particularly snarky reporter corners me as I wait, asking, "Are you eloping with Bronson tonight?"

I want to smile and answer, "No, we're on our way to an NFL orgy." But answering, "We're celebrating the win with friends," feels equally evasive and erotic.

Am I feeling cute, wearing a demure knee-length shell pink dress that Colt bought me from Christian Dior? Yes. Am I wearing the gold, non-piercing labia ring that Beau gave me, too? With little bells on it. Is it hidden by my surprise panties that say "Place Beard Here"? You can bet your I'm-the-bottom dollar tonight.

I can't stop smiling. My cheeks hurt from it until Malik Goodwin steps out of the locker room. He sees me waiting and pulls me aside, whispering, "Something's wrong with our boy."

My face falls. My heart drops. "What do you mean?"

I like Malik. He and his wife, Brianna, come over a lot for steaks and beers. They're fun.

"I mean, Bronson's not talking," Malik answers. "Not to us. Not to reporters. It's not like him. I mean, we just won, but he looks like he lost. Like he lost everything."

"Is he okay? Did he get hurt?"

"Don't think so. He ain't talking to Hawke either, which is weird. Something's off. He loves you. I'm sure you'll make it better, but heads up."

I give Malik a quick hug before gluing my eyes to the doors of the locker room. It's guarded. I can't go in. It makes me sick with worry. I want to help Beau.

What's wrong?

Usually, the guys don't make me wait this long. It's like every player, and most of the staff leave until finally Beau appears, pushing the doors open.

He's showered and dressed. He looks sexy and powerful

in his light grey, tailored dress pants and a loose white V-neck T-shirt. Usually, he comes out smiling and looking for me.

"Hey," but I rush to him, reading his face. It's like he's seen a ghost. "What's wrong?"

He snarls, "Let's get out of here."

"Where's Colt?"

"Fuck Colt."

I pull back, reading his face. He's not kidding. "Beau, what happened?"

"Not now, Blair. Not here."

I look over his shoulder, and Colt appears in the doorway, his eyes aimed at us. He's in his usual style—cream joggers and a matching sleeveless shirt. With his hair knot and dark ink, it's a deadly look.

So is the expression on his face.

It makes a chill drop through my veins. Even when we were in Belize, these two never looked like this. Like if the other were drowning, they'd walk away.

But I won't.

Not now. Not ever.

I plaster a smile on my face. We're still under watching eyes. "Come on. The limo's waiting," I tell them. "We got a party to attend."

"Just us," Beau mutters, grabbing my hand.

"No," I softly answer, squeezing it.

Beau looks surprised, but I turn my head, my eyes and voice pleading, "Colt? *Please.* Come with us. Our friends are waiting."

Colt wavers, like he doesn't know what to do, his eyes glaring at Beau while Beau glares back.

They won't budge.

So I drop my voice to where only they can hear. "I swear

to God, if you two don't smile and get in that damn limo together, I'll go back to dating my plastic boyfriends in Charleston."

Silently, we walk toward the exit. Beau holds my hand, but I glance back and let Colt read my eyes. "Are you okay?"

The chauffeur holds the door open. We slide inside, and once it's safe, I ask, "What the hell happened?"

Beau doesn't speak. Neither does Colt.

They just snarl at each other like it's about to be a shank fight.

"Fine then." I reach, popping open the champagne chilling in the silver bucket. I pour myself a glass and toast, "Here's to a great win against Philadelphia. And here's to my amazing men. The first one who tells me what's going on gets a blowjob."

Beau snarls, "It's not fucking funny, Blair."

"So then get serious and tell me what's going on."

"I just saw Reese," Beau sneers, "holding Colt's *son*."

Have you ever had lightning crack overhead? Like it's so loud that it shakes your skull? Your brain vibrates, exploding all your logic away?

"What?"

That's this moment.

That's this shock.

"Reese was at our game," Beau explains, his stare burning holes in Colt. "And she had a little boy in her arms. What is he now? About eight, maybe nine years old, Colt? Is that how old your son is?"

"Fuck you," Colt mutters, turning his stare toward the window, at the city blurring by.

"No, it was *you* who did the fucking," Beau's furious, "of my college girlfriend and now you have a kid together."

"Wait." I grab Beau's hand. "Stop."

This can't be true.

Colt would never betray Beau. He'd die for him. And yeah, Colt might've been a sexy man-whore in the past, but he'd never lie, he'd never do someone wrong.

"Colt." I reach across for his hand, too. "What's going on? Was Reese at your game today?"

I haven't seen her in almost a decade. Maybe Beau's mistaken. Maybe it was another gorgeous blonde, the typical Bama prototype. It's easy to confuse them. They all look alike.

"Yes," Colt answers, his eyes glued to the glass.

I feel the punch, the same shock as Beau. "Does she have a son?" I can barely ask.

"Yes," Colt confesses, not looking at us. He's tugging at his beard, chewing on his lip, like he's lost in painful thought.

Something's wrong.

I can read it in the pain marring Colt's handsome face. It hurts me too to ask, "Is he *yours*?"

A tear falls down Colt's cheek. He closes his eyes. Another tear falls, but he won't answer.

"You gotta be fucking kidding me," Beau mutters. "All this time. All these years. You lied to me. You cheated on me."

"But," I argue for Colt, "y'all weren't together back then. You were with Reese."

"He knows what I mean," Beau growls. "He betrayed my trust. It was the one thing we could have. We couldn't be together, but I always believed in him. Him and you. You were the only people I trusted."

Cynically, Colt rumbles, "Then why did you date Reese if you knew you couldn't trust her?"

"Are you fucking kidding me?" Beau lurches forward. "You knew why I dated her."

Colt snaps, "You didn't love her."

"So what?" Beau asks. "*You* did?"

"No, I loved you."

"You have a fucked up way of showing it."

"Of course, you'd say that." Colt flares his nostrils. "Of course, you'd see it that way. Who's the one who doesn't trust?"

"Doesn't *trust*?" Beau shouts. "That's all I've ever done with you. That's all we've ever had—trust. It was me and you against the world. We've always trusted, we've always *loved* each other, and now?" His voice cracks. "Now, it's a fucking lie."

"Wait. Wait." I kneel on the floorboard between them, one hand on Colt's knee, the other on Beau's. It's crazy. I know. But something's off. I can't shake the feeling. "Colt, you love Beau. You'd never hurt him. You're not telling us something, so what is it? What happened with Reese?"

He mutters, "Just drop it. It doesn't matter. He hates me now."

I look at Beau.

Yes, he's so angry and hurt that it looks like hate, but it's not. It's so much love breaking across his rugged face.

These two? They're so deep in love and pain. They're in that dangerous spot where they want to keep hurting each other instead of healing.

Colt won't speak.

Beau looks away, too.

So, I won't leave my spot with my hands on their knees. Like out of sheer will, I can hold them together.

I keep us connected until the limo clears the private

airport's gates. It parks alongside a gleaming white Gulfstream jet.

In minutes, we're buckled into our ivory leather recliners. Beau sits diagonal from Colt, as far away as he can. So, I sit in front of Colt and across the tiny aisle from Beau.

The flight attendant serves us a round of Glenlivet, per Ruby's instructions, I'm sure. This flight is for us, so that means we're secure. Whoever can hear us has signed NDAs.

Good. Because I'm feeling NDA, too—No Dumbassery Allowed.

I can't stand it when they fight, when they don't talk.

Adolescents fight. Adults talk.

"Alright, now," I warn as we taxi, "I'll tell this pilot to fly us to hell and back. I don't care. However long it takes for us to talk this out."

Though, secretly, my pulse starts racing. My pits start sweating.

I hate flying.

"There's nothing to say." Beau stares at his tumbler, swirling it. "The only man I ever loved betrayed me. What more do I need to know?"

Colt huffs, shaking his head like Beau has no clue.

"You need to know what happened," I answer their cynicism. "You need to let him tell us."

"I don't want to tell you," Colt answers. "It ain't gonna change anything."

"Yes, it will," I say, tears suddenly welling in my eyes. "If you two don't talk, it'll change everything between us."

The G-force of the little jet taking off slams me back in my seat. Any minute, we'll crash into a frozen mountainside, and Colt and Beau will have to eat my carcass to stay alive, so they need to get along.

Okay. Different decade. Different sport and team. Different continent.

But still, it's a true story.

So, this bitch ain't dying without knowing her men will be okay without her.

"I won't lose us," I insist, the nose of the plane aiming toward heaven. *That's our next stop.* "I won't lose our love. I won't pick one of you over the other." The plane jumps. *Apparently, there are potholes to heaven.* "And I sure as shit—before I die in this goddamn tin can in the sky—won't let you two kill your love, too." *Nope, this isn't heaven. It's a non-stop flight to hell.* "So, talk before we're engulfed in a falling fireball."

A hint of a smile lifts Colt's lips. "You'll be okay, Raven," he says. "I got you. God's fingertip, remember?"

"I'm about to give y'all my middle fingertip if you don't talk."

We hit a bump.

And another.

Apparently, you God or you Devil. One of you fuckers has allergies! Because you're sneezing like a bitch when we need a ride on a steady fingertip to heaven or hell or Charleston.

I don't give a shit, just get us there. Right. Now.

Beau reaches to hold my hand, white-knuckling my armrests.

"Please!" I pray, staring at the woodgrain and ivory glowing ceiling of my flying coffin. "Please, someone talk because now I know why they call it 'going to hell in a handbasket' because this is hell, and I'm in your hands. Your big, sexy hands that I love so much. I love you guys so much, so say something." The plane bumps. "Hurry! Before it's too late. Before we die! The Devil is calling my slutty ass home!"

"Is he mine?" Beau's voice ends my rant; he ends my panic. "Or is he yours?"

"I don't know," Colt mumbles.

"When was it?" Beau presses. "That night we played beer pong? Or did you cheat on me more?"

Colt shakes his head, staring at the sunset outside the oval window.

"Look at me! Answer me!" Beau sounds hurt. "Just tell me the fucking truth. How many times?"

"Once!" Colt whips his glare at him. "Once!"

"Okay, y'all," I ease. "I said talk, not yell and summon a federal air marshal."

Beau drops his tone to a controlled fury level. "So I got drunk and passed out, and you what? You flirted with her? You came on to her? You kissed Reese and fucked her? Right under my goddamn nose?"

Something, not guilt, twists Colt's face. It bends his eyes. *He's hurting.* He's holding back. He won't answer.

"Colt." I reach for his hand. "Colt, what's wrong? I can tell something's wrong."

He barely answers, "I didn't want to."

Beau growls, "And yet, you did. You hurt me and had a son with her when I dreamt it would be me and you one day." He yells at Colt, "I dreamt *we* would have a child together."

"I thought it was you!" Colt shouts, pain welling in his eyes. "I was drunk and on your sofa, and I thought it was you touching me and making me hard. I was half fucking asleep and so goddamn happy to be near you again. My heart wanted to believe it was you. That we were in love. That we were finally together. It was like a dream, but then

I woke up to the nightmare of her, of *your* girlfriend on *me*, and it was too late. She was—"

I yank my seatbelt off. "Colt." I leap into his arms, wrapping my hands around his neck, and he squeezes me back. So tight. He doesn't need to finish.

I understand.

"Wait. What?" Beau's still processing. "You mean Reese—"

"Yes," Colt mutters into my neck. "She did."

"But.. but.. why didn't you tell me?" Agony cracks Beau's voice. I hear the click of his seatbelt before he kneels beside me, reaching for Colt, too. "Why didn't you say something?"

"I didn't think you'd believe me," Colt answers, lifting from my embrace to tell him, "I couldn't believe it myself. I was in a daze. Then, weeks later, she told me she was pregnant and begged me not to tell you. She said she was sorry. She had so many issues and addictions, so she went into rehab and got her life together, and she met her husband there. He thinks the boy is his."

I cup Colt's cheek. "But are *you* okay?"

"Yeah," Colt sighs while I sit on his lap, searching his sincere face. "Yeah, I forgave Reese a long time ago. Once I held that baby in my arms, I couldn't hold any hatred in my heart."

"So, is he yours?" I ask Colt. "I mean, he could be. He could be either of yours." I ask Beau, "Right? You were with Reese around the same time, too?"

"Rarely," Beau answers. "But yeah, it's possible."

"Has she ever found out for sure?" I ask Colt.

"No," he answers. "Reese wants her husband to believe her son is his. And he's a good guy. Jake's been there. Like you said, he's his *real* dad, even though she doesn't know who his father is."

"Colt, baby." Beau cups his cheek, too. "I'm so fucking sorry. I'm so sorry I got mad. I didn't know. I just wish you would've told me so you wouldn't have to go through this alone."

"I didn't think I could tell you."

It twists Beau's face. "Why?"

"Because I had just gotten you back. I didn't want to lose you again, but that didn't last because we got into another fight. All I've ever felt like since we were eighteen is that life wouldn't let us work. That our love was doomed," he squeezes me, "until now."

"Yes." I nuzzle my forehead to his. "We work. Our *love* works, so we'll figure this out."

Beau reaches, pulling Colt's cheek to meet his lips, then Colt turns, tenderly kissing him back.

"I'm so sorry," Beau murmurs over their lips. "I'm so sorry, baby. Are you okay?"

"I'm fine," Colt answers. "Really, I am. I had my mom. She knew about you, about the baby. We talked for years about it, and I got my shit together. I found a way to forgive Reese because you should see him. He's the sweetest little boy."

"What's his name?" Beau asks.

"Forrest."

Beau flinches. "Forrest? After *Forrest Gump*? Does that mean he's—"

"I don't know," Colt repeats. "Dude, I really don't. Sometimes he looks like me. Sometimes he looks like you. I don't know what's real except that I love him. And I love you. And I'm sorry I didn't tell you. From the beginning, I feel like I never had control in this."

"Because you didn't." I kiss his cheek. "But now you do."

Colt looks at me. "How do you figure?"

"Because I'm calling my old friend, Reese Langley," I answer. "We'll talk, woman-to-woman, and I'll show her who has control. I'll make this right."

BEAU

CHAPTER THIRTY-TWO

I don't want to let go of Colt's hand. I want to wrap around him and take away the past nine years he suffered alone.

I'll never forget the first time Colt touched me. The time he rubbed sunscreen on my neck. His warmth washed through me then, and it's filled my heart ever since.

It was me feeling love for the first time.

I feel the same way he does. Like life wouldn't bless us until now, until we loved Blair, too.

I want to hold him, but the jet swings like a trapeze as we land, so we buckle up, and I hold Blair's hand.

Our woman hates to fly, but she'll get used to it. We'll have years of traveling together because I'm never leaving Blair again and never letting Colt go.

Despite what Blair says, this time *never* applies.

Do I have a son? Maybe.

Do I have my forever loves? Definitely.

When we enter the gold and glass doors of The Mercier Hotel, I don't care who's watching. I reach for Colt again. Lightly, I brush my fingertips over his hand.

He turns his chin, aiming his sexy, scruffy grin my way. "You flirting, Bronson?"

I cock a brow. "Goddamn right, I am, Hawke. You're mine tonight."

I'm so flooded with love. I want to make everything right. I want makeup sex all night long.

I can't believe I got mad at him, but I didn't know. But now we're free of that secret, while the biggest remains.

Blair wedges between us, hooking her arms through ours. "Time out before you score in his end zone," she teases. "There are some people you need to meet."

She guides us through the white-marbled lobby toward the intimate bar while the bellhops whisk our bags to our suite. It's like they were expecting us.

And they were.

We're getting the VIP treatment in a five-star hotel.

Because there Ruby sits on a blue velvet barstool, flanked by another stunning auburn-haired beauty who has to be her sister.

And the two men who stand beside them? They can rule the world with their hot smirks alone.

I recognize Luca Mercier—dark hair, tan skin, body like a marble statue, and the face of a Grecian God. Anyone with a screen knows who Luca is—a billionaire hotelier.

But should you escape his imposing image on the cover of magazines about the rich and powerful, you can't escape his glacial eyes when they're aimed at you.

The man could command the sun to rise in the west.

He doesn't even introduce himself.

He greets us, "Mr. Bronson. Mr. Hawke," his massive hand demanding our shake. "Welcome to The Mercier." Then he aims his lips for Blair's cheeks, kissing both. "And Ms. Monroe. We meet again." *They know each other?* "And you're in love, I see." Luca smiles, glancing from me to Colt before dropping his voice like it's a secret with Blair. "As I knew you would be."

Colt darts his eyes at me.

What was that about?

But Ruby chuckles. "Okay, okay. Forgive my brother-in-law. He can be so cryptic and formal when we're all friends." She gestures to her left. "This is my sister, Scarlett Mercier, Luca's smarter half."

Scarlett greets us, looking as formidable as her husband. She just makes it look breathtaking, too, like her sister, Ruby, who gestures to her right. "And this is Zar Rollins. *Their* best half."

"Well now," Zar cocks an easy grin, "I don't know about their best half, but I sure am the best-looking."

That's no lie.

Zar's as tall, dark, and handsome as Luca. But where Luca exudes European elegance and an accent, Zar has Texas swagger. Like he's as comfortable in a boardroom as in a barn.

I take the sight of our hosts in, and I'm having a hard time breathing.

It's like we've stepped into steam, and it's not from the humidity outside. It's the heat, the energy, the mysterious, invisible bond cracking and pulling us to them.

You don't have to see a net for it to be there, waiting to catch you.

It's not unnerving.

It's as safe as it is thrilling.

"Mr. Hawke." Zar shakes Colt's hand. "Mr. Bronson." He shakes mine. "Helluva win today. Congratulations. That running pass in the first quarter? Twenty-one yards to Hawke, who dove into the end zone? Dayum, y'all are faster than a prairie fire with a tailwind."

I laugh. I keep shaking his hand.

Suddenly, I sense who Zar is—*he's the one Ruby protects.*

"Thank you," I answer. "So you're a big fan?"

"Oh," Zar grins, his dark eyes dancing, "I do *love* the sport."

Luca orders us a round of Ouzo, a traditional Greek liquor.

Blair huddles with Ruby and Scarlett. No telling what those women are laughing about.

"Your restaurants in Atlanta." Luca hands us our drinks. "I'm impressed. We dined there last month. You have an innovative menu; classic meets cutting edge."

"Thanks." Colt leans on the gleaming wood bar. "Next time you're back in A-town, let us know. It'll be our treat."

"Would you ever be interested in another venture?"

"Yeah," Colt answers for us. "We're looking to expand."

Colt has an appetite for risk. Me? I prefer more secure investments, but that's another thing that makes us a perfect match.

"We're opening a property in West Palm Beach," Luca explains. "Let's talk more if you're interested." He nods to Zar. "My CFO has all the numbers."

"I have the numbers," Zar adds, "and I have an invitation."

But my eyes are drawn to the way his arm brushes Luca's. How their intimacy is covert. How it's like what Colt and I share. How it surges the heat in my veins. Oddly, I feel safe *and* seduced.

"Tomorrow," Zar continues, "let Ruby bring you to my beach house for a Lowcountry boil. There are some others I'd like you to meet."

Colt glances at me. I know the look. We've exchanged it so many times when we fear we've been outed.

But we don't need to fear Zar. Right?

"These others," I ask. "Can they be trusted?"

Zar nods. "As much as they need to trust you."

Trust.

It's the most valuable emotion today.

I've trusted Colt from the moment he told me that my fly was open on the first day of our sophomore year. And yeah, it turned me on that he was staring at my dick.

I knew I could trust Blair when I was about to step into my Anatomy class, but someone stepped on the back of my Jordans. "What the...?" I almost tripped, whipping around to see her grinning.

"You got a shoe comet." She saved me from certain embarrassment before I walked in front of a hundred students with toilet paper on my shoe.

Toilet paper that was her fault, I reminded her while she scooped it up. "Yeah, well," she winked, "Bronson, I may give you shit, but it's safe with me."

That's why it hurt so bad. For two long hours today, I thought Colt had betrayed my trust in the worst way. I felt sick. But now I know what Reese did, and all I want to do is show Colt tonight how he can always trust me.

He can always trust us.

Again, despite what Blair says, this time *always* applies, too.

So, if Zar is friends with Ruby. If Blair knows Luca Mercier, and it seems she knows his wife, too. Then, yeah, I'm learning to trust.

"Alright." I nod to Zar. "We'll be there."

We finish our round of drinks. They wish us a good night. A gold elevator whisks us to the top floor, to the same suite I shared with Blair on Valentine's night.

"Did you plan this?" I swipe our guest card, holding the door open for her. "Did you tell Ruby about our night here?"

"What about your night here?" Colt flops down on the lavish sofa in the suite's living room.

"Oh," Blair shrugs, "I fucked myself in front of that mirror for Beau." She points to the massive, gold-framed one on the wall opposite the windows to the Charleston harbor outside. "And then we fucked for the first time on that bed." She smiles, pointing to the one in the adjoining bedroom. "That's where he tied me up and gave me my blue cock alien fuck fantasy, too. So, to thank him, I fucked Beau in the spa shower before we fell asleep."

Did I just blush?

Yep, I did.

"You *fucked* Beau?" Colt sounds intrigued. "When is it my turn?"

"Damn, y'all." I unbutton my shirt. "Can we catch our breath first? It's been a day."

"Which part?" Blair curls up beside Colt. "The part where you kicked ass and beat Philadelphia in the last forty seconds? Or the part where you discovered either you or Colt has a son with Reese? Or the part where you just met the sexy Texas nexus of a network?"

"All of the above," I answer.

"I wanna talk about this network." Colt slings his arm over her shoulder, asking, "What was that between you and Luca Mercier downstairs? And before you answer, can I just say—damn, that man is fine."

"I'm standing *right* here." I toss my shirt on a chair.

"I know you are, sweet cheeks." Colt grins, admiring my abs. "I can look but never touch. And don't tell me you didn't look either because Zar Rollins is fine as fuck, too."

Blair laughs. "Watch out because Zar Rollins belongs to Luca Mercier."

"Wait? What?" I'm sounding like a broken record today. "Someone, please tell me which end is up."

"Alright." Blair kicks off her heels, curling them under her while she curls into Colt even more. "Here's what I know. Luca Mercier is madly in love with his wife, Scarlett, and she's also his proud sub. So is Zar. They shop at Delta's, and when I worked there, they made my panties wet with every kinky BDSM purchase they made."

Colt grabs his crotch.

Noted: my man may be down for more bondage.

"But obviously," Blair explains, "Ruby is not with them. They're family. So, she's with someone else. And that's what I've been trying to figure out. I keep wondering if it's my sister and her secret man, but Ruby and Vale swear they're not together. Not sexually, at least."

"Holy, poly puzzle." I aim for the bar in the room. "I need a goddamn offensive play diagram."

Colt laughs, "Sure sounds like a lot of coverage, line holes, and slot backs."

"No," Blair chuckles. "We'll wait and find out more tomorrow. Because somehow, Zar connects them all. That much I can tell."

"But Zar's the CFO of Mercier Hotels," Colt asks what I'm thinking. "So, how the hell is he connected to NFL players?"

"Don't worry your sexy hair knot," Blair answers. I glance over my shoulder. She's turning to straddle Colt, to kiss him. "We just need to focus on you tonight. We want to make sure you're okay."

Blair always does this.

She feels what I feel.

And it's all love.

"I'm dandy," Colt teases. "I want to hear more about you fucking Beau. I thought I was his first."

"You were," I answer, taking a swig of Glenlivet. *We are getting the VIP treatment.* "But Blair was the first to play with my ass and make me admit that I liked it, that I wanted more."

Damn, my dick is a circuit breaker.

It just turned on, and the electricity travels from me to Blair kissing Colt, to Colt undressing Blair. Then to me, minutes later, holding Colt's naked back to my chest while I can't bury my cock deep enough inside him.

I press my lips to his ear. "Fuck, I love you so much." He gets so damn hard, his dick bobbing swollen and long, while I fuck him for Blair to watch.

She drives us insane. She's fucking beautiful, naked, and fingering her pussy while she sits on the sofa, witnessing our love, our trust.

"Gimme that pussy, too," Colt growls. So Blair lets him suck on her glistening fingers before he's overcome by what we feel—our need for her.

He bends over, burying his mouth in her taste while she writhes over his tongue, never taking her eyes off of me while I fuck Colt and praise her.

"Yes, Kitten." I grab Colt's waist. I pound inside him. He moans into her sex while I lock my gaze on hers. "Rub that sweet pussy all over his sexy face." Colt moans. "He loves it when you soak his beard with your cum." I reach around, matching my thrusts to my fist, stroking Colt's hard cock.

He's dripping; he's moaning for us.

"Feel it, Kitten?" Blair moans for me, too. "Feel how every time I pound my dick into his ass, it shoves his tongue up your sweet cunt?"

"Oh fuck." Blair's about to come. She's breathtaking when she does, and it makes me savage, wanting to take her there. I crave taking Colt, too. Our bodies belong connected. My thrusts make Colt grunt. They make Blair grab his hair, suffocating him in her lust.

"Come for us, Kitten." My voice makes her eyelids drop. "Yes, that's it. Be our dirty little girl and come for your daddies while you watch us fuck each other before we fuck you, too."

Blair bucks. Her eyes roll. Her thighs shake while she comes, and that makes Colt's cock swell, rigid, and aching in my grasp.

"Fuck yes, baby." My free hand palms Colt's sweating back. "Fuck yes, come for me, too. Always, Colt. You're always mine to fuck."

Colt groans, his thighs shaking against mine. Shamelessly, he spurts, coming on the carpet, and I love it. It gets me off. It makes me pound harder. It makes me give him everything I have because he can take it.

He can take so much, and he already has, and I cry out, kissing his back while I come, too.

"Baby." My lips brush over his skin before I gaze up at Blair, who's caressing Colt's head between her legs. "Baby," I tell them, "we'll have our own kids, I swear."

CHAPTER THIRTY-THREE

"**I**F YOU'RE GONNA BE A DICK, THEN SHOW IT."

"Oh my god."

Sleep. I need sleep.

"Put the pussy poker away."

That's Beau's cock.

His morning wood is a tail splitter. So, I shake my ass, trying to shoo him away, but that only makes it worse.

"Come on, Kitten." Beau nuzzles my neck, rutting against my backside. "Just a little boom, boom."

My lips are smashed against the pillow, declaring, "There's nothing little about your boom, boom."

Silence falls over our hotel bed. I close my eyes, desperate for another hour of sleep, but...

"Uh-huh," Colt grumbles on the other side of him. "Old Faithful needs to sleep, too."

"If it's Old Faithful," Beau sounds so husky with lust, "then this long rod erupts every hour."

He must be stroking Colt's cock, while grinding on my ass. Yes, I love my men. Yes, I will shamelessly fuck them senseless.

But no human alive can take as much as Beau wants to give. It's sweet, but we're sore.

"Damn, y'all," he huffs, almost sounding mad about it. "You're giving me blue balls."

I roll over, cracking an eyelid open. "If you're gonna be a dick, then show it."

Beau shoves the white sheets down, showing off his angling, thick erection, and my kitty pops her head up. Like a big juicy mouse just crossed her line of sight.

Hmmm. Am I feral or fatigued?

"See what I mean," he says, making his cock jump. "I keep thinking about this beach house party, and I get hard. I'm horny as hell."

"Well then." I yawn. "Save it for the party."

"Hell no," he scoffs. "Ruby says we gotta have skin in the game. And if other pros are gonna see my skin flute in a game with y'all, it's gotta last. I'm not gonna pop one off like a rookie."

Colt mumbles, "What *are* we doing this afternoon? Like, what's the game plan? What's the play?"

"Hell no," I groan. "Don't turn group sex into a group sport with practice, plans, and plays."

"Why not?" Colt sits up, tousling his long hair. "I'm with him. We gotta be pros, not like we're back in college and jackhammering every hole we can have."

"So you were a bad lay in college?"

"Yeah!" Colt schools me, his brows all bent up. "Every man is a bad lay in college. We don't know what the fuck we're doing. We're just too damn excited to be doing it. It is like a sport. It takes practice. It takes knowing some plays. I'm just now getting to be a pro at it."

"Yeah, you are," Beau growls, rolling toward him, but Colt laughs, gently shoving him away.

"Tackle her," he says. "You played my ass hard last night."

Beau rolls my way, grinning, but I press my palms to his chest. "Whoa, there. I need a break, too. At least a couple of hours. At least until we eat breakfast and I call Reese."

"Fuck." Beau falls back on his pillow. "Congratulations. That's an instant boner-killer."

"Maybe so." I toss the sheet off me. "But I mean it. I'm fixing this shit today."

I open our bedroom door to find a gold cart, brimming with brass-covered breakfast dishes, waiting for us in the living room. A folded notecard reads.

THANK YOU FOR TRUSTING US.
SEE YOU SOON,
ZAR

Colt ambles naked my way, reading the note while scratching his abs like he's starving. Then, he lifts a lid. "Hell yeah! Blueberry pancakes."

"Blair!" Beau shouts from the bed. "If they sent us blueberry pancakes for breakfast, that means you told Ruby about our blue alien fucks."

I munch a slice of bacon. "I'm an innocent virgin. I don't know what you're talking about."

"Raven," Colt grabs a plate, "you make guilty as fuck look gorgeous as hell."

"What?" I shrug, turning to find Beau staring at me with a *you're busted* grin. "We're about to have skin in the game with Ruby, remember? What's wrong with sharing our alien fuck tales? Hell, I write about them all the time."

We pile onto the bed with our plates. The guys don't want to be rude. They eat everything on the tray.

While they lie back in a food coma, I've had three cups of coffee, so I'm more than ready.

Colt places the call on his phone then hands it to me.

"Hey," Reese answers.

"Hey," I reply. "It's me."

She pauses before she shrieks, "Blair! Is that *you*?"

"Yep, roll tide roll and all that shit."

"But... " she stammers, her tone dropping along with her logic. "This is Colt's number, so that means—"

"It means I know, and so does Beau."

"Beau? Wait? You're with Colt right now? *And* Beau?"

I could almost feel bad for her. This is an ambush. But all is fair in love and war and secrets.

"Yes. I'm with Beau, *and* I'm with Colt. We're in a loving throuple. That's our secret. What's yours?"

"Blair," she murmurs, "I don't want any trouble. I got my life together. I have a son."

"Yeah, I know. And honestly, Reese, I'm glad you got it together. I'm glad you're happy and healthy. Truly. But what about Colt? What about his son? Or is he Beau's?"

I hear laughter, like lots of kids in the background. She must be at a park somewhere.

So, she whispers, "I have a husband. My son has a dad who he loves very much. I can't rip their world apart."

"So you'll rip Colt's apart instead? Like you haven't hurt him enough?" Damn, what I want to say. How I want to shred Reese with my words. I know I can, but there's been enough damage done. It's time to heal. And there's a child involved. "Reese, we know what you did to Colt."

I reach for his hand and squeeze it. He's wrapped in Beau's arms, squeezing my hand back.

"I'm sorry," Reese almost sobs. "I'm so sorry. I've told Colt so many times. I know it was wrong. So wrong."

"Well, it's time to stop *saying* it was wrong and *act* to make it right."

"I can't. Jake thinks Forrest is his, and Forrest loves his dad. He's a good man."

"Yeah, that's what Colt says because *Colt* is a good man, too. He's protected your lies for too long."

"This will ruin my marriage. This will break Forrest's heart."

"No, Reese. The longer you lie, the more it will hurt. One day, Forrest will know the truth and think of how hurt he'll be that you kept his father from him all that time. You're not protecting him. You're punishing him. And your husband? Well? Love tells the truth. He deserves to know, too."

She's silent while I turn to see Beau kissing Colt's shoulder.

And the irony hits me.

How our love isn't a lie, but it's a secret. So, how long before it hurts, too? How long can we hide?

And why should we?

Why, when Beau is holding Colt so tight while Colt holds my hand, should we hide our love? While marriages like Reese's or my dad's get to parade around, all public and praised, under the guise of being moral and good?

Because we're moral.

We're good.

The way we scarf down blueberry pancakes together. The way Beau swiped maple syrup across my nose for Colt to kiss off, making me giggle. The way we solve a crossword puzzle together in bed or sit in a row, reading our books at night. Or roll over and turn off the light.

Why are three mouths kissing the other goodnight so wrong, but two mouths are so right?

"Look, Reese." I break the silence. "We'll give you a month. We'll pay for a counselor for you to consult with or one who can facilitate these conversations with your husband and son. We don't want to destroy your family. We just want to have ours, too."

She rushes, "I don't think I can do this."

"Yes, you can and you will," I answer. "You're strong. You got sober. I always knew you would. Now get it right."

"Mommy?" A voice chimes. "Where's my ball?"

It's so quiet on our end, Beau hears him. He hears Forrest for the first time, and his expression is a storm of emotions. It matches Colt's: wonder, love, ache.

"Right here, sweetie. In my backpack," Reese answers. "Tie your shoe first. And don't throw near the little kids. Go over there where I can still see you."

I wait until she asks, "You there?"

"Yes, Reese. We're here, and we're not going anywhere." I draw a deep breath, feeling so damn protective, too. "Listen, you love your husband and son, and I love my men. So don't make me be a bitch. You know how nuclear that can be. This is happening the easy way or the hard way. It's your choice. What'll it be?"

"Okay," she sighs. "Just give me a few days, and I'll call back. I promise. Just let me do this my way. I mean... the easy way. Let me talk to my husband first."

We end the call and I drop the phone on the bed.

Colt holds his arms open, and I crawl over, snuggling his chest. He kisses my hair while Beau reaches over Colt, gently brushing his hand up my back.

"I love you." That's Beau, and I smile against Colt's beating heart.

"I love you, too."

In our world, *you* is plural. There isn't one. There's three.

Silently, we hold each other until Colt murmurs. "I'm getting hard."

"Really?" I start laughing. "Can't we have a sweet moment?"

"We did," Colt answers. "It's so damn sweet watching you go all Blair on someone. It turns me on."

I pull back as Beau appears over Colt's shoulder. "Yeah, baby," he agrees. "It's hot."

"Hot?" I huff. "You just turned me into a verb."

"Woman," Beau grins, "*Blair* is a verb. It's a full body and mind fuck. In the best way."

"Speaking of... " Colt rolls on top of me.

"Flag on the field!" But I point to the clock on the nightstand. "Ruby will be here in an hour, and we have to get ready." I bat my lashes. "You gotta be ready for some pro-NFL butt-balling."

"See what we mean!" Beau laughs, tossing the covers aside. He aims for the shower, proclaiming over his shoulder, "That's a classic Blair!"

COLTON

"No more silence."

My brain is blitzed.

Can anyone tell?

I'm casually leaning against the deck railing of a swanky beach mansion, the Atlantic sparkling blue on my right. I got a chilled beer in my hand. I look relaxed, my ankles crossed, all casual in my black shorts and a weathered gray T-shirt.

But I wish I didn't leave my shades at the hotel. They'd hide my roaming eyes.

There's an outdoor dining table covered in brown paper, with a pile of seasoned shrimp, smoked sausage, half corn cobs, and red potatoes steaming on it.

It's a traditional Lowcountry boil while I'm steaming, too. And it's not from the bright afternoon sun.

It's the crowd of beefy bodies milling around. It's the

faces I know, the names, too, ones I've played against on the backs of jerseys. It's the laughs and jokes and ease.

It's a dozen NFL players, along with other guests, men and women, who are so relaxed, I can't believe what I'm seeing.

All of these players are gay or bi?

Blair mingles with Ruby. Beau is talking to Nick Barinov, the tight end for Carolina. Our host, Zar Rollins, swigs a beer, too, working the crowd. He catches me staring, probably with my jaw hanging open, flies buzzing in and out, so he grins, aiming my way.

"Cat got your tongue?" he asks.

"Uh, there ain't many cats here. It's the dogs I'm shocked about."

"They're good men. Like you."

Zar has the braun of a fast player, like a running back, but he's not one. He's a C-suite executive.

I can't make sense of it.

"Just how are you involved though?"

"See that man talking to your man?" Zar subtly points his brown bottle toward Nick Barinov. "He's mine. He's how I got involved. He's why I care so damn much."

He must clock my confusion. How I thought Zar's with Luca and Scarlett Mercier.

So he cocks a half grin, using that sexy Texas drawl. "Being a sub ain't the same as being a spouse." He shrugs. "Not always. I serve Luca, and I'm loyal to his wife. But I belong with Nick. As soon as we can, we're getting married."

I nod, letting the dust fall over my logic.

"And you and Bronson?" he asks. "You're with Ms. Monroe. Equally? Exclusively?"

I don't waver. "Yes, and yes. We're not... What does

Blair call it... Open? Yeah, we're not open. We're closed. It's just the three of us. Hope that's okay."

I don't know what the expectation is. I don't know what these guys think of us being here. I've heard of swinger parties, and I've done several threesomes, me and two women before I found my forever throuple, but this is a whole new world to me.

"That's quite alright," Zar answers. "Most here are in closed relationships. That's why we're here. We want to protect them. To celebrate them."

"How? None of us can be out. How can we celebrate *that*?"

Zar tilts his head toward his lavish living room on the other side of the open accordion glass doors. "I think it's time we all meet. It may answer your questions."

He gestures for me to lead the way, then he calls the others to join us.

I find an overstuffed chair. The room is full of them and sofas, all draped in beachy white slipcovers. Blair joins me. She sits on my lap while Beau sits on the wide arm of the chair, draping his hand over my shoulder.

At first, I flinch. We don't show our affection in public. But here?

I exhale. I try to relax and enjoy it.

Other guests settle into seats while Zar stands beside Nick with the ocean gleaming behind them. They look like a true power couple.

"Thank y'all for joining us," Zar begins. "We know it's not easy finding a day off during the season."

"Fins up!" Shouts Booker Davis, the nose tackle for Miami.

"DUUUVAL!" Carter Smith, Jacksonville's safety, shouts back, and we laugh.

"Exactly," says Nick, who plays for Carolina. "And may the best team win, but we're here to talk about *our* team." The room gets quiet. "The one that finally deserves to win, too."

Eyes dart. Not guilty. Not ashamed. Just understanding. Just feeling the weight of our secret. The injustice of it.

I scan all the players. How their trained muscles are tense. Their steel jaws clenched. I can imagine what they hear in their locker rooms, too. The homo-erotic jokes. The mocking teases. The outright slurs. We have thick skins, but we have hearts.

Hearts we've been hiding for too long.

Beau cups my shoulder, asking Nick, "So what's the play?"

And goddamn, I fall even deeper in love with this man.

I know his gruff tone. I know his firm grip. I know when Beau puts his nose down like that, glaring up through his eyebrows, he's ready to fight.

To fight for *us*.

"Leave it to a QB to ask," Booker jokes, and it's true. QBs can't live without a plan or a play.

"Bronson's right, though," Brayton Jervis, the QB from Tennessee, adds. "I appreciate the support." He holds the man's knee beside him. He's not a player. He must be his partner. *Huh, I never knew.* "Having this group means a lot. And adding to it helps." He nods to me and Beau. "The world is changing, but not fast enough. Not for the NFL."

Beau glances at me. I glance back.

That's what Dr. Gary said.

"So what are we gonna do?" Brayton continues. "Stay closeted until we retire? Or worse, we get outed? Or do we just stay silent until we die?"

"Imagine," Booker says, his tone grave, "how many

already have. It has to be hundreds after a hundred years of the league. Probably some of the legends in the sport, but we'll never know."

Nick answers, "That's why we're here today." Zar coughs. "Oh, and for our host's top-notch Lowcountry boil and party later." He hooks his arm around Zar's waist. "We're here to support each other, to relax and be ourselves, but also to propose a play, a plan. Just hear us out."

A curious rumble ripples through the crowd.

"Who's *us*?" Beau asks.

It raises Zar's eyebrow. As Blair said, we know it's not just Zar. He and Nick are connected to others in a bigger network.

"You're a secret group." Zar gestures to us gathered. "And there's another. One that wants to help."

"Who?" Booker asks, rightfully suspicious. "And why?"

"Some are family," Zar answers. "Some are friends. Some are *partners* for a few."

Blair elbows me like I'm supposed to know what the fuck is going on, but then I remember Ruby and Vale, and however they're a part of this, too.

Vale, Blair's sister, isn't here, but Ruby is. She sits like a referee on the sidelines of our conversation.

"It's a group that can help," Nick says. "They'll provide resources and protection should we do this."

I'm jumping out of my skin. I can't stand the suspense. "Do what?" I ask.

Nick looks at Zar, then Ruby, before he answers, "Before we come out together."

You can hear a pin drop on the other side of the planet.

"Fuck," Blair huffs. "That's fucking brilliant."

"That's fucking crazy," Booker says what most of us are

thinking. "You expect me to be Black *and* out as gay in the NFL?"

"Or married to a man?" Brayton gets his back. "Jim and I already married. No one knows, and you expect us to come out about it?"

The room descends into grunts of protest and riled side-chatter until Beau calls it like a play on the field.

"Stand together or fall alone. We got a choice. And I'm fucking tired of being alone. Of being silent. Of hiding who I am and who I love. I'm bi and a better player because of it. I'm fucking winning because I'm finally in love. I'm finally living my life."

"Me, too." My throat is burning. *Fuck, I love him,* so I speak up, too. "Since we were sixteen, we've been in love and had to hide it. And now we have to hide the woman we love, too. It's bullshit. We play. We perform. We make them billions. And then what? It's a matter of time before one of us gets outed, and then it'll be brutal. If the rest of us wait to come out then it looks like we were ashamed of our love when we're not."

"But if you come out *now*," Blair adds, "you look proud and powerful."

"Exactly," Ruby chimes in. "You do it on your terms, under your control, and you do it together. No more silence."

"We do it as a team," Nick announces. "Then they can't single us out. Then, they have to confront the closet. The one so many are in."

"Yeah," Blair asserts, "then you become a movement. Other players will come out, too. It'll change everything for good."

"So what?" Beau asks like he's ready, like it's war. "We hold a press conference next week?"

"No," Zar answers. "We wait. We make a plan. We work with the other group that wants to help. Legally. Financially. PR. Security and such. We get ready for the ultimate power play."

"Then," Nick adds, "we do it at the end of the season. We come out on the day of the Super Bowl. When one hundred million people and the league will have no choice but to see us. And to watch us win."

Eyes turn to me and Beau.

Like they know it, too.

We'll make it to the Super Bowl. We'll be the ultimate example.

Half of me is fearless. I'm proud to do it.

The other half of me knows it could be like a war, where people I love can get hurt.

"Well, shit," Beau scoffs with his cocky grin. "We got this. It's just a game."

The crowd laughs low, still processing the shock. Me, too.

Do we really know what we're agreeing to?

"Look," Zar adds. "It's like every smart business deal or political plan. Think about it. Don't decide now. We got three months to chew the fat, to see if this dog will hunt."

"What my man is saying," Nick pulls him in closer, "is let's eat. Let's have a good night. Let's see how we feel in the morning... three months from now."

COLTON

CHAPTER THIRTY-FIVE

I peel a seasoned shrimp, watching Ruby do the same.

"You behind all this?" I ask.

Beau sits beside me. Blair sits beside Ruby. We're at a table on the deck, under a white umbrella, watching the sunset while the mood of Zar's party is darkening, too. It's enticing as I clock people disappearing upstairs.

"In a way, yeah," Ruby answers. "But it's not just me. I'm like a representative."

"So you work for someone?"

"Work? Fuck? Love?" She dances her brows at me. "It all comes together, right?"

"Any minute, I expect to see my sister walk through the door." Blair spins a corn cob over a stick of melting butter. "That plan? That's something she'd come up with. She studies this for a living. I know she's in this other myste-rious group."

But Ruby won't talk. She smiles, popping the shrimp in her mouth.

"But why do we need so much time and help?" Beau asks. "I'm ready to do this shit tomorrow. They're right. If we do this together, it works. We'll finally be free."

"Because think about it. We're making history," I answer. "Hordes of press will stalk us. Fans will be in a frenzy. Our organizations will freak out. Then there are the haters and the homophobes. We'll lose endorsements. And some of us have contracts up for renewal, too. Zar's right. We need time and a plan."

"I can't believe you agreed that quickly." Blair smiles in awe at Beau. "You always said you couldn't come out while you're playing. What changed?"

"Love," Beau answers. "I didn't know it'd be this good, and I don't want to hide it. And I don't want to be busted again like your dad did. I want to step on a field or hell, even at the fucking gas station, with my chin held high. I got one season left in me, and I'm gonna make it fucking count."

I turn to him, shocked, "Whatdaya mean 'one season?'"

"I mean my shoulder. I know you can tell. It's not gonna last. So I'll sacrifice it. I'll make it give me everything it's got until the very end. Until we win the Super Bowl, then I'll retire."

"But Beau," Blair pleads, sounding as shocked as me, "you *love* football. You can't stop playing."

"No, I love being happy." He reaches across the table for her hand. "I thought only football made me happy, but I was wrong. You do. He does." He nudges my shoulder. "It's just a game. Yeah, I've played it since I was a kid, but it doesn't last." He pauses. The sexy fucker is getting choked up. Dammit, it chokes me up, too. "*We* last," he says. "*We're* forever."

"Ahhh," Ruby sings, bouncing in her seat. "Can I be a bridesmaid?"

Blair blushes. It's easy to see with her milky skin.

It makes Beau lean over the table, cupping her cheek, taking a long, tender kiss from her buttery lips and a little tongue before he sits down and turns to me.

He kisses me, too, for the first time in public, with others watching, and I moan against his scruffy lips. I grab him, holding him by the neck. I can feel his pulse in my grasp, our tongues relishing this moment.

Yes, this is desire, but it's more.

It's relief. It's pride. It's freedom to love him. To love us.

"So," Ruby eases, "maybe it's time I tell you about the second part of the party."

Beau lifts from my lips, demanding, "Tell me we have a bedroom upstairs where we can fuck because we're dying to."

"I've prepared something for you," Ruby answers. "The room at the end of the hall. It has a red and a black tie on the door handle. Leave the red tie on the handle if you want privacy. Hang the black tie if others can join you."

My dick starts swelling. "Join us *how*?"

"You can peek in some other bedrooms upstairs with black ties, too. You'll see how we join. Some are open with others tonight. Some aren't. Some watch. Some join in by doing their thing in the same room."

"Like an orgy?" Yep, my dick is raging hard.

"Like freedom," Ruby answers. "Here, that's what we are: free and safe."

"But you said you've prepared something." Beau lowers his brow. "What?"

"I might've gone shopping at Delta's," Blair answers,

coquettish and cute. "I might've sent some things over ahead of time."

"And this might not be the first rodeo here," Ruby adds.

"Whoa!" I hold up my hands. "We can do some kink, and I'm already hard about an orgy, but hell-to-the-no on horse stuff."

"Settle down, Trigger," Blair teases, wiping her lips with a napkin. "What about latex?"

My cock answers for me. "Keep talking."

"What about me doing to you what I did to Beau?"

"Oh fuck." I scrub my face, nudging Beau. "We better put a ring on her finger soon because she's never getting away."

We take turns freshening up in the restroom downstairs before Ruby leads the way, escorting us upstairs. She grabs the doorknob of the first bedroom on the right. A red tie hangs from it.

"This one's for me," she winks, "so y'all have fun," before she disappears into the dark room.

But the hallway is wide and bright and airy with light wooden floors and a white rug running down the center. There must be at least five bedrooms up here. Then I turn, spotting another wing on the opposite side of the landing. That must be the owner's suite where Zar and Nick are. There's a red tie on that door, too.

"Do you want to see?" Blair's hand is suspended over the first doorknob on the left, a black tie swinging from it.

I look at Beau, who answers, "Real quick, because I'm too damn ready for our turn."

Slowly, Blair opens the door, and I'm shocked by how my pulse soars, by how my dick surges. I feel like we're doing something wrong, but we're not.

They want to be watched.

We stand in the doorway, and I sway, lust hitting me so hard at what we see.

Booker is topping Carter. They're naked and kissing on the lavish bed, not even looking up. They're so lost in the moment together, they don't care.

God, I don't want to assume, but it looks like they're in love—like they've been together for a while.

And Brayton's with his husband, too. They're beside Booker and Carter on the bed. Brayton has his husband on all fours so they can watch. Then, they glance up and see us doing the same.

"Come in," Brayton coaxes. "Watch us."

I get it. I get how our stare makes his carved pecs tense. His muscular hips thrust harder. He grabs his husband's shoulders, pounding into his backside.

It makes my mouth water how hard Jim's dick hangs, bouncing as he receives his husband's fuck.

He loves him. He wants us to see it.

"We'll watch you come," I answer, feeling Beau cup my dick. He's reaching behind him where I stand, stroking his palm over my hard shaft, hidden by my shorts, while I rumble, "We like watching, too."

It makes Brayton lock his eyes on us. Like he's proud, his muscles puffing up. Like's he's proving his primacy. Like he wants us to witness their love.

We're making Booker and Carter do the same. They're grunting as Booker's hips thrust into Carter, his tempo almost matching Brayton's while he fucks his husband beside them.

"Damn," Beau sighs. "Damn, they're fucking hot and beautiful." He wraps around Blair, pulling her back against his chest while I hold Beau against mine.

This is new for us. But when we're connected like this,

I'm not afraid. I finally feel like I belong. Like I'm safe. I'm validated.

Men just like me love like me.

All the isolation I felt for years melts away.

The heat of our bodies and the heat of what we're watching makes me sweat. I start rutting into Beau, my control slowly slipping.

"It's my turn with your ass tonight." I tease Beau, but Blair murmurs, "No, big boy. It's *my* turn with your ass."

"Our naughty girl." I reach around Beau, moving his arm aside so I can palm Blair's luscious breast.

Damn, our woman has the best pair. Full and lush like her hips, like her ass.

I love everything soft and curving on Blair's body and everything hard and rigid on Beau's.

She moans at my touch as I reach, tugging the strap of her dress down. When she wears dresses like this, all retro and sexy with a built-in corset, she doesn't wear a bra, so I tug the fabric down, exposing what I want, gently pinching her nipple, palming the weight of her breast while I grind into Beau's ass.

They moan for me. They're panting, and the sight of us, of our arousal, makes Brayton grunt and growl, his husband crying out like he loves it, too. Quickly, they come. They're loud about it, which makes Booker and Carter come, too.

I guess having new members and a new audience, one that supports them and relishes what we see, really turned them on.

"Have a good night," Blair softly says, wedging her body so we can ease back out of the room.

We close the door behind us.

"Now," I growl. "I don't need to see more. I need to get fucked."

As we walk by the other bedrooms, we hear moans. We hear soft laughter. We hear voices easily chatting. Two doors, Ruby's and Zar's, I assume, have red ties. The others are all black.

I wonder who's in them. I wonder what they're doing, but I need this more.

I need us.

When we open the door to the bedroom Ruby said was reserved for us, I'm surprised.

I expected to find bondage furniture or, hell, even ropes from the ceiling. There's no telling with Blair. Add Ruby into their cock and cunt cahoots, and I wouldn't be surprised to find a room full of breeding benches.

But no.

It's just a sumptuous king-sized bed with white linens in a room decorated like a modern beach retreat. The balcony has a splash tub and loungers. Lamps glow in the room as night begins to twinkle outside.

I toss the red tie from the doorknob onto the carpeted floor, leaving the black one to swing like an invitation.

But I'm confused. "Where are our surprises from Delta's?" I ask.

"*I'm* your surprise," Blair answers so sweetly that I'm suspicious.

Beau chuffs, "Oh, hell, Colt. Get ready."

I lick my lips, reaching over my back to tug my T-shirt off. "Oh, I'm ready." I make quick work of dropping my shorts, then my briefs next, kicking off my flip-flops, too.

I hold my arms out, buck naked and dick hard, daring her, "Surprise me, Raven."

She smirks, demanding, "Take the nice duvet off the

bed. I want you both naked and waiting for me on the mattress. I'll be out in a few minutes."

Beau strips his clothes off while I strip the bed, a deep moan crawling up my throat when I find a fitted, black latex sheet under the innocent, white bedding.

"Oh, hell," I mutter, staring at it.

"Told you." Beau chuckles.

I set the pile of linens down on a bench by a dresser before I turn back for my shorts on the floor. "I need my phone." I pluck it out of my shorts pocket. "We're recording this. Whatever she does to me, I never want to forget."

"Trust me. You won't," Beau taunts, nude with his cock jutting hard for Blair's next kinky surprise.

I prop the phone on the dresser across from the bed. If we angle our bodies sideways across the mattress, we can capture almost everything.

What that'll be?

Bring it on. I'm game.

Beau strokes off by the edge of the mattress. "Lie down, baby," he orders me, though I'm two inches taller, and I love it.

"I hear you!" Blair shouts from the adjacent bathroom. "I'm in charge. *Both* of you lie down."

I smirk. I love her. I love lying down beside him. We stare at the ceiling, a wooden fan lazily whirling above.

"Did you ever think we'd be here?"

"You mean fucking?" Beau asks. "And getting fucked? And loving you and loving her? Only in my wildest dreams."

"I mean the other thing," I answer, my hand reaching for his. "Did you ever think we'd agree to be the first NFL players to be out as a couple when we win the Super Bowl? Because you know, we will. We'll have to win."

"Don't jinx us."

"I'm not afraid of a jinx. I'm afraid of someone hurting you or Blair. About what some will say or do. That's all I care about."

Beau grips my hand. "The only thing that hurts is us hiding our love. All these years? I'm so sorry we did. I wish from our first kiss we could've stayed together."

I turn my head. He turns his, too. The blue storm of his eyes gets me every time.

"All these years," I answer, "we did stay together. My heart never left yours."

He cocks a grin. "You're making this really fucking romantic when I'm trying to stay hard."

I laugh. "You mean you can't stay hard while I melt your heart?"

Beau glances down. "It confuses Mr. Big. You make me feel all soft on the inside and hard on the outside."

"Need some help with that confusion?" I rise, grabbing his base, leaning over to take him between my lips, my mouth watering for his taste. I'm all soft and hard, too.

"Put that big cock in your mouth, and you'll get a spanking."

I snap my glance up to see Blair standing in the threshold, the light behind her illuminating her silhouette like a halo. Like she's our dark angel of orgy heaven.

"Holy fucking latex," I sigh.

Because Blair's wearing it for me with a shameless smile.

Black, high-heeled, thigh-high latex boots zip up her legs. No panties cover her thin black landing strip. A black latex corset laces tight around her waist. It has no cups, leaving her breasts magnificent and exposed, her nipples raging hard. Long, black latex gloves draw my eye down to the black strap-on dangling from her grasp and something hidden in her other hand.

"Oh, shit," Beau half moans, half laughs. "Welcome to the club. You're about to love getting so fucked tonight."

Blair stalks our way. "Did I hear you two being bad?"

Drool pools in my mouth. "Fuck yes, Raven, I'm guilty." My cock leaks. "Punish me with a life sentence of you dressed like our Dominatrix. Damn, woman, you're hot."

"You want to be my bad boy tonight, Colt?" She stands by the edge of the bed, the strap-on swaying from her grasp. "Do you want what I gave Beau?"

"Uh, baby," Beau mutters, eyeing the dildo, "that's *not* what you gave me."

"No, it's not. You weren't ready for this, but now you are." She lifts it, kissing it. "This is an eight-inch, vibrating, curving strap-on with three speeds and a wireless remote. Quite a popular purchase."

"Sold!" I shout, loving her professional sexpertise. "Woman, you could sell semen to seamen."

I make her grin. "But maybe you want what I gave, Beau? He loved it so much he almost passed out when he came."

"True story," Beau confirms as Blair reveals what's in her other hand.

Along with the strap-on remote, she's holding a smaller black dildo with a black strap and two holes.

"This is a prostrate massager," she explains. "I put one of these inside Beau for the first time, and he was mine forever."

"And it made me fuck you so hard while I was wearing it that I'll love you forever, too." He smirks, shaking his head, patting my shoulder. "Man, good luck. That's a hard call."

Me and my dick agree. Having Beau inside me feels like a calling fulfilled. Having Blair inside me? That's a fantasy fulfilled. "I'm curious about both," I confess.

She sets them on the bed. "I'll give you one tonight and promise the other tomorrow."

Crawling over me, she rings her tongue around my belly button, just like she did in Belize. That afternoon feels like a lifetime ago because that's what we have together.

A lifetime of this love.

I feel it vibrating like light through my skin.

I know they're giving me this night, too, because of the past couple of days we've shared. And I've never felt this free, this loved before.

I know this forever.

I glance left to find Beau watching us. Arousal and love flood his hooded gaze while Blair worships my nipples, knowing exactly how to lick them, blow on them, suck and bite them until I'm fisting the sheets, bowing my back, and growling for her.

I love her dominating me.

I could flip her over and hold her down, breeding her sweet pussy all night, but no, I need her like this. Blair has my love. She has my trust. For me, it's as seductive as sex.

So, like no woman before, I let her take me.

It's what I want.

She rises, straddling me, exposing her pussy, glistening and splayed over my chest pounding for her. She gazes down at me, playing with her nipples hoisted high in that corset while she rolls her hips, driving me mad.

I grab her waist, loving the slick, tight, naughty fabric she's laced in.

Damn, I don't know why I have such a fetish for this latex shit, but I do, and Blair makes it look like she's the brand ambassador for it. She looks like a pin-up girl, like every man's fantasy, and women's, too, I guess. Her curves squeeze and spill. Her milky skin and rosy nipples make my mouth water.

My cock aches.

"Fuck, Raven." I reach, lacing my hand through her hair, spilling over her shoulders. "You're so goddamn beautiful. Take whatever you want from me because I'll take forever with you. With him, too."

Beau's lying beside me, propped on an elbow. He's hard. He's stroking off to us.

"What does my big Daddy want tonight?" she asks. "Does he want to be bad for me?"

With latex fingertips, she pinches my nipples, and I writhe. "Fuck, yes." I smack her ass above me, ordering her, "Spank me. Fuck me. Make me do whatever you want because I will for you, woman. Always."

"Fuck," Beau growls, his stare combing my body. "You're so hard for this, Colt. I had no idea you had this kink."

"Hell yeah, I do. Look at our woman." I reach, pinching her nipples, too, and Blair throws her chin up, moaning as I tug hard. "She looks like our Bad Kitty we can fuck forever. She drives us crazy." Her hips roll, begging for more. "She loves us. She satisfies us. She gets so fucking dirty for us. She gives us that sweet pussy that's so wet for us, too."

"Fuck yes, she does." I set Beau off.

He jumps up like we're on the field, and he's rushing the play and can't be stopped.

He climbs behind her, straddling me, too. Grabbing her neck, he fists his base, and Blair doesn't fight him. She arches open for him.

I lie beneath them, still pinching her nipples, while I

watch in awe, with my lips parted at how Beau guides his swollen crown into her glistening pink entrance. It's so fucking hot, beautiful, and natural, watching as his thick cock starts fucking her pussy, pumping hard inside her.

He taunts Blair, thrusting while he snarls, "You want to fuck my man, too?"

He squeezes her neck, and she groans, "Yes. Yes, Beau. Fuck me so I can fuck Colt."

Holy shit, they're taking this next level, and I love it.

I love how he's possessive about me. I love how he loves her. I love how Blair takes us. She gives us so much while Beau delivers, too. Thrust after thrust, I watch her cream smear up and down his shaft.

I lick my lips to it, and Beau sees me.

"Taste us," he demands. "Be our bad boy and taste our fuck."

Damn, that does something to me.

Suddenly, I crave obeying, sliding down, and lining my mouth to where they're joined. To where I can watch Beau's thick shaft splitting Blair's slick folds open, his cock pumping slowly inside her.

I can smell their feral musk. I can see their milky lust. I can hear the smack of their arousal. So, I lave my tongue over the tender spot where Beau's shaft disappears inside Blair's sweet cunt.

Their moans could crack walls as I taste them. Dragging the tip of my tongue up to Blair's hard clit, I circle it over and over, making her sound feral before I lick down to Beau's stiff, veiny shaft, needing the deep sound of his moan, too.

"Dayum." I hear a Texas drawl. "My kinda people."

Now, I moan because that's Zar.

His voice is so distinct, dripping with power and sex

and honey. It makes my exposed cock so fucking hard, knowing he's watching us.

I don't know who else is in here. I can't see. I'm lying on my back, trapped between Blair's thighs, watching as Beau pulls out.

Palming my skull, Beau orders me, "Suck her cum off my cock. Taste what a sweet little slut she is for us."

"Yes, Colt," Blair sighs, palming my skull too. "Be my bad boy. Suck his cock for me."

I groan, loving their dirty commands and her tangy sugar. I love sucking it off of Beau's tip, letting others watch while I clean it off his shaft before I take control. I reach, guiding his tip inside her again.

I'm so hard for this, I feel my tip dripping, too. I feel my cock so naked and heavy under the eyes of others watching while I taste my lovers' lust until Beau has Blair so close.

Her thighs shake by my cheeks. "You're such a dirty girl for us," he coaxes, strumming her clit while I flick his base. I swear Beau can take Blair with his words alone. "You want to fuck my man? You want to fuck Colt's tight ass, Kitten? You expect me to share him with our sweet slut?"

"Yes," Blair gasps. "Yes. Please, Daddy. Please let me fuck him, too."

"Oh fuck me." A man's deep voice groans, seduced by our kink, too.

I don't know who it is, but I agree. I'm starving for it.

I pull Beau's fingers aside before taking Blair's hard little nub with a ruthless suck while Beau hammers inside her.

We make her buck, shaking and soaking my beard with her arousal. The quake of her thighs gets me off. I keep licking her clit until she stops. Until she's huffing for breath. Until she can order, "Turn over, Colt. Now it's my turn with your ass."

Beau holds her, twisting their bodies off mine before I flip over.

Looking to my left, I groan, finding a sight I'll never forget.

Six men are watching us.

Carter stands, holding Booker with his back to his chest. Brayton sits with his husband, Jim. They're on the small sofa in the room. And Zar stands beside Nick, closer to the bed. They're not touching yet, but their cocks are so hard, aching like they will be soon.

This is the ultimate act of pride. Of trust. Of love as I lie and receive Blair.

"Do you want to be bad, Colt?" Blair taunts, spanking me, "Do you want me to fuck you, too?"

"Yes," I grunt.

"Then spread your ass for me."

I lie prone, my cheek pressed against the slick sheet, watching the other men as I reach behind me and open myself for her. It makes me raging hard, feeling the cool drizzle as she douses my ass in lube, covering me and the latex sheet. It makes everything slippery and erotic.

I'm a big man in every way. I don't have to take this; I want to. I want them to watch our beautiful woman do this to me. It thrills me, letting her finger my ass, her slick digits in those latex gloves plunging and twirling, making my back arch, making me beg for more.

"Oh fuck, yes, Raven," I growl. "Fuck my ass, baby, please."

Forever, I'm seconds away from coming on the rubbery sheet, but I edge.

I hold back until Blair finally gives it to me. So slow. So

damn good my eyes roll. I grunt, feeling the toy she chose, stretching to her careful penetration, her strap-on dildo vibrating in my ass.

She lies over me, pressing her breasts to my back. Beau lies beside us, watching us, watching Blair fuck my ass. He's still so hard, licking his lips to it, and it makes me lick mine.

But I turn my head back to our audience.

I let them watch me receive my woman. To love her. To need her. I want to come for her. I'm aching and fucking the slick mattress to do it. "Yes," I taunt us. "Yes, Blair, fuck my ass like a dirty girl. Spank me." She does it three times with stinging smacks, and I groan. "Yes. Show them how I'm such a bad boy for you." I make her moan, too.

"Damn."

I hear more voices than Beau's admiring our kink.

I'm so close, but Blair's closer. I can hear her thinning breath. She can't even speak. Her slick hands grab my hard glutes, spreading me wider. She must be watching me take her thrusts, and I love her so much I give her this. I take her there. "Yes, fuck me, Blair. I'm yours, too. Fuck me so hard and come in my ass."

She falls over me, her lush breasts and soft body shuddering over my back as she comes. "Colt," she sighs against my flesh. I know the sound of her orgasm. It drives me wild. "Colt, oh my god." She kisses my back, but we're not done.

I need her, too.

I need us.

I pat her leg, signaling for her to pull out, and she does. Then, in a fast blur, I flip over, taking her petite body, too. I turn us, putting our feet toward the edge of the bed, toward our audience with our bodies on our sides.

I lie behind Blair, hooking my arm under her knee, lifting her thigh so high the whole room can watch my aching cock sink inside her splayed slick pussy. I make her groan while I start rolling my hips, gliding my hungry length up and down her swollen walls.

Damn, she feels so good. Damn, she's so wet and ready for me.

"Did you like that, Blair?" I steam over her ear. "Are you Daddy's dirty girl? Did you come fucking my ass?"

"Oh god, yes, Colt," she sighs.

Like he can read our desire, Beau joins us. He lies behind me, on his side, too, hooking his beefy arm under my knee. I help him. I lift my leg so he can guide his fat tip into my ready ass. He starts thrusting inside me, taking me like Blair did while I fuck her wet pussy.

The moans. The connection. The show we give of our love. We lift our legs, letting everyone see our bodies joined.

Blair cranes her chin, looking over her shoulder, seeking my languid kiss, and I give it to her. Our lips are lush, tender, and sharing while my thrusts inside her are hard, driven by Beau's force.

He's more brutal, more aggressive with his relentless fuck, and I love it. I love how he takes me like an animal, like I'm his mate. It's him controlling our tempo, our feral fuck, while others watch, almost speechless and in awe.

I look, a groan escaping my heaving lungs, when I see Nick sucking Zar's cock. He's kneeling before him, his head bobbing. Nick's hands are grabbing Zar's thighs, his throat *glucking* on his cock, while Zar's lusty stare won't abandon our spectacle.

We make Brayton and his husband hard. They're slowly stroking each other's cocks to our show.

Carter and Booker still hold each other, but Carter is raging hard, like another round is coming between them.

There's something about this give and take. This trust

and claim. I'm seeing it. I'm feeling it. To let them watch us. To allow ourselves to be seen. To demand that our love be witnessed.

I won't suffer a life hidden anymore.

It has me craning my neck for Beau's scruffy, passionate kiss, taking it before I turn my chin, sharing his kiss, still tingling on my lips with Blair's plump waiting mouth.

"Fuck, yes, baby." It starts taking Beau first. He bites my shoulder, his bicep lifting my knee, so I have to take him. He's getting off on them watching him fuck my ass, I know him. I feel him everywhere. I take his brutal fuck while I fuck Blair's tight wet heat.

Her moans turn into gasps. She's going too, so I lift her leg higher. I open her for all to watch my length start driving deep into her, and that claims her. She's proud and shameless about our sex, too. In soft mewls, she comes, gushing over my dick.

Beau hears her.

Her pleasure always makes him come.

With a final grunt, with a brutal thrust, he buries his thick cock so hard in my ass I see stars. I explode. I shout as I release, collapsing between the bodies I'll love forever.

Minutes we spend catching our breath. We spend time holding each other, kissing lips and shoulders, and watching the love of others around us.

Brayton and his husband leave to start fucking, I assume. Carter and Booker do the same.

But Nick and Zar finish, their passion sealed with long kisses before they aim our way.

We're all nude. We all trust. We're all in this together.

Now, I feel what Ruby means, my heart not finding an ounce of fear.

We have skin in the game.

We have our hearts in the game.

We have the game of our lives to win for everyone like us. For everyone to feel this free.

Zar lies at the foot of the bed. Nick joins him. They spoon, Zar holding Nick's chest while he drapes his thigh over Nick's, and we chat about the next few months—our next games and plans.

I want to share more with them. Not sex. Not my body. But I want this friendship.

I look at Beau. I look at Blair. Their eyes are full of trust, too, and I know my partners. We need this support, this community.

So when Zar mentions a private Halloween party hosted by people like us. When he asks if we'd be interested in going?

I'm already imagining the masks and latex costumes we'll wear.

Blair

CHAPTER THIRTY-SIX

Beau keeps staring at me, cocking his head to the side. He's making me nervous as if this day isn't a test of super-strength Xanax as it is.

Others stare at us, too. They recognize Beau and Colt.

It's the day after Thanksgiving in this coffee shop full of retail warriors who need more caffeine before they return to battle.

Me? I'd rather be stuck on a puddle-jumping plane, flying through a hurricane, listening to Amber Kostas bitch about drugstore eyeshadow while I barf fried pickles than shop on Black Friday.

Clearly, I'm not a fan.

But this is worse.

Colt blows his hot chocolate, looking so damn cute because he's got whipped cream on his beard, while Beau sits beside him, across the cafe table from me. He's staring like praying mantises are mating on my forehead.

"What?" I finally huff. "What are you staring at?"

"Nothing." He's not blinking.

But I am. A lot.

I look away, but his stare gives my cheek a dermatological laser peel. "Beau Willuf Bronson," I mutter. "If I have a booger in my nose that you're not telling me about, I'll—"

"I'll tell you," Colt jumps in. "That's our code, remember?"

"Then what is he staring at?" I ask Colt, who starts doing the same.

Yes, I'm blinking a ridiculous amount, like I've been exposed to tear gas, but nothing else is different about me.

I'm the same.

My hair is down, smoothed, and curled to one side. I'm wearing high-waisted jeans that Vale swore do not make my butt look three feet long. Maybe that's what they're staring at, but I'm sitting on my ass.

That can't be it.

I glance down.

I didn't spill peppermint latte on my white cropped turtleneck sweater. Sure, I'm showing a little belly. It accentuates my curves. My men are used to that.

I dressed for this. I carefully planned it, actually. I look cute and casual while we wait for Reese to join us.

We're stuck in the corner of a coffee shop in Birmingham, Alabama, patrons gawking and snapping pics at us. I've gotten used to that, too. Fans and press don't bother me.

Atlanta is 10-1. The hype is so loud, honestly, I don't hear it anymore. Beau and Colt are deaf to it, too.

They say they're just having fun playing ball. It's like since they secretly know it's Beau's last season, the pressure is gone. They're soaking up every moment on the gridiron like they're back in high school. Half the time they play, they smile like they huffed laughing gas.

It's so damn cute. I'm so proud and happy, but not now.

Beau is so sexy, annoying the shit out of me.

Finally, I can't take it. I lean toward him, trying to widen my eyes while I demand, "What are you staring at?"

"Kitten, if I tell you, you'll get mad."

"If you don't tell me, I'll start putting toothpaste in your golden Oreos again. Or make more caramel candied onions instead of apples for Halloween."

Colt chuckles. "Fuck, that was funny."

The memory of our Tricks and Treats Halloween trip with Zar and Nick to that private island of fucks and fun with their friends gives Colt the belly laughs again.

"Dude," he says, "her candied onions made you cry for an hour. No boom, boom for you that night."

Beau rolls his eyes, smiling at the memory, too, but I'm focused on this annoying minute.

"Just tell me, Beau. *Please. What is it?*"

Am I whining? Yep, I sound like a rich housewife on a reality show.

He lets out a long exhale, his face tender while I blink and blink and blink, the suspense killing me.

"Kitten," he sighs, "what did you do to your lashes?"

"What?" I blink like a frog. One eye oddly, slowly, lazily blinks before the other blinks with an amphibious twitch across my face.

It makes him fight a smile. I see his nostrils flaring while he asks, "What did you do to them?"

"Nothing," I lie, making it worse. I try not to blink, straining my eyelids. You know, like when you suddenly smell a fart and it wasn't yours?

"They look different," Beau softly says. "They make you blink like you have conjunctivitis."

Colt snorts, then looks away. *Smart man.* He's avoiding my blinking death stare.

"My lashes are perfectly fine."

No, they're not. They're sticking like gooey price tags attached to my eyelids.

"They look pretty as usual," Beau eases. "But you keep blinking like you're caught in a dust storm or like you're an animated character or like—"

"Okay, okay. Enough with the similes." I fight the instinct to blink and my eyes fight back, filling with water. "I might've tried something new. I wanted to look nice today. We're meeting Forrest for the first time, and I wanted to make a good impression."

"Babe," Beau chuckles, "with all that blinking, the only impression you're giving is that you're a compulsive liar."

"*Beeaaaauuuu.*"

"*Blaaaiiiirrrr.*" He keeps laughing. "Babe, love tells the truth, right?"

"I need you to support the lies I tell myself. My lashes look perfectly natural."

Just then, the top corner of my left eyelid, which has a super long lash that requires its own zip code, welds itself to my bottom lid, sticking like flypaper.

I can't open my left eye, and I'm not even in TLC.

This morning, I tried gluing on individual lashes. You know, since one of my boyfriends, who's arachnophobic, shit his shorts at the sight of my usual lash strips.

And this is the thanks I get for being a lashified, sensitive girlfriend.

"He's going to like y'all." Colt's chest is shaking. The cute fucker is trying not to laugh, either. "Don't worry."

"Fine," I huff. "Gimme a minute."

I stomp up, wedging my way through the crowd, seeking the ladies' room to yank these damn things off because Colt's right. Forrest won't care. He'll barely notice I'm there.

He'll be so focused on Colt or Beau.

We don't know who Forrest's biological father is. Reese did the test. She got the results, but we don't know them yet. They're sealed in an envelope because Colt wanted to find out this way—in person, with me and Beau here.

Like once and for all, his haunting question will be answered.

But more importantly, Forrest has been told about babies and biological parents. Reese said she and her husband worked with a counselor on how to do this. They've had many talks to prepare for today when we'll follow her home.

Today, when Forrest meets his father.

We just need to know if it's Beau or Colt.

Staring in the bathroom mirror, I curse, plucking off the fake lashes.

I guess I did this dumb shit because I'm nervous, too.

This won't be easy. I'm so mad at Reese. So is Beau. I'm surprised if he'll even speak to her today. He's not angry about her cheating on him. He's enraged about all she's put Colt through.

Yes, Colt is the size of a Viking, but his heart is even bigger. He's just a giant, ink-covered, muscle-wielding cinnamon roll with a very hard, ripped, long, smooth exterior.

Did I mention hard? Because Colt is. A lot. I'm surprised he doesn't pass out from blood loss due to erections.

But then again, Beau would be in a coma by now. He's equally guilty.

And yes, Beau can be so tender, too, but not when he's protective.

Then, he's evil.

Like last week when he had enough of the photographers stalking us.

They follow Beau's truck everywhere. So he pulled through the Starbucks near his house and ordered a round of coffees for them. Then, he strolled up to their cars parked behind us, carrying a drink tray of steaming cups, and said, "Here you go, boys. You've been up all day, following me around. I thought you might need a good jolt."

Oh, it was a jolt.

Beau stirred three tablespoons of unflavored laxative powder into each one.

"Do this shit to me," I warned, laughing while I watched him do it over the center console of his truck, "and you're dead."

"Kitten, I may give you shit." He kissed my cheek over his piping hot cups of revenge. "But it's always safe with me."

Cute asshole stole my line from college.

When I return to our table, I see Reese pushing open the glass door. She searches for us, and I wave.

It's weird. Reese looks great. She looks healthy, and I'm relieved. We were best friends once. Deep down, I care. But I can't forget what she did. I just hope to be like Colt and forgive her in time.

Beau struggles, too. "Hi," is all he says to her as she sits with us at the table.

"I got you a chai latte." I slide it to her. "It used to be your favorite. Hope it's not cold."

"Thanks." Her hands wrap around the paper cup. "And thanks, y'all, for meeting me like this. I thought we should talk before we go to my house. It's just around the corner."

"Does he know we're coming?" Colt asks.

"Yes," Reese answers. "I told him that his biological father, the man I made a baby with in college, is coming to meet him today. Forrest keeps asking what his name is, but I said his father wants to tell him."

Colt nods, but Beau is fuming, staring at her like he can't accept it.

He seethes, asking Reese, "Why did you name him Forrest? Was that to fuck with Colt's head or mine?"

Reese drops her gaze, spinning the cup in her hand. "No. It was never to hurt you, either of you. After I realized what I did, I wanted to give him a happy name. A name I associated with hope and unconditional love. The name of a good friend, a good father, a good man, and all that."

She wipes a tear off her cheek. "Beau," she lifts her eyes to him, "I'm so sorry I hurt you, too. You were always good to me. You saved me until I could save myself. And there's no excuse for what I did. I've told Colt I'm sorry so many times, but Blair's right. I need to make amends with actions, not just words."

She turns her watery eyes to Colt. "Whoever Forrest's father is, I promise you can see him as much as you want. Jake agreed. This has been hard on our marriage, but we'll get through it. He knows it's best for Forrest."

"Do you have the test results?" Colt sounds gruff, like

he's choked up, so I reach for his hand. He holds it while Reese pulls a manilla envelope from her bag.

"I haven't opened this," she says. "I respected your wishes. You'll be the first to know."

She hands it to Colt. I let go of his hand so he can open it.

The papers tremble in his grasp, and I glance at Beau. He sees it, too. How Colt has waited so long for this.

"I hope Forrest is his." That's what Beau told me this morning in the shower. Colt was still asleep. I crawled out of bed, and Beau followed me. The weight of this day hung over us, so he held me in the shower, nuzzling his forehead to mine while he confessed, "I'll love Forrest if he's mine. Heck, I'll love that boy no matter what. But I love Colt so much; I want Forrest to be his. I can't ever hurt Colt. I can't take his son from him."

We hold our breath, watching Colt read the letter, his hand crumpling the paper. A tear falls over his lashes, streaming down to his beard, making me cry, too.

He closes his eyes and lifts his chin. He's praying to his mom, I know. I do the same when I need help.

More of his tears fall, and I grab Beau's thigh, squeezing to hang on. To will this to finally go right for Colt. To finally give him peace.

"He's mine," Colt sighs, another tear escaping. "Forrest is mine."

I exhale, a stream of tears pouring down my cheeks. Beau sighs with heavy relief, wrapping his arm around me.

"Your mom always believed it," Reese gently adds. "She said Forrest may look like me, but he has your soul. She said she could see it in his eyes."

Colt nods, clenching his jaw. I can see him fighting his flood of tears that wants to escape.

"Can we go see him now?" He coughs, begging, "Please, I can't wait anymore."

It's five quick minutes around some turns, driving up hills through a tree-lined neighborhood to Reese's home.

Autumn leaves dot her front lawn. Her home is quaint and craftsman-style, with a holiday wreath hanging on her door. You can tell it's a warm, loving home.

The day is sunny and crisp. Beau parks his truck by the curb in front of Reese's house, but we wait. Reese asked us to while she disappears through her front door for a few minutes.

"We'll stay here for an hour, and then we'll meet him, too." Beau looks in the rearview mirror, telling Colt, "Okay, babe? You tell him and take your time with him. You've waited long enough for this."

"I'm nervous," Colt mutters. "What if he hates me?"

I turn around in my passenger seat. Colt won't let me ride in the back, but now I wish I were there with him, holding him. Instead, I reach, holding his knee. "It'll be okay. He's going to love you. Heck, he already does. He's your biggest fan."

The front door opens, and the little boy emerges with his parents behind him.

"Oh, god. Your mom was right," I gasp, seeing him in person. "Forrest does look like you, Colt. He's you up one side and down the other."

Colt coughs, clearing his throat. "Alright, I got this. I can't lose my shit in front of him."

"It's okay to cry," Beau says. "He's your son. It's okay if he knows how much you love him."

Colt cups Beau's shoulder, leaning forward to peck his cheek, and then he pecks mine before turning to open the car door.

And when he does?

When Colt emerges from the back seat of the truck, his massive body landing on the sidewalk with a gentle thud, a sob escapes my throat.

Because I watch Forrest.

I watch the boy's eyes get so big as if he can't believe it. It's like he's witnessing every childhood miracle. I'd feel sorry for his dad, Jake, but that boy will always love him. Jake raised him. He's been there.

"Hey, Forrest," Colt calls out, shoving his hands in the front pockets of his jeans.

I climb across the truck's cab to sit in Beau's lap to watch this together.

Beau cracks the window a bit so we can hear, too.

"Colton Hawke?" The boy sounds surprised but looks confused. He's frozen on the brick step of his porch. "Are you here to play with me? With your ball?"

"I sure am." Slowly, like he's afraid he'll scare him away, Colt walks across the grass, closing the distance between them. "I'm here to throw the ball with you all day if you want. But I'm also here to tell you something if that's okay."

"Go on, sweetie." Gently, Reese urges Forrest down the front steps. "Go say hello. Colton came to see you."

Forrest's dad, Jake, watches. He's stoic but not mad. You can read it in how his eyebrows bend. He's just worried about his boy.

"But," Forrest turns back to his mom, "we're waiting for the man you made a baby with. The man who's my father, not my dad."

Colt struggles. His voice cracks. "That's me."

Forrest turns back to him, and in the boy's eyes, Colt drops to his height. But to us... we witness love so profound drop Colt to his knees on the grass before his son.

"Forrest, I'm your father," he says, his tone strangling with emotion. "I'm the man your mom had a baby with. And I'm really happy to finally meet you like this. I'm here today because I hope we can be friends if that's okay with you."

I bite my lip, salty tears spilling over their seam. I nestle my head against Beau's. He's squeezing my waist. He's crying, too.

The boy tilts his head. It's so cute. It's like he's seeing Colt for the first time. "Is that why I run so fast?" he asks. "Because you're my father? I'm like you because I'm the baby you made me with my mom?"

Colt huffs a laugh. It's so tender. It's so he won't cry; I can hear it. He's fighting back tears.

"Yeah," he answers. "That's probably why you're so fast. But I bet you throw so good because your Dad taught you. Right? He's teaching you to be a great football player?"

"Yeah," Forrest answers, his proud chin jutting high. He's an innocent kid. For him, it's simple. "Can we play now? Me, you and my dad? Can we play with the ball you gave me? It's in my room. Wanna see it? I have posters of you, too. And I have your jersey. You and Beau Bronson's, but you're my favorite. Don't tell him. He's your friend, right?"

"Yeah." Colt clears his throat. He rises from his knees. "He's my *best* friend. But I won't tell him I'm your favorite. I'll let you tell him."

I kiss Beau's cheek. It's wet with tears.

"Come on." Forrest holds out his little hand for Colt's. "Come see my room. And my Legos. And my—"

The boy's excited, rambling on, tugging at Colt's massive hand like he's found his new best friend. Colt smiles, glancing over his shoulder at us, and we wave. Then he climbs the porch, shaking Jake's hand before following his son into the house.

We watch as Reese disappears, closing the front door behind them.

Wind rustles the autumn leaves while we're silent, while love swirls around us.

Gently, Beau presses his lips to my ear. "We're going to have a baby together, Blair Monroe." He whispers, "Please, say yes."

Tears won't stop filling my eyes. "Yes." I can see it, too.

Tenderly, he murmurs, his beard tickling my flesh. "We'll have a girl who loves books, and then we'll have a boy who loves football. Two boys, actually."

I turn, nuzzling his nose. "Or the other way around."

"Sorry." His eyes sparkle, searching mine. "I forgot my feminism."

"You're a hot alpha male with a big dick and a sexy smile. Feminism says I have to forgive you."

He laughs. "Not in the books I read."

"And since you read books by Virginia Woolf and Toni Morrison, too, my feminism says I have to give you really hot, kinky sex every single night."

"It doesn't take hot, kinky sex for us to make lots of bookish babies."

"It does if you're making babies with me."

Laughter fills our kiss. I taste the salt on our lips, too. The happy tears we shed for Colt.

Something about this moment makes Beau cup my cheeks, and I cup his back, loving his whiskers in my grasp. It deepens our kiss, our hearts beating together, our breath intertwined like our connection.

It takes me full circle, back to the night Beau showed up at my dorm. When he had a busted lip and a broken heart over Colt. I could feel his love, wanting to take away his pain. And we wanted to kiss, too. We wanted to share everything together, but we couldn't.

We waited until now.

"Marry me," Beau sighs into our kiss. "Marry me, Blair Monroe."

The sweet shock stops my heart. I pull back, searching his deep blue eyes. I can't believe my ears. Or my luck.

"Is this a prank?"

"Never." He won't let go of my face. "I'll do it right one day. I'll surprise you with a huge ring and everything, I promise. But I can't sit here and see Colt with his son and not see every day of my future with you and him and our kids, too. It's all I want now. More than the Super Bowl."

"Such goddamn blasphemy." I gently smile. "I'm telling Coach you said it."

"Go ahead." He pecks my lips. "It's the truth. I'm not going to win the Super Bowl for myself. I'll win it with Colt for every kid like us in school. For every closeted guy in a locker room. For every lonely college athlete who's not as lucky as I was." His thumb brushes my cheek. "Because I loved Blair Monroe. I survived hell because she made my life heaven when she was around."

I'm so proud. I'm so in love, too, I have to prank and pout, "But you said *I* was the pain in your ass who made your life hell. You said *I* was the best at it."

"You are, baby." His smiling lips seek mine. They're soft, kissing and vowing, "You're my heaven and hell forever."

"So, you want me to be your wife, your WAG?"

"Yep."

"You want me to wear an obnoxiously massive diamond ring, size five by the way, on my finger. It'll be so big, twelve carats to be exact, that I'll have to do bicep curls to pick my nose with my left finger?"

His deep laugh is so sexy. "Yep."

"You want me to decorate our house any way I want, as well as our vacation home in Key West?"

"Key West?"

"Yeah. Where Hemingway lived. I have a love-hate relationship with him."

"Yes, Kitten. We can buy a house in Key West."

"And you want me to be Mrs. Beau Bronson?"

"Hell, no." He shakes his head. "I love Blair Madison Monroe way too much. Don't you dare change your name or the other naughty ones I call you."

I search his eyes, remembering the morning after Valentine's when I made Beau leave. When I wanted him to have his dream. Even if it wasn't me.

But now, I am.

He dreams of our love.

I nuzzle his nose. "Okay, I'll be your wife, your better half, and ball-and-chain. I'll be the mother of your children, too. I'll spend all your money on books and—"

"Uh, you make money, too."

"Yeah, but it's more fun spending yours."

I feel his smile as he kisses my neck. "This is the prenup from hell."

"Beau." I lift his gaze to mine. "I'll be your wife forever under two conditions."

He cocks a grin. "What's the game plan?"

"Ask me next time in a way that melts my panties and makes me snot cry."

"Done." He kisses me. "What else?"

"Marry Colt, not me."

I watch it light up his blue eyes. I watch the dream dance across his gorgeous gaze.

"Right?" I ask. "It feels right, you marrying Colt, doesn't it?"

His brows bend. "But I want to marry you, too."

"But you can't. Not legally. So marry your high school sweetheart. The one you've loved for so long. Do that, *and* you can have the wife of your dreams, too. I don't need for it to be legal, for it to be real." I touch his chest. His heart is pounding. "But think about it. You and Colt need it. You deserve it. You don't need to hide. You deserve to celebrate your husband, your love, and for the whole world to see it."

"Blair." His hand glides through my hair, tugging my lips to his. "Baby, I love you even more for saying that. You know I love Colt. I've always wanted to marry him, but I want to be your husband, too. I wanted you for so long. I need you to be my wife."

"I am." I chew my lip, fighting the sweet tears, but *fuck it*. Today is the time to let them flow.

"Beau, from the moment you showed up at my door, saving my friend with her passed out in your arms. Or the time you knocked on my door with a busted lip, missing *your* friend and needing me too. Or the morning I made you leave me alone in a hotel room, so you could have your dream. It's like you said; there's always been an *us*. We've always been together. I've always loved you, and good fucking luck making me stop."

He kisses me so deeply a tiny sob catches in my throat. I can feel it in how he clutches me so tight. *He's in the moments with me, too.*

Like that's where our love resides, not in rings, paper, or names.

"But there's this girl from college," he murmurs over my

lips. "For my birthday, she made a paper rose for me from the pages of a Harry Potter book and left it on my pillow without a note. But I know it was her. I still have the rose, and she still has my heart. How do I show her I'll be devoted to her forever?"

My fucking happy tears won't stop, so I kiss his lips. *I won't ever stop kissing Beau's lips.* "I'm sure you'll come up with a game plan."

BEAU

CHAPTER THIRTY-SEVEN

THERE'S THIS GUY FROM HIGH SCHOOL I FELL IN LOVE WITH.
THERE'S THIS GIRL FROM COLLEGE WHO SAVED ME.

E veryone knows the feeling of people watching you. Most of the time, it's no big deal. It's a fleeting moment.

But today, millions are watching us make history.

It would almost be surreal, like I'm living in a dream, but I've been getting the shit sacked out of me during the first half.

So it's very real.

It's the Super Bowl.

We're matched up against Philadelphia again. Although we're favored to win, we're down 14-24 at halftime, and the pressure is immense.

Everyone not only expects us to win.

Too many *need* us to win.

It's not just the victory that matters to so many. It's the

legacy we'll create for generations, for everyone like me and Colt.

I stand by the locker assigned to me, and I stretch, trying to breathe through the stress, the expectation that I'll lead us there. I keep my muscles warm. That's what I usually do during halftime, but the halftime of the Super Bowl is longer, and the extra minutes are torture.

We can distract ourselves. We can watch the halftime show on the flatscreens in the locker room.

I glance up at the screen to my left and watch as the lights drop in the stadium. The singer is about to take the stage.

It's about to be an epic performance and not because the performer is the number-one-selling woman pop artist of all time who happens to date another NFL player.

It's because she's pulled off a last-minute wardrobe change. It's because, in addition to her glittery Louboutin boots and signature Versace bodysuits, she stands in the spotlight, wearing a sparkling rainbow pride tailcoat.

Don't ask me how she got it so fast, but she's doing it. She's taking the stage in strong support of me and Colt.

Of "The First Fourteen."

That's what they're calling us—the first fourteen NFL players to come out as gay, bi, or queer.

Yes, a few have come out over the years, but not like this —not together, not as a movement, not before they play in the Super Bowl.

We waited until after our team's morning at the hotel.

The Pact—that's what Zar's group informally calls itself —strategically selected ten reporters. They were invited, with their camera crews, to a meeting room rented in our team's hotel.

Speculation flew as to what the impromptu, secret press conference was about.

Great lengths were taken to sneak the other players, who are not playing in the game, into the hotel and into the meeting room where reporters were waiting.

We wore black or white button-up shirts with black pants. No colors to signify teams or causes. Some suggested the pride colors, but we decided not today.

Today, we let our voices speak.

Nick went first and kept it short. Over the months, there will be more time to speak. We have group interviews, feature stories, documentaries, and more planned.

But today, it was simple.

The words were poignant and planned.

"There are almost seventeen hundred players, like us, in the NFL today," Nick spoke into the microphone at the podium. "If our numbers match the world we live in, that means about one hundred men in the league are gay or bisexual. That means too many are in the closet. Too few are free. Until now.

"Today, we are the first fourteen players to say we are proud. We hope we inspire others to speak up, too. My name is Nick Barinov. I am one of many. I'm a football player and a proud gay man."

Then, each player stood at the mic and proudly came out, too.

Colt and I went last.

"My name is Colton Hawke. I am one of many." His voice didn't waver. "I'm a football player and the son of a devoted mother. In her memory, I am proud to say I am a father and a bisexual man in love."

Then I took the mic last. "My name is Beau Bronson. I am one of many." I looked straight into the camera lens of the largest sports network in the world. "I'm a football player who's always loved the game, and today, I'll win the Super Bowl for everyone like me. For everyone proud of who they love. I am a bisexual man in a loving, committed partnership with Colton Hawke and Blair Monroe."

Questions erupted.

We didn't answer any.

We stood in line, broad shoulder to shoulder, our hands crossed in front. We lifted our proud chins and stood in solidarity, fourteen men out at once in the NFL.

That photograph, that moment, will go in the history books. We could feel it.

Then silently, we left the room, one by one, while Ruby became our spokesperson. It seems The Pact had been hiding her as their secret weapon all along.

Word, of course, spread like wildfire.

Colt and I weren't even on our team's bus, waiting to take us to the stadium for the game, before tens of millions knew, including our teammates.

I stepped on the bus before Colt. Under my black tailored Dior suit, I was sweating. But I lifted my chin, ready for hateful glares, cruel jokes, or disgusted eyes that wouldn't even meet mine.

It was the moment I feared the most.

The one that kept me silent for so long.

But Malik Goodwin stood up and started clapping. Then David Martinez. Then Patrick Smith. Then Coach. The entire bus gave us a standing ovation.

Yeah, it fucking choked me up. Colt too. From our teammates, we got hugs and back slaps instead of hate.

But from others? We know what's coming, too.

"Rise up!" Malik shouted. "And let's win a mother-fucking Super Bowl!"

We've been focused on the game ever since.

Should I be worried we're ten down at the half?

Yeah.

All season, I've felt it in my heart. I've felt the joy and love on the field.

It's just a game.

I tell myself when I'm in the pocket, and huge defensive linemen aim for me, trying to score a hit so hard that I'm on Injury Reserve or worse.

But hell, no, I won't let them. I've fought too hard to make it this far. Ice baths with Colt. Heat therapy with Blair. Acupuncture and sheer will have me pushing my right shoulder to the limit. It feels like hot razors slicing my tendons every time I throw.

Still... I fucking throw, and we win.

But today, when we took the field, I didn't know what to expect.

I saw a sea of sixty thousand people. And maybe it was all in my head because their noise usually sounds like a jet or a trumpet; it depends on the stadium. I'm used to the cheers and jeers, but this time, it sounded different. It felt different.

It was different.

It's not just a game.

Atlanta's flags and colors were smeared with Philadelphia's. From where I stood on the gridiron, they filled the horizon. I expected that.

But then I saw the rainbow flags. Then I saw the cruel homemade signs. "BRONSON BLOWS HAWKE." "HAWKE WIDE RECEIVES BRONSON."

You get the idea.

No, it's not just a game. It's not just my *last* game.

It's THE GAME.

It's every rap song about owning one shot, capturing one moment. That song plays in my head on a loop—the proud burden pounding through every cell in my body.

Because if we lose, it won't be blamed on missed blocks or mistakes or holding penalties. And it won't be about our completions or our offense or defense.

It'll be blamed on me. It'll be blamed on Colt. It'll be blamed on our love. On everyone like us.

But if we win?

We'll change "America's game" forever.

I can only imagine what's being posted online—what fans, haters, and commentators are saying about me, Colt, and Blair.

We agreed that I'd reveal our relationship since I was the last to speak. I'd never out them without their permission.

Besides, who are we in love with?

Blair had a T-shirt made. She's wearing it right now. It's Atlanta's colors. It's white with a black infinity symbol proudly circling her breasts with BEAU and COLT in red over each.

Our woman's so cute. She's proud and shameless. That beautiful woman will put our love in your face until you feel it, too.

And you're welcome.

Love like ours feels amazing.

Cameras keep cutting to her, cheering in the box suite with my family. We told them months ago. They're in full support of us. Blair's sister and father are here, too, along with Ruby, Zar, and Nick. Lots of our friends are here. We only surround ourselves with the people who love us.

Stretching my right shoulder, tugging it tight across my chest, the tension burns as I search across the locker room and find the other half of my heart, my other love, with his nose down.

Colt's on his phone.

Usually, we put them away during a game. We need to stay focused.

Yep, no distractions.

But then, as if he senses me, Colt looks up and shakes his phone like, "Check yours."

So I turn, digging through the front pocket of my backpack. I swipe my screen to our group text: Blair, Colt, and me.

KITTEN

> New Rule: White football pants must be worn at home. You're making my ovaries explode

COLT

> New Rule: Black latex must be worn in bed. It makes my dick explode

KITTEN

> New Rule: We wear it but don't sleep in it. Talk about boiling in man-soup all night

I know what they're doing, and it works. I relax, laugh, and chime in.

> New Rule: We win and get matching tattoos of blue cocks

KITTEN

> I worship your blue veined throbbers but I'm not erecting them on my skin

COLT

> Erect blue veined throbbers? That's going in my sleeve

Big blue gamecocks. Like for our galactic games

And we ink our names together

KITTEN

Rookie, that's a jinx

COLT

True Story

No jinx

It's good luck

We'll get our cocks and names

KITTEN

Beau Bronson, if you tattoo my name anywhere on your hot body I will lick your ass

Colt looks up from his phone, smirking all sexy at me like, "*Dayum.*" So, I wink back before replying.

Kitten, LICK my ass, and I'll tattoo your name right on it

KITTEN

Typo

I'll KICK your ass

Too late

NEW RULE: Blair licks ass with her name on it

COLT

Spreading my cheeks for the ink now

KITTEN

New Rule: Win this Super Bowl and I'll

Then nothing. No dots. No text.

What?

She'll what?

I glance up at Colt again, and he shrugs. On the flatscreen, the crowd is going wild for the halftime singer and her final song about touchdowns and love as my phone vibrates in my hand with Blair's answer.

KITTEN

I'll write your names on my heart forever

That's a classic Blair.

That's the best line before we smile, tucking our phones away.

"Alright, goddammit," Coach calls us into a huddle, and here we go.

In the third quarter, we orchestrate a heart-pounding, ninety-two-yard drive that ends in Goodwin scoring a touchdown. I'm feeling hopeful, confident.

We're 21-24 going into the fourth.

When the offense takes the field again, we move to huddle as I catch Colt waving to the midfield. He spared no expense getting Forrest, along with Reese and Jake, seats to see our game.

"A-town. A-town. Coors. Sixteen," I shout the call, the trick play where I'll hand off to Goodwin, a Coors fan. Then he'll trick defense and turn, passing to Colt, Mr. Sixteen Candles, who'll be waiting.

And it works.

The crowd goes fucking wild for Colt as he struts across the end zone.

With the field goal, we lead 28-24. Victory is in our grasp. I can finally breathe.

But I'm lying to myself as our defense takes the field,

and I stand on the sideline, trying to stay calm. I mutter, repeating my mantra, "It's just a game. It's just a game."

But it's not. Philadelphia's offense can execute like ours. They look ready to kill our lead. I watch, cursing as they get their first down. They're in our red zone and about to score.

And I feel sick.

And, *oh fuck.*

Coach storms my way with a fierce look I've never seen in his eyes. With his play sheet, he blocks his mouth. Cameras can't read his lips as he growls at me, "I've never been so goddamn proud of you, Bronson, as I am today. And goddammit, I'm not just talking about this goddamn game. I'm talking about you. I'm talking about Hawke. That was some goddamn brave shit today. You've put it all on the line, so go win this game because you're the best goddamn player I've ever coached."

Goddamn, I'm shocked.

I just nod, smiling from ear to ear. "Yes, Coach."

He marches away as I stare at the stands and the rainbow flags.

This time, I notice the signs that read "LOVE WINS," and "THE FOURTEEN FOREVER," and "YOU SCORED AN ALLY," and "BRONSON, WE LOVE HAWKE TOO!"

"Need your mom's binoculars?" Colt elbows up beside me, catching me taking it all in.

"Yeah," I answer, "I can't find our Tufted Titmouse."

"Oh, she's in the box suite with your mom, hearing all about our love of Puffs Tissues."

I chew my mouthpiece, laughing. "Nah, I'm still a Kleenex man."

"Liar." Colt slings his arm over my shoulder. "Kleenex ain't got shit on me because you're *my* man now."

Players hug on the sidelines all the time. It's no big deal.

But this is, and we know it. I'm sure every camera is aimed at us.

So fuck it.

I turn to Colt with a smile and let the cameras lip-read the words I say to him. "Love you, too."

"Love, love, love," it repeats in my head like my new mantra as we take the field with fifty-five seconds remaining in the game. In the game so many people need us to win.

I can't fail them.

Because Philadelphia scored and got the field goal, too.

We're down 28-31.

We need a touchdown.

I scan our opponents and all defensive eyes are on Colt. Their aim, too. They won't let him move a yard. Goodwin's been suffocated by defense all quarter as well.

We're running out of plays. We're running out of time.

I scan the end zone, "Love, love, love," chanting in my head. With my heart pounding, my vision tunnels to a girl with her parents. A smiling girl with black hair, wearing my number four Atlanta jersey, waving a rainbow flag.

Colt believes in signs.

So do I.

Smiling as we huddle, I call the play, "A-town flip. Raven. Raven. Birds Fly Home."

To our offensive line, it's code for what to do.

For me, Hawke, and Blair—it's everything.

I take the snap and fall back, seconds running down. Inhaling, I hold the pocket one last time, acting like my right shoulder, all swollen and on fire, is twitching to throw to Goodwin on my left.

Then, I pivot right like I'm going to throw to Hawke instead, while Hawke and Goodwin run like decoys in opposite directions, drawing Philadelphia's defense their way while our offensive line clears the way for me.

They clear the path for me to put my nose down, my nostrils flaring, my jaw clenched, my muscles exploding as I fly up the field, running home with the ball tucked in my grasp.

I sprint fourteen yards, smirking when I see a defensive tackle. *I love this.* With a front flip, I jump over him, landing in the end zone for the winning touchdown. *It's just a game.* It's just my old trick from high school. Pointing to the girl with the rainbow flag, I wave and pump my fist for her.

For everyone like us.

Then it's a blur.

Players storm the field. We pile on. We celebrate. We hug, ripping off helmets and slapping pads. Then I find Philadelphia's players and shake hands. A few seem to hate me, but I don't care.

The press surrounds me. I'm ready for the after-game interviews. I know what to say and repeat it over and over.

"Man, it's about our team tonight," I huff. I smile and praise, "It's about our players, our organization, and this incredible game. I'm proud to talk about the rest later, but let's talk about how they crushed it tonight."

I won't answer questions about Hawke. He won't answer about me. The Fourteen have spent too long planning and practicing this. We know what to say. We're in control.

It seems like forever until, finally, I'm seeking Blair by the sidelines. Staff and security have her waiting for me.

Her smiling red lips. Her cute glasses. Her sexy black hair. Her T-shirt with our names on it.

That's my woman.

I run to her. I pick her up, spinning her around, kissing

her for all to see, just like I was dying to that night when she opened her dorm door to me.

When she opened my heart forever to her.

"I love you, Beau. I love you," she shouts, tears welling in her silver eyes. Even though I'm soaked in sweat, she doesn't care. She wraps her arms around my grimy neck as cameras surround us.

"I'm so proud of y'all," she huffs against my beard, so I whisper in her ear, "It's no joke this time, Blair Monroe. You have my devotion. I'm gonna love you forever, I promise."

I kiss her pillow lips again and know we'll share an incredible night and an amazing life together, but it's not complete. Not until we turn, looking for him, and there he is, just as brawny, sweaty, and proud as me.

I hold my arms open for Colt. With our pads still on, we practically smush Blair between us, but she laughs.

Yes, when players win, they hug.

But Colt and I are more than players. We're in love.

We waited forever for this moment, smiling nose-to-nose. Gently, I grab his neck, and he grabs mine. Our eyes lock before... we kiss, his whiskers soft against mine, his lips salty like mine.

It's not long, but it says *everything.*

It changes *everything.*

Every camera captures it, and we hope they do.

Yep, this picture is going on our nightstand.

Then I feel Blair gently tugging my hand. Her warm hand, which I love so much and plan to hold every day, slips something smooth and circular into my grasp.

This was our game plan.

I've waited too long for this, too.

And I'm not talking about a Super Bowl win.

With my chin up, I lower to one knee before Colt. He's

shocked. Then, instantly, I see the dream fill his brown eyes, too. He knows what I'm about to do, what we've always wanted, and he lets me.

The camera shutters hiss. Microphones hover. People gasp, then freeze around us like they're holding their breath as screams in the crowd erupt at the sight.

But they all fall away except for Blair, who Colt tenderly pulls into his grasp. He holds her tight under his right arm, her hand on his chest, while I take his left hand.

There's this guy from high school I fell in love with.

There's this girl from college who saved me.

"Colton Hawke," I vow, "you never gave up on me. You never gave up on us. You always believed in our love, and now I'm asking you to always believe in me. Let me win your heart every day. Will you marry me?"

His thick lashes wet, his brown eyes welling with tears, just like mine, his voice dropping gruff. "Yes, Beau Bronson. Proudly, I will marry you."

I slide the perfect gold band on his thick finger, knowing we'll say so much later. But that's private, and for us to share with Blair without the cameras and fans.

And I know that next week, after the three of us go to Disneyland, where I'm sure we'll share many rides and pranks, we'll go to Charleston.

Luca Mercier is letting Ruby organize the most lavish surprise takeover of his luxury hotel.

Five hundred white roses, along with five hundred paper roses made from Blair's books, the ones inspired by our love, will fill the white marble lobby. Hundreds of flickering candles will glow in glass votives while all the lights will drop as I drop to my knee and propose to Blair, too, in front of everyone we love.

Yes, I already have the twelve-carat emerald-cut

diamond ring, size five, by the way, for her. Yes, I'll buy her any beach house she wants. Yes, she can have my bookshelves, but I'll always control the remote, and Colt commands the thermostat. So yes, she'll want to snuggle with us and have our babies, too.

And yes, I know Colt will try to outscore me.

He'll orchestrate his lavish proposal to Blair and surprise me with one, too,

And that's my new game plan.

I hope we never stop trying to win each other's hearts... shamelessly.

NOT THE END

Blair

EPILOGUE

WHY GIVE AN OLIVE BRANCH WHEN YOU CAN PROVIDE ORGASMS?

Eight years later

"**P**apa!" Azora shouts across the field. "Will's licking the ball again!"

I smile at our daughter.

I still love teasing Beau, "Hey, Daddy." He sits beside me, trying to drink his coffee in peace. "That's got you written all over it."

"Goddammit," he mutters, wedging his cup in the holder before climbing out of his navy folding chair. "Willuf Bronson-Hawke!" He shouts, storming across the grass. "Quit licking the damn ball and throw it!"

But Beau loves this. He loves watching our kids play, even if our son likes to lick the football instead of throwing it half the time.

Colt laughs on the other side of me. He's always the

pragmatic parent. "Maybe," he wonders, "if we tell him there's dog poop in the park, he'll stop."

Colt holds Val, our youngest, in her baby carrier, content and sleeping on her Dad's chest while our oldest kids try tossing a football like their fathers taught them.

But when kids are seven and five, you're missing a few buttons off your shirt if you think that'll last longer than five minutes.

"Well," I beam, watching the spectacle as Beau starts running after Will because Will's fast like Colt, squealing and thrilled by the chase. Other Charleston families peacefully enjoy their fall morning in the park while ours turns it into training camp every time. "Beau's the one who told him about the Super Bowl and the *sweet taste of victory*. Now all that boy wants to do is lick every ball, thinking he can taste the flavor like chocolate ice cream."

It makes me laugh, glancing at Colt, who smirks back with that sweet, devilish look in his brown eyes. It's the same one he gets when he pinches my ass or slaps Beau's when we're washing dishes.

Cupping our daughter's downy hair, holding her close to his brawny chest, Colt leans my way. "Speaking of thirty-one flavors and banana splits."

By the huskiness in Colt's voice as his tender kiss takes mine, he's as excited about tonight as I am.

Aunt Vale is babysitting because it's the parents' night out. We've booked our suite at The Mercier. We'll have dinner and drinks there with friends before we have a long overdue night of kinky games.

I've weaned Val. I'm back on birth control. I went shopping at Delta's for new toys to spice things up.

But honestly, I'd really just love an uninterrupted night in my husbands' arms. They need it, too.

Lately, Will's been climbing into our bed at ungodly hours. Then Azora, like a Tawny Owl, hears him and gets jealous. She climbs in, too. I swear, Val is nine months old and the only one who sleeps through the night.

I tease over Colt's whiskers, "Don't forget to pack the whipped—"

But in the usual happy hell of parenting life, we're interrupted.

"Mama!" Azora stomps our way, making her long brown ponytail swish. Her pretty cheeks are all flushed, her blue eyes squinting and mad. "I can't practice with him. He's such a brat. He licks the ball to annoy me."

"Your brother is not a brat, pumpkin. He's a boy." I school our daughter—our wise elder. "The difference is brats grow out of it. Boys don't. They'll always an—"

"Um," Colt chuckles, jumping in, "what your mother means to say is *I'll* practice with you."

"But, *Daaaadddd*, you're holding *Vaaaallll*." Azora's dancing on the edge of a whine. I'm glad I packed cheese sticks to go with it. "She never lets you put her down. She always cries."

"She's teething," I calmly remind her. "You were the same way."

Azora rolls her eyes at me, and I flick my stare at Colt. He looks back, cocking his brow, our eyes speaking without words.

You know—Parent Telepathy.

"Oh hell, no," we agree. "We're not raising snobs or snowflakes."

That's another rule in our playbook.

"Azora Celeste," I drop my tone, "what did we tell you about rolling your eyes at us?"

"Don't make me turn this car around."

"Nope, the other thing."

"Keep it up, and I'll cancel your birth certificate."

I snort, choking down my laugh because when kids have three Southern parents, they say the darnedest things because we do, too.

"No, Azora." I hold my coffee like a chalice. Like I'm a queen on a throne, not a folding chair. Like I'm teaching our pissed-off princess how to rule the world. "I told you if you're going to be a smartass, young lady, then do it right and look the person in the eye."

Our daughter doesn't want to, but she smirks.

I swear, she looks like Beau, all brown hair and blue eyes, but she has my sass and Colt's big heart. She's a good big sister. Her little brother just tests her.

Because Will? Our five year old? He has my black hair and Colt's speed. But damn if he's not like Beau, always planning a prank, always trying to annoy her.

Hell, Beau still does it to me.

Last week, he left me a sweet note by the coffee pot to check under his pillow. I thought I'd find his usual gift, a paper rose made from our books. But no. It was another note that read,

"TOUCHDOWN. I FARTED ON THIS PILLOW. LOVE YOU!" XO, WILLUF

Don't worry.

I got him back.

I wrote on his truck's bumper,

"PLEASE HONK + WAVE. ANNOY ME LIKE I ANNOY MY BEAUTIFUL WIFE."

But Val? Our nine month old? She has Colt's brown eyes, tracking him like a hawk. If I'm not holding her, she reaches for him. But then she's always smiling for Beau and has his brown hair. Either way, she's got their grip. She's already yanked out three pairs of my earrings.

"Come on, pumpkin." Carefully, Colt rises from his chair beside me, one hand cupping Val in her carrier, the other reaching for Azora's hand. "I'm an NFL Hall of Famer. I think I can manage throwing a ball with our daughter while holding the other one."

I swoon, warmth flooding my heart for the umpteenth time at the sight before me. Every day, I fall more in love with my husbands and our kids.

Ultimately, whose child is whose?

The answer: they're ours. Beau is Papa, Colt is Dad, I'm Mama, and... *I'm done.*

No more kids.

Azora came fast. We had our lavish wedding at The Mercier in Charleston, and I swear they got me pregnant that night.

Will was a surprise. I think he was our treat after the tricks we enjoyed at the annual Halloween party hosted by Silas & Eily Van de May.

Damn, those parties are worth waiting for. And damn, like every mom, I need a break sometimes. Give me some shameless holiday sex to keep me sane.

But Val? I think she was my birthday baby, and we had to fight for her. The doctors put me on bed rest for the last three months. Of course, my husbands took care of me and our kids. And yeah, I wrote two books while I was stuck in bed, but still.

We didn't want to lose her, and I can't go through that fear again.

Besides, forty is around the corner for us, and our life is full.

Beau's a leading NFL game analyst for ESPN. He's a fixture on Monday Night Football.

Colt retired a few years after Beau and then got busy expanding our restaurants into almost every Mercier hotel property worldwide. He's also become quite a chef.

And me?

I'm on book number thirty-eight. I even have another pen name—Raven Hawk—for my kids' books. They're about a flock of young birds with rainbow feathers who make a pact. They learn if they fly together, they're safer and stronger.

"Mama! Mama!" Will runs my way. I hold out my arms and let him leap into my lap. "Papa said when we get home I can have a popsicle if I stop licking balls."

Oh, the jokes I want to say as Beau jogs up behind him because he smirks at what our son just said.

It's still so sexy how Beau's blue eyes can read a dozen puns on the tip of my tongue without me saying them.

"Alright," I tell Will, kissing his sweaty, flushed cheeks. "Go play on the slides until it's time to leave. We have an hour before your brother's game starts."

Forrest, Colt's son, plays football for Clemson University. He's their star tight end.

You see, Colt can't be mad Forrest isn't playing for Auburn or Alabama because Clemson is so close to us in Charleston; we see Forrest all the time. The kids worship their big brother.

And Reese? We'll never be close friends again, but Beau and I have found the forgiveness Colt has.

Our lives are too blessed to be bitter.

"Damn, that kid," Beau huffs with a smile, plopping

back in his chair beside me. "I don't care how it looks. We're leashing him when we go to Disney next time. That cute fucker is fast, and I'm almost forty."

Actually, Beau's gotten hotter with age. So has Colt. They were just on the June cover of Sports Illustrated, celebrating Pride month and their wedding anniversary as the first married couple in the NFL.

And yes, I sent the kids to Ruby's for a playdate the afternoon of their cover shoot.

Because when Beau and Colt came home, I put on my bridal lingerie from our honeymoon and made them put on their tuxes from the cover shoot.

No, their tuxes weren't rentals, and yes, we ruined them. Because vanilla cake icing mixed with blue body paint and cum, stains fine wool.

Can I get points for that pun?

Sipping coffees, our gaze bounces from Will, whizzing down the sliding board feet away, to Colt, tossing the ball with Azora while Val sucks her fingers on her Dad's chest.

"Look at her," Beau admires our daughter as he reaches for my hand. "Our girl has a golden arm."

Azora is the football player Beau said we'd have. And Val? Obviously, it's too soon to say, but she sure does love story time. Will is the wild card. Is taste-tester a job? We'll see where life takes him.

We soak in our dreamy, chaotic life, his warm thumb gently brushing over mine before his phone in the side pocket of the chair pings with a text.

"You better check it," I tell him. "It's probably about the house."

We're remodeling a beach home on the Isle of Palms. Once we became so close to Zar and Nick, we bought a house near them. I didn't want a place in Key West. We don't want to leave the Lowcountry. Luca and Scarlett are only a few doors down, too, and Vale's nearby on Johns Island. So is Ruby. All of our family and friends are close.

"It's Ruby." Beau smirks, reading his screen.

"What?" I ask because he looks guilty AF. "What's so funny?"

"She's trying to plan our Halloween costumes with The Six," he says. "And she doesn't want me to tell you. Like I can lie to my wife. But she and Eily Van de May *really* want you to be one of the kinky treats this year."

"The little cunt candies," I huff, shoving down my grin. "Go ahead. Play along. Y'all plan something, and I'll act dumb about it."

Dumb?

No.

The trick is on Beau. And on Colt, too.

Ruby, Eily, and I are going for the long prank. Of course, Zar and Nick are in on it, too.

The Six are Eily and Silas Van de May and their polycule. They host fun, family-friendly parties every month. I love our community of dozens now.

But it's their adults-only events when we get shameless. Like every year, for their Halloween bash, when we plan elaborate taboo tricks and very kinky treats. It takes plans, plays, and practice.

The NFL would be so proud.

The National Fucking League, that is.

It makes me smile, cuddled in my chair beside Beau, holding his hand. I'm all warm and cozy in my old Atlanta football sweatshirt—the one from *that* Super Bowl.

The game that freed us forever.

Do we get haters? Do we get judged?

Sure.

But don't hate back. They're just miserable non-fuckers. So, whenever I can, I send our critics vibrators, dildos, and prostate massagers from Delta's. Oh, and lots of flavored lube.

Why give an olive branch when you can provide orgasms?

"Damn, look at her spiral." Beau's in awe, watching Azora throw to Colt.

Yes, Colt has talons for hands. He can catch anything, but Azora has Beau's aim. It's incredible to watch.

"It's in the blood," I agree. "Maybe she'll be the first woman quarterback to play for the NFL."

Beau nods like he can see the future while he teases me, gently squeezing my hand. "You sure we don't want another one? Eight more, and we'll have an offensive team."

"Hell, no!" I laugh, answering, "But I'm always up for some blue alien breeding."

Like he can sense our loving vibe, Colt turns our way, jutting his chin all sexy before blowing us a kiss.

"Damn, our husband is hot," Beau rumbles. "And I saw the two Lover's Cages you bought at Delta's. Let's call Aunt Vale and see if she can babysit a few hours early."

"She *does* owe me," I answer, feeling the same urge, the love, the need to just hold my men without a pile of kids on us. Though I live for that, too.

"Good job, pumpkin!" Colt praises Azora's last throw. "But let's get going. It's game time."

Of course, we won't miss Forrest's noon game. It's playing on College GameDay.

Everyone knows now that Colt is Forrest's father. With that and Colt's marriage to Beau, the pressure on Forrest is immense, but he handles it well. Still, we only go to Clemson's home games. Colt doesn't want to steal the light from Forrest. He wants him to shine on his own.

So I start packing our family bag while Beau folds our chairs and calls for Will.

"Excuse me."

A deep but shy-sounding voice lifts my focus from the orange slices I'm cramming in the cooler pouch. The voice gets Beau's attention, too, as Colt joins us.

Our little family gathers around while a strapping teenage boy stands before us with a girl beside him.

"Excuse me," the teen says again, "but aren't you Beau Bronson and Colton Hawke?"

"Yes, we are." Beau sounds wary, almost protective. It's in his Dad DNA, but this kid isn't a threat.

"I, uh… " The teen stammers, but the girl—she's got to be his little sister—nudges him with her elbow, so he continues, "My name is Josh, and I'm a big fan. I have your posters and jerseys. I grew up watching you guys play, and I want to thank you."

Beau stands, his massive hand cupping Will's little head to keep him still while his other hand shakes the teen's. "It's nice to meet you, Josh."

Colt shakes his hand next, asking, "Josh, do you play, too?"

"For his high school!" His sister interjects. "He's the quarterback! He's the best in South Carolina!"

"But I hope to play for Bama," the teen adds. Then he smiles, eyeing Colt, whose arm is wrapped around Azora, his other patting a waking Val. "Or Auburn," Josh rushes. "It doesn't matter to me. Either would be my dream. I just want to be like y'all one day. I'm gonna play for the NFL, too." He stammers, all shy again, "Would you… Uh… Would you guys sign my ball?"

Warm, proud tears bite at my eyes as I stand safely nestled between Beau and Colt. As we stand as a loving family, smiling at the teenage boy cradling "The Duke," a traditional Wilson football in his arm.

It's the new edition made in their honor.

It's an official NFL football emblazoned with a proud rainbow flag.

Want the story of the tricks & treats at the
Halloween party for all?
Get HALLOWEEN FOR SIX.

Did you read Beau & Blair's sweet and spicy prequel
novella?
SHAMELESS PLAY is free in Kindle Unlimited.

Want to meet Luca, Scarlett, Zar & Nick?
Get MAKE HIM.

Want more romance in this spicy, interconnected world?
Enjoy the books ALSO BY KELLY FINLEY,
the "Queen of Spice."

ALSO BY KELLY FINLEY
"THE QUEEN OF SPICE"

-Interconnected Books & Audiobooks

Available in Kindle Unlimited & Audible-

BELLES & BRATVA BEASTS

NASH

AXEL

SIRE

LOCH

JACE

FEATURING RUBY, VALE & MORE IN A CROSSOVER SPICY MAFIA ROMANCE

MAKE HIM

featuring Luca & Scarlett with Zar and Nick

A BILLIONAIRE DOM, MMF, WHY CHOOSE ROMANCE & AUDIOBOOK

TEMPT HER

featuring Stacey & her husbands

MMMF, WHY CHOOSE REVENGE ROMANCE & AUDIOBOOK

HOLIDAY FOR SIX

HALLOWEEN FOR SIX

with cameos of MCs from characters above and below!

VERY SPICY, LOTS OF FRIENDS TO LOVERS ROMCOMS & AUDIOBOOKS

ALL FOR HIM

featuring Silas & Eily Van de May with Cade and Redix

ACKNOWLEDGMENTS

My husband and best friend: I wake up to our coffee and your sweet notes. Your love and support keep me writing. Thanks also for being a football player who can answer my questions. I'm lucky I found you, Silver Fox.

My Book Team: Deborah, you are a Proofreading Goddess and always so encouraging. Thank you, Lori, for another gorgeous cover design. Thanks to Katie Cadwallader for the great photograph of model Cole Forsgren. And as always... big hugs to my BTS team, Bree and Brit.

My Beta Team: Dani, Deborah, Heather, Jay, Jessica, Katelyn, Marsha and Rachel. I love y'all! Thanks for your comments, edits, and texts. They either crack me up or crack the whip.

My Spicy Gals & ARC Team: I love the family we're building. I cherish your posts, reviews, and support. I love our DMs and chats, too. I truly can't do it without you all.

#Bookstagram & #BookTok Followers: It's true. There *is* a community and a world of friends online. I'm overwhelmed by the amazing people I've met. Every day you make me smile. You keep me writing. Thanks for your comments and love.

Author Friends & Mentors: You inspire me. You school me. You help me. Thanks for the Zooms, emails, and chats. You keep me strong.

Best for last - You, my readers: Thank you for giving your time to share this story with me. I welcome your messages, posts, and emails. They are the greatest gifts. And I promise to keep giving you more spice. Big hugs.

Xoxo,
Kelly

ABOUT KELLY
"THE QUEEN OF SPICE"

Kelly Finley hates writing bios but appreciates that you made it this far. So here you go...

She lives in the Carolinas with her sexy husband and cherished family. A rebel with many causes, she fancies black leather, dirty jokes, big hearts, and smart mouths.

Her books are so spicy that her readers started calling her **"The Queen of Spice,"**...and she wears her crown with pride.

Dedicated to writing books with proud love and shameless heat, she's most likely at her keyboard putting the next spicy story on the page for you.

Want to connect with Kelly and her readers? Get her newsletter at KellyFinley.com, join her Spicy Book Babes on Facebook, and share the fun on her socials.

instagram.com/kellyfinleybooks

tiktok.com/@kellyfinleybooks

facebook.com/KellyFinleyBooks

bookbub.com/authors/kelly-finley

goodreads.com/goodreads_kelly_finley

amazon.com/author/kellyfinley